Dreamless

First Paperback Edition: May 2016

For information on subsidiary rights, please contact the publisher at rights@jollyfishpress.com. For additional information, write us at Jolly Fish Press, PO Box 1773, Provo, UT 84603-1773, or visit us online at www.jollyfishpress.com.

Printed in the United States of America

THIS TITLE IS ALSO AVAILABLE AS AN EBOOK.

Library of Congress Cataloging-in-Publication Data

Names: Wardell, Jenniffer, 1981- author.
Title: Dreamless / Jenniffer Wardell.
Description: First Paperback Edition. | Provo, Utah : Jolly Fish Press, 2016.
Identifiers: LCCN 2015046086 | ISBN 9781631630422 (paperback)
Subjects: | CYAC: Princesses--Fiction. | Blessing and cursing--Fiction. | Fantasy. | BISAC: JUVENILE FICTION / Fairy Tales & Folklore / Adaptations. | JUVENILE FICTION / Fantasy & Magic.
Classification: LCC PZ7.1.W368 Dr 2016 | DDC [Fic]--dc23
LC record available at https://lccn.loc.gov/2015046086

10 9 8 7 6 5 4 3 2 1

To Rachel.

Sorry, but this is what happens when your best friend is a writer.

Also by Jenniffer Wardell

Fairy Godmothers, Inc.

Beast Charming

JENNIFFER WARDELL

JOLLY
FISH
PRESS
Provo, Utah

CHAPTER 1

Mindfulness

"So, how are we feeling today?"

Elena was fairly certain that Dr. Flyte knew exactly how annoying the question was and kept asking it in the hopes that one day when she would snap and hurl something at him instead of answering. The fact that he was a magic mirror and likely wouldn't survive the experience didn't seem to faze him.

Thankfully, Elena was more practical than he was. She let her eyes linger on the pale taupe walls of the small office, wondering if the color was supposed to be soothing. "Actually, I'm a little tired. A spell book I'd been waiting for finally arrived yesterday, and I'm afraid I stayed up later reading it than I should have." Her smile was an old defensive reflex, well-used and entirely meaningless. "I assure you, Alan gave me a suitably firm talking-to."

Had her personal bodyguard been close enough to hear them, rather than standing at attention on the other side of the thankfully sound-muffling wooden door, he would have given her that look that made it clear he could see right through her.

Dr. Flyte, however, carefully had no expression at all. "Shall I talk to Commander Merrick? Given the damage he did to his leg during that incident with Prince Nigel, it would comfortably fall within the range of post-trauma employee evaluations."

Elena would have sworn she kept her face blank, but one of the doctor's eyebrows still twitched upward. It was, she knew from experience, his version of a smirk. "Of course, questions about his job duties would naturally come up, particularly about the mental state of the princess he spends his days guarding."

That was the problem with verbally fencing with a true magic mirror, the sentient entities that were so much more than the mass-produced communication devices they'd inspired. Though some continued their traditional work assisting particularly lucky sorcerers or sorceresses with their spells, many of the original mirrors had gone on to have second careers in a variety of fields where information and perceptiveness were more important than arms and legs.

Elena lifted her chin slightly, abandoning evasion for simple stubbornness. "What makes you think Alan could tell you any more about how I feel than these endless years worth of sessions have? After poking and prodding me all these years, surely you've figured me out by now."

Dr. Flyte sighed, his ghostly face sagging gently into something she refused to acknowledge as sadness. "Elena." The disappointment in his voice was worse than chiding would have been. "I'm only trying to help."

She pressed the palms of her hands flat against her legs, refusing to let them betray her emotions. "Curses are supposed to help you attract a royal spouse, or temporarily punish a business rival when a lawsuit doesn't quite get the message across. The worst ones are supposed to simply kill people." Elena couldn't keep the edge out of the words. "And then there's *me*."

Her mother, a sorceress who had decided to take the "evil" track after grad school simply because her beloved older sister had, decided to leave the family business when she fell in love. It was a common enough situation, normally nothing more serious than a story told at parties. This time, though, that older sister hadn't taken it well. As a result, Elena had inherited both her mother's talent and the curse that would eventually shut her down.

Thankfully, Dr. Flyte was an old friend of her mother's, which meant she didn't have to go into detail.

"Elena, you know perfectly well how unusual your situation is. The 'evil' part of an evil sorceress' title is often nothing more than a marketing tool, and the Worldwide Council of Sorcery is quick to punish those who would do irreversible harm outside the boundaries of a contract. Though there are any number of scholarly papers out there debating the merits of this, curses are generally seen as instructional at their worst and helpful at their best. Not . . ." The word hovered alone for a moment, the doctor's normal verbal acuity apparently having failed him. He was a magic user in his own right, as knowledgeable about sorcery as anyone she'd ever met, and had studied her curse intently. Despite all that, it still pained him sometimes to talk about the curse.

To Elena, that meant they should all stop talking about it. No one ever seemed to listen, though. "Cruel?" Elena finished, feeling the old anger stir and forcing it back down. It never helped anything. "Appallingly vindictive to both her supposedly beloved younger sister and her only niece?"

"Yes," the doctor said quietly. "What happened to you is terrible, Elena. Which is why your mother and I feel it's important that you talk about what you're going through."

Elena took a deep breath, smoothing the non-existent wrinkles out of her dress as she ordered her emotions to steady. "I'm exactly like I was yesterday, Dr. Flyte." Then she pushed herself further back into the too-cushioned chair, deliberately turning the conversation towards a particularly relevant bit of gossip she'd been saving. "So, I ran into a particular young lady we both know who was asking about you yesterday. You know, I think she still hasn't gotten over her crush on you."

There was a flash of eagerness across the mirror's face, quickly suppressed. "You saw Maladicta?" There was a brief, very telling hesitation. "What did she say?"

She smiled, far more warmly this time, easing the sharp lines of her face into something that might have been welcoming. "Braeth is the one who saw her. He said that she's looking for a tutor to help her with a graduate course, and was so disappointed to find out you weren't still teaching."

"Well, I—" Catching himself, Dr. Flyte scowled. "For a supposedly eldritch nightmare, Braeth is entirely too fond of generating gossip."

"He's dead." She lifted her shoulders, long pale hair shifting as she moved. "There's only so many entertainment options available to him."

"I am, unfortunately, familiar with that." There was a definite undercurrent of sympathy in his voice, and Elena made a mental note to send him mirror copies of some of the harder-to-obtain magical journals she'd hunted down. Then his gaze sharpened on her again, and her impulse for generosity faded somewhat. "We are not, however, here to talk about either Braeth or Maladicta."

She held her hands out in a conciliatory gesture. "I was just attempting to be friendly. You always tell me I should take comfort from my relationships with the people around me." They'd had nearly a half hour-long argument about that particular piece of advice, consisting mostly of tense silences and disapproving looks on both sides, but there was no need to bring that up now.

The doctor, however, clearly remembered it, and he gave her a look that suggested he could see through her just as well as Alan Merrick. "I don't offer advice simply as some kind of complex scheme to torture you, Elena. Or," he added as her mouth opened, "because your mother pays me to."

She'd stopped using that particular argument when she was sixteen. Her mother had found out, and the guilt and sadness that had been on her face had robbed the accusation of any pleasure. "She is the queen, though. Maybe you do it out of fealty to our tiny little kingdom's tragic, beloved leader."

The mirror snorted disbelievingly. "I was manipulating kings and queens long before even your mother was born, princess. If I hadn't been foolish enough to teach you all my tricks, we'd be having a very different conversation right now."

Elena smiled again. When the good doctor was feeling particularly expansive, she could even get him to tell stories. "Oh, I'm sure there's a trick or two in there somewhere you haven't told me about yet."

Dr. Flyte started to nod, then caught himself. "You're distracting me again. If you won't talk about yourself, you can tell me more about the incident with Prince Nigel. Tell me, how did you feel . . ."

~

Finally, mercifully, the session was over. Closing the door to Dr. Flyte's office firmly behind her, Princess Elena Augusta Randall let herself simply stand there and take slow, deep breaths through her nose until she stopped wanting to hit things.

"Every time I see you leave a session, there's a part of me that waits for you to at least kick the door behind you." Voice gentle and just a little bit amused, Commander Alan Merrick stepped away from the wall to follow her out of the office. The enormous cast freezing his leg into place made movement far more awkward than it normally was for the lifelong soldier, and Elena sent a dozen more mental curses in Nigel's direction for causing the injury. "I know better than anyone that it won't happen, but you remind me so much of my oldest daughter sometimes that the picture of it is always there."

Elena sighed, sending him a weak but real smile. "I will never understand why everyone seems so excited by the thought that I'll explode one day." She lifted her hands, some of the wariness leaving her hazel eyes. "When a sorceress gets angry, there's a lot more at risk than a few dishes. I might actually take a mountain down with me if I ever snapped, or at the very least blow huge chunks out of the castle walls."

Alan paused as he held the door open for her, as if genuinely considering the question. "Well, it might inspire them to update the décor a little."

She was surprised to find herself chuckling, and she held onto the feeling for a few precious extra seconds as they stepped out onto the street. Almost immediately they were surrounded by the bustle of a busy weekday morning, the noise of the people around them almost enough to disguise the brace of guards carefully positioned throughout the immediate vicinity. Normally, Alan guarded her alone, which was more than enough security to handle whatever dangers slipped past her magical defenses. But Nigel had used a curse charm on Alan, which meant no healing spell could fix her guard's leg, forcing him to be at diminished capacity until it healed naturally. He wasn't taking it well.

Elena, taking in a deep breath of the sausage-scented air surrounding the cart they just passed, had learned to accept such things. "I'll explode in Braeth's office, then get an interior decorator to redo everything in pink." Her smile widened at the mental image. "He'd kill me, but it might be worth sacrificing my last eight months just to see the steam coming out of his nonexistent ears."

Alan was the only one who didn't flinch when she joked about the curse, and she hoped he knew how much she cherished the freedom that gave her. "Actually, for all we know he might have enormous clown ears hidden under that—" He stopped, eyes going distant, then blinked and refocused on her. "We're being followed."

Had it been anyone but Alan, there were a number of smart comments she would have been tempted to make. Since it wasn't, she began scanning the crowd. "Won't the other guards be able to handle it?" Alan felt that most of the castle guard was poorly trained—he and the guard master had arguments about it all the time—but surely he had some faith in the group he'd requisitioned himself.

He caught her gaze when it moved past his, and the seriousness in his eyes made her go still with wariness. "Maybe." His hand moved to the hilt of his sword. "But I'm not about to trust either of our lives on it."

With the smallest tilt of his head, he gestured back to the alley they had just passed. They moved toward it with a deliberate casualness that only the person following them would even notice, then ducked inside. Alan went first, making sure whoever was following them hadn't chosen it as their own hideout, and at his signal Elena slipped in behind him. A search spell would be useless since there were likely to be more than a few perfectly innocent magic users on the street, and she didn't have enough idea of what she was looking for to narrow it down. Offensive combat spells would draw too much attention, and depending on who was following them potentially lead to assault charges if they were seen as unwarranted. A paralysis spell would be simpler and more effective, pinning whoever it was in their tracks and saving her guard from fighting with his broken leg. She just needed to know who she was aiming at.

A moment later, Alan answered that question for her. With no signal she could see or hear, he suddenly pivoted around on his good leg and slammed what seemed to be absolutely nothing against the wall. His arm stopped about six inches away from the bricks, resting on something solid despite the distance, and Elena shifted tactics and muttered the words needed to disable an invisibility spell. One quick yanking motion later, an embarrassed-looking young man wearing far too much silk was standing in front of them. "Well." He cleared his throat, then tried an overly bright smile. "How . . . how lovely to see you both. Have you been having a pleasant afternoon?"

Elena's fist clenched as she stared at Prince Nigel, who had been officially barred from the castle grounds but was unfortunately still allowed to wander the streets without supervision. "You fool," she hissed, stalking towards him. "What did you think you were doing, following us like that?, The only reason you escaped after the last time you tried to knock me unconscious is because I was too busy worrying about Alan to punish you suitably. Now you actually bring me a knife? Do you want to die?"

Nigel's cheeks reddened. "I told youthat was just a terribly unfortunate accident! The curse charm was meant for the wall, not his leg!"

Alan, who was far too calm to punch the idiot like he deserved, kept the nobleman pinned in place while he used his free hand to check for any weapons. When he pulled an old spindle out of the young man's vest, he turned back to Elena. "Has this been enchanted?"

She waved her hand over it, murmuring the key word, but there was no responding glow. "Nothing, which makes no sense. What use would—" Remembering, Elena narrowed her eyes at Nigel. "You know that was a rumor, right? Started hundreds of years ago by a sorcerer whose ex-wife specialized in making spinning wheels." She grabbed the spindle out of Alan's hand, holding the pointed end uncomfortably close to Nigel's face. "They're far more capable of damaging, say, someone's eye than setting off a sorceress's curse."

"I just—it seemed so much more civilized." Nigel swallowed, his cheeks starting to get red. "The man at the junk shop was more than happy to sell me a spindle, and I thought—"

"No. You didn't think." Alan's voice was hard as he yanked Nigel away from the wall, giving the prince his best "Commander" glare. "And if I see your face again, I will tell the Queen that you're stalking her only child with the intent to harm. I don't believe she'll like that."

Nigel's eyes widened. Elena's mother was generally a quiet, responsible, faintly sad woman, the kind of queen people felt protective towards rather than afraid of. But rumors, rumors were powerful things. Especially when there were still scorch marks on the castle walls that had been there as long as Elena could remember. "I didn't —I never meant to harm Princess Elena! I just, I wanted—"

"To start my curse early, so you could be the one to break it," Elena finished for him, the words flat to hide the bitterness behind them. "Kiss the poor cursed princess and everyone will be thrilled enough to forget what made her lose consciousness in the first place." She paused as his face turned an even more crimson. "Of course, it never occurred to you what would happen if your kiss didn't work, did it? You wouldn't be the hero. You'd be nothing more than the bastard who trapped the princess in a century of sleep months before she had to be, just because you'd decided to be clever." A quick spell was enough to make the spindle transport away as he watched. "Unless, of course, I decided to take care of you first."

Nigel couldn't say a word, just staring at her like his voice had been stolen. Looking disgusted now, Alan shoved the prince back out onto the main street. Once he was safely gone, Elena pressed the heels of her hands against her eyes and reminded herself to breathe. "If you don't want to kill him," she said quietly. "I'm sure Braeth would be willing to do it. We could say it was an early death-day present for him."

"He's not worth it," Alan smoothed a gentle hand against her hair. "Besides, I need to get you home. I have to explain to several supposedly skilled guardsmen why they need to start looking for work in the food service industry."

That last part was a little too edged to have been directed at her, and she lowered her hands to see three guardsmen standing at the entrance to the alley looking far more embarrassed than even Nigel had managed. Alan jerked his head back in the direction of the castle, and the three disappeared as quickly as if he'd barked an actual order.

Seeing them flee, Elena was surprised to find a smile tugging at the corners of her mouth. "It's not really their fault, you know." She glanced over at Alan. "The fool was invisible, remember. You can't expect all the guards who work for us to be as frighteningly talented as you are."

Her guard was still frowning in the direction his men had escaped, brow lowered as if he was already yelling at them in his head. "I can damn well expect them to figure out when you're being followed." He turned back to her, genuine worry in his eyes. "Until this leg finishes healing, you won't be protected enough."

She knew what he was really saying. "I don't need a different guard," she said firmly, trying to pretend that her chest didn't clutch in panic at the thought. Alan understood so much without either of them ever needing to speak about it, but to trust someone else to be that close? There would never be a time she could relax. "Nigel's horrible, but mostly because of his incompetence. After this he might even have the good sense to continue his ridiculous 'quest' somewhere far away from here." He'd called it that in the one grand announcement he'd made, before anyone realized what a danger he was, and she cursed whoever his father was for inflicting him on the rest of the world without even any body guards to stop him.

His hand on her shoulder made it clear he'd heard the panic in her voice and understood the reason for it. "You remember the other supposed 'suitors' who've tried to attack you as well as I do. Nigel isn't even the worst of them, and there's nothing to say they won't come back."

Elena made herself take a deep breath as she felt her options slip away from her. "I know, but—"

The world shut off.

When she opened her eyes again she was on the ground, staring up at Alan's terrified face. He was cradling her in his arms, checking for a pulse, and for one disoriented second she wondered how he'd managed to catch her with that broken leg of his. She hadn't fainted—you swooned first, when that happened. You weren't just snuffed out like a candle that someone else was done with.

Elena felt her body go ice cold. "How long was I . . ." Her throat closed up, unable to finish the word. The curse wasn't supposed to work like this—the spell was designed to put her to sleep for a century, not mere minutes—but it had felt exactly like every nightmare she'd ever had about her non-existent future.

She forced the thought from her mind as Alan helped her sit up. "Twenty seconds. Maybe thirty." His voice hadn't quite steadied all the way yet. "You stopped speaking, and your eyes rolled up in the back of your head. Then you dropped straight to the ground."

She shook her head, more to deny reality than anything he'd said, then made herself stand so she could help him up. He didn't accept the offer, watching her face the entire time as he got to his feet on his own. "We need to tell your mother."

"No." Elena focused on her breathing, forcing it into a slow, steady rhythm. "We can't even be sure that was the curse." Alan's eyes narrowed, and she held up her hands in supplication. "Not yet, then. Let me—let me at least find out more about what's happening."

He put his hand back on her shoulder. "It's not supposed to work like that, is it?"

"No." She covered his hand with her own, giving it a squeeze as a silent thank you. "Another special surprise from my aunt, I would guess."

Alan swore softly. "I wish Nigel had been the worst thing to happen this afternoon."

Elena sighed. "Me, too."

CHAPTER 2

Phone Home

At the sight of the crate full of smuggled pixie rum slung over Cameron Merrick's shoulder, Captain Parker made a face. "Deever again? Already?"

"Yep. Matt's processing him now." Cam set the crate down on the table, working out the kinks in his neck as he grinned at his superior officer. The leather armor had helped protect his shoulder, but there was only so much it could do when the crate was as heavy as both of his younger siblings combined. "He asked if your back was feeling any better."

"Oh he did, did he?" The captain leaned back in his chair, glaring at the crate as if it had disobeyed a direct order. He'd tried to pick up last week's crate to prove a point. It hadn't worked out well. "And it's just barely under the limit that would let us throw him in the prison. Again." He was getting that pinched look that meant a headache was on its way. "If he didn't keep getting caught every time he tried to cross the border, I'd think the man was a blasted genius."

"Hey, no one ever said the life of a border guard was all

danger and excitement." Grabbing the necessary paperwork—if he didn't fill it out for the alcohol, the captain would make him copy over all fifteen pages of Deever's arrest record—he dropped down into an open chair. "There's also the comic relief."

Captain Parker pinned him with a glare. It wasn't nearly as terrifying as the one Cam's father could manage, but he had long ago decided it would be wisest to not point that out. "It's you kids who get the excitement and the comic relief. All I get is the blasted paperwork."

"At least you don't have to suffer through it all alone." Cam held up the form, his grey-blue eyes artificially innocent. "And I'll let you take one of my patrols tomorrow, just out of the goodness of my heart."

The captain's eyes were still narrowed, but there was amusement in them now. "You say that now, kid, but you'll be sorry when I actually take you up on it."

"Hey." Lee, another one of the guards assigned to the station, ducked his head in through the open doorway. "Mirror call for Cam. Says she's his mom."

The Captain immediately perked up, then pretended he hadn't. "Tell Marie 'hi' for me," he said gruffly. "And if she asks when I'm going to pay her the twenty credit slips I owe her, tell her I'll do it the second she gets her butt back out here and starts doing her job again."

"Yes, sir." His mom had served with the border guard around the same time the Captain had been out on patrols, but after she'd met his dad, she quit to go adventuring with him. If even half the stories they'd told were true, they'd had some dangerously exciting years before settling down to raise a family.

He'd loved the stories as a kid, but he definitely didn't want to have that conversation with the Captain. They never talked about it, but Cam was pretty sure the captain had never quite forgiven her for leaving. "I'll use those exact words."

Cam stopped by the station's main mirror, transferring the call to his private mirror before ducking into the bunks to grab it. He took a second to smooth out his messy hair before pressing the glass. When the mist cleared, it revealed a stunning woman in her early fifties who could still arm-wrestle his dad into submission. "I'll be home for dinner this weekend, Mom, I swear it. You know I'd never risk your wrath."

Marie Merrick showed off exactly where her son had gotten both his sun-blond hair and lethal grin. "That's because you're a wise boy who doesn't start fights he can't win." She took a deep breath, her expression far more serious than Cam liked to see. "And I'm a wise mother who knows which parent her son is more likely to listen to. So I'll cut to the chase—please take some leave and come home. Your father needs you."

Cam expected annoyance, his instinctive reaction to pretty much anything to do with his father since he'd turned sixteen. He was surprised, then, that the first thing that hit him was fear. "Is Dad okay?" He couldn't think of a reason his father might actually need him—they argued about eighteen hours out of every twenty-four, and that was only because they spent the rest sleeping. But if he was dying, he'd want the entire family with him. "Is he sick?"

"No, no. Other than the leg, he's completely fine." She leaned a little closer to the mirror, everything from her voice to her posture meant to reassure. "If it was something like that, I promise I would have told you right away."

Cam leaned his head back against the wall, closing his eyes at the sudden wash of relief that filled him. Now that he knew nothing was wrong, he could go right back to being annoyed. "Then are you sure it's me Dad wants? Laurel called me a few days ago—her and Mason's mercenary outfit is still only a few days away from here. I'm sure he would have asked you to call one of them if he'd known that."

Marie narrowed her eyes at her second-oldest son. "Your father was perfectly willing to make the call. I suggested that I be the one to do it, because I knew the conversation would devolve into an argument and I'd have to take the mirror anyway. And we both already knew where your brother and sister were stationed—they may be too far away to come home for dinner, but they're no more interested in risking my wrath than you are." She sighed, giving him her "What am I going to do with you?" face. "If you won't do it, he plans on asking your sister. But only if you say no."

Cam rubbed a hand over his stubbled chin. He wasn't quite sure he believed his mother but was too smart to actually say that out loud. "Okay, but what does he need me for? Because if this is some weird backwards way to get Robbie off his magic kick, I can just tell him no from here. The kid wants to be a witch, and if he keeps working as hard at it as he is now we all know he'll be the best one in the kingdom."

She gave him her motherly glare again, then her expression gentled. "It's about Elena."

Cam cursed. Everyone knew about Elena, the only child of Queen Illiana and the great tragedy of their tiny kingdom. What most people didn't know was that she was a silent, disapproving slip of a girl his parents had semi-adopted ever since the King had died just after her twelfth birthday. He'd occasionally had to spend time with her during family events, the last of which had thankfully been almost two years ago, and he could definitely say he had no interest in repeating the experience. "You can't be serious."

The sudden sadness in her eyes had him bracing for the news. "Your father thinks Elena's curse has started early."

Cam blew out a breath. That was about the one thing he couldn't argue against. "He thinks?" He kept his tone carefully serious, not wanting her to think he was making light of the situation. "I was always under the impression that the curse would be pretty obvious once it kicked in."

"Robbie thinks all of the spells that have been thrown at it over the years might have degraded the pre-established initiation trigger Elena's aunt set up."

Cam thought about trying to translate that himself, then decided he needed to reserve his brainpower. "In words I can understand, please?"

"She collapsed, Cam. It wasn't for very long, but Alan said there was no warning. She just . . ." The hesitation said more than the words did. "She just dropped. Like someone had yanked all the life out of her."

He could feel the walls start to close in on him. "And he's absolutely, one hundred percent sure she didn't just faint."

"Yes. Your father has had more than enough experience with fainting women. You remember your great-aunt, don't you?"

He did, at least well enough to effectively kill the hope that his dad was wrong somehow. Cameron scrubbed a hand down his face, torn between wanting to comfort his mother by promising he'd come help and running away from all this so fast he left a trail of singed ground behind him. His parents had been the ones to sign up for this particular tragedy, not him, but it looked like it was going to catch up to him anyway. "What exactly does Dad think I can do? This is magic we're talking about. Unless something shows up I can stab, I'm not sure how much help I'll be."

"With his leg broken, he doesn't feel he can protect Elena as well as he needs to. It wasn't as much of an issue when all he had to worry about was idiot members of the nobility, but now that she might become incapacitated at a moment's notice—"

He just stared at her, eyes going wide as he realized what she was getting at. "He wants me as backup? I know he thinks the castle guard are all idiots, but—"

She shook her head, cutting him off. "No. He wants you to take over his duties until his leg heals."

It took real effort to keep his jaw from dropping open. "Me?" He tried to find a single part of the idea that made any sense, but he couldn't come up with anything. "Are you sure you heard him right?"

His mother rolled her eyes. "This is why I knew I had to be the one to make the call. You and your father inspire each other to say the stupidest things." She shook her head. "And I'm not entirely sure what happened, but even mentioning the rest of the castle guard inspired his 'Commander Death Scowl' and made him go almost mute for the rest of the evening. I decided it wasn't worth it to ask for details."

There had been a few years there where he'd actually counted inspiring the "Commander Death Scowl" as one of his favorite hobbies, but he could see why his mother wouldn't feel the same way. "And he really thinks having me there will help the situation."

As impossible as the idea seemed, it left a weird, hopeful

spark in his chest. No matter how much he tried to deny it, he wasn't immune to the desire to make his father proud of him. The idea that Dad had asked for his help specifically . . .

Her expression was bland enough that he knew she was hiding amusement. She had him, and she knew it. "Yes. He does."

"And Dad's sure he doesn't want to ask Laurel?"

"Absolutely."

He sighed, rubbing a hand along his jaw. This was a really, really terrible idea. "Fine. I'll talk to the captain."

~

Days later, Cameron stood outside the castle's main gate and decided that coming was probably even more of a mistake than he'd originally thought. The building had been practically carved out of the mountainside, as much inside the dirt and rock as on top of it, and one of the previous kings had decided that meant the hallways should be as ludicrously twisted as your average mountain passageway. He'd heard his dad joke that the royal family punished criminals by sending them downstairs to try and find the kitchens in the middle of the night.

He hadn't been inside in over a year, and he'd never had cause to spend any real time there. Even if he didn't get completely lost in his first fifteen minutes—and wouldn't that make dear old dad proud—Elena could probably give him the slip whenever she wanted. She knew the territory; he didn't. He'd been working the border long enough to know who that gave the advantage to.

"You here to see your dad?"

Cam blinked, refocusing his attention on the gate guard who had spoken. "You can't seriously tell me you recognize me."

The older man grinned. "I've seen the picture collection

your mom keeps on her mirror. Only person I've ever met who has more than my wife."

Cam groaned, suddenly aware that the princess had probably seen his baby pictures. The only way any of this could get worse was if he'd dated her briefly and there was a messy breakup to worry about. "Yeah, I am. Any idea where he might be?"

"Princess has been holed up in the library for the last few days. Can't imagine the commander's too far away." He hesitated, then leaned forward slightly. "They're both in kind of a mood. Be careful."

Cam forced a smile. "I will." He looked back over at the castle. "Now, can you give me really detailed directions to the library?"

~

He only made one wrong turn, opening the door to find a cramped, paper-filled office rather than the books he'd been expecting. When he tried to shut the door as quietly as he'd opened it, the pleasantly round-faced man at the desk lifted his head from his paperwork. "Lost?"

"Yes. I'm looking for my dad, Commander Alan Merrick. I was told he might be in the library, but I'd like to be sure before I plunge back into the void."

The man smiled. It was only then that Cam noticed the pointed ears that were visible against what now seemed like a surprisingly short haircut. He didn't look at all like any of the other elves Cam had met—they tended toward long hair and formal clothing, while this man looked more like a rumpled accountant.

"As of twenty minutes ago, he and Elena were still in the library," the elf said, hopefully unaware of Cam's inner monologue. "Which, I noticed you carefully not asking, is down at the hallway and around the corner on the left."

"Thank you." Cam made sure his relieved sigh was obvious enough to be humorous. "I'm Cam, by the way. If I don't manage to escape Dad's evil plot, you'll probably end up seeing me again."

"I knew who you were. I recognize you from the pictures your mother keeps in her personal magic mirror. When Cam groaned, the elf's smile widened. "I'm Bishop." He stood, leaning forward over his desk far enough for the two men to shake hands.

As he headed for the door again, Cam hesitated. "Secret Stream clan?"

Bishop's eyebrows lifted in surprised approval. "Good eye. Most people try to place me in the Windy Peak clan."

Cam shrugged. "Most of the Windy Peak elves I've run into are kind of annoying. You're not."

Bishop chuckled. "I won't tell them that." Then he sobered. "Are you here to help your father with Elena?"

Now it was Cam's turn to be surprised. "I'm afraid so. Any friendly warnings you might be able to pass on in advance?"

Bishop leaned back in his chair. "We're fond of each other here in the castle, but none of us are terribly comfortable with sharing our innermost thoughts. All I know is something happened a few days ago, and neither she nor the commander will speak to her mother about it," he said, looking hopeful. "If you might be able to pass on some news—"

Cam held up a hand to stop him. "I can't promise that."

The other man shook his head as if he regretted even asking. "Of course not, of course not." He put his elbows on the desk, still looking at Cam. "Then I will simply say good luck."

With that incredibly comforting thought, Cam left the office and made his way to the library. When he arrived, he noticed the door was firmly closed, which could mean either that it was empty or that there were people inside having a conversation they didn't want others to hear. Deciding that the only risk was looking like an idiot, he cracked the door open slowly enough that it didn't make a sound.

Of course, the people inside were so focused on their argument that they might not have heard him anyway.

"It's magic that's the problem, Alan, not the threat of physical violence." The voice was female, young, and frosty enough to chill a campfire. Yes, that was definitely his least-favorite princess. "My aunt isn't going to suddenly step out of the shadows with a knife, and Nigel is more of a threat to innocent bystanders than he is to me."

"Then tell yourself Cameron is here to protect both you and the innocent bystanders." His father never actually raised his voice unless you got him really ticked off, but Cam recognized the tone. Once Commander Alan Merrick had decided something, a team of giants wasn't enough to drag him away from it. Apparently, during his younger "hero for hire" days, one set had actually tried. "But he is either temporarily taking over my duties as your primary guard, or you are to be confined to the castle for the next six weeks." There was a pause. "I will have each and every one of your escape routes blocked, and the blocks will be immune to magic."

She had escape routes? Cam closed his eyes, forehead dropping against the wall. Maybe his father had asked him to come here purely as some kind of weird punishment.

From inside the library, there was an inhalation of breath that sounded like it really, really wanted to turn into a curse word. "You wouldn't dare."

From his hiding spot, Cam cringed for her. Clearly, the princess was dumber than she looked.

His dad didn't respond at first, which usually meant he was using the silence to really build the terror of anticipation in whoever he was glaring at. Then came the voice, quiet enough that you knew you were in serious trouble. "If I tell your mother, it will happen whether or not either of us ask for it."

More silence. Cam was surprised to feel actual sympathy for the princess. He'd always thought of her as being stuck-up, but no one was immune from parental pressure.

Naturally, it didn't last very long. "Fine." The word sounded like it had been physically dragged out of her. "But don't think I'm going to automatically grant him your level of authority simply on your say so. And I won't let him work around me, either—your son's not nearly as charming as he thinks he is. He'll do what I say."

Cam narrowed his eyes. Now he had to take the job, just so he could prove to the stuck-up little brat how incredibly wrong she was. He only took orders from people he respected, and right then she was about a million miles away from qualifying.

Deciding that the tactical advantage with the princess was worth potentially inciting his father's wrath, he pushed open the library door and stepped into the room. Elena jerked her head around to face him, long blond hair flying, and gave him a look that promised a quick and violent death. His dad, on the other hand, looked calmer than he'd sounded at any point during the last twenty minutes, and Cam suspected that he'd known someone was outside the door the whole time.

Luckily, he was kind enough to stay silent and not blow his son's surprise opening. Taking advantage of the generosity, Cam gave the princess a slow grin. "If you've spent any time with my parents, you know I'm not that good at being obedient. So no, I can't promise to do what you say. If it's going to get in the way of keeping you safe, I may end up ignoring you completely."

She glared at him, chin lifting in automatic defiance that actually earned her a few points. Elena was a good four or five inches shorter than he was, but that didn't seem to faze her at all. "It's not smart to challenge me."

"Challenge you? Never." His grin widened, taking on an angle that had caused more than a few people to try and punch him over the years. "I'm just explaining the situation." Then he turned to his dad. "Hi. I know Mom was probably vague on the subject, but it turns out that I am most definitely willing to take the job."

His dad looked at him for a second, then his mouth quirked upward briefly in what Cam could have sworn was a smile. It threw him more than any other response could have, and he started to doubt that he'd ever seen it almost the moment it disappeared. "I'll tell your mother not to expect you home for dinner," he said calmly. "Though gods help you if you miss the big family meal this weekend."

Then, without another word, he left the library. Cam watched him go, pretty sure he'd been conned somehow, then glanced over at the princess. She was staring at the door, a little bit of shock mixed in with the frustration in her eyes, and Cam suspected she was thinking the same thing.

When she realized he was looking at her, Elena turned her glare on him. "Do not even think about following me," she snapped, slamming her book closed. Then she stalked out of the room, her long hair flying out behind her in a huff.

Cam waited until she'd disappeared beyond the edge of the doorframe, then started following her.

CHAPTER 3

The Terrors of Unpredictability

Elena realized her mistake the moment she noticed someone was following her. It was embarrassing how long it had taken her—Cameron had apparently inherited his father's tendency to move as quietly as the undead when he wanted to. Unfortunately, he also seemed to have inherited Alan's stubbornness.

She whipped around to face him, hands gripping her skirt tightly to keep from bunching into fists, but he just smiled at her like he was taking a stroll through a picturesque mountain valley. The idea of throwing something at him was a powerfully tempting one, but he was probably perverse enough to enjoy it even more than her therapist would. "Fine. I didn't know I was dealing with a stubborn five-year-old rather than a rational adult." She grit her teeth, directing all her willpower to not shouting at him. "Now that I know otherwise, let me point out that nowhere in your job description does it say that you have to follow me around the palace like a trained puppy. I am surrounded by thick stone walls and the entire palace guard—no one's going to leap out of the shadows at me."

Cameron, who was no less insufferable since the last time she'd seen him, simply folded his arms across his chest. His hair, obviously not at all familiar with a brush, fell over his forehead in a way she was sure all the women just found adorable. "My dad seems to think otherwise."

Wasn't this supposed to be the son who never did anything his father said? Why of all times did he have to pick now to suddenly become obedient? "I'm not sure what he or Marie told you, but I can assure you it was an exaggeration. Even if he defies his banishment, Nigel is more of a natural disaster than an actual threat. No one else has made an attempt on me in months, and if—" Her voice betrayed her by failing briefly. She could only be grateful there was no change in his expression as she wrestled to control her emotions, forcing her hands to relax. "If the curse is starting early, there is absolutely nothing either you, he, or any of the rest of us can do about it." She lifted her chin, re-gathering her completely deserved anger. "So go home. Staying just to defy me is only going to waste your evening."

"No." The word was calm. Elena had a terrible feeling it was the guard in him answering this time, not just the childish troublemaker. "I'll be the first to tell you my dad isn't right all the time, but when it comes to his job he usually is. And he wants me to stick close to you."

Her eyes took on a dangerous glint. "So you had a detailed tactical conversation about me at some point? I suppose you'll tell me next that there are battle plans somewhere."

The corner of his mouth quirked upward. "Actually, that might not be a bad idea. But no, he didn't share any tactics." He didn't say anything at first, then relaxed his stance a fraction. "He said he didn't expect me home for dinner. Translated, that means he'll make the necessary excuses to Mom so that I can stay here and keep an eye on you the rest of the evening."

"That's where you're getting your instructions from?" The terrible thing was, it made sense. That was exactly how Alan thought. "Does your family have some secret psychic bond you refuse to tell anyone about?"

"Sweet mercy, no. What a terrible thought." Genuine horror flashed across his face. "I don't know which would be worse—hearing my parents think dirty thoughts about each other or having to be near Gabby when she starts getting interested in boys."

Elena just stared at him, confused by the sudden side-step in the conversation. Was he incapable of keeping a single thought in his head long enough to have a proper argument? *Oh.*

She scowled. "Is this your way of refusing to argue with me?"

"Were we arguing?" Cameron asked. "I thought we were just having a spirited discussion about the basic facts of the situation."

The sudden mood shift was disarming, leaving an unsteadiness that was far more dangerous than anger. Her fingers flexed almost involuntarily, and she felt the faint but unmistakable build up of magic around her. Appalled at the lack of control that implied, she gave both her hands a fierce shake and took a deliberate step away from him. Thankfully, they were alone in the hallway—she hated the thought that someone else might have seen that.

When she met his eyes again, there was enough wariness in them to make it clear that he had at least some idea of what had just happened. Apparently, he'd spent enough time with magic users to be able to identify some of the more common gestures used in spell casting.

She made herself take a deep, steadying breath. "I'll be suitably protected, I promise you. Braeth watches me in the evenings. Feel free to go home and go enjoy your mother's cooking."

"Braeth?" Cameron asked.

"He was a powerful evil sorcerer, back in the days when 'evil' was less a professional certification and more a sign that you were in the habit of slaughtering random villagers." She watched carefully for any sign of surprise or alarm on his face, and was forced to give him grudging points when she couldn't find it. "The centuries since his death have made him much more pleasant to be around, though. My mother gave him a workroom to tinker in, and he repays the favor by helping with the castle's magical defenses and looming at anyone stupid enough to be rude to her."

Cameron hesitated, and Elena could see at least five or six different questions flash across his eyes before he settled on the one he'd presumably decided was the safest. "He's not a zombie, is he? I mean, I'm sure they're perfectly fine people, but I'm really not looking forward to the possibility of a co-worker politely asking me if I could help re-attach their body part."

Elena only realized she'd snickered when the sound reached her ears, and when Cameron's eyes widened she only barely resisted the urge to clap a hand over her mouth. Instead, she lifted her chin and prepared to lie through her teeth if he tried to call her on it. "He's a wraith, actually. He used to haunt an abandoned tower, but moved into the castle at my mother's request."

The corner of his mouth quirked up. "Braeth the Wraith?"

She was flatly determined not to give him the satisfaction

of making her smile. The fact that it was taking some effort was already annoying enough. "I wouldn't call him that if you enjoy having all your appendages. He may technically be incorporeal, but he's never let that stop—"

The world shut off again.

When it came back, her head ached and she was being carried in someone's arms. There was a single, blissful moment where she didn't know where she was or what had happened, but it lasted barely enough time to take a breath. Then there was only the ice in her stomach, and the realization that she could no longer pretend her collapse in town had been an isolated incident.

The curse was coming for her early.

Pushing the fear aside, she tugged on the front of Cameron's shirt to get his attention. "I can walk." She squinted against a pounding headache, deciding whether or not trying to get down on her own would be worth it. "I'm serious. Let me go."

He stopped, looking down at her with a carefully evaluating expression. "Is this what happened last time?"

Elena bit back an instinctive sarcastic comment, knowing he didn't deserve it. "That depends," she said, struggling once more to get down. This time, he let her go. "How long was I out?"

"Almost two minutes." She couldn't read his eyes, but he didn't sound happy.

That was at least four times as long as her last collapse. If they kept growing at the same rate, she had less than a week before she would be unconscious for hours at a time. Then it would be days. And all of it would crash down on her without even a breath of warning.

She wouldn't even have time to tell anyone goodbye.

"Elena." Cameron touched her shoulder. "You have to tell someone. I was getting you out of the corridor so someone didn't trip over you, but I got the impression you wouldn't be too keen on the idea of me hunting down your mother."

"What would I tell her when I woke up?"She pressed the heels of her hands against her eyes, telling herself it was the headache that was making them sting. "Sorry, Mother, but we don't even get those last eight months we were promised? You'd better get your mourning clothes ready, and oh, by the way, don't get upset if I collapse on you in the middle of dinner. It's been happening a lot lately." There was so much she and her mother tried to hide from each other. To make her reveal it like that seemed particularly cruel to them both.

For a moment, neither of them moved. Then Cameron squeezed her shoulder, immediately pulling his hand away so they could both pretend he hadn't done it. The fact that the small gesture had been surprisingly comforting wasn't something she cared to think about.

Instead, Elena took a deep breath, lowering her hands and opening her eyes as she steadied herself. She brushed her fingers across her forehead, murmuring an incantation to ease pain, then turned back around to face Cameron. "We should introduce you to my mother, though. I'm not sure Alan told her who he'd chosen as his temporary replacement." And her mother probably wouldn't have asked, trusting Alan's judgment.

"He probably didn't." The corners of Cam's mouth curved upward. "Dad's usually good about chain of command, but—"

The pause seemed too deliberate not to be an invitation, so she finished the joke she'd first heard from Marie. "Only because he sees himself at the top." It was such an obviously soothing gesture that she searched for even the slightest sign of pity. She couldn't see any, but her nerves were too tightly strung to even take the risk. "I'm sorry, but don't be nice to me. Not right now."

She could practically see the impending argument spark in his eyes. Rather than give voice to any of it, though, he settled for shaking his head. "I bet you're really fun at parties."

"It depends on how comfortable I am lying to the other guests." She smoothed her hands over her hair and down the front of her dress, then let her expression soften. "Thank you." At the surprise in his eyes, Elena smiled a little. "I'm serious. Most of the other guards in the castle would have panicked or immediately gone running to my mother."

Cameron didn't say anything, face still enough that she wondered if she'd said the wrong thing. Then he huffed out a breath, letting the humor back into his face. "Can you imagine that conversation? 'Your Majesty, I'm sorry, but your daughter's collapsed. We think the curse has started early.' 'Oh, no, Elena! Wait, who are you exactly?'" He winced. "She'd chop off my head before I could even finish getting the explanation out."

She could already feel herself relaxing, the muscles in her chest easing as a result of the same ridiculous patter she'd tried to deflect barely a minute ago. This time, she took a risk and let herself tease him back, telling herself she was only doing it because it would be exhausting not to give in. "We haven't chopped off anyone's head in years, and then she'd have to go through the inconvenience of holding an actual trial. She'd probably just use magic to make your head explode."

There was that surprise again, then he grinned as they started down the hallway. "You're such a comfort."

~

It took a little while to find the right meeting room. Cameron, naturally, joked that she had gotten lost, but the truth was that Elena could barely keep track of her mother's schedule. The queen met with at least eight different committees or various community leaders on any given day—sometimes she marveled at how a kingdom this small could have so much bureaucracy—and would often hold the meetings in whatever space happened to be available.

Finally, she found the room she needed, pressing her ear to the door to gauge what point of the meeting they were at. "Small talk. Either the meeting is taking forever to get started, or it's already ended and no one's smart enough to move on with their day. Either way, it turns out we might actually be doing my mother a favor." Besides, if she waited for a rare moment of privacy with her mother, she'd risk being asked questions she didn't want to answer.

She laid her hand on the door handle, glancing over at him. "If anyone in there looks like a former military man, try not to meet their eyes. We're familiar enough with each other here that most of them have run out of people who haven't heard their stories. You're a new enough face they might actually chase you down."

He simply raised an eyebrow at her, amused again. "It's very hard for me to tell right now if you're being serious."

She shrugged, fighting the temptation to smile. "Don't say I didn't warn you."

As she opened the door, eight different pairs of eyes swung around to focus on her. From the way they were sitting it seemed like the meeting hadn't started yet, unfortunately, and even an unexpected visitor served as a distraction from the boredom of waiting.

Elena shoulders tensed, a movement subtle enough that no one ever seemed to notice. "Forgive me for the intrusion, Mother, but I wanted to introduce my new personal guard." She stepped aside so he could be seen. "Cameron Merrick, the commander's son. He'll be taking over the position temporarily while the commander's leg heals."

Most of the people at the table expressed some form of polite interest in the news—from the look of them, this was apparently the Harvest Celebration committee—but her mother pressed her lips together. "He and I discussed the matter. Quite briefly, unfortunately."

Elena recognized the wariness in her mother's eyes, as familiar to her as the long, white-blond hair tightly bound in a knot at the nape of the queen's neck. She was her mother's daughter in several ways, and could pick up on the unspoken implication that her mother still had several unanswered questions.

Thankfully, she wouldn't press the matter here. "You know how concerned he's been ever since he injured his leg." Elena kept her voice light, but decided not to risk her camouflage smile. Her mother used one too often herself not to be able to identify it.

Cameron, who had stepped forward to stand next to her, cleared his throat. "My mother is actually the one who asked me to come," he specified, head ducked slightly to make him look even younger than his twenty-one years. "Honestly, I'm not a hundred percent sure Dad even knew she asked me. She just wanted him to stop worrying."

It was a bald-faced lie—the Merricks talked more than any

two people Elena had ever met—but relief smoothed her mother's expression back out. "There's nothing to worry about, then." She smiled briefly, a real one, and Elena was overcome with the highly dangerous impulse to go over and hug her mother.

If she did, however, there was a very good chance that her mother would burst into silent tears—it had happened, once—and then she would start and there would be no stopping either of them.

Instead, she tried her own smile before giving everyone else at the table a dignified nod of acknowledgement. "Ladies, gentlemen, I apologize for interrupting the meeting."

"No need to apologize, Your Highness." Duke Halton—a booming man who enjoyed the distinction of being the kingdom's only duke—waved away the apology. "Even if you hadn't made an appearance, we can't get started until Bishop shows up. Man's got his head buried in his numbers again."

"We sent a page to fetch him, but it's entirely possible he's gotten lost as well." This was from Ruth Hatarni, who held a great deal of unofficial power among the kingdom's guilds. "If you would be a dear and stop by his office, it would be a great help in moving things along."

"I'm sure he'll be here shortly," her mother said calmly, taking a little too much care to keep any warmth from showing in her voice. It had been a habit of hers, these last few months, and some of the servants started to wonder whether the queen and her trusted right hand had suffered a falling out. Elena, however, knew that it really meant quite the opposite. "Given how much he does for all of us, I think we can spare him a few more minutes."

"If I see him, I will let him know," Elena said. Then, careful not to spark any more casual conversation that might pin her there any longer, she quickly slipped out of the room.

Cameron, thankfully, was right behind her, and shut the door with an expression that suggested he'd thought of something unpleasant. "How many of those meetings do you get stuck in during an average day?" He hesitated, as if bracing himself for the worst. "Also, I didn't see anyone else in there with guards, including your mother. What's the protocol for where your guard has to be standing during these things, and do you know of any tricks my dad used to keep from falling asleep in the middle of them?"

Elena kept them both moving down the corridor, torn between relief that Alan hadn't gone into this much detail with him and dreading the fact that she was going to have to. Cameron was in the habit of asking questions, and if she tried to stonewall him she suspected he'd just go out and find the answers on his own. "Don't worry—you'll be spared the subtle tortures of committee meetings. I don't attend any of them."

He was far enough behind her that she couldn't see his expression, but the sound he made was pure relief. "So how'd you pull that off? Is your mom being nice, or did you somehow manage to talk your way out of it?"

She hunted for the simplest lie. "She's just being nice."

Behind her, Cameron abruptly stopped moving. Elena took a few more steps down the hallway, trying to tell herself that the pause had nothing to do with the conversation, then gave up and turned around to face him. "What?"He narrowed his eyes at her, the seriousness of a professional guard mixing with a fundamental stubbornness that kept cropping up at the most annoyingly unpredictable moments. "If you don't want to talk about something, tell me it's none of my business. Tell me to shut up. Don't say anything at all. I don't care." His voice was almost angry. "But don't try to shut me up by saying what you think I want to hear. If I'm supposed to be protecting you, I can't spend half my time trying to figure out when you're lying to me."

She stared at him, eyes wide, then it was her turn to glare. "What makes you think I'm going to give you any special consideration?" she snapped. "I lie to everyone."

He gave a disbelieving snort. "I doubt that. You're not good enough at it."

"People want me to lie to them, you idiot." She might not be able to stop herself from getting angry, but she flatly refused to show it. "The fact that I never tell people what I'm really feeling is the kindest thing I could possibly do for them, especially when they're stupid enough to ask. The people who want to be kind to me are smart enough not to."

Cameron just watched her. "So everything's off limits, basically," he said, the humor gone from his voice.

Elena lifted her chin, unnerved by how much she'd suddenly unloaded on him. "Yes." She smoothed an uncertain hand down the front of her dress. "But you're also right. I'll try to confine my responses to 'no comment' rather than a lie of some kind."

They stared each other down for what seemed like a small eternity before Cameron finally broke the silence. "Fair enough." He inclined his head down the hallway. "May I ask where we're going?"

Elena turned to look in the direction they'd been heading, trying to remember. "Bishop's office," she decided, leaping for the first coherent sounding answer. "I said we'd see if he'd left for the meeting yet."

"And then?"

She turned back to look at him, wary at the ultra-even tone

he'd adopted. Somehow, he seemed even more unpredictable like this. "I'm not sure yet."

He gestured ahead of them. "Then you'd better lead the way."

CHAPTER 4

Justifiable Lightning Strikes

It was easier this way.

Firmly reminding himself of that fact, Cam dutifully followed Elena down the hall to Bishop's office. The elf had apparently left already, and when the princess turned down another corner Cam didn't ask where they were going next. He'd put in enough grunt time on sentry detail—stand there, look forbidding, learn how to embrace boredom—that he could probably make it through the next month without speaking more than eight words to the woman he was supposed to be guarding. Clearly, she would prefer it that way, and if she could keep from lying to him he could certainly do without the small talk. It wasn't like he could do anything about the curse, anyway.

Cam narrowed his eyes at the back of Elena's head, trying to figure out what was bothering him about all this. He was sure his dad expected him to do more than play shadow, but from what his parents had said, Nigel sounded more like a pest than a serious threat. Even if he had been, Cam was no better with a sword than either of his older siblings, and yet for some reason his dad had still wanted him on the job.

He wasn't even exactly sure what the real job was. The biggest threat against Elena was obviously the curse, but Robbie was the closest thing the family had to a magic expert. If this was some insane scheme to get the princess a friend—what a nightmare that would be—he hoped they would have at least tried to throw twelve-year-old Gabby at her first. What was Cam supposed to do that no one else could?

He hated trying to figure out what his father was thinking.

"Wait here," Elena ordered, stopping in front of one of the castle's seemingly endless doorways. The faint chemical smell emanating from the other side suggested the room was hiding something considerably more interesting than a meeting. "I'll only be a few minutes."

He was fine with following rules. Dictates, however, were a different matter. "I don't think so." He stepped forward before she could argue and grasped the door handle. "A good guard always enters a room before the person he's protecting."

Cam opened the door just as Elena was drawing breath for a response, moving into a room that was almost pitch black. He waited for his eyes to adjust, and when there was absolutely no improvement, he became suspicious. Then there was a faint crackling sound, only a little bit louder than the bubbling, and he yanked Elena behind him as he lunged for the wall.

An instant later, a bolt of lightning shot out of the darkness and sizzled as it left a burn spot on the wooden door.

"This is why I wanted you to wait outside," Elena snapped, hitting him on the arm as she stepped away from him. "Braeth doesn't like strangers."

There was a deep, foreboding voice from the darkness "Oh,

I have little trouble with them." The words had an odd echoing quality, suggesting they were being made without the benefit of actual vocal cords. "It's a poor sorcerer who hasn't learned to work around a charred corpse or two."

The darkness thinned, just a little, and Cam could just barely make out a hooded figure on the other side of the room. From the little Cameron knew about wraiths, they didn't actually need to stay in the shadows, but it definitely upped the drama factor. "I bet you really annoy the housekeeping staff."

Braeth—at least, it better be the Braeth Elena had mentioned—chuckled again. "Oh, I do approve of this one." When Elena made a disgusted noise and pushed passed Cam, the darkness thinned a little more as the wraith floated toward her. "Though if you were hoping to put your potential suitor through a trial by fire, I would be pleased to make him bleed a little."

The princess made a choking sound, presumably at the word "suitor" rather than "bleed," but Cam had grown up with older siblings. "Pleased to meet you, sir. My name is Cameron Merrick, and Elena and I are very much in love." As he gave his voice the extra drama such a ridiculous statement required, he could practically feel Elena's temper climb a few more notches. He fought a grin. "It means so much to me that you could sense the emotion we have for each other."

This time, Braeth gave in to a full laugh. "Oh, you *are* an entertaining creature." Cam could make out just a hint of a skeletal face in the shadows beneath the cowl. Braeth's bony fingers peeked out of the edge of his sleeve as he motioned toward Elena."I suspect young Elena is already considering what portion of the cellar to bury your corpse in."

Cam glanced over at the princess, deciding he could squeeze in one more joke before his life would be genuinely at risk—from

Elena, not the wraith. Surprisingly, he felt comfortable around Braeth already."If she kills me, she'd have to deal with my mother."

Out of the corner of his eye, he could see Elena's hand twitch in that same way it had before. Though he couldn't be sure of the specific meaning behind the gesture, it looked remarkably like a woman fighting the urge to toss a spell at his head. He gave her an "Oh, really?" look, making it clear he'd seen the aborted gesture. Her jaw tightened, eyes sliding away from his.

When he turned back to Braeth, the wraith was watching them both. Nothing of his face was visible, and Cam realized how much he usually relied on reading people's expressions. "As entertaining as that was, we have other matters to attend to," the wraith said, the humor that had been in his voice now completely absent. "Did you come seeking wisdom or death from me?"

Elena hesitated, then folded her arms tightly across her chest. "I think the curse is coming early."

Braeth went utterly still, even shutting off the wind effect that made his cloak perpetually rustle. "If it did," he said, "You would already be unconscious. Sleep curses are designed to take effect as soon as the target date or scenario is achieved. The one your aunt constructed is very definitive."

Cam saw Elena flinch a little on the last word, but she lifted her chin. "Well, it's becoming less definitive. I collapsed for thirty seconds in town a few days ago, and in the hallway for more than a minute about an hour ago. I dropped in mid-sentence, without reason."

Braeth was silent as she finished speaking, then lifted a hand towards a row of bookshelves against an opposite wall. One of the books floated up off a shelf and headed for the wraith, opening in front of him and hovering there obligingly while the pages turned. "If this was an intentional feature of the curse, there will be a specific pattern to the incidents. Only fools think it possible to generate true chaos."

Elena sighed, her entire body drooping a little. "So you're saying I need to wait for more incidents so I can see what the pattern is. Because there will be a pattern, and this is just a nasty little feature of the curse we somehow haven't found until now." The fire that had been in her voice was gone, and she sounded tired and sad enough that Cam felt an uncomfortable twinge inside his chest. He liked her smiling, and he was used to her ice queen routine, but this, this was just wrong.

Braeth didn't say anything as he slowly returned the book to its place on the shelf. "I fear so," he said finally, sounding oddly regretful despite the echo in his voice. "We focused on the inherent structure of the curse, not flourishes such as these. Whatever this proves to be, it is likely nothing more than cosmetic."

"This feels a little more than that, Braeth." The edge was back in her voice. Cam tried hard to pretend he wasn't relieved to hear it. "After we find the pattern, will there be any way to get rid of this particular flourish? She's getting the rest of my life—she shouldn't be able to mess with the last few months I have left."

The cowl nodded. "I cannot imagine it will be too difficult, once we understand the structure of the alteration. I will consult my books." He slid towards Elena, lifting a hand to brush almost but not quite along the top of her hair. The fine hairs fluttered, caught in the same invisible wind that he used on his cloak. "There is little need to ask if you've consulted with your mother about this."

"No." Elena closed her eyes, looking tired again. Cam was sure she'd completely forgotten he was in the room. "No one's going to. There's no reason to break her heart any more than it already has been."

Braeth let out a long, rattling breath. "You know full well I do not share the secrets given into my possession." His bony fingers moved near her face, once again almost but not quite touching her. Then he floated away again. "You must be careful until we resolve the matter, however. Keeping your secret is useless if she sees a collapse with her own eyes, and the queen is a skilled enough sorceress that she would undoubtedly detect any attempt on my part to wipe her memory."

Cam's brain registered all the possibilities in the last couple of words, and he turned to Elena with a steely look. "If you were thinking about it, don't."

Elena had jumped a little when he'd started speaking—he'd been right about her forgetting.Her face shifted from confused to appalled to annoyed in a matter of seconds. "Why would I bother going through the effort of wiping your memory? You already know everything useful there is to know about the curse, and I'm certainly not going to let you get the opportunity to find out anything else I want kept secret." She huffed out a breath. "Besides, it speaks poorly of you that you immediately assumed a threat from a casual conversation."

"Casual? Hah!" Cam made a disbelieving noise. "You're apparently comfortable enough with the idea of wiping your mother's memory that the terrifying wraith felt like he needed to be the voice of reason, and you don't even like me. Don't try to tell me the idea wouldn't have crossed your mind at some point."

She sputtered for a few seconds, clearly trying to find a reality where he wasn't right. "I don't know why I'm even trying to explain myself to you," she snapped, taking a definite step away from him.

"If you could manage some reasonable explanation for why you are the way you are, I'd love to hear it! There are entire five or ten minute stretches where you're a fairly pleasant human being, but then it's like some sort of signal goes off in your head and you insist on doing something specifically designed to drive me insane. You make less sense than anyone I've ever met in my life, and that includes my little sister who spent a good three months of her life wanting to be a frog."

Her glare sharpened. "You think I'm the one who doesn't make any sense? You clearly don't want to be here, and yet no matter how many chances I give you to leave you insist—"

"Silence!" Braeth's voice thundered as he cut them both off, the echo in his voice making it seem like it was coming from all sides of the room at once. Both Cam and Elena fell silent, and the wraith let the stillness settle in before he spoke again. "Good. If I had needed to expend further effort to get your attention, you would not have appreciated the consequences."

He looked back and forth between them, then focused on Cam. "I assure you that your memories will remain unharmed while you reside in this castle. I cannot make the same promise for all of your limbs if you continue to vex my goddaughter, but I suspect you are already well aware of that."

Then his gaze swung to Elena, tone softening in the same way it had earlier.Really, the whole "goddaughter" thing made a lot more sense than it probably should have. "It will do you good to be vexed on a more regular basis." He paused, considering. "In time, I suspect you will realize that as well."

Elena stared at him, appalled, then shook her head as if she'd given up hope of finding any common sense in the immediate vicinity. "Why does everyone like it so much when I get upset? You'd think a centuries-old sorcerer would have better things to do with his free time." Still looking annoyed, she gestured to the wraith's bookshelves. "Can I borrow Eskalion's Treatise on Magical Forms'? I think it has something in there on exponential curse structures."

When the book floated over to her outstretched hand, she turned and pushed her way out of the room without another word to either of them. Cameron resisted for only a second before hurrying after her, pride temporarily bowing to the knowledge that he had no chance of finding his way to the dining hall alone.

~

Several hours and one very stressful dinner later, all Cam wanted was a little sleep. His dad didn't have a bedroom in the castle—there was a perfectly good one with a wife in it waiting for him at home—but there were a few rooms in the princess' suite meant for ladies-in-waiting. Since Elena had talked her mother into reassigning all of hers to other parts of the castle, his dad had commandeered one of the beds for those few nights he'd had to sleep over.

One of the maids had already brought his bag in and set it on the bed. Cam shoved it onto the floor as he sat down and scrubbed his hands through his hair. Elena was safely ensconced in her room, after deliberately locking the door on him, and he left his own open to make it that much harder for her to sneak past him.

He let out a long, tired breath. Just six more weeks.

"If he can't see us, do you think we can sneak away and eat his pie?"

Mood lifting at the familiar voice, Cam opened his eyes again to see his little sister and no-longer-quite-so-little brother standing in the doorway. Gabby was holding a covered dish that probably held a slice or two of the aforementioned pie, and both of them were flashing grins that matched the one he was wearing. Apparently, Mom had been letting Robbie practice his transportation spell.

"I think he's caught us, Gabs," Robbie said easily, leading his younger sister into the room. He sat down on the bed next to Cam, his lanky teenage legs only an inch or two shorter than his older brother's, while Gabby held the dish out to Cam. "Two slices of bloodberry pie, your favorite," she announced. "I helped mom make it, so it's more delicious than usual."

Robbie leaned over. "Don't let that scare you off," he said in a stage whisper, making Gabby scowl at him just like he'd wanted her to. "It's definitely not poisoned. We've all tested it."

"Hah hah." Gabby kicked Robbie in the leg. "I'm a good cook. I've decided I'm gonna be a big fancy chef."

"And I'm sure you'll be a great one," Cam soothed, rubbing at an errant smudge of flour just underneath his sister's ear. She changed what she wanted to be when she grew up about once a month, throwing herself headlong into every new profession. His mother had been profoundly relieved when the juggling urges had passed, but so far Cam had been particularly delighted by that phase. "Now give me the pie."

She handed the dish over with a big smacking kiss, then started poking around the room looking for anything interesting enough to occupy her attention. Grateful for both the pie and the company, Cam started eating.

"Wow, you really needed the pie. You look wrecked." Robbie watched his brother with an analytical, sympathetic expression. "Since Mom didn't mention that she was worried about anything, I'd say it's the princess who's been running you ragged."

Cam shook his head, swallowing his mouthful before attempting to say anything. "I can't talk about it. If I do, I'll start shouting, and it'll make it harder to keep drowning my sorrows in pie."

Robbie winced sympathetically. "Sorry. I know Dad was pretty insistent on dragging you back here, but I thought the fact that he'd managed to convince Mom meant it was probably safe."

"She loves him," Cam grumbled, taking another bite. "That sometimes leads her to make poor choices."

Robbie chuckled. "Because I love you, I promise not to tell either of our parents you said that." He patted Cam on the leg, expression sobering. "Honestly, though, I'm here for you if you think there's anything I can do. You backed me up on enough of those magic fights between me and Dad that I probably owe you about a hundred at this point."

Cam was about to say no, not sure that there was anything anyone could do to make his life easier, when his mind went back to the rows of books lining Braeth and Elena's shelves. He wasn't going to get involved in the technical details of the curse—what a nightmare that would be—but he desperately needed to understand something that was going on with these people. "Do any of your books have anything about curses?" he asked, not sure if he'd be able to understand the books even if Robbie did have anything to hand over. Even if he couldn't, though, this wasn't the first time the kid had helped him with his homework. "How they're put together, the basic features, that sort of thing?"

"Witchcraft doesn't really do curses, but there are a couple of theory books that might have something. It depends on what you're looking for." Robbie hesitated. "You know that a whole bunch of really serious sorcerers and sorceresses have studied the curse over the years, right? No one's been able to figure out how to even get a look at the inner workings of the thing, let alone start on untangling it."

Cam looked at his brother in confusion, knowing Robbie was trying to politely say something but not sure what it was. When it hit him, he laughed. "You think I've got designs on fixing the curse? I'm not stupid, Robbie." He returned to his pie. "I'm the first person to admit that the only thing I know about magic is what you've told me over the years. But there are about twenty different things going on here that no one wants to talk about, and you're the only person who I'm sure will give me a straight answer."

Robbie's expression cleared in understanding, but before he could say anything, Gabby's voice cut in. "Cam? Robbie? I don't think that's a bird."

Both brothers turned to look at the girl, who had stuck her body halfway out the window to get a closer look at something in the night sky. Suddenly suspicious for no reason that made logical sense, Cam hurried to the window to try and get a look at whatever his sister was seeing. Gabby, obliging, pointed at the tree line just in time to catch a dark shape disappearing just beneath the tips of the pines.

Cam turned to his sister. "Did you see what direction it came from?" Elena had seemed a little too calm about him being able to watch her door, now that he thought about it.

When she pointed in the general direction of the princess's room, Cam swore and turned to Robbie. "Do sorceresses know flying spells?"

"Not as far as I know. It's usually easier to just ask a dragon to give you a lift." Robbie's brow lowered as he thought. "Witches use a spell to make their broomsticks fly, but—"

"Close enough." Cam bolted out the door, then went a few feet and swore again. He spun around on his heel, then poked his head back in to look at his confused brother and sister. "Does anyone know the quickest way out of this stupid building?"

CHAPTER 5

Joyriding

Elena stared intently at the book sitting on the desk in front of her, willing herself to open it. Studying this new feature of the curse was the sensible thing to do, even if it wasn't likely to get her anywhere without more blackouts to help her figure out the pattern. She couldn't let Braeth do all the research work, even if they were the only two people who would know it. It would be irresponsible.

Oh, how she wished she could be irresponsible right now.

She sat back, pressing her fingertips against her eyes. It should probably comfort her that Braeth hadn't seemed more worried about the blackouts, but now that the fear was gone the sheer inevitability of it all seemed that much more crushing. The blackouts were simply another cruelty that had always been waiting for her, one more facet of the curse's labyrinthine, multi-shielded structure that she'd somehow failed to discover even after years of study.

All her talent and effort had gotten her was a lifetime of beating her head against the wall, and the daily reconfirmation that she'd been a tragedy from the day she was born. If Cameron knew what was really going on inside her head, he'd be grateful she was kind enough to lie to him.

Sick of herself and everything else, she stood and went to the chest at the foot of her bed. Digging down to the false bottom, she flipped the release catch and pulled out a leather harness and bracelet set that was absolutely soaked in magic.

Changing into black leggings and an undershirt, she buckled herself into the harness and snapped on the bracelets. Pulling a dark blue tunic on over the whole thing, she put her hair up into a knot and tucked it under a black stocking cap. Then she opened her shutters and climbed up onto the window sill, swinging her legs down over the edge. Carefully surveying the scene spread out beneath her, she watched the rotation of the castle guards around the castle's front perimeter. Alan had browbeat the guard master into changing their rotations nightly, but there were only so many possible combinations that the same number of people could move in. Over the years, she'd seen all of them.

Within a few minutes, she'd figured out the current patrol rotation they were using and picked out the soldier she was looking for. Robertson had neck trouble, and wasn't terribly fond of bending her head back when she didn't have to. And it didn't matter which of them ended up just beneath her window, because no one ever looked straight up.

Admittedly, she could have simply used a cloaking spell and eliminated any threat of discovery. But where was the challenge in that?

Elena moved up into a crouching position, murmuring the words of the spell while the guardsmen moved into position below her. She felt the magic take effect, the lift of the harness pulling her slightly upward. When the moment was right, she pushed off into open sky.

There was a slight lurch as the harness accepted her full weight, then she was arrowing off towards her favorite patch of trees. She'd adapted the spell from the one witches used to make their brooms fly, spending months tinkering on it whenever she didn't want to be alone with her thoughts.Later, after a few practice runs that had edged into the comical, she'd added bracelets that gave her better control of her steering.

Elena coasted carefully over the guard's heads, staying high enough to avoid the light and moving quietly enough that she made no noise. Only Braeth and Alan knew she made these flights,with Alan following her out whenever he stayed over at the castle and Braeth using his magic to watch her. Even without them, she was wrapped in so many protective spells that she never worried about being caught out on her own.

Once she was out of range, she celebrated by doing a loop in the air. Her stomach flipped in the best possible way, and she let herself grin like an idiot before indulging in another one and speeding off as wind brushed against her face, she closed her eyes and let herself savor the sensation before ducking down beneath the tree line.

Playing beneath the huge canopy of branches didn't offer as much freedom as the open sky, but it was considerably better protected from overly concerned guards or annoying princes who wanted to take advantage of the curse. She landed carefully on an exposed tree branch, disturbing an owl who gave her an annoyed hoot as it vacated the premises.

Whispering an apology as it flew off, Elena pushed off again to weave a slow, curving path through the moonlit trees. Some nights were for experimentation or training—with this rig, flying straight down took a lot of leg strength—but right now she just wanted to relax and enjoy this beautiful section of forest. A quick spell cast a faint glow, giving her just enough light not to run into anything.

A walk might have been simpler, but girls who walked through the woods alone in the dark tended to be either kidnapped or accosted by mysterious creatures intent on making trouble. Flying through the woods, however, not only did you have an immediate escape route, but it tended to confuse people just long enough to let you use that escape route.

She dipped low to the ground, fingers brushing lightly over the bright blue blossoms of the wild fairy bonnets that grew wherever sunlight made it all the way to the forest floor. Her dad had loved nature far more than he'd loved being a king, and she could still remember the stolen sunlit mornings when they'd take walks together through the woods around the castle and he'd teach her the names of all the plants and flowers: hyssop, Witches' Nails, fairy bonnets, sweet ivy, dragon's breath.

Sometimes, her mother would join them. Witches had a much wider range of herbal knowledge than sorceresses, but Illiana Randall had known a few stories designed to impress the wide-eyed young girl Elena had been. Her mother had smiled so much more in those days, even though the curse was already a part of their lives, and if she concentrated she could still remember the sound of her parents laughing together on those long-ago walks.

The memory was a sweet-sharp ache, deep in her chest.

Pushing it aside, she kicked her legs and headed upward to weave in and out through the branches. It was unlikely that Cameron would think to bother her while she was out—he was watching her doorway, not the window, and had absolutely no reason to be scanning the skies looking for her. Besides, he'd seemed drained enough when he'd gone to his own room she couldn't imagine he'd have any interest in crawling out of bed. She'd been surprised to find herself faintly disappointed—from everything Alan said about his children, she would have thought Cameron would be at least a little better at keeping up with her—but it meant the next few weeks would be easier than she thought. All she'd have to do was wait him out.

"I hate to say it, but I'm actually kind of impressed."

Elena jerked around in the direction of the unexpected voice, forgetting that she hadn't given herself a great deal of clearance when she'd gone under the last branch. She smacked straight into it, immediately getting scraped arms and a face full of leaves, and there was an endlessly embarrassing minute while she fought her way free and flew out into the clearing.

Cameron, who had now officially earned the title of the most annoying man in this world or any other, was standing in the middle of the undergrowth looking up at her. He'd taken off his uniform jacket at some point, along with most of his weapons, and he had his hands in his pockets like he'd been watching her for awhile. When she strengthened her light spell—it was always important to see your enemy clearly—there was a grin on his face like someone had just told him a really fantastic joke.

If she killed him now, she could probably blame it on wild animals. "If you laugh at me, I'll set your internal organs on fire."

"I'm sure you could, but then you'd have to explain what happened to my older sister." When he stepped closer, however, she realized there was no mockery in his expression. "Besides, I'm way too thrilled by the fact that you're secretly a free spirit to even think about mocking you for it."

She blinked, not having expected that response. "You're not going to yell at me for sneaking out of the castle in the middle of the night?"

"Oh, at first I wanted to kill you." He gestured slightly behind him with his head. "I actually brought some rope, in case I needed to tie you up and forcibly drag you back to the castle."

She flew upward a little, glaring down at him. "You could have tried."

Cameron just laughed. "Remind me to get you out into the sparring ring at some point. If your mother asks, we'll call it self-defense training."

Without anything to push back against, Elena felt the righteous anger she'd been gathering slip through her fingers. She clung to it, intent on making Cameron respond to something in a way that made sense to her. "So I defied you, snuck out, presumably made you steal what had to be the quietest horse in the stables to chase me out here, and yet somehow you've decided this is all wonderful news." She'd gotten him shouting before, and he had to be exhausted right now. It shouldn't take too much work to make him yell at her again. "Did you hit your head when you were riding after me?"

He shook his head, still looking far too pleased about the whole thing. "That ice princess routine isn't going to work anymore, Princess. Game's up."

Elena didn't understand what he was talking about, but that didn't stop a thin trickle of panic from working its way through her chest. "You're babbling."

"And you sneak out of your room at night to go flying through the forest when no one else can see you." He watched her face, looking for a reaction. "I bet you even do loop-de-loops."

She loved doing loops. "Don't be absurd."

Triumph lit Cameron's eyes. "I knew it." Mercifully, he turned to scan the forest around them. "I used to fight ogres."

It was exhausting trying to keep up with the man. "When you were with the border guards?"He snorted as he turned back to look at her. "No, when I was twelve, on nights I couldn't sleep, I'd sneak out into the shed Dad used for practice and use one of his staves to beat up on the practice bag. In my head, though, I was saving a town from a ravaging ogre. I did a pretty good impression of a cheering crowd." He laughed. "Still do, actually."

For just a second, she could see him as that little boy, hitting a practice bag with all the determination he was currently pouring into driving her insane. "And you think this is my version of your late-night practice fights? That I'm living out some secret fantasy of being a dragon I haven't told anyone about?"

Cameron cocked his head to one side, looking at her as if trying to sort out a riddle. "At what point did you decide that there wasn't a single person in the entire kingdom you could relax around?"

Elena had hoped that being able to loom over him in midair would give her some advantage, but if anything he seemed even more determined to control the conversation than usual. She let her feet touch the ground, murmuring the word that would shut off the spell. "I find your father very relaxing."

"See, I know you're lying now, because I know my dad." His voice was easy, and no matter how much she wanted to Elena couldn't detect even a hint of frustration. "But nice try."

Unfortunately, he was doing a wonderful job at annoying her. "You may know your father, but you don't know me at all." She lifted her chin, aware they were arguing in circles. Flying off in a huff, however, would only relocate the conversation someplace where too many people would overhear it. "You're in no position to decide whether or not I find something relaxing."

Cameron pulled his hands out of his pockets. "If you were the ice princess you try so hard to seem like, you would have come out here in the first place solely as some sort of annoying mind game. When I showed up, you would have said something cutting about my reflexes or my reaction time and flown off again. Which is why I brought the rope." He moved toward her suddenly, and when she stepped back he reached out and plucked something off the top of her head. When he pulled his hand back, he was holding a single leaf. "You definitely wouldn't risk getting leaves in your hair, or touch all the branches as you flew by like you were telling them hello."

She hadn't been aware she did that. "I still defied you."

"Yeah, but now I'm starting to understand why you did it, and since it's for the exact reason I would have I can't be too annoyed about it." Cameron said, dropping the leaf. "I'm not gonna start yelling at you, so you might as well stop trying to push me into it. I will ask how you pulled off the flying trick, though."

Her first stubborn impulse was not to tell him, but there was no reason not to. "I enchanted the leather with the basic spell witches use to make their brooms fly," she said, lifting up her tunic just far enough to give him a look at the harness. "Then I tweaked it for more directional mobility, and added the leather bracelets to improve the guidance system."

Cameron looked impressed. "Would the bracelets work on their own? Like if a squirrel stole one, would he have his own little magical flying belt?"

Elena's lips twitched at the image, though she did her best

to repress the response. “I hooked all of the enchantments together, so one won’t work without the other. That fact can be fairly annoying when I misplace one of the bracelets, but it’s safer in the long run.”

“Probably true.” He hesitated. “I feel I should probably warn you that Robbie knows you can fly now. He’ll be polite about it, but he’ll pester you until you indulge him in a full-on technical discussion of every single tweak you made. He’ll take a lot of notes, and maybe even bow.”

“Robert? Really?” Cameron’s brother was only a year or so younger than she was, and Elena had always thought of him as the safest of the Merrick siblings. They’d had a few discussions about magic over the years, but nothing too terribly involved. “I’d be happy to.”

“See? This is why I can’t be mad at you.” He nodded, satisfied. “Whenever we were forced to be in the same room before, you’d just sit there all stiff and quiet like you didn’t know how to interact with the rest of us.Every time I tried to draw you in, you’d freeze me out.”

“I was always perfectly polite to you,” Elena said.

“Politeness can be its own weapon.”Cameron sounded amused. “Now that I find out you’re using it to hide a playful side, though, I’m seeing it in a whole new light.”

The panic was back, and as usual it made her voice sharp. “Because you think you know some big secret about me? For all you know, this whole inner life you’re so sure you see in me is nothing more than a construct inside your own head.”

He smirked. “Another thing I’ve figured out about you. You bluff with absolutely no cards in your hand, which can be either frustrating or funny depending on my mood.”

She narrowed her eyes at him. It would serve him right if she *did* start being honest with him. A few weeks of hearing all the details of her life and he'd be begging her to go back to the "ice princess routine" he was so dismissive of.

As Elena turned the thought over in her head, it started to genuinely sound like a pretty good idea. It wouldn't be quite as easy as it sounded, of course. His father could handle the occasional morbid joke without becoming uncomfortable, which meant she'd have to dump everything on Cameron's head to have any chance of properly scaring him off.

The thought sent panic sliding through her chest again, a cold slither that felt like a warning. But he clearly wasn't going to give up and wander away on his own, and it didn't seem like she had another option. "Maybe I am quite sweet and sensitive in reality." Her voice was sugar sweet as she spoke. "When I start crying in the middle of the night, should I knock on your door so you can come comfort me?"

She had the distinct satisfaction of seeing his eyes go wide for a second. It didn't matter how tough a man was—a crying woman rattled every single one of them. "You have crying fits in the middle of the night?"

"You tell me." Elena folded her arms across her chest. "After all, you're the one who knows me so well."

He made an exasperated noise. "Look, the verbal sparring is fun, but it's giving you the wrong impression. I can promise you I have no interest in reading your psyche or walking you through some confrontational therapy mumbo jumbo." He held his hands out in a "What can you do?" gesture, looking far more tired and harried than furious. "I just want to spend the next six weeks without feeling like I offended you by existing. I don't like that feeling, and I definitely don't like the fact that feeling that way makes me want to yell at people."

For some reason, it was incredibly hard for her to stay mad at the man. "All I asked was that we leave each other alone. After spending the entire evening arguing with me, I would think you'd jump at the opportunity."

"Normal people don't stop talking when they leave each other alone!" Cameron moved closer, expression suggesting that he was seriously thinking about shaking her. "Sure, you tiptoe around the really painful stuff if they want, but random, pleasant conversation about the weather, crazy families or what you did over the weekend is a basic part of being a human being." He took a deep breath, deliberately making himself calm down. "And, now that I'm 100 percent certain you are a human being, I'm going to wait patiently until you figure that out, too."

Ignoring the frisson of worry that snuck through her, she tightened her jaw. "I don't believe you're capable of being patient."

"Okay, relatively patient." He smiled again, the charm firmly back in place. "Will it help if I answer the question you asked Braeth earlier?"

Her brow furrowed at the sudden change in topic. "What question?"

"Why everyone likes seeing you upset." When she narrowed her eyes at him, he shrugged. "I'm serious. I haven't interviewed the 'everyone' you were referring to, but my guess is that seeing you shout is the only time they have any idea what's going on inside your head."

Elena huffed. "You just think that way because your family's insane. You're all far too comfortable talking about your feelings."

His responding grin was warm and genuine, though Elena wasn't entirely certain she'd been joking. "We've been called insane for a lot of reasons, but never that." He turned around, looking back in the direction where he'd presumably left the horse. "So, have I annoyed you enough you'll be flying back, or did you want to hang out here a few more hours?"

"Don't think you have to lose sleep because of me," Elena said carefully, the warning bells going off in her head. "Alan was usually home with Marie during my flying trips, and I'm so wrapped up in protective spells it's practically impossible for someone to kidnap me."

He met her eyes. "Do any of those spells fly you home if you have one of your blackout episodes in midair?"

Elena didn't bother trying to answer, not wanting to admit that she hadn't thought of that. "I'll see you back at the castle." She re-activated the spell, pushing herself upward. "We'll re-visit the question of whether or not you're coming with me next time when I have some actual evidence to argue with."

Looking not at all bothered by this prospect, Cameron he headed back to his horse. Our of the corner of her eye, she could see him wave at her as she flew off.

The idea that he was following her back, that he'd notice if she fell, was a weirdly comforting one. She firmly ignored it.

SUMMER

19 years ago

Illiana didn't think of herself as evil, though she had all the training and proper certification to advertise that she was. As her older sister Ariadne put it, being "evil" simply meant that you attracted a more interesting range of clients and were exempt from the normal community service requirements.

Having only recently graduated, Illiana had little firsthand experience with clients of any sort. She was currently working as an assistant to her sister, handling research duties and providing a second pair of hands for more complicated spells. Ariadne, who had already been practicing independently for a few years, dealt directly with customers and handled the creative experimentation that had given her such a long client list. Both sisters were happy with the arrangement, which appealed to their personal strengths.

Illiana had first been promised the job when she was nine years old, a blood-oath made by a twelve-year old Ariadne in her first throes of passion over what she swore was her destined profession. She had said as much to their parents only hours before, interrupting an evening cocktail with other elegantly dressed people to do so. Their indifference to the news, a common response when it came to their inconvenient children, had infuriated Ariadne into a spectacular rant about her professional future.

"I'll be the greatest sorceress the world has ever seen!" she had shouted, throwing out her arms wide. "And not a stupid good one, either. No one tells evil sorceresses not to do something because people will gossip about it. Evil sorceresses love gossip."

It was Illiana's job to be the audience to such proclamations, a duty she was always happy to fulfill when it came to her sister. The world was full of people infinitely more bright and shiny than she was, and Ariadne was the only one who ever tried to include her little sister in the glow. "Don't you have to be scary to be an evil sorceress?" Illiana asked then, a pillow clutched tight against her chest. "I want to be one, too, but I don't know if I can be scary."

Ariadne had seemed a little startled at that, as if she'd forgotten anyone else was in the room. Then she'd jumped down from the dresser she'd been standing on and sat next to Illiana on the bed. "I'll be scary for both of us, and you can help me with stuff," Ariadne said, putting an arm around her little sister. "We'll be the greatest evil sorceresses the world has ever seen."

A decade later, it was still the best offer Illiana had ever received. Ariadne had her own tower, payment for one of her more spectacular jobs, and she'd given her little sister an entire suite of rooms and free run of the well-stocked library. Illiana had been in the library for most of the afternoon, researching illnesses that could be induced by sorcery and were almost, but not quite, fatal.

She had just started her notes on a curse that would make everything a person ate taste like spoiled milk when Ariadne burst into the room. "Ana!" There was a slight theatrical edge to her voice that meant she wasn't in any genuine distress. "You're the only one who can save me!"

Smiling slightly, Illiana carefully finished the sentence she'd started before looking up. "Have the ravens gotten out of their cages again?"

"No, nothing so boring as that." Long black sleeves fluttering as she made a dismissive gesture, Ariadne dropped down into the seat opposite Illiana's. "I've got a client that's going to make our fortunes, but I've run into a bit of a snag."

Illiana's brow furrowed. "I thought you weren't taking clients for a little while so you could focus on a special project."

"This is the special project! I didn't want to tell you about it until I was sure it would be as fabulous as I hoped." Ariadne leaned forward across the table, the excitement in her voice entirely at odds with her precise upsweep of white-blond hair. Illiana often wondered if she was the only person her sister allowed herself to be giddy with. "We're going to curse a king."

Illiana hesitated. "Killing royalty brings powerful enemies, Ari, especially if whoever hired us makes sure the blame falls on us as well."

Ariadne's eyes narrowed, her voice dark enough that it sent a chill through Illiana. "Oh, I've taken care of that." Then her expression cleared again. "Besides, we're not going to kill him. I've been working on this genius curse that will keep him asleep for a hundred years. The second cousin once removed can cry with everyone else when he takes the throne, making solemn promises that he won't rest until a cure is found for his poor whoever it is."

Personally, Illiana preferred the curses that involved giving someone boils or terrible fashion sense. Ariadne always told Illiana that she thought too small. "What will he do if someone does find a cure? Wandering princesses are less common than princes, but the odds are that someone will try and convince the curse that this sleeping king is her true love."

"That's the best part!" Ariadne dropped her voice to a conspiratorial whisper, delight evident in every line of her face. "The first thing I did was disconnect the True Love's Kiss trigger. Unless some sorceress can make it through all my shields and unwind my whole knot by hand, there is no cure for this curse!"

Illiana blinked, a little unnerved by her sister's happiness. Ariadne, however, would have no interest in hearing about that. "You'd be known as the most ruthless evil sorceress in all the kingdoms." She reminded herself that such a reputation would be a clear advantage in their business, and that evil sorceresses weren't supposed to care about being seen as horrible people. "I'm not sure I see where you need me, though."

Now Ariadne's expression turned frustrated. "I need to tie the curse into the king's blood. It's the only key deep enough to make the spell truly unbreakable, but I have no idea how to actually get some."

"Why not the second cousin who hired you? Family blood is a common enough substitute."

Ariadne shook her head. "The connection is too distant between them for his blood to be any good. If that was my only option, I might as well just tie the curse to the king's hair and be done with it." Then she tilted her head to the side, lowering it just enough that she could look up at her sister. She didn't flutter her eyelashes—it was too much of a joke between them—but she did widen her eyes just a little. "Lucky for me, I have an incredibly smart sister who can pretend to be one of the scholars the king allows to use the palace library. You'll get a sample of his blood and bring it back to me, and I'll make sure everyone knows we created the curse together."

Illiana hesitated. She'd never admit to her sister, but she didn't like dealing with either client or their targets. She'd met a few of their clients, and most of them seemed like the kind of people who could stand to have a few more painful swelling boils in their lives. It had been hard to do the research for those assignments, though she'd never told her sister about it. She hadn't wanted to disappoint her.

Ariadne recognized the thoughtful expression in her sister's eyes but thankfully misinterpreted its meaning. "See, you're already thinking of ways to do it." Leaning further across the table, she pressed a quick kiss against Illiana's forehead before standing. "Oh, this will be brilliant."

Ariadne swept out of the room without the formality of her sister's official agreement. Both of them knew it hadn't really been needed.

CHAPTER 6

Both Sides of a Deal

The next several days passed in relative peace, though that was due more to Elena's distraction than any actual truce between her and Cam. The collapse she and Braeth had been expecting never came, and both were churning out pages of numbers they would then immediately swear at and throw away. They'd meet again, consult more books than it should be physically possible to fit in either of their rooms, and start back on the math. The swearing became more creative as the days passed, though Elena's were more entertaining since Cam didn't understand half of what Braeth was saying.

Cam refrained from saying this out loud, though. He doubted either of them would take it well.

They'd made another visit to Braeth's lab that morning, and Cam was trailing Elena back to her rooms with half of the inconveniently enormous stack of books she'd borrowed. Elena was yards ahead with the other half of the stack, clearly ready to bowl over anyone not quick enough to get out of her way.

Normally, Cam was huffing after her rather than risk taking a wrong turn into a closet. However, since this was the twentieth time they'd made this particular trip over the last three days, he pretty much had the route memorized.

He'd just rounded the second corner at the top of the first staircase when Bishop walked by, looking more harried than the first time Cam had seen him. When their eyes met, the elf shifted his route to match Cam's. After a few steps, he held out his hands. "Need some help with those?"

Cam hesitated, knowing that Elena wouldn't want Bishop to find out about the blackouts, then handed over half the stack he'd been carrying. The elf would get the chance to read the spines anyway, just by walking next to him, and at least this way Cam would have a lighter load. "Thanks. My manly honor stupidly insisted I take the bigger half, so right now I'm more than happy to annoy it by accepting help."

Bishop smiled as they kept walking. Though he generally looked as ageless as most elves, the expression made him look surprisingly young. "I've found that my manly honor rarely has my best interests at heart." He glanced over at the books Cam was still carrying, then down at the top book in his own stack. Cam had made sure it was one of the older ones, with a complicated symbol on the cover instead of a title. "I notice that Braeth and Elena seem to be working quite intently on a special project of some kind," Bishop said, as if deciding that the subtle route wasn't getting him anywhere. "Should I be warning the staff to prepare for an explosion?"

Cam had no doubt what the other man was asking, but he wasn't ready to break Elena's trust without her life being at risk. He'd come to respect her too much. "There's a lot of math," he said, face as blank as the time his parents asked who had broken his grandmother's favorite vase. "I mostly listen to them argue and carry her books when she asks me to."

Bishop gave Cam a sideways look, the elf's expression turning rueful. "And that's the second polite 'no' you've given me. I should reclaim my dignity by respecting your decision and leaving you in peace." The way the sentence was phrased, and the pause that followed it, it was obvious that Bishop wasn't likely to follow his own advice.

Cam watched the older man's face, trying to figure out what was behind Bishop's urge to know. He understood how frustrating it was to be left completely in the dark, but he wasn't about to hand over all his cards just to make the elf's job a little easier. "The queen making your life miserable until you find out?"he asked, thinking about his own parents.

Surprisingly, the question seemed to throw Bishop. He opened his mouth, then closed it, and something painful flashed briefly across his face. "Illiana doesn't know I ask." The softness of his voice hinted at a thousand other things he wasn't saying. "But I can see her worry, and I'm happy to do whatever is necessary for an opportunity to ease her mind."

Cam blew out a breath. Now he *had* to give the man something. "Elena's on top of the problem," he offered, pretty sure he wasn't lying. "They've hit a roadblock, but Braeth still seems confident he knows what's going on." When Bishop seemed to relax a little, Cam decided to risk getting something in return. Elena was still determined to keep her mother in the dark about her blackouts, getting this awful closed-off look every time it was brought up."Is everything okay with Elena and her mother?" When wariness lit the other man's eyes, Cam hurried to clarify himself. "I'm not looking for dark family secrets or anything.

I just want to know the basics so I don't accidentally stick my foot in my mouth."

Bishop mulled the question over, clearly working out how much he was willing to say. "They're too much alike," he said.

Cam snorted. "Oh, that's helpful."

Bishop's mouth quirked upward at the corners. "My people believe quite strongly in making sure that both sides of a deal are proportionate. Appearing generous means no one will ever take you seriously in politics or business again."

Cam shifted his books, elbow brushing against a tapestry hanging on the wall. "But since I'm not an elf, you should be able to make an exception."

Bishop shook his head, looking a little too serious. "Exceptions are the keys that end up altering the course of lives. I have no interest in changing my current life."

Cam saw the second-to-last turn coming up ahead, which meant he only had two more hallways and another turn before they'd be at Elena's rooms. Knowing that wouldn't be nearly enough time to get anything useful out of the man, he stopped them both before they made the turn. "You have to understand where I'm coming from, here. If I tell you, you'll tell the queen, Elena will find out, and she'll—" He tried to remember what her most recent threat had been, then gave up and shook his head. "I think it involved something painful happening to all my appendages." He raised an eyebrow at Bishop. "Are your appendages at risk if you don't tell the queen?"

Bishop gave Cam a long, analytical look, as if trying to decide whether or not the younger man was serious. Then he shook his head. "There's not much more I can tell you. Think of every problem you've had with Elena, then imagine a conversation between two people exactly like that."

Cam could, all too easily. "Okay, that does make sense. Elena's in therapy, though. Can't the mirror guy make them talk to each other?"

"He tried," Bishop said, deftly edging past a suit of armor on display. "I could never get the complete story out of Dr. Flyte, but I do know that he developed a rather disconcerting nervous tic for several months after the attempted group session."

"Okay, so scratch talking it out." Cam glanced in the direction of Elena's room, listening for the sound of her stalking back for the rest of her books. He didn't hear anything, and he was willing to bet she was too obsessed with the research to be lurking around the corner listening to him. "Is there some sort of truth serum spell we could hit them both with?"

"That they wouldn't be able to guard against? No." Bishop sounded amused, which Cam decided to take as a good sign in the long run. If nothing else, it was better than pity. "Though I'm encouraged that you care enough to be asking me these questions."

That stopped Cam short, nearly making the top few books slide off the stack. He caught them before they fell, but it didn't help him feel less flustered. "Listen, this isn't some kind of secret crush we're talking about. I just need whatever I can to diffuse the mine field that is Elena Randall."

Now Bishop didn't show a trace of emotion. It was a trick all elves had, a sort of basic armor for all the little social games they played, and it gave some people the impression that the entire race was cold and unfeeling. "Actually, most people find her remarkably easy to get along with."

Cam glared at the other man. "I was being serious."

"So was I. Elena's better at meaningless polite conversation than anyone I've ever met, except for her mother." Still, Bishop's smile returned as he resumed walking towards Elena's room. Cam followed, pleased to note that he'd been right about Elena not lurking anywhere. "Though Elena's never been tested by an eight-hour meeting, so it's entirely possible her skills might not hold up as well under pressure."

"Why doesn't she go to meetings?" Cam lowered his voice, walking more slowly in the hopes that it would get him a few extra minutes. "Everyone else seems in the castle seems to get stuck in them."

Bishop shook his head. "She has no official title, so there's no need for her to have any involvement in matters of state."

"So she's not really the princess?"

"Being a princess is a condition of birth. It doesn't necessarily have anything to do with your position in the ruling government." Bishop was solemn. "Elena and her mother are reluctant to have her declared heir, since the curse will take effect long before she would ever take the throne. It would also leave her open to unscrupulous young men more interested in utilizing the curse to further their own ends."

"Do I dare ask who will take over?"

Bishop hesitated. "For the record, I am the official heir to the throne, though I tell you this mostly so that you won't ask Elena. The king has no extended family left to challenge the decision, and in extreme circumstances the law allows a member of the royal family to designate in advance who will take the throne." He shifted the stack of books in his hand. "I believe a king several generations ago had a deranged elder son he wanted to make absolutely certain never had power."

Cam wondered what it would be like to be able to think

with that kind of cool practicality about something so terrible. Not fun, he imagined. "You don't seem too happy about maybe being king one day."

An old grief flashed across Bishop's face. "I would give everything I own to never have to take the throne." By the time Bishop dropped his books into Cameron's hands, however, his expression was clear. "And now, I will do you a further service by not following you into Elena's room. I suspect she would be less than pleased to see me carrying these books, and would correspondingly subject you to a suitably intimidating interrogation the moment I left the room."

Cam sighed. "True." As the elf turned to go, the younger man shifted the books enough to reach out and catch Bishop's arm. "Hey, thanks." He felt the urge to say more rise up inside him, then decided it wouldn't hurt to say it out loud. "If I get to the point where I don't think she and Braeth can handle this on their own, I promise I'll tell you, okay?"

Bishop closed his eyes then opened them again. "Thank you," he said quietly, then disappeared down the hallway.

Once he was gone, Cam took a deep breath and made his way to Elena's rooms. She was right where he expected her to be, bent over a book with a glower on her face, and as he pushed her door open he could hear her muttering to herself. "Ridiculous nonsense.I know that— you said the same thing twenty pages ago. Okay, now he's just babbling."

Cam cleared his throat—he didn't want to see firsthand how she reacted to being startled—and set the books on the desk next to her. "You do know there's nothing forcing you to keep reading, right?"

Elena rubbed the bridge of her nose. "Yes, but if I don't, the answer will be on page 643 in the margins of a diagram that looks as though it was drawn by someone who was clearly inebriated."

He looked down at her, almost sympathetic. "And if it's not there?"

"It will have been if I don't keep reading. The universe hates me like that." She opened her eyes, meeting his, briefly matching his sudden smirk with her own. "It took you awhile to find your way back here. Did you get lost again?" Then the humor faded and two small lines formed between her eyes. "I shouldn't have left you behind. I forget what the castle is like for people who didn't grow up in it."

The sudden concession made him hesitate, trying to figure out whether being honest would kick them both into another fight. Still, it seemed wrong to insist that she not lie and not give her the same in return. "Bishop offered to help me carry the books. I took him up on it."

Elena tensed. "He asked about them, didn't he?"

Cam nodded, relieved that she hadn't accused him of spilling the beans. They'd gotten that far, at least. "I told him that you and Braeth were working out a problem without telling him anything about it." When she winced, he put a hand on her shoulder. "I had to tell him something, Elena. He knew there was a problem even before I got here, and he does a really good worried face." Cam paused. "Bishop seems to care a lot about both of you."

There was the briefest hesitation from Elena, just like there always was when she was about to tell him something at all personal. "I wish he didn't try so hard with me. It would be easier." She sounded tired, as if just thinking about it exhausted her, and Cam squeezed her shoulder in comfort without being at all aware that he'd done it. "But I'm glad he's there for my mother. She needs him so much, and no matter how much she tries to hide it it's obvious how happy he makes her. I'd suffer through a thousand of his worried looks rather than part the two of them."

Cam thought back to his conversation with Bishop. "Does he know that?" he asked, picturing the expression that had been on the elf's face when he talked about the queen.

Elena looked at him like he was an idiot. "Of course he—" Then she stopped, studying whatever her brain was presenting for inspection. Then she closed her eyes, just like Bishop had done earlier. "Fantastic," she said quietly, clearly not thrilled with whatever she'd just decided.

Realizing he'd stirred up more than he'd meant to, Cam picked up one of the books and sat down on Elena's bed to flip through it. He knew he didn't understand enough to help look, but annoying her would distract her from whatever she was thinking. "So, I'm thinking you and Braeth have been sitting on a secret cure for insomnia and haven't told anyone."

Rather than glare at him, she made a small sound that could have been a weak chuckle. "Sadly, no. Even the dullest spell books are so frustrating and convoluted that you end up furious at the people who wrote them. It actually makes it harder to go to sleep."

Cam smiled at her. "I felt exactly the same way about school books. Needless to say, I didn't end up at the top of my class." He set the book back down on her desk. "I take it you'll be flying tonight?"

"I wish I could," Elena said. She'd been incredibly prickly the second night he'd followed her out, but he'd tried hard to be on his best behavior. By the third night, she'd accepted his presence as one more step in the process. "But if I let myself get distracted, I won't have the energy to push my way through the rest of—"

The words cut off abruptly as her head dropped forward, then her entire body started to slowly fall sideways. Cam swore and dove for her, but just as he caught her he felt her body tense up with renewed awareness. He let her go as she pulled herself back up into a sitting position. "How long was I out that time?" Elena asked, expression grim as she pushed her chair back to get a little more breathing room.

"Fifteen seconds." More watchful now, Cam moved back to his position on the bed. "Maybe less."

Elena pressed a hand to her forehead. "That's less time than my first blackout, which makes no sense. No matter what the pattern is, the time should be inc—"

The minute the words broke off Cam was moving again, but Elena dropped faster since she no longer had the desk to partially hold her up. He caught her at an odd angle, holding her there for a few seconds to see if she would wake up as quickly as last time. When she didn't, he picked her up and laid her down on the bed. He checked her pulse, fighting off the same brief panic he felt last time she collapsed then took her chair and sat down beside the bed.

As the seconds turned into minutes, the panic snuck back in. She was still breathing, her chest rising and falling slowly enough that you could miss it if you looked away, but that didn't mean the curse hadn't hit. Cam brushed a hair away from Elena's face, trying to figure out when he would have to tell her mother. A half hour? Longer? He kept his eye on the clock, trying not to imagine how the queen or his parents would react if Elena didn't wake up again.

So he waited. Some of it involved sitting, some of it involved pacing, and there was one brief stretch when he seriously considered going to get Braith. Eighteen painfully slow minutes later, Elena sucked in a sharp breath and opened her eyes. Then she blinked, swore softly, and pushed herself up into a sitting position. "I presume that one was longer."

Her eyes widened when Cam told her how long it had been. He tried to smile. "You should really think about sitting in a chair more often, though. It was a lot easier to make sure your head didn't hit the ground."

"That explains the headache I had when I woke up in the corridor."

He gave an exaggerated shrug, grateful she was going along with the joke. "Hey, they didn't cover princess catching in my guard training."

Elena twisted her mouth."Your father could do it with a broken leg," Elena said, a faint hint of humor lighting her eyes.

Cam just grinned. "You never met my great aunt. He's had a lot more practice than I have."

She made the appropriate disbelieving noise, but frustration overwhelmed her. "This makes no sense. When you add the timing of these blackouts to the earlier ones, it's nearly impossible to get any kind of exponential pattern out of them." She shifted sideways on the bed, reaching for the nearest book and rapidly flipping through the pages. "The timing seems like absolute nonsense, which shouldn't be possible in a curse. They have to work according to a pattern. It's how they're built."

Cam watched her, ready to get out of her way if she decided she wanted the chair again. He considered telling her that she should take it easy after that long a blackout, but Elena didn't usually take well to that category of suggestions. "Maybe this one's broken."

Elena shook her head, not looking up. "As far as anyone who's studied it can tell, it's functioning perfectly." She stopped on a page, scanned it quickly, then slammed the book closed in apparent disgust. "Maybe it really is just a sadistic little twist that no one's been able to pick up on before now."

"Why?" He hadn't meant to say the word out loud, but when Elena lifted her head he thought he might as well go with it. "Unless she's lurking around here somewhere in the shadows—"

"No." Elena shook her head, cutting him off. "There's no way she could have gotten past all the alert spells my mother has up for her."

"Okay, then. If she's not close enough to enjoy it, there's no reason for her to mess with you." He made a slicing gesture to emphasize his point. "And if she's scrying on you or something, she'd time it for moments specifically designed to hurt you instead of just driving you nuts."

Elena narrowed her eyes at him, but she looked speculative rather than angry. "What are you saying?"

He held his hands out. "What if the pattern makes no sense because it doesn't actually exist? What if you and Braeth have been chasing—pardon the pun—a ghost?"

She considered the idea, then shook her head again. "If it's not a lead-up like Braeth thinks, the blackouts would have to mean that the curse was malfunctioning somehow. There hasn't been anything that could have broken it since we last examined it."

"That you know about," Cam corrected, leaning forward. "What would it hurt to look again?"

The silence that followed was deeper this time, and Elena's fingers flexed on her knee. Cam's own hand lifted a fraction before he realized he'd even moved. Deciding that Elena would definitely not appreciate him touching her right now, he firmly put his own back down on his knee.

Seemingly unaware of this, Elena let out a long breath. “I’ll think about it,” she said finally.

Cam knew that the look on her face really meant no. But now didn’t seem like the time to push.

CHAPTER 7

Tall, Dumb, and Dangerous

Despite what Cam might have thought, Elena didn't just dismiss what he'd said.

In fact, it was hard to think about anything but the possibility of re-examining the curse. When she'd told Braeth about her newest blackouts, he had looked as genuinely confused as was possible for someone who technically no longer had a face. He'd never heard of a curse breaking without either the involvement of a cure or real effort on the part of an enemy sorcerer, but he promised to consult his books to see if he could find some kind of precedent.

A proper look of the curse, however, could answer the question so much quicker. The kind of detailed examination they'd need would take hours to set up, and traditionally involved more than one sorcerer or sorceress to handle all of the different spells involved. Still, she knew Braeth and Dr. Flyte would be willing, and she could conceivably ask her mother to be involved without telling her why they were doing it. Lying was also a perfectly acceptable alternative, as it always was.

But as soon as she asked any one of the three of them, she'd be committed to going through with it. And the hope that something might have changed, that after all this time there might actually be a loose thread they could use to pull it all apart—the idea was absolutely terrifying.

To escape having to think about it, she focused on Cameron.

"I promise you, people don't regularly jump out of the shadows to accost me," Elena told him the next day, a little amused as she watched Cam survey the busy street the same way his father did. They were making the short walk from the castle to Dr. Flyte's office, and Cameron was treating the trip as if they were heading into enemy territory. "I also feel I should point out that there aren't a great number of shadows in the immediate vicinity."

Cam slanted her a look that said volumes about how hilarious she was. "As happy as I normally am to call Dad paranoid, the walk to and from your therapist is the only time you're regularly outside the walls of the castle. Though you help that by not having your appointments at a regular time—"

"Alan's idea, if I recall correctly."

Cam snorted, eyes still scanning the passers-by. There were several people out shopping, their conversations an easy buzz as they flowed in and out of the nearby stores. "Notice my shock. Still, it's the best time for someone to come after you. I wouldn't be doing my job if I didn't take that into account."

Elena didn't respond, looking away so he wouldn't think she was staring at him. She was beginning to think that traumatizing him with the truth wouldn't have worked, even if she'd felt brave enough to actually go through with it. Cameron Merrick was as unshakeable as his father, in his own way, and if she suddenly turned into a twenty-foot-tall dragon his only response would probably be to ask if she wanted him to find her a nice tasty cow for lunch. Once she'd stopped fighting it, Elena found the attitude weirdly comforting.

Not, of course, that she was about to tell him that. "I don't think even Nigel would be stupid enough to defy his exile." Elena kept her voice low as an older man passed, acknowledging his friendly nod with one of her own. It wouldn't help her mother if people thought of her as cold. "The next step is prison."

Cam shook his head. "Anyone dumb enough to go up against Dad twice isn't smart enough to think that far—" Catching sight of something, he broke off with a muttered curse and grabbed her arm. He then pulled them both into the nearest store, where the proprietor was busy trying to convince a rather ample woman that his dresses were enchanted to make her look twenty pound lighter. Thankfully, they were both so intent on the sale—or the promises that came with it—that neither looked up.

"What is it?" Elena whispered, gathering the magic she'd need for a paralysis spell.

"A very large man who looks like he punches people for a living was headed straight for us." Cam had pulled Elena behind him, his focus on whatever was happening just outside the front entrance. "Either he'll pass right by and I'll look like an idiot, or he'll follow us in here and I'll have endangered innocent civilians."

"If I get a clear shot, I can freeze him," she offered. "The spell doesn't last very long, but it should give you time to hit him over the head with something heavy."

Cam glanced over at the woman. "Hopefully, all either of us will need to do is stand here."

Elena shifted just enough that she could see the street as well, just in time to see a living mountain of a man stop on the street in front of the dress shop. She tensed, ready to fight, as he glared at the spot where they had been walking. Then back and forth along the street, as if expecting them to suddenly materialize. When they didn't, he moved toward some nearby shops, leaning down to peer in through any convenient windows. Anyone else who had been out on the street was taking this as their cue to scurry out of the man's immediate view.

Still, they could be at risk. Elena touched Cam's shoulder. "If he decides to start hunting for us—"

"He might find some innocent bystanders," Cam finished, voice serious. "I know." He tensed, reaching down for his sword. "I'll distract him and give you that clear shot you're looking for. While you're doing that I'll try to find something heavy, and hopefully by then the other idiots who are supposed to be watching you will finally catchup to us." He rolled his eyes. "I swear, those guards of yours move like molasses. I'd have better luck calling the city guards for backup."

"What if he's not actually looking for me?" she whispered. It didn't seem terribly likely, but she felt obligated to bring it up before he risked himself by going out there.

"He clearly wants to make sure someone gets hurt." Cam looked back at the store owner and customer, who had just now realized something might be amiss. "Sir, Ma'am, I ask that you please retreat to a back room until we make sure this is taken care of."

They froze, staring at Cameron as if they couldn't process what he was saying, and Elena impatiently waved them into the back. "Go! There's a very large man outside who might rip your front door off at any minute."

That got the appropriate response, the owner swooping up an armful of his most expensive dresses as he and the customer hurried into the back. When they'd disappeared, Cam took a step outside. "Make sure to stay as much in cover as you possibly— for pity's sake, not like that."

The person Cam was speaking to was one of her other guards, who had apparently wandered by to check on the situation. He was striding towards the large man right up the middle of the street, hand on the hilt of his sword. "Sir, I'm afraid I'm going to have to ask you—"

The big man's fist, swinging around like the castle's front gate, cut off the rest of the sentence. The guard crumpled into a heap, and Elena felt a twinge of sympathy as Cam swore. "Hasn't anyone taught these guys that you never go after the bad guy one at a time? I know my father's their co-worker rather than their boss, but I'm still amazed he hasn't staged a formal takeover out of sheer exasperation."

When he talked like that, he sounded just like his father. Realizing that now was not the time to distract him by pointing that out, she poked his back. "Technically, you're going after him one at a time."

"No, *I'm* going to wave my hands around like an idiot while you sneak attack him. Completely different." Then, squaring his shoulders, Cam headed outside.

Elena took his place near the edge of the door, fingers moving through the first part of the spell so it would take less time to fire it. She kept her eyes on Cam, who was wisely staying well out of arm's reach of the thug. "Hi!" He made sure his voice was cheerful as possible. "Mr. Big, Tall, and Scary? Can I have a minute?"

The enormous man's eyes fixed on Cameron. "You." He was silent for what seemed like an eternity, obviously waiting for his next thought to arrive. "Where's the girl?"

"Sorry, but I'm afraid you have me confused for someone else. I've been single ever since my last girlfriend decided I wasn't funny enough." As Cam spoke, he slowly moved around their target in an arc. The big man kept shifting around to make sure Cam stayed in sight, putting Elena's doorway further and further out of his field of vision. Cam's plan was wonderfully brave and far too dangerous, and Elena's fingers itched to go out and help him. "Before you knock me unconscious, can I maybe ask what your name is?"

The man's brow furrowed. Clearly, he wasn't used to small talk. "Bill." He paused, while up and down the street the rest of the town was peering through windows and around corners to watch the scene. "You're lyin' about the girl, ain't ya."

"Still don't know what girl you're talking about, Bill, though I can't imagine why any lady wouldn't fall all over themselves trying to get to you." Cam's patter continued even though he'd stopped moving, and Elena presumed that was the signal for the spell.

As she lifted her hand, however, Cam met her gaze for just a second. Reading the 'not yet' in his eyes, she withdrew her hand while he returned his attention to Bill. Still shielded by the doorway, all Elena could do was wait. "Is this girl you're looking for someone you've been dating? Or just someone special you have your eye on?"

Apparently, Bill also didn't deal well with confusion. "What're you talkin' about? Some guy hired me to knock her out and bring her to him." Looking angry now, Bill took a step forward. "Won't get paid for you, but that's okay."

Pushing down the edge of fear that skimmed through her, Elena raised her hand again as Cam took a step back. "What's the man's name?" When Bill didn't say anything, Cam looked chiding. "You really ought to know who's offering to pay you, Bill. If nothing else, it'll help you track them down again if he refuses to follow through with his end of the deal."

"Nigel somethin.'" Bill said, taking another step forward. When Cam shook his head, looking disappointed, the other man lifted an arm. "What do you care? I'm doin' you for free."

Deciding that she was going to kill Nigel slowly, Elena finished the spell and aimed it squarely at Bill's back. The man froze, muscles locking together in a single instant, and she strode out into the middle the street to stand next to Cam. "You have thirty seconds," she told him, watching as he reached into his pocket. "And if we see Prince Nigel again, I'm going to murder him long before he ever sees the inside of a prison cell."

"Fair enough." Cam pulled his hand out, now wearing a well-used set of brass knuckles, and walked over to Bill. Without breaking stride, he leaned forward slightly and delivered a solid uppercut straight to the man's unmentionables, then took a single step back. Even from here, Elena could see the agony flooding Bill's eyes, and she felt the corners of her mouth curve upward. Maybe they could do this to Nigel.

The street was still mostly quiet, most of the people wisely deciding that the danger hadn't passed yet. However, one old woman poked her head around the doorway of a hat shop. She hesitated, then lifted a hand to catch Cam's attention. "Young man, you might want to back away from him. Once he can move again, he's going to be very angry about what you just did."

"I know, Ma'am." Cam smiled, eyes never leaving Bill's. "Don't worry. I have everything under control."

When the spell released him, Bill's entire body curled inward as he clutched himself and dropped to his knees. Before he could get further than that, Cam stepped forward and delivered another solid right hook to the man's cheek. As Bill toppled over like a tree, Cam dropped the brass knuckles back into his pocket and turned to Elena. "See, cheating is much more effective."

It was impossible not to smile back at him, and it seemed ridiculous to try and fight it. "As impressive as that was, we should probably get this mess cleaned up." Cam gestured down the street. "I believe I hear the cleaning crew coming as we speak.

Hearing the sound of running feet, she turned to see two of the city guardsmen coming to join the part. When they got close enough, she gestured to Bill's unconscious form. "Get him to the nearest holding cell. He assaulted one of the castle guardsmen." The guardsman in question was just now coming to, groaning and holding his head. Cam crouched down beside him, having a quiet conversation that likely focused on the finer points of sensible fighting.

The other guardsmen were still trying to haul Bill away by the time Cam , walked back over to Elena. "You shouldn't be too late for your appointment, but I'll apologize to Dr. Flyte if you want." There was a crashing sound from behind them, followed by a round of cursing. Apparently, Bill was as heavy as he looked. "Bill should probably do it, but it's probably best that he stay unconscious for the next little while."

Elena hesitated briefly, not wanting to show that she'd entirely forgotten they'd been on their way somewhere. "He should be fine. He leaves the hour before and after my appointments free as a basic security measure." She watched as the guardsmen backed a cart into position, then attempted to hoist the unconscious criminal into place. The guard who had been knocked unconscious, now wearing a very familiar set of brass knuckles, had been assigned the job of making sure Bill didn't wake up.

"I hate to say it, but I was wrong." She turned back to Cameron. "I should have taken Nigel more seriously."

He shrugged. "You had no reason to. Dad always says that he's paranoid so the rest of the world doesn't have to be."

Elena's temper flared at the memory of Nigel's thin, apologetic face. "That's no excuse for me to be one of those idiotic princesses. He just seemed so ridiculous that I underestimated—" Realizing something, her gaze focused back on Cameron. "Why didn't you? You pretend like you're the kind of person who gets by entirely on charm, but you knew exactly what to watch for with Nigel. You've never even met the man." The logic of it all unfolded in her head, making so many things she'd dismissed about Cam slot neatly into what was suddenly a much larger picture. "You do that to everyone, don't you? You say just the right thing to make sure they don't pay attention, and while they're looking away you study them like a battle plan."

Cam's eyes widened a little. "I don't know if I'd say that."

"No," she said firmly, watching his face change as he tried and failed to find an argument. "You're better at hiding than you look, Cameron Merrick." She smiled a little at the thought. For the first time, she understood how Cam had felt when he'd caught her out in the woods that night. "You really had no right to be annoyed at me for lying, though. Just because you're more subtle than I am is no reason to yell at me."

Now he looked almost alarmed. "Wait, I'm not sure what—"

But she had already turned, heading towards Dr. Flyte's office at a brisk pace. "Are you coming? As you so kindly pointed out, we're running late. I'd hate to have to do any apologizing today."

~

"I've never known you to be late before," Dr. Flyte said thoughtfully, motioning for Elena to sit down once all the polite greetings had been made. She and Cam had only been fifteen minutes late—the man knew how to run when he needed to—but the mirror wasn't about to let even that small an aberration go unnoticed. "Did something happen?"

"Cameron and I ran into a little trouble on our way here." Elena settled back in her chair, having already decided that full disclosure would be the best course of action. Particularly since she would need the good doctor's help. "Apparently, Nigel's decided that hiring people to kidnap me is the best way to make a good impression."

Alarm crossed the mirror's face, though he was quick to collect himself. "I didn't notice any injuries on you or young Mr. Merrick," he asked, examining her for any sign of a bruise or tender shoulder.

"There was only one man, though he was about half as big as Cameron. Together, we managed to knock him unconscious and get him carted away without either of us being the worse for wear." She felt like she was shorting Cam's part in it, but she didn't dare sound too complimentary around Dr. Flyte. He'd make far too much out of it. "The problem is that I doubt this is Nigel's last brilliant idea."

"No, I can't imagine that it is." The mirror was solemn. "Are you planning to tell your mother?"

Elena hadn't decided the answer to that question yet. "She knows about the other two incidents and didn't lock me inside the castle. Cameron and I proved as competent together as Alan and I were, so I'm at least as well protected as before."

Dr. Flyte raised an eyebrow at the entirely non-committal response. "Clearly, you're still giving the matter some thought."

Not able to properly argue, she waved the chain of questioning aside. "What's really important is that we find out more about Prince Nigel. He told us he was a younger son from Long Ago, but right now I think it's safest not to believe a word that's come out of his mouth." She leaned forward, letting herself look hopeful. "You have more contacts than anyone in the kingdom, including Bishop. Is there any way you could talk to them? Even if we can't figure out where he's really from, it's might be possible to find out where he's hiding."

Dr. Flyte considered this. "If he's still within the boundaries of the kingdom, your guardsman might be more useful in this particular quest."

"He's not—" Elena snapped her mouth closed, realizing that the term was technically accurate. And arguing against emotional shadings he likely hadn't even meant would only make her look like a fool. "Alan and Marie will likely be even more helpful. I'll ask Cameron once the appointment ends."

"And I'll see what I can do on my end. An old friend of mine, a dragon named Mandrake, may know something—I believe he has relatives near Long Ago." Dr. Flyte's voice was pleasant, but his gaze was alarmingly focused. "So, it sounds as though you and Cameron Merrick are getting along better than you were during our last appointment."

She lifted her chin, refusing to be baited. "He's less infuriating than I'd initially thought he was. There's no longer any threat of me snapping and killing him." She smiled deliberately, deflecting. "Which I know must disappoint you."

Dr. Flyte sighed. "I just want you to talk to me, Elena. I'm supposed to be here to help."

Inconveniently, the memory of Cam's comment flashed across her mind. *Seeing you shout is the only time they have any idea what's going on inside your head.*

Elena softened her expression. "You are helping me. Information is what I need most right now, and there's no one at it better than you." Once she'd admitted that to herself, it seemed childish to let her fear stand in the way of getting that information. She took a deep breath. "I would also like you to be involved when we do another full examination of my curse. You've been involved in all the other examinations, and I want this one to include only those I trust the most."

The doctor's ghostly face went absolutely still. "You're planning another examination? Full projection, protection circle, a full complement of study spells?" Only when she nodded did he allow his surprise to show. "We haven't held one of those in—"

"Years, I know," she finished for him. "I haven't told anyone else yet, and I ask that you don't say anything until I do." He opened his mouth again, and she held up a hand. "Yes, I will ask my mother. With all the alert spells she has up, there's no way I could hide such a large spell casting from her."

"She's also the finest sorceress in the kingdom," Dr. Flyte said mildly.

"I'm going to ask her, Doctor. I promise."

The mirror nodded. "Then I would be honored to participate. And I won't say anything to Braeth or your mother until you've figured out the way you want to present the situation." He paused. "I would suggest honesty, however."

She rolled her eyes at him. "Of course you would."

Dr. Flyte simply smiled in response, making the image of a monocle appear over one of his eyes. "Now, my dear, let's talk about any dreams you've been having."

CHAPTER 8

Exploding Socks and Pirates

Cam still didn't know what on earth Elena thought she'd figured out from his showdown with Bill—he'd been babbling, basically, and the man was dumb enough a rock probably could have fooled him. But when he'd explained both very logical points, she'd just smiled at him in the way his mom did when his dad didn't have the slightest chance of winning an argument.

So, wisely, he stopped arguing. He comforted himself with the thought that she was just getting him back for ambushing her that night in the woods. Sure, his version was genius insight while hers made no sense, but he could let her pretend she had something.

Still, in the days following, he found other things to argue with her about. Nothing serious—no need to remind her how good she was at pushing his buttons. Just enough to keep her from going quiet on him. She hadn't said a word about the timing of the blackouts for days now, despite the fact that she'd had two more brief ones, and Cam could only imagine what was going through her head.

He didn't feel he could push the issue again—she'd already shut him down once—but seeing a spark in her eyes made him feel better.

"So, is this the Sunday I'm going to come back and find that you and Braeth have blown up half the castle?" Cam perched on the edge of Elena's desk in what he was starting to think of as his spot. "Everyone keeps talking about the possibility, but I have yet to see decent wreckage out of the two of you."

"I don't see why everyone can't just let that go," Elena huffed. "It was once when I was eight, and the crater wasn't nearly as big as people make it out to be."

It was easy to picture her as a kid, glaring at everyone because they were overreacting to one measly little fireball. "The one thing no one's ever told me is how it happened."

She didn't say anything, looking stubborn. Then the corners of her mouth twitched upward. "Braeth was helping me make some warming socks, but I decided they took too long to heat up. I tried tweaking the spell."

"And accidentally blew up the socks." He couldn't stop the chuckle. "I should ask you to make me some for my birthday. We've got a guy back at the station with a nasty habit of borrowing people's things without asking."

"If I could control when they exploded, you would have gotten a set your first night here." Still, her smile widened. "Your parents would have been upset, but it would have been worth it."

"I should probably be relieved you put all of that in past tense, but I'm definitely going to start checking my socks from now on."

Elena shook her head. "It's no fun now that you'd see it coming." Closing the book he'd spent the last twenty minutes distracting her from reading, she turned to the clock sitting on the fireplace mantle. "Speaking of your parents, you should really leave now if you don't want to be late for Sunday dinner. Mrs. Feeney's daughter's in town, so she's going to drag out filling your bread order as long as humanly possible."

Cam winced, remembering Mrs. Feeney's rhapsodic mentions of "bubbly, fun Tamara" that he'd somehow managed to repress. Then his brain caught on a more immediate question. "How do you know about Mrs. Feeney's daughter? Do you sneak into town and chat with random villagers after I go to sleep?"

She shot him a look that held equal measures of amusement and pity. "Mrs. Feeney makes early morning deliveries to the palace. She asked me if you were seeing anyone."

"And you told her?" He swore under his breath, shaking his head. "I know I said I didn't want you lying to me, but for me is a completely different thing. It's basic kindness when you see someone like Mrs. Feeney coming."

Elena gave him a faintly chiding look. "If I'd invented a girlfriend for you, Mrs. Feeney would have told everyone in the immediate vicinity before the week was out. Then you'd have everyone in town harassing you about your secret girlfriend, someone would ask your parents about it, and you'd have to admit what happened to any real girl you might be interested in dating."

Cam wanted to argue, what Elena said made an unfortunate amount of sense. "Okay, you have a point," he said, less than thrilled with his list of options. He could avoid the bakery entirely, but when he showed up at home empty handed he would then have to explain the entire story to his parents. There was another bakery a half-mile away, but it would take him three times as long to make it home and he'd still have to explain.

The only way he wouldn't have to explain was if he went

by Mrs. Feeney's, let Tamara giggle all over him, and escaped as quickly as he could. Of course, if he offended her at all Mrs. Feeney would probably start poisoning the bread. So he'd have to go through with the date, and hope that "bubbly" wasn't code for "so inane you want to choke yourself just to stop listening to her." And then he'd have to keep dating her, because heaven help the man who broke the heart of Mrs. Feeney's little angel.

"Cam." Elena's voice, a little surprised and far more serious than it had been, broke his train of thought. "Is it really that bad? You just have to flirt with her daughter for a few minutes. Even if she's unattractive, I'm sure your charm can stretch that far."

"No, I will have to date her daughter, who her beloved mother describes as 'bubbly.' I've dated bubbly girls, and while it's cute for the first five minutes after that you want to smother them with a pillow." He rubbed a hand across his eyes. "Do you know how hard it is to say no to an old lady who knows exactly where both you and your parents live? Unless I start acting like a jerk, I'm probably stuck with at least one date. And once I go out with one old lady's daughter, every other friendly shopkeeper with single children is going to be expecting the same thing. I'm setting a *really* bad precedent."

She leaned her chin on her hand, just watching him now. "If I knew an old lady could rattle you so much, I would have put more effort into protecting you." The corners of her mouth quirked upward again. "Of course, this could all be for nothing. You might meet this girl, stare into her eyes, and fall instantly in love."

Still perched on the edge of the desk, Cam gave her a disgusted look. "That doesn't happen unless black magic or potions are involved."

Elena's lips twitched in a way that made her look like she

was suppressing a chuckle. "I'm amazed you haven't considered the possibility that she may not like you. It would solve all your problems."

That caught him short for a second. The truth was, he *hadn't* considered the possibility. He made a good first impression with everyone, unless you were Elena,and if he defaulted to his usual charm he couldn't see any reason why she'd say no right away. It was only after he'd been seeing a girl for a couple of months that they started tallying up the reasons why he was a bad idea.

This time, Elena let the laugh slip out as she straightened. "You truly didn't think of that, did you? I don't know whether I should be impressed by your self-confidence or start making fun of your ego."

He made an exasperated noise. "Fine, so maybe I'll get off scott free. Would you blindly trust a 'maybe' that you couldn't do anything about?"

She hesitated, then lifted a hand in acknowledgement. "Fine. I'll apologize. Next time this happens I'll create an obsessively jealous fake girlfriend for you. I wouldn't want you to have to face the sweet old lady all alone."

Cam's brain, desperate for something he could work with, seized on the last few words. "Or you could come with me."

She blinked, surprised, then glared. "I'm not pretending to be your girlfriend."

Cam shook his head, grimacing as he imagined the disasters that would spring up if they tried that little lie. If nothing else, her mother might eventually hear it. "No, no. That would just be asking for trouble. But if you come to dinner with me, you can go in and get the bread." He stepped closer, a cajoling edge to his voice. Just because it was harder to charm Elena didn't mean it was impossible. "I get to avoid meeting Tamara, and you get an evening of my parents' cooking. As a bonus, you can mock me all the way there. We both win."

She still wasn't convinced, but she'd clearly started thinking about it. "So I'm supposed to go in and chat with Mrs. Feeney and Tamara while you, what, hide in the bushes? The windows of that store are big enough they could both see you standing outside."

He sighed, knowing she was right. Still, the thought of having backup made him dread the entire situation a little less. "It'll still be better if you come inside with me. If nothing else, I'll have the excuse to leave early because you're a guest."

Elena met his gaze. "Would your parents really be okay with me—" She cut off the sentence before Cam could shoot her an incredulous look. "No, I can't even make myself finish the question."

"You always struck me as a smart woman," he said dryly. "Now that we have that taken care of, what's your next excuse?"

"Maybe I just don't want to go with you. As happy as I normally am to spend time with your parents, your regular Sunday dinner routine is one of my few chances to get a break from you."

He leaned back against the edge of the desk, not at all offended. If the edge of frost wasn't in her voice, she didn't really mean it as an insult. "I admit that you're weirdly immune to my powers, and I suppose it's possible that I'm annoying enough to counteract the majesty of my mom's marinated chicken. Given both those things, it makes total sense that you'd want to stay here and have a tense, awkward dinner with your mother and Bishop."

She almost winced, then stopped herself. "I'll just have dinner in my room. I did it last week, and spent a very restful evening studying."

"You've had dinner in your room every Sunday since I've gotten here." He let the sympathy come through in his voice, knowing how frustrating it was when the facts stacked up against you. "You keep it up, either your mother or Bishop is going to snap and make you tell them what's wrong."

Elena mulled that over. "She'll still wonder why I went to your parents' house. Alan didn't usually get me out there unless there was a major holiday or he was worried about me." At Cam's questioning look, smiled a little. "He always said it was your mother who was worried, but your father has this way of herding people. The few times that Marie actually has been worried, she always just called and invited me herself."

"Oh, Dad's had Mom call before, but it's really just an expansion of the herding thing," he said, thinking of the mirror call that had gotten him here in the first place. Luckily, it had turned out to be way less of a torture session than he'd thought it would be. "And she only agrees to play herd dog if she thinks you should be going in the same direction."

"Your parents are mildly terrifying when they team up." Elena sounded amused as she said it, but her expression made it clear she was still thinking too hard. "I can't imagine my mother hasn't picked up on the pattern, however. If I go to dinner at your parents' house, she'll think they're worried about me. Given the fact that she and Bishop are already worried about me, the results will be almost as bad as if I ate alone in my room."

Cam shook his head, ready with a counter for this line of reasoning. "My dad hasn't seen you in a couple of weeks, and he hasn't been hovering over my shoulder checking to see if I'm doing his job right. Even if it's not true, anyone who knows him will believe he's asking you over to get a sense of whether I'm screwing up or not."

That seemed to surprise her. "He hasn't been by the palace once since you got here. I know he's controlling, but I thought the fact that he's virtually disappeared meant that he at least trusts his children."

"That, or my mom threatened him." Privately, he wasn't sure he wanted to know which was the real answer. "But is your mother going to know that?"

Elena opened her mouth, then caught sight of the clock out. "Okay, now you're going to be late anyway." Her voice firmed as she made shooing motions with her hands. "Go. Mrs. Feeney should let you go fairly quickly if you say your family won't start dinner until you get there. No good son wants to hold up the family meal."

He glanced at the clock, realizing that he'd talked away most of his travel time. If he was smart he'd leave now, and even then he'd have to be really quick with the bread pick up. Even Tamara probably wouldn't have time to cause him too much trouble.

And Elena would be here, either alone or sharing that awful chilly silence with her mother, while he was at home, eating delicious food and enjoying his pick of at least three different conversations going on at once. Even if you didn't take part in any of them, they made for an interesting soundtrack.

Besides, his parents really would enjoy seeing her.

"If you don't come with me, I'll tell them I asked and you said no." He held out a hand, voice teasing enough that it sounded like less of a threat. "Think of the guilt you'll be sparing yourself if you just come now."

She narrowed her eyes at him, but he could still see the spark. "Fine. Clearly, it's the only way to get you to stop talking."

~

They made it out of the palace with admirable speed, pausing only to tell Bishop where Elena was going. Though Cam didn't actually stop talking as they walked, he did try to restrain himself. He preferred to get Elena talking, anyway—it was a good distraction from worrying about the Tamara situation.

The buildings in this part of town were old but well-cared for, marked by the generations of people who had lived there. They got several waves from people on the street, since they were both familiar faces. Normally, Cam would stop and chat, answering the inevitable questions about various family members, but today Elena had his full attention.

When they got to the bakery, the only person they could see through the windows was Mrs. Feeney. Her head was down, and she was scrubbing the counter like she was trying to teach it a lesson.

"Maybe her daughter's hiding in the back," Cam said, trying to shake the feeling that someone was about to jump out of the shadows at him. They'd both been in this bakery often enough to be considered regulars—to get nervous now was ridiculous. "Trying to catch me by surprise."

"Seriously?" Elena shot him a pitying look, then hooked her arm through his to pull him forward. "I have no idea how you managed to survive this long."

When they went inside, there were no suspicious sounds coming from the back room. Mrs. Feeney looked up at the sound of the door opening, the scowl on her face instantly clearing at the sight of Cam and Elena. "Your Highness! What a lovely surprise. Let me get you one of those cinnamon buns you like, free of charge. And Cameron! Here to pick up your dear mother's harvest bread." She dropped the cloth, bustling around with what Cam realized was just a little too much enthusiasm.

Cam had spent enough of his childhood watching his mother to know that something had gone wrong. That made him start feeling guilty, even though there was no reason for it, and like most guilty people he compensated for it by being stupid. "Is Tamara around? I remember you mentioning that she might be by this week."

Out of the corner of his eye, he could see Elena shoot him a look that suggested he was insane. Mrs. Feeney, thankfully, was too busy scowling at a heart-shaped twist bread to notice. "She's not feeling well," the woman said, making her voice sound sweet again through sheer force of will. "Poor dear had to cancel the visit."

Anyone with half a brain could tell that the two women had fought, and that the only sensible solution was to stay completely silent and get out of there as quickly as possible. Cam's mouth, however, had decided that being sensible was not on the day's agenda. "It's okay, Mrs. Feeney. I'm sure I'll run into her next time."

This was, naturally, the wrong thing to say. "I cannot believe that girl!" Mrs. Feeney burst out, a sudden explosion of temper that actually had Elena taking a step back. "She's seeing a pirate, can you believe it?" Ever the businesswoman, the old woman kept working as she continued the rant. "Oh, she tries to tell me it's serious, and they're really in love, but he's a pirate." There was a slapping sound as the harvest bread hit the paper. "What kind of future can they have?" The cinnamon bun hit harder, getting squished nearly flat in the process. Cam couldn't help but wince. "People who spend their days pillaging on the high seas aren't known for being steady, faithful spouses." She grabbed one corner of the paper hard enough that the bun rolled off it entirely, skimming dangerously close along the edge of the counter. Mrs. Feeney didn't seem to notice. "Takes this long to tell me, says I 'wouldn't understand.' There's nothing for me to understand! I'm not going to get grandchildren like this!"

"Let me get that for you," Elena cut in, dashing around the counter and grabbing the bun before Mrs. Feeney could take out any more of her frustration on it. Shooting Cam an amused look, she tossed the bun to him for safekeeping before rescuing the bread. Cam, fighting his own smile, stole a few extra papers out of the basket. Wrapping Elena's poor damaged bun in one of them, he exchanged it for the loaf when Elena slipped back over to stand by him. "Maybe you should sit down, Mrs. Feeney."

That seemed to catch her off guard. "Sit down?" The old woman blinked, as if the thought had never occurred to her. "I can't sit down. I still have the counter to clean. And I haven't finished your orders yet." The words trailed off as she looked around, finally realizing that the bread was missing.

Knowing it was his turn to help with the escape plan, Cam held out the loaf of bread he had finished wrapping behind his back. "No, see, you already took care of it." He gave her his most reassuring smile, the kind he used when assuring supervisors that there had been absolutely no trouble on patrol that night. "Now we just need to pay you."

He was very careful not to sound amused, no matter how much fun he was having.

Mrs. Feeney stared at the bread for a moment, as if trying to fill in the gaps in her memory, then gave Cam an exasperated look. "Here, let me have that," she said, motioning to the loaf. "I can't believe I nearly let this go out of the shop wrapped so poorly." She set the bread on the squeaky clean counter, smoothing and re-wrapping the paper while Cam went for his money. He traded it for the newly wrapped bread with a mental sigh of relief.

"And thank you so much for the bun, too," Elena added, holding it up as evidence that part of the to-do list had been taken care of as well. Then she tucked it behind her back, before Mrs. Feeney could examine Cam's wrap job too closely. "We'll get out of your way now so you can get back to that counter."

They escaped without giving the other woman time to respond, ducking out the door and around the corner with a speed normally used to flee from people brandishing battle-axes. When they'd gone a sufficient distance that there was no chance of being either seen or heard, they both collapsed against someone's garden wall and burst out laughing.

When they were able to get some air back into their lungs, Elena wiped her eyes. "You're right. That was—" She paused here, inhaling for more breath as a lingering chuckle overcame her. "Absolutely terrifying. I don't know how you could have survived it alone."

"Hey, I was right about needing backup. You were the one who thought to save the bread." He straightened, letting himself bask a little in the feeling of having fun. The whole situation probably would have been as funny if he'd been alone, but he didn't think he would have enjoyed it quite so much. "I'm pretty sure I was in shock. By the time I snapped out of it, the poor thing would have been flattened."

"Speaking of the bread, we really should be getting it to your parents." She smoothed her hair with her free hand as they started off again, the glow of a really great joke not quite gone from her face. It was a good look for her. "If we're really late, your family might start worrying that I've done something awful to you."

"We'll just tell them we were accosted by pirates."

He was quite pleased when she laughed again.

CHAPTER 9

Shop Talk

The Merricks lived on the edge of town, in a simple but well-loved home big enough to house all seven members of the family and a few guests. The yard was large enough for a garden, training area, and workshop, since even people who loved each other needed a little breathing room sometimes. Marie had told her that, during a quiet moment when a younger Elena had needed to escape the warm but overpowering bustle of some family event. The thought had been surprisingly comforting.

When they got closer, Elena could hear the sounds of conversation through the open window. "They've already started, haven't they?" she asked, belatedly wondering if she should offer her bun as part of the meal or if they'd let her set it down on a counter. The polite thing to do would probably have been to eat it on the way here, but then she would have had less room for dinner. "Tell me you at least told them I'd be coming."

"That would be lying to you, which at this point just seems hypocritical," Cam said cheerfully, pushing open the front door. Elena hesitated, trying to figure out the most polite way to crash a family dinner party, when he turned around gave her an exasperated look. "Come on. If we're any slower Gabby will have finished off all the potato salad." Then, before she could say anything, he grabbed her hand and pulled her inside.

The sound of conversation enveloped her the minute she stepped into the house, a cheerful back-and-forth about cackling techniques, chocolate cake, and whether or not someone could have seconds. When she and Cam appeared in view of the table, however, they immediately had everyone's attention.

"Elena! Cam didn't tell me you were coming!" Marie stood up, pulling Elena out of Cam's grip and into a hug. "What a wonderful surprise. It's been too long since we've had you over for dinner."

"Robbie, get your brother a chair," Alan said, squeezing Elena's hand and ushering her into an available seat. "Elena, dig in. You don't eat enough."

"You haven't seen her with cinnamon toast," Cam chipped in, sounding completely unconcerned about the fact that she'd just stolen his seat. He took the wrapped bun out of her hand, setting it down on a sideboard as Robbie came back in with another chair. "It's as bad as Gabby and potato salad."

"I helped make it today. It's delicious," Gabby piped in, adding another helping onto her own plate before pushing the bowl towards Elena. "You can have some, but not all of it. Mom said I get all the leftovers."

"If there are any," Robbie added, scooting his sister over so there would be room for Cam's chair. They both took their seats, reaching for the cheese-covered vegetables a second after Cam had already snatched them away. "Fine, then. Dish me some while you have it."

"Fair enough." Cam gave both of them big helpings, then passed the dish across the table to Elena.

Noticing that the serving dishes were piling up around her, Elena started filling up her plate. The move earned a smile of approval from Marie, who added a piece of chicken to Elena's growing collection of food. "Here. You can't just eat Alan's part of the meal."

"Dad's really careful about chopping things, so he does the inside stuff," Gabby explained, as if Elena hadn't already been aware of the family's cooking arrangements. Then again, maybe the girl simply liked explaining things. "Mom's more of a free spirit."

"Besides," Alan added, sending a secret smile across the table to his wife. "She likes the fire."

"Of course I do." Marie grinned back at him. "You can have so much fun with it."

"People, please," Cam cut in, the humor evident on his face. "Not in front of the children."

"Are you using physical or mental ages to define children?" Robbie argued, looking so serious Elena suspected the expression must be its own joke. "Because if it's mental ages, that includes everyone at the table but Elena."

The conversation settled back into a rhythm as everyone began eating again, giving Elena time to re-acclimatize herself. She'd been to the Merricks' at least a few times every year since Alan had become her guard, but it was still a little disorienting to step into the world they made. They talked more to each other in a single hour than she and her mother did in an entire week. Maybe even a month.

She felt both Alan and Marie watching her out of the corners of their eyes, giving her the time she needed. They always did, waiting for whatever secret signal they used when they decided she'd finally relaxed. When they saw it, Marie smiled at her again. "It's been too long since we've had the chance to sit down and really talk, Elena. How have you been?"

Marie knew about the blackouts, which meant Elena thankfully didn't have to mention them. "Same as usual, really. Dr. Flyte says hello."

"I'll have to give him a mirror call." The two sometimes talked about Marie's students, many of whom went on to top positions with the city guard. She'd tried to talk them into joining the castle guard, if only so that Alan would stop complaining so much. Given the castle guard's reputation, however, they'd all refused to take the bait. "How about Cam? Hopefully he hasn't been causing you too much trouble."

Elena glanced over at Cam, who was debating with his brother the question of who had been given the worst childhood chores and didn't seem to be paying any attention. "No. He's been good." She didn't mention the not-quite-fight with the muscle Nigel had hired, not certain how much Cam had told his parents. "We had some disagreements at first, but he's very skilled at his job."

"Ah." There was laughter in Marie's eyes, and Elena suspected she'd heard a far less polite version of the story. Honestly, Alan could have told her—she had started yelling at Cam from essentially the moment he arrived. Still, it wasn't her right to talk about any of that with his parents, no matter what she threatened or teased Cam with in private. Besides, she hadn't lied—Cam should appreciate that, if nothing else.

Before she could decide what else she could safely add to her answer, Elena felt someone watching her. Turning, she caught Cam sending her a look that was somewhere between disbelief and what appeared to be worry. She sent back an expression meant to ask him what the problem was, but he just shook his head and returned his attention to the meal. Alan and Marie were now watching both of them, and to Elena's frustration they seemed to have a far better sense of what had just happened than she did.

Wanting to distract them, she turned to Alan. "Have we heard anything more about Nigel?"

The older man's face darkened. "Cam told us about the local muscle he hired. No one's spotted him in the city limits, but that doesn't mean anything."

"The city guard's had to cut back on witch assistance due to budget cuts," said Marie."He may still be using an invisibility spell, which would make him difficult to find during the sweeps they've been making."

"I'm finishing up a set of charms they can use to pick up that specific spell," Robbie added surprising Elena. She'd studied some witchcraft over the years, and giving a non-magic user the ability to detect invisibility was definitely not one of the standard charms. In fact, she wasn't sure it was a standard spell. "If he's still here, they should help the patrols find him."

Elena nodded, watching Cam's younger brother. She remembered Cam telling her how excited Robbie would be to hear about her adaptations to the broom spell, and she wondered why he had stopped asking her about magic. She couldn't imagine his curiosity had waned, and in her experience a Merrick was never too afraid to ask a person anything.

Maybe he, too, had been trying to be polite.

"Cam tells me you're in your third year of studying witchcraft with Dame Beacham," Elena said, directing her attention to Robbie. "I've never worked with her personally, but I did know her mentor, Dame Kadrey, before she died. I've heard that Dame Beacham is just as skilled and exacting a teacher. You must be a rare student for her to have continued working with you for so long."

Robbie's eyes went wide at the unexpected compliment, and he even blushed a little before clearing his throat. "I—it's an honor to work with her." He hesitated, his eyes surprisingly hopeful. "I have a lab out back, where I'm finishing up the charms."

He didn't say anything else, but Elena used almost-questions often enough to recognize when one was being directed at her. She hesitated, knowing that it would be safer to pretend she hadn't heard it. Private workrooms were a line of familiarity, and it would do no one any good if she crossed this one.

But surely it wouldn't do too much harm to simply talk a little shop with someone. It was unlikely she would live long enough to take on a student—it would be nice to pass on at least a few of the tricks she'd learned to someone so eager to learn. "I would love to see it, if there's time after dinner," she told him, taking another sip of her drink before glancing at Alan and Marie for approval. "Cam mentioned you might also be interested in some work I've done adapting a witch's broom spell to a flying harness."

Robbie's face lit as Alan nodded. He seemed pleased, as any good father likely would be when someone took an interest in his children. "We'll make Cam help with the dishes."

"I'll do it!" Gabby piped in, trying to sneak in another

serving of potato salad. When Marie stopped her with a stern look, she gave her mom a sheepish grin and put the spoon back in the bowl.

"You can't. You've been banned from dishes ever since the juggling thing." Cam sighed theatrically, but there was definite approval in his eyes. Possibly, she realized, because this was the first sign she'd given that she'd actually listened to him about anything. "Okay, fine. I'll do it."

Marie's smile included everyone at the table. "It touches a mother's heart to see her children sacrifice like that."

~

As soon as Robbie swallowed his last mouthful, he hurried outside so he could "get everything ready." Elena offered to help with the dishes, but Marie told her to sit down and relax. Cam schooled his face into an expression of exaggerated suffering as his mother teasingly dragged him into the kitchen, and Elena wiggled her fingers at him as he disappeared.

Gabby disappeared, no longer interested once there was no potato salad to hold her attention. That left only her and Alan at the table, and as soon as they were alone he turned that focused gaze of his in her direction. "So, how's Cam doing?" he asked quietly. "Honest answer, not what you'd say to please the parents. It'll be awhile before my leg is fully up to speed."

Elena wasn't sure if she was amused or annoyed that Cam had been right. More surprising, however, was the odd sense of defensiveness that sent a little spike along her shoulder blades. "I was being completely honest with Marie," she said, watching Alan as closely as he was watching her. "In his own way, Cam is just as scary as you are."

Alan smiled at that, the expression so close to a grin that

it instantly melted Elena's defensiveness. "I know. He cheats, just like his mother."

The last was said with such approval that it briefly brought a smile to Elena's own lips. Still, it wasn't the response she'd been expecting. "I thought you two fought all the time."He settled back in his chair, clearly having obtained the information he was looking for. "We do. He also has his mother's inability to follow basic instructions," he said, his face becoming solemn. "Cam could make captain in a few years if he'd just focus himself a little." It sounded like an old argument between them, one she wasn't familiar enough with to even consider touching."

If he moved over to the castle guard, he could have made captain a year ago. They're in desperate need of men and women who actually know what they're doing."

Alan's disapproval of the basic training methods utilized by the palace guard was legendary, which had led to more than a few shouting matches between him and the guardmaster over the years. As her personal guard, Alan was technically outside their command structure, which was the only reason he hadn't overhauled the entire system years before. "So why ask me if Cam's doing a good job?" she asked, knowing she wasn't likely to get a straight answer out of him. Still, she had to try. "It seems pretty clear to me that you already knew the answer."

He looked amused. "I knew the truth. That didn't mean I knew what your answer would be."

She was tempted to prod the man further. Before she decided whether or not to make the push, however, Robbie reappeared. "Everything's ready," he said, his breathlessness suggesting he'd run back inside. As if he'd realized that himself, he stopped and made himself breathe more slowly. "You can come out whenever you want."

There was only one acceptable answer to give. Standing up, she tried hard to make sure her expression didn't slide into its usual defensive mask. "I'll follow you out right now."

Robbie kept up a steady stream of explanation all the way out to the lab, the semi-familiar technical language doing a great deal to make her shoulders relax. She asked a few careful questions, always designed to set off a new round of explanations, and made a mental note to copy her harness notes and send them along with Cam the following Sunday.

The lab itself was small, full of plants and different bits of wood and metal. There weren't quite as many books as in her own work area, a sign of the differences between the two disciplines of magic, but the ones that were there looked well-read. "I like it," she said. "You must accomplish a great deal out here."

Taking that as a sign of approval, Robbie hurried over to his worktable. "I wove together the basic magic detection and lost child charm spells, then calibrated it to seek out the invisibility spell instead of the blood match like it usually does. It's kind of blind, though. The one time I tested it, the spell tried to make Mom walk through the side of a building. I was wondering if you had any techniques to maybe refine the guidance system a little better."

It was impossible not to jump in with him, offering suggestions from her own work and fascinated by the ideas that Robbie seemed to pull directly from his own imagination. At some point he sacrificed his chair so she could sit down, instead using an overturned mixing cauldron generally used to make basic household potions in large batches. Elena immediately asked him where he'd purchased it—Braeth had recently dissolved his, and they were hard to find in the city.

A casual mention of the flying spells set the conversation

off in an entirely different direction. Soon various practice rounds of the spell—purely for testing, of course—had the invisibility-detecting charms dancing in a circle above their heads. Once Robbie came up with an idea, they used a basic wind spell for propulsion and guided the charms into even more complicated tricks. It was almost as much fun as flying.

"As much as I hate to interrupt, it's getting dark. We should probably be getting you home soon."

Elena jumped at the sound of Cam's voice behind her, accidentally causing an eddy that sent one of the charms sailing towards the door. Cam caught it easily, his smile warm and a teasing light in his eyes. "Has anyone ever told you you're pretty cute when you get caught up playing?"

Giving him her best haughty expression in response, she sent the breeze to pick the charm back up and return it to Robbie. "We weren't playing. We were conducting serious magical experiments." It was only then that Elena realized that it had been "getting dark" for at least a solid hour by now. She had been out here for far longer than she realized. "I really should be getting home. My mother doesn't hover when she's worried, but Bishop somehow senses it and hovers for her." She smiled at Robbie. "Thank you. I should probably apologize to your parents for avoiding them all night, but I had a wonderful time."

Robbie's cheeks colored a little, but the grin on his face reminded her of Cam. "Hey, my door is always open for anyone who has the transitive properties of quartz memorized." Then his expression sobered a little, becoming more earnest. "Seriously, I would love to do this again any time you'd be interested. I don't have a lot of friends who are as in to the technical details of all this as I am."

Elena knew exactly what he meant, and was briefly,

powerfully, tempted to name a date. Then guilt hit, crushing the desire. She and Robbie could become good, close friends, but she had no right to be making those when she had so little time left. Even though she'd decided to examine the curse again, the odds that anyone would find something to help her were miniscule.

A thought clicked quietly inside her head, and the words were out of Elena's mouth before she had any idea they were coming. "Do you know anything about deep spell analysis?"

Robbie paused. "Yeah. Sorcerers and sorceresses use them for intense study sessions on really complicated spells. They set up this whole circle so nothing accidentally explodes or backlashes while they're poking at it, and aren't there usually like three or four people on the outside sending in probes and doing different tests?"

"There are." Elena took a deep breath, telling herself that this was an entirely practical decision. It was always good to have an extra set of knowledgeable eyes during an analysis, and the fact that Robbie was a witch gave him a perspective no one else in the circle would have. "I'm doing a deep spell analysis on a particularly complicated spell construction sometime in the near future, and I would like you to be in the circle. If you're willing, of course."

Behind her, Elena sensed Cam go still. Robbie, however, was paying absolutely no attention to his brother's reaction. "That's, I—" Blinking too-wide eyes, Robbie stopped and made himself take a breath before trying again. "Yes, of course. I'd be honored. But don't you want somebody with more experience? I haven't even finished my training. I'm sure if you asked Dame Beacham she'd—"

Elena stopped him with a lift of her hand, deliberately ignoring Cam. Whatever he was feeling, she could deal with it later. "I'd need you for your observational skills, not your spell casting, and those are already excellent. It's also important to me that I absolutely trust everyone who will be involved in this circle." She smiled a little. "The only witch I know of who fits that qualification is you."

Their eyes met for a long time, then Robbie swallowed. "Of course, just tell me when." Then he hesitated. "Is this something I shouldn't mention to Mom and Dad?"

The question gave Elena pause, and she was annoyed at herself for not having considered that particular wrinkle. But if her own mother was eventually going to have to be told, it seemed wrong not to tell Alan and Marie as well. "I would never be so foolish as to try and keep a secret from your parents," she said.

It was only when the worry left Robbie's face that Elena realized it had been there in the first place. He started cleaning things up, and when she offered to help he gently shooed her away. "I've got a secret organizational system no one else can understand," he said, smiling.

"He really does," Cam cut in, trying to sound as light and easy as he had only minutes ago. But she could hear the tension, and braced herself for whatever argument he was going to try as soon as they were alone. "Come on. Mom and Dad will kill me if you don't say goodbye before you go."

Elena followed him outside, carefully shutting the lab door behind her so that Robbie couldn't overhear. Expecting Cam to jump on the relative privacy, she started with the counterattack. "I have every right to involve your brother." She sounded angrier than she'd meant to, but it bothered her that Cam thought

Robbie had to be protected from her. "If you want Alan and Marie to weigh in first, that's fine. But he's intelligent and attentive, and I need his input."

She stopped where she was, not wanting the rest of the family involved until they'd hashed out a few things. When Cam turned around, however, it wasn't to yell at her. "You didn't tell me you were going to take another look at the curse," he said quietly.

Her frustration abruptly deflated in surprise. "It didn't occur to me," she admitted, feeling her way around the unexpected conversational turn. "Is that what this is about?"

Cam's jaw tightened briefly, and for a while there was nothing but silence. Then he sighed. "I didn't think you'd listened to me."

There were so many ways she could take that, some of which would start conversations she wasn't ready for. Elena kept her voice light, not letting herself wish for anything more than the simplest version. "I enjoy not listening to you."

The corners of his mouth quirked upward. "Believe me, I know." His expression went serious again. "But this was important. And before you try to yell at me again, Robbie was a good call. Mom and Dad won't have any problem with it."

There was no safe response to any of this, except for a simple and dignified apology that she'd gotten mad at him in the first place. "I'm sorry."

Cam's smile widened. "Let's not start that." He held out a crooked arm. "People might think you're possessed."

After a moment, she slid her arm through his. "I don't know what came over me."

CHAPTER 10

Connections

Cam's good mood lasted until the next morning.

Elena was always awake earlier than he was. Cam could make himself get up whenever he had to—when you were a member of the border guard, sometimes shifts started before dawn—but he didn't like the process. Here his duties officially started at eight a.m., which meant that Elena had been wandering around the castle for at least an hour before that. No matter what she did, though, she always made sure she was back in her suite by the time he opened his eyes. She'd tried to give him the slip that first morning after he'd discovered her little flying habit, and he'd ended up in three separate meetings and two guest bedrooms attempting to look for her. After that, she'd decided he was a menace when left to his own devices.

Now, though, there was no sign of her and her bedroom door was firmly closed. He knocked, stomach sinking when she didn't respond, and when the silence continued he pushed open the door.

Elena was lying peacefully in bed, eyes closed like she

simply hadn't woken up yet. But it took a small eternity for her chest to rise and fall even once, and he felt a little sick as he laid his fingers against her pulse. Finally, he felt the too-faint beat that he'd already become painfully familiar with.

Cam reminded himself that they'd done this plenty of times before. It was a blackout, just like all the others, except this time it must have hit while she was asleep. It was his job to keep watch, deflect anyone who tried to talk to her, and have the numbers as close as he could for when she woke up.

He pulled the desk chair over, sat down, and made himself wait. He'd mentally composed his explanation to the queen over a week ago, and though there was a small chance it'd get him on the execution block it was too important not to handle himself. The news that Elena planned to re-examine the curse meant that some changes were required, but Cam was happy to make them.

By the second hour, he was too angry to focus. It was like the curse was slapping back at Elena, punishing her for even thinking about taking a swing at it. For hoping, even a little, that there was a way out of the future dropped on her by an insane relative who she'd never even met.

He wanted to hurt someone, but the only person who deserved it was probably hidden in a tower somewhere thousands of miles away. Besides, Elena was the one who deserved to take the shots. When she woke up again—anything other than "when" wasn't an option here—he was going to figure out some way to give her that chance.

It was about the only thing he could do to help her.

Cam jumped at the sound of someone knocking, and he hurried to answer it before whoever it was invited themselves in. "What?"

When she saw the look on his face, the maid took an involuntary step back. She held the breakfast tray out in front of her like a peace offering. "I— I was just bringing some food up to the princess. Normally, she's already sent for it by now. The cook thought she might be hungry."

Cam kept himself from swearing through sheer force of will, reminding himself that the poor woman didn't deserve it. "She's not feeling well." His words were biting, and he made himself stop when he heard how he sounded. "I told her to get some more rest."

The woman looked concerned. "Do you want me to fetch the doctor, sir?"

He shook his head, taking the tray out of the maid's hands. "I already tried that, and she said no. But you can send Braeth up, if he's willing."

"No, don't." Elena's voice cut into the conversation, firm and only a little disoriented. The sheer relief of hearing it hit Cam hard enough that he almost fumbled the tray. "I'm fine. But tell him I'll be down this afternoon."

The maid bowed her head. "Yes, Your Highness." Then she glanced at Cam again, still looking a little spooked, and hurried down the hallway.

He almost slammed the door in his hurry to turn around, dropping the tray on the desk before returning to Elena's side. She was a little pale, her breathing slow and focused like she was trying to calm herself. But she was sitting up, and right now that was the only thing that mattered.

Cam sat back down in the chair, taking one of Elena's hands in his. When she squeezed it, holding on tight, he realized she was even more shaken up than she was letting on. "It was a blackout, wasn't it?" When he nodded, she closed her eyes. "How long was I out?"

"At least two hours." He tried to make his voice as steady and reassuring as possible, hoping it could counteract what he was saying at least a little. "Probably longer—I think the blackout hit while you were still asleep."

"Fantastic." Her shoulders sagged. "I need to set up the analysis spell soon, don't I?"

"That might be a good idea," Cam said quietly, trying to figure out if there was some way he could fuss over her that she would accept. He wasn't all that good at it, anyway—Mom had always been the champion fusser, meaning that his duties extended only to dumb jokes and other related distractions. Right now seemed way too soon for that.

Facts, however, might do the same thing. "How many people do you have left to talk to?"

Elena sighed, dropping her forehead into her free hand. "Just my mother." She lifted her head again and squared her shoulders. "Which means I should probably get it over with." She tugged on his hand, just a little, then blinked and looked down at their joined hands as if surprised to see them so firmly attached. He let go immediately, but if anything that seemed to disconcert her even more.

Cam grabbed the tray off the desk, ignoring how cold his hand suddenly felt. "Eat something first." He set it down on her lap, hand twitching as he resisted the urge to give her shoulder a comforting squeeze. "It'll give your cheeks a little time to get some of their color back."

It took a second, but she smiled a little at that. "Are you saying I look less than breathtaking right now?"

If she was teasing him, she was okay again. "Well, I didn't want to say anything."

"Hush." Her smile widened as she shooed him toward the door. "Now go away for a second. I need to put on my battle armor."

~

Fifteen minutes later, she emerged from her bedroom pressed, polished, and without a single hair out of place. It was her ice princess look, which had never impressed him, but the warmth in her eyes called up a similar warmth in his chest. "When you said battle armor, you weren't kidding."

She lifted her chin, giving him her best haughty expression. "A warrior must be prepared for every eventuality."

He headed toward Elena, shooting a quick glance behind her to see if he could see the breakfast tray. When she caught him doing it, the humor crept back onto her face. "Are you this much of a mother hen to Robbie and Gabby, too?"

"I'll deny it to my dying day." He held his arm crooked out again, just like he had the night before. "Shall we?"

Taking a deep breath, she slid her arm through his. "If Bishop isn't already with her, I'll need you to go find him while I'm talking to her and bring him back with you."

They started walking, Elena leading the way. Maybe it was because they seemed intent on avoiding each other as much as possible, but she always had a surprisingly good sense of where her mother was. "In case you two start fighting and need someone to break it up?"

Elena shook her head, looking solemn. "No. But there's a fifty-percent chance I'm going to break her heart, and I want him to be there for her."

He briefly tightened his arm around hers, giving her a squeeze without being obvious about it. "She'll be glad you're telling her now."

When they got to the meeting room, however, the queen wasn't there. In fact, the only person in the room was one of the little army of assistants that seemed to swarm the palace at all hours, carrying paperwork from room to room. When he saw Elena, he snapped instantly to attention. "Your Highness—I did not expect to see you. How may I be of assistance?"

"Wasn't there a meeting scheduled for this room?" Elena asked, making the question sound like nothing more than mild curiosity. "Something about property taxes?"

"There was, but Bishop informed us that the queen was ill and could not attend," the man said, his voice solemn. "The meeting is being rescheduled for tomorrow morning."

Cam felt Elena go tense, though none of it leaked through into her voice. "Ill?"

"I apologize, Your Highness." The man bowed slightly in apology. "I'm afraid we were not given details as to the nature of the queen's discomfort."

Elena practically pulled Cam out of the room at that, and when they were safely out of sight she slid her arm free of his and started hurrying down the hallway. He followed her, the pair of them almost but not quite running. "I take it your mom doesn't get sick very often?"

She stopped, whirling around to face him. "No, she never misses meetings." The worry was all over her face. "And the only way even Bishop could have convinced her to miss one was if something was seriously wrong." She squeezed her eyes shut. "I was so busy trying not to tell her about the blackouts that I completely missed the fact that she was in trouble."

"Hey, it's okay." He caught her by the shoulders, leaning down enough that his eyes met hers when she opened them. "You'll figure out what to do."

It wasn't exactly useful or original, but it seemed to help. She squared her shoulders, then pulled away again to continue hurrying down the hallway. Cam followed her, hoping she knew where they were going. After three turns, two sets of stairs and another turn, he recognized the queen's chambers. The guards that were normally stationed outside had been sent away, which normally meant she was having a private meeting, but the door had been left partially open.

When they got closer, Cam could hear both the queen's and Bishop's voices.

He caught Elena's arm, but she just nodded and moved around to the side of the doorway that would offer them some cover. Faintly exasperated that the two women still wouldn't just talk to each other, he settled in behind her so he at least wouldn't give her position away.

"Bishop, I told you. I feel perfectly well." That was the queen, her usually restrained tone not quite able to mask either the affection or exasperation in the words. "I let you cancel the meeting because I knew how worried you were, but I'm up to handling even the most stubborn council member."

"You feel perfectly well now because your symptoms mysteriously disappeared less than an hour ago." Bishop's voice was insistent, with just enough passion behind it that Cam suspected the elf would rather be shouting. "After three full hours of nausea, disorientation, and chills, which is by far the longest episode you've had. You're a sorceress, Illiana. You can't tell me you don't find this at least a little bit concerning."

Cam's eyes narrowed. Elena had been awake for less than

an hour. If they compared the exact time to the moment the queen recovered, he had a sudden suspicion they'd match. In front of him, Elena had gone absolutely still. Had the same thought occurred to her?

Inside the room, the queen sighed. "You know why I can't see a doctor. If news were to get around that I'd fallen ill, the council would become difficult."

"They'd panic, you mean." The words were blunt. "No one is pleased by the thought of the kingdom falling into my hands, me more than anyone. We all want you safe, Illiana."

"The council members simply want me around to keep them all in line." The words were light enough that they sounded like an old joke. "If any of them ever saw you whipping the departmental budgets into shape, I'm sure they'd understand that you're more than sufficiently terrifying enough to maintain order."

"Illiana." Bishop's voice had gone sharp. Cam sympathized completely. "You've been having these episodes for weeks now, striking at random times with absolutely no notice. For all we know, this morning was a sign that they'll all be that long in the future. You must see someone!" He exhaled, the anger seeming to drain out of him. "Please."

Elena's shoulders had gone tense, confirmation that she'd come to the same conclusion he had. Inside the queen's room was the kind of all-encompassing silence that either meant a serious emotional moment or lethal levels of embarrassment, both of which meant that now was not the time to interrupt.

Finally, the queen spoke. "I'll talk to Braeth," she said softly. "He knows some of the basic spells witches use to sense illness. If he agrees with you, I'll see a doctor."

And that was their cue. Cam reached forward to pull the

door further open, then pushed Elena forward until she was visible. Luckily for everyone's dignity, she didn't fight it. "Mother?" she asked, stepping inside the room fully under her own power. Cam slipped in after her. "I was wondering if I could talk to you about something."

"Of course," the queen said, her face shifting subtly as she collected herself. She sat up very straight, as if bracing herself a little, and Cam realized that the queen had to know they'd overheard at least part of the conversation. There was no sign of illness on her face, but her dress was more rumpled than she normally allowed it to be. "What did you need?"

Elena took a deep breath. "I'm going to perform a full analysis on the curse, and I would like you to be a part of it."

The queen went absolutely still, and Cam couldn't read her reaction at all. Bishop took a step towards the queen, almost involuntarily, but she stopped him with a small shake of her head before turning back to her daughter. "Of course." Then she paused. "I was wondering, however, what inspired this. We initially put a stop to them because you were quite vehement that they weren't doing any good."

Now it was Elena's turn to go silent. At her side, her fingers clenched briefly. "I've been having blackouts." The queen's eyes widened, but Elena pushed ahead before her mother could say anything. "Initially, I thought they were just an unfortunate extension of the curse, but now I think it's because the curse has been affected somehow. Maybe—" Here, she faltered a little, and Cam moved closer to her. "Maybe it's breaking down somehow. I won't know for sure until we examine it."

Neither woman even breathed for what felt like far too long, but Cam knew they were the only ones with the right to break the silence. Then the queen let out a long breath, blinking away a suspicious sheen in her eyes. "That sounds like a very good idea," she said, holding out a hand to her daughter. "Thank you for asking me to be a part of it."

Elena took her mother's hand, squeezing it tight. "We can't be sure without double checking the times, but I think your bouts of illness are happening the same time as the blackouts."

Bishop froze at that. Surprise flashed across the queen's eyes, followed by what Cam could only describe as intellectual interest. In the next instant, that was chased away by deep, deep fury. "Ariadne."

Elena jumped on that nugget of information. "Why are you so sure? Is she doing this to hurt us somehow? And how is she getting at you?" She crouched down in front of her mother. "She can reach me through the curse, but I know how good your shielding is. Both Braeth and I keep adding to it when you're not looking."

The queen froze at that, pressing her lips together. The wetness in her eyes was getting harder to blink away. "A blood sample was needed to activate the curse. Since you hadn't been born yet, there was no way for Ariadne to obtain yours. Her only choice was to the blood she and I shared as sisters, and that you and I share as mother and daughter."

Elena shot to her feet, but she still didn't let go of her mother. "So the curse is going to affect you, too? Seventeen years and you never thought to mention this?"

The queen's expression looked remarkably similar to his mother's when one of the kids started panicking about something ridiculous. "Other than breaking my heart, the sleeping curse won't have any effect on me. Braeth triple-checked. But if it is Ariadne, she might be using the blood as a conduit to alter the curse somehow. That would have an effect me, since I'm the access point between you."

Elena's shoulders were still stiff. "How can you talk about that so calmly?"

The queen glared at her daughter, the look surprisingly similar to the one he'd seen so often on Elena. "The same way you hid the blackouts from me and the rest of the castle for weeks."

She glanced past her daughter, briefly meeting Cam's eyes, and he could see that the queen was aware of just how much he knew. She didn't look angry at him, but the Randall women were too good at hiding their emotions for Cam to let himself relax completely.

Elena, surprisingly, wasn't doing quite as good a job of that as usual. Her shoulders hadn't relaxed at all, and when he put a steadying hand on her back he realized there was plenty of tension there as well. He kept waiting for her to say something stupid, which was what he and his siblings reliably did when they were angry for no reason, but she made herself exhale. "I didn't schedule a time for the analysis with anyone, but we need to do it soon." He could hear the worry in her voice. "You talk to Braeth, and I'll let Dr. Flyte and Robbie Merrick know. Hopefully, they'll have some free time before the end of this week."

The queen tensed a little at the mention of Robbie—clearly, several people had known before she did—but she didn't say anything about it. "I'll speak to Braeth today." She leaned in close to her daughter. "We will solve this, sweetheart. I promise you."

For a minute, mother and daughter just looked at each other. Then Elena slid her hand free of the queen's, laying both her hands on the sides of her mother's head. She pressed a kiss against her hair. "I love you, too."

She turned and left the room. Cam hurried to follow her, watching the tension that Elena no longer bothered trying to hide. Once he was sure they were safely out of earshot of the queen, he moved close enough to talk to her. "You have no right to be mad at your mom, you know. She was doing exactly the same thing you were."

Elena whirled on him, mouth open to snap something at him. Then she froze, as if she'd actually thought through whatever she'd been about to say, and closed it again. "I'm going to die at eighteen," she said. "What is there left to protect me from?"

If that was the milder version, what had she held back from saying? "Her only kid's going to die at eighteen because of her sister. What is there left to protect her from?"

Elena didn't say anything for the longest time, jaw tightening. She met his eyes. "Do you have any idea what it's like, knowing you're going to break the hearts of everyone you ever cared about? I don't—" She caught herself again. "I was trying to make it easier."

Cam wished he didn't know what she was talking about. "Love doesn't work that way, princess." He shook his head, feeling a sympathetic ache in his own chest. He'd never met two people who needed a hug more in his entire life. "I know my parents have at least half adopted you. Why haven't they told you that at some point?"

The exasperation in her eyes was better than the pain had been. "Because I don't ask them. I know how they would want me to handle things, and I—" The words trailed off as her shoulders sagged. "I can't."

It hurt just listening to this. How on earth had he ever gotten sucked up in the middle of it? "Maybe your mom can't, either." Needing to focus on something else, Cam started moving again.

He nudged Elena into continuing down the hallway ahead of him. "Now, that's enough of me being insightful. You have some people you need to call."

LATE SUMMER

19 years ago

Getting King Randall's blood was becoming complicated.

The technical challenges were only a part of the problem. As she'd suspected, a visiting scholar didn't have easy access to any of the king's medical tests or leftover bandages. She'd pretended to be a witch studying the human body, hoping that it would lead to some time with the castle doctor, but all of the king's medical needs were taken care of by a witch named Dame Kadrey. They had met once, briefly, but it was enough to make it clear that route wouldn't be effective. Kadrey was suspicious, perceptive, and highly protective of anyone in her charge. Any bandages or biological samples were burned instantly.

The king himself was surprisingly private, appearing mostly in administrative meetings and the occasional public function. In each circumstance he seemed quiet, intelligent and unfailingly polite, which was the other part of the problem. It was hard to concentrate on hurting someone who seemed determined not to hurt anyone else.

She told herself that he didn't spend enough time in his library. It was a small, ridiculous fault, but she clung to it.

Illiana found her own time in that library stretching later and later into the evening, preferring the peace and quiet that came after the other scholars had left for the day. It also allowed her to plan without anyone asking her inconvenient questions, spreading notes and diagrams out in front of her that would have required yet more lies not to seem suspicious.

A sudden sound near one of the shelves startled Illiana. Her head shot upright to scan the room, which at first seemed as empty as it had been last time she'd looked up. Then a head emerged from behind a table as a man slowly pushed himself to his feet, dusting himself off and picking up a few books that had fallen to the ground. It took a moment to put the scene together with the sound she'd heard, and she realized he must have tripped somehow. "Are you hurt?" she asked, closing the architectural book and pushing it beneath a stack of other volumes.

The man met her eyes, looking embarrassed, and Illiana faced the far more startling realization that she was alone in a room with the king. "Only my pride. I didn't expect anyone to be in the library this late."

"I like the quiet." Illiana swallowed, horrified to have been dropped in the middle of what her sister would have described as a perfect opportunity. "I'm sorry, Your Majesty. I didn't know I'd be interrupting you. You don't come into the library very often."

She hadn't had a great deal of opportunity to study him this closely. He was perhaps five years older than she was, with a lean face and a black goatee that she felt made him look distinguished. The servants all adored him, perhaps in part because she'd never once heard of him raising his voice during the time she'd been at the castle.

Looking at him, she decided that his kind eyes also probably had something to do with it.

"Call me Thomas. When your kingdom is as small as this one, the people care far less about propriety than that you do your job properly. As such, I've never really felt comfortable with the title." His voice was surprisingly warm as he returned the books to the shelves, carefully sliding them into their proper spaces. "As to your apology, you're not interrupting me. I can hardly fault someone else for enjoying the library under the same conditions I do."

After his arms were empty, the king—Thomas—set about refilling them again. She watched him pluck several books from the nearby shelves, scanning the nearby titles only briefly before finding the ones he wanted. He was clearly far more familiar with the library than she'd imagined, and demonstrated a care and respect for it that she could only admire.

When he had gathered a small stack, he hesitated by the table. "What are you studying?"

Illiana blinked, so caught up in watching him that she'd briefly forgotten her cover story. "The human body. Specifically, magically-induced illnesses and how to cure them."

"Not an easy course of study." The admiration in his voice sounded genuine, which only made the situation a thousand times worse. She told herself that she should leave now and try to forget about all of this by the morning. She could find another place to work, some place where she could think of him as just a king instead of a kind man who loved books as much as she did.

Instead of doing any of that, she refocused on what Thomas was saying. "Are you planning on going into teaching?"

"No." Here, at least, she could be honest with him. "I prefer not to deal with too many people. I'm much more comfortable with facts."

"A feeling we share." His voice was soft, and it seemed like he was about to take a step towards her. Then he stopped himself, turning instead to set the volumes he'd collected down on the table. "Isn't it lucky for us that books are such excellent company?"

"Yes." Her own voice had softened as she watched his eyes widen slightly, as if surprised that someone else might feel the same way he did. She had learned to read people by watching her sister's mercurial shifts of mood, but she recognized his movements because she saw them so often in the mirror. "What are you reading?"

Even as his eyebrows lifted in surprise, she saw Thomas's shoulders relax a little. "A bit of a mix, really. Some legal histories, the journal of an ancestor who apparently held off an invasion with nothing more than a toothpick and a clever cat, and a few of my favorite botany guides." The corners of his mouth curved upward briefly. "The last are a reward for me when I make it through the others."

Illiana couldn't remember the last time she'd rewarded herself. She wasn't even sure how to go about it. "I always wished I had a firmer grasp of botany. I know a great deal about the different plants, but I'm useless to identify any of them without a diagram in my hands."

Thomas smiled suddenly, as if she'd made a joke, and at the sight of it she felt a treacherous warmth blossom in her chest. "I'm sure you deserve more credit than you're giving yourself." He hesitated again, just for a minute. It was only when he took a step forward that she realized she'd been holding her breath. "I could help you become more familiar with some of the local plants, if you'd like."

Later, Illiana would tell herself that she'd stumbled across the perfect plan. Nature, full of the possibility of thorns and sharp branches, would offer any number of ideal opportunities to get a sample of the king's blood. The offer to tutor her made it apparent he trusted too easily, which would only help her achieve her goal.

At that time, however, she hadn't yet thought up that particular lie. "I'd love to." The words were breathy, as if they'd come out before she'd been ready for them. "When?"

Pleasure instantly lit his face. "Would tomorrow evening be too soon?"

"No." She smiled at him, wondering if this was what rewarding yourself felt like. "Tomorrow evening sounds wonderful."

CHAPTER 11

Tangled Web

They were using her mother's workroom, a bright space full of books and potions that had been mostly cleared for the analysis. Elena hadn't felt comfortable about using her own workroom, which she'd intentionally kept small to discourage company. Braeth's was too dark, and full of things that might be lethally annoyed if someone accidentally tripped over them.

Elena was kneeling in the middle of the newly cleared floor, drawing the protective circle. Its main function would be to keep the curse from unleashing any nasty surprises on the people prodding it. Though the protection would do her little good—she and the curse would both be within the containment—there was something oddly comforting about it.

Or there would be, as soon as she could draw the thing properly.

"The glyph is fine, princess," Braeth chided her, the shadows that surrounded him wildly out of place in the sunlight-filled workroom. "I suspect even the original spell caster did not worry quite so much over each individual line as you have."

Elena, whose hand had already been twitching to erase the glyph and start over, narrowed her eyes at the wraith. "You know as well as I do that even the smallest mistake can make the circle completely useless." Still, she made herself stop, sitting back on her heels to examine the circle one more time. She hadn't slept a great deal the night before, and didn't want that fact to affect her work. "We haven't done this in a few years, and now is the worst possible time for me to become careless."

"You're not capable of carelessness, my dear," her mother said, sitting at one of the long worktables and checking her own notes for what Elena suspected was the thirtieth time. She met her daughter's gaze, a world of understanding in her eyes. "Stubbornness, perhaps, but never carelessness."

The tension inside Elena eased a fraction as she let herself be distracted. "I should be more considerate of Braeth's feelings, though. I'm sure it must be hard for him with all this sunlight, and not nearly enough bubbling things to make him feel comfortable."

"That is true." Her mother glanced over at Braeth, lips curving upward a little. "If you'd like, I can run down and grab a few of your potions to help you feel at home. Maybe even a skull or two."

"Impertinent children." The humor was obvious in the wraith's voice. "It is fortunate for you both that I have forgiven you for your tragic wit long ago."

"We're eternally grateful," Elena said, leaning over and redoing a curve on one of the sigils. She hadn't made it quite sharp enough. "If it helps, I'm sure Dr. Flyte and Robbie will be much better behaved than we are."

Braeth's shadows snuck upward, collecting around the skylights and dimming the entire room a little. "The good doctor is always well behaved, which is another way of saying 'profoundly uninteresting.'"

"If you could resist sniping at him during the analysis, I'd appreciate it." Elena took another look at the protective circle, which also included the projection spell that would make all magic performed within its boundaries visible to everyone.

Intelligent people generally assigned two people to draw the circles for the most complicated spells, since the stress of getting everything right was generally enough to make even the most well-adjusted sorceress snap. Elena, however, had decided it was the only project large enough to keep her from panicking.

As she brushed away a microscopic bit of chalk dust, nerves twisted her stomach just a little tighter. Unfortunately, her theory hadn't been entirely accurate.

"I assure you, Elena," Braeth responded solemnly. "I have never approached a task more seriously than I do this one." She sensed the wraith floating closer to the circle. When she looked up, her mother's eyes were on her again as well. The sheer concern she could feel radiating from both of them was a pressure against her chest, and she hated that she couldn't seem to hold on to such a simple thing as light teasing.

Clearing her throat, Elena returned her gaze to the circle and tried again. "I'm not worried about that. I would just rather you not scar Robbie." Knowing she'd done all she could with the glyphs, she made herself sit back on her heels and review the spells for her portion of the analysis. "He's still relatively new to the craft, which means he thinks that people who have mastered it are wise, thoughtful people. I'd hate to have you and Dr. Flyte be the ones to disillusion him."

"Oh, it's better that it happens now." Her mother stood, deliberately turning away from her notes. "Someone like Braeth comes as such a shock later in life. The young are far more resilient."

Before Braeth could reply, the door swung open. Robbie appeared, his shoulder against the door and his arms full of the bottom half of Dr. Flyte's mirror. Cam came through the door next, holding onto the mirror's other side with a long-suffering expression.

Elena realized why as soon as she caught what the doctor was saying. "Personality has far more influence on sibling dynamics than birth order, but younger siblings cannot help but be influenced by the older children. For example, it's likely that Robbie initially sought out witchcraft simply because it's so drastically different from the more martial pursuits of his elder siblings. Cameron, on the other hand, may be carrying a great deal of—"

"And we're here," Cam announced, talking over the top of Dr. Flyte as he kicked the door closed behind him. "Which means you can stop talking any time now."

The mirror huffed. "You and your brother are the ones who started the conversation. I was simply offering my professional insight."

"Which I found fascinating," Robbie said lightly. "It's not your fault Cam can't appreciate your genius."

Elena smiled when she heard Cam's response. "Maybe I could if I wasn't killing myself hauling that incredibly heavy genius down fifteen miles of hallway."

"I'll have you know this frame was hand-carved by blind mystics from the mountains of Barren. Every pound of it is priceless!"

"Of course it is, doctor," said Elena's mother smoothly, rolling the empty mirror stand to the appropriate place in the circle.

"But you should thank them both for carrying you up here. You remember how stressful it was for you the last time the pages tried to maneuver you up that staircase."

Dr. Flyte shuddered. "I will never understand what birds find so fascinating about flying. I'm much more comfortable when I'm firmly attached to something solid."

Robbie set the bottom end of the mirror down on the stand, leaving Cam to lever it upright and secure the fasteners in place. "There now," her guard said soothingly. "No flying down the stairs or sudden bouts of therapy. We're both happier." Then he turned to Elena, flashing her an easy, gentle grin. "You thought we'd drop him, didn't you?"

She smiled back at him as the knot inside her loosened again. When had the sight of him become such a comfort? "No, I didn't. I know how responsible Robbie is." She stood, brushing off her skirt as everyone moved into position. Cam would be near the door, watching everything and making sure they wouldn't be interrupted. "Robbie, you'll be between my mother and Dr. Flyte. She'll be studying energy signatures, Braeth will be looking at the curse's structure with a magnification spell, Dr. Flyte will be monitoring the the biological effects of the spell on Elena, and I'll be tracing the energy paths. You're welcome to offer commentary on any of the tests we'll be performing."

Robbie took one quick glance back at his brother before facing the center of the circle. Elena stole one more reassuring glance of her own before turning to her mother. "Is Bishop coming? I know you talked about him possibly wanting to observe."

The queen's shoulders tensed for the briefest moment. "He decided against it," she said quietly.

Elena watched her mother's face, certain there was far more to it than that. She would definitely need to find time to talk to the elf alone. "Fair enough." She moved to her own point inside the circle, lifting her hands to activate both spells. "Shall we begin?"

"Hold on," Cam said, leaning towards the door as if he could hear something on the other side. He opened it, held a murmured conversation with the person on the other side, then moved back to let them in. After a hesitation, Bishop stepped through the door. "My apologies," the elf said, clearing his throat as he found a place next to Cam. His eyes went to her mother, full of apology and something else Elena didn't feel she had the right to pry into.

She turned to see her mother's reaction to this sudden appearance. The queen's lips were pressed together, holding back words or something even stronger, but her eyes shone as she met Bishop's. Then she turned to her daughter, giving her the nod to begin.

Nodding back, Elena raised her hands again. She activated the illumination spell first, the faint blue aura of her magic appearing around her as she finished the necessary gesture, then murmured the words for the protection spell. When she shoved both hands downward, palms flat, the spell flared upward briefly in a wall of shimmering golden light before vanishing again.

The shadows deepened against the skylights, darkening the room even further. Then Elena activated the projection spell, designed to make magical energies visible so they could be studied and manipulated more easily. It was harder to manipulate magic without the structure of a spell or pre-established guide, but working with the raw energy was the only way to create a new curse or spell. It was also a diagnostic tool, designed to study never-before-seen spells and curses to figure out how they work.

As it always did, the projection of Elena's own curse formed around her body, a visual representation of how profoundly it had trapped her. As if she were adjusting the lens on a magical scope, Elena murmured a key word that allowed her to shift the projection far enough that she could step outside it to get a better look.

As she stared at the all-too-familiar image of a large, impossibly complex knot glowing in the air in front of her, Elena felt the world rock under her feet.

The last time she had seen the curse, both the knot and the tendrils shooting out from it in all directions were stretched tight and completely still. Now the thing seemed almost alive, the different strands of her aunt's magic sliding restlessly against one another. Pulses of energy shot back and forth inside some of the individual strands, coming in from the different tendrils and zipping around before shooting back out again along a different strand. The curse's outer shields flickered in and out, as if overloaded by everything that was happening.

It was Robbie who broke the silence. "That's terrifying," he murmured. "I know I'm not as familiar with sorcery, but aren't cast spells supposed to give off only a quiet hum of magic? There's a big burst when it's activated, but nothing like this."

"You're correct." The chance to impart information helped Dr. Flyte recover. "Once a sorcerer's spell is completed, it generally leaks even less ambient energy than witchcraft. This—I've only ever seen its like in spells that are actively being constructed."

"Or dismantled," Elena breathed, eyes widening as she heard the words she certainly hadn't meant to say. She resisted a childish impulse to clap her hand over her mouth.

"We cannot be certain of that." Braeth's voice, completely free of emotion, seemed more otherworldly than usual. "This could simply be an attempt to strengthen the curse, or activate it early."

He carefully used no names or even gender pronouns. Elena's aunt was the most obvious suspect—no one else would have such easy access to the curse, or even know enough about it to have this kind of effect. But why would her aunt bother with a pre-emptive strike? She'd waited almost eighteen years for her revenge—surely she could wait a little longer.

And if it was indeed an attempt to stop the curse, the question of why it was happening now still needed to be answered. Her aunt having a sudden change of heart after all these years and wanting to make amends made for a lovely story, but not a terribly practical one.

Elena shook herself, forcing her mind back to the task at hand. "I'm going to follow the energy pulses," she announced, giving herself an order as much as she was informing everyone else. She prepared a simple tracking spell, the kind used in charms to help parents keep track of their children, then shot it into the nearest pulse of light.

Everything else was pushed aside as she followed the pulse, pinging along a serpentine path in the upper levels of the curse. It stayed far away from the area of the core, though nothing in the tracker suggested why, and disappeared along the same strand it had entered by. Interested now, she sent a tracking spell into another pulse. It, too, avoided the core, and Elena set her jaw and forcibly nudged the next spell directly at the core. When it hit, the spell smashed against an invisible barrier and ricocheted in the opposite direction. Immediately, she felt dizzy, swaying slightly as the world spun around her.

"Elena?" It was her mother's voice, sharp with worry. "What just happened? Are you all right?"

"I registered a spike." Dr. Flyte's voice was equally firm. "Who just made direct contact with the curse?"

"It was me. I tried to access the core, and it bit back." She paused, realizing what her mother's immediate response probably meant, and fought a twinge of guilt over forgetting that her mother was also affected by the spell. "Did you feel the counterstrike, or just see me react?"

"I felt disorientated, and after our discussion I decided the curse was the most likely culprit." The technical nature of the discussion seemed to steady her mother. "I think it would be best for all of us not to try that little experiment again, however."

"The question I find myself wrestling with is why the curse does not seem to be tied to your mother, despite the echo effect that is often the result of such a tie." Braeth spun the curse projection to get a better look at it. "None of the tendrils are even attempting to reach out for her."

"Was the effect on the queen part of the original intention of the curse, or a side effect?" Robbie asked, his voice soft. "Because when a witch's spell has accidental side effects, they're most often found in the core. It's the one part you can't fix as easily."

For a minute, everyone in the circle went silent. "Well, there's one way to test the theory," her mother said finally, lifting up her skirts and stepping into the circle even as everyone else moved to stop her.

The second her foot touched the inside of the circle's boundaries, thin streams of teal and purple light flared out from between the tendrils from of the curse's knot. The unfurled tendrils were drawn toward the queen, as if pulled, while the knot itself went chillingly still.

Everyone moved at once. The queen stepped back, and Braeth and Robbie reached to help pull her out. Elena, her panic immediately replaced by frustration, moved straight through the projection to push her mother outside of the circle. Once she was back outside the boundaries, the tendrils hit against the wall of the protective spell. The golden light flared, refusing to let the magic pass, and the knot writhed again as the tendrils retreated back into their original positions.

"Well," Braeth said. "That was interesting."

Her mother, however, was still staring at the knot as if she'd seen a ghost. "It is Ariadne." Her voice was strange. "I was right about her using the blood."

Elena felt a chill, the frustration that had been building over her mother's risk smothered at the mention of her aunt. "That's why the tendrils attacked you?"

The queen took a deep breath, steadying herself. "I don't think it was an attack. Ariadne's magic passed through mine to touch the curse, so my energy was familiar to them. It makes sense that they would be drawn to me." Her control faltered, the bitterness and grief slipping out. "Ariadne always said our magic was compatible. It's what made me the perfect assistant."

"So now we know who is responsible for the alterations to the curse." Dr. Flyte used his therapy voice, designed to calm and analyze. "The next question is why Ariadne would even attempt to alter the curse at this point. None of the effects we're seeing correlate to anything that might strengthen the curse, unless something went terribly wrong on her end."

"I would guess an enormous power surge." Braeth deepened the shadows against the skylight, bringing the knot into even clearer focus. "But any sorceress with even a modicum of training would know that would only wreak havoc on a complex structure such as this."

"Ariadne would know that better than anyone." Her mother

sounded dismissive, but it was better than the grief had been. "But I'm not ready to believe she's trying to undo the curse."

"If she is, she's trying to fix it blindly," Robbie said thoughtfully, moving closer to Braeth in order to get a better look at something. "Without being close enough to initiate a full analysis, she's doing it all by feel."

"That's insane." Her mother's voice had gone sharp again, but this time it was anger providing the edge. "Even if she is trying to help, she could kill my daughter completely by accident."

"She may see it as her only alternative," Dr. Flyte said. "She knows you'll kill her if she comes near Elena again."

The pain that flashed in the queen's gaze was raw enough that Elena felt tears sting her own eyes. For both their sakes, she made herself look away. "I won't let her hurt my daughter again," the queen whispered.

An uncomfortable silence fell over the circle that was finally broken by Braeth. "Death may not be the only option."

Everyone's head snapped around to stare at him. "I don't believe we were actually considering it as an option," Dr. Flyte said. "It was more of an abhorrent worst-case scenario."

"Fortunately, I have what may be a more effective one." The wraith's voice was as calm as it ever was, but something about it set warning bells off in the back of Elena's brain. "If we use the new activity in the curse to trace the location of Illiana's sister, I can force her to take the brunt of the sleeping curse once it activates. The magic itself will still exist in Elena, but it is this other sorceress who will lose consciousness for a century."

All the breath seemed to leave Elena's body as she tried to make herself comprehend what Braeth was saying. Dr. Flyte, who had no breath to worry about, was far more capable of responding. "That's impossible. If such a spell existed, I would know about it."

"It is an old spell, used by dark sorcerers to deflect the attacks of their enemies onto unsuspecting prisoners. One of the enemy's own loved ones, held hostage, was usually an ideal choice." The shadows were even thicker around Braeth, making it almost impossible to see him at all. "Its use died out more than a century ago, when the darker branch of sorcery became more civilized. But I can assure you that it is remarkably effective."

The silence was almost choking this time. "And you wait more than a decade to tell me this?" The words sounded like they'd been ripped out of her mother, full of the same dangerously overwhelming swamp of feeling that echoed in Elena's own chest.

"The spell requires Ariadne's blood, which we have not had before now," he said simply. "Her failings as a sorceress do not extend to her ability to hide herself well enough that neither we nor the council could find her. Once I trace her magic, however, she'll be ours."

"No." Elena's throat was raw. "We don't know enough to even think that yet." She hated that she'd used the word "yet," even giving that small credence to Braeth's suggestion. But sheer practicality made it a necessity. "I agree we need to find my aunt somehow, bring her here and make her talk to us. But we can't—"

The rest of the words died as purple light began streaming down the tendrils of the curse, pouring into it from some outside source. The tendrils pushed inward, shoving aside the other strands as if attempting to burrow their way into the curse's core. As if they were trying to untangle the knot by themselves.

Realizing what it meant, Elena half-stumbled into a sitting position so she would have less far to fall when she blacked out. Once again, someone else had to give voice to what she was feeling.

This time, it was her mother. "Ariadne," the queen breathed. "She's trying to affect the curse again."

CHAPTER 12

Getting Around It

Cam would rather have had a thousand swords coming at him. Swords were easy. He knew what moves they were capable of making, all the ways they could potentially hurt people, and everything that needed to be done to stop them.

Watching everyone do what was supposed to be a simple magical analysis, however, was making him crazy. He didn't know how to stop magic from attacking people, but that didn't stop his muscles from jerking in reaction every time the lights flared or the tendrils reached for someone. Bishop, on the other hand, had gone so still Cam wouldn't have been surprised to find out the elf had stopped breathing.

It was Cam's turn to nearly stop breathing when Braeth suggested turning the curse back on the aunt. Protective instincts that had previously been reserved for his family rose up inside him, completely approving of what seemed like the first solid plan to get Elena free of the curse. She clearly didn't feel the same way, but surely she could be outvoted.

When Elena half-fell into a sitting position in the middle of the circle, however, Cam forgot about everything else. He knew that look on her face, a mix of practicality and dread that made it obvious she knew the next blackout was coming and he saw her move closer to the ground. He watched the purple light, the strands digging their way toward the center of the curse, and remembered that it was a hit to the core that had made her dizzy the first time. Having something go all the way through would hit both her and the queen a lot harder.

Braeth, seeing this, was already planning ahead. "Illiana, prepare the back trace before the core is breached and the illness hits. I will maintain the energy levels and ease the worst of the symptoms, but my magic cannot still be active while the spell is cast. There's a chance it may infect the trace, and it is to our tactical advantage to keep Ariadne unaware of my presence."

The queen nodded, hands forming the necessary gestures. "It's a simple spell," Bishop murmured, voice so low it was almost impossible to make out the individual words. It took a second for Cam to realize that the other man was talking to himself. "She's talented and shielded enough that Ariadne won't be able to hurt her. She won't even notice her."

Taking pity on the elf, Cam nudged him. "We should be closer."

Bishop hesitated, then agreed. They moved to a few feet outside the circle, the elf staying near the queen while Cam gravitated to the open space near his brother. It was the most immediate route to Elena, and he could ask Robbie questions without interrupting the main action.

The strings were about halfway to the core now, the rest of the knot looser but still fighting back. Watching this with a grim expression on her face, Elena made a gesture and touched her hands to her chest. Murmuring something, she filled her hands with blue light and sent it flowing to her mother. "Use this," Elena said quietly. She looked even more tired than she had a second ago. "I won't be able to."

She'd moved to a point in the exact center of the circle, arms tucked tight against her so she wouldn't smudge the circle no matter where she fell. She'd accounted for that little technical detail, but not the fact that she still had a few feet to go before she hit the ground. With the way the blackouts dropped her, there wasn't even a chance she'd catch herself.

Lie down, he mouthed at her, willing her to look at him. It was insane that she wouldn't cut herself even that much of a break. You'll hit your head if you don't.

Elena didn't even glance in his direction. "If all of my blackouts began only when she hit the core, the curse should have taken a lot more damage by now," she said, folding her hands in her lap.

"The outer shields are almost destroyed," Dr. Flyte said. "When they were at greater strength, I suspect they would have had a similar response when attacked."

"The trace is locked in," the queen said, eyes on the strands still digging into the curse. As far as Cam could tell, they were almost to the core. "Now all we can do is wait."

In a story, there would be a convenient coat or drop cloth lying around, no matter how little sense it made for either thing to be in a well-organized workroom in the middle of the summer. Seeing neither, Cam swore softly and headed toward his brother. "Would it mess anything up if I went into the circle?" he asked, voice low.

Ripping his eyes away from the curse, Robbie said, "Not if

you didn't smudge any of the lines or sigils. But you can't take her out of there, Cam. We need to see what's happening with the curse."

"I figured that part out, genius," Cam muttered, deciding that he was the only one who was going to care if he looked like an idiot. Everyone else had more important things to worry about.

When he stepped into the circle, Elena looked up at him like he'd lost his mind. "Cam, you can't—" The words trailed off as he sat down next to her, taking care not to smudge the circle at all. "What are you doing?"

"You're going to bounce your head against the floor." He kept his voice gruff, reminding himself that this was still better than being able to do nothing. "Lie down before you give yourself another headache."

Her eyes widened as she realized what he meant. "Cam," she said quietly. "You don't—"

"Elena." He let the helplessness he was feeling out into his eyes. "Lie down."

It took some shuffling, but if he moved over there was enough room for her to curl up on her side and lay her head down on his leg. He laid his hand on her shoulder as they both looked up, all their attention on the projection of the curse.

A few seconds later, the strands slammed hard into the core. Elena went boneless as the blackout took her, cheek pressing against his leg. At the same time, the queen swayed and pressed a hand against her stomach. Still, the teal light of the tracking spell stayed solid, her eyes fixed on the projection. She didn't look away even when Bishop moved to her side, but she leaned into him a little as her arm curled around his.

The strands being controlled by Elena's aunt kept digging

into the core, violently enough now that the entire knot started shaking a little. The only other effect was a faint shimmer from inside the knot, and Cam heard Dr. Flyte murmur something about it possibly being a reaction to the shielding around the core.

Finally, the purple light disappeared, vanishing as if it had been sucked out of the knot. The tendrils floated out of the tangle again, stretching out into the distance, while the rest of the knot shifted and writhed like it had before. The queen had straightened completely, eyes distant and hands stretched out as if pressed flat against an invisible wall. Under his hand, Elena inhaled and opened her eyes. "How long was it this time?" she asked, sitting up and brushing her hair back from her face.

"Not long," he murmured, smoothing an errant bit that she'd missed. "As far as I can tell, she tried a big push rather than an extended assault this time."

Elena rested her hand on his leg as she moved closer to him. "Whatever my aunt's trying to do, she'll never be effective if she can't see it."

Above them, the queen blinked as her eyes refocused. "Ariadne is in Yonder, along the border of Lake Sorrows." She lowered her hands, shoulders sagging a little as the strain ended. "She must have moved there only within the last few years. Thomas and I routinely sent investigators through that whole area."

"If you sent soldiers now, they could probably get to Yonder in a few days," Robbie said. "My older brother Mason sent me a postcard from there once. He said the kingdom is small enough that the king still has time to keep his winery business running."

Cam remembered it now, mostly from Laurel's sarcastic commentary about how much of that wine their captain was drinking. "I know a mercenary unit who could pick her up," he offered. "We'd probably need royal backing and an official charge just to make sure the paperwork was all in order, but I know their unit's close to wrapping up their current contract."

"Call them," Elena said, any sign of unsteadiness from the blackout carefully eradicated. "I'll pay for the contract out of my private accounts so we don't have to wait for mother to push it through committees. I spend so little of my yearly stipend that there should be plenty of money."

"There are any number of formal charges we could use, most of which would have the direct backing of the Council," Dr. Flyte said. "I could have them drawn up and sent to your mirror within the hour, Cameron."

"I'll have a map to you around the same time, along with a royal order to help speed things along." The queen cast the simple spell that shut down the curse projection, then let out a long breath. "And if the captain needs to contact me, feel free to send him or her to my private mirror."

"He won't need to," Robbie answered, watching his older brother with an odd expression on his face. "Laurel and Cam will take care of it."Realizing he was still sitting on the floor, Cam hurriedly stood up before holding out a hand to help Elena do the same. He felt surprisingly relieved that he'd been able to do something to help, even if it had just been to make a suggestion.

"So we're done?" Elena asked, looking around at everyone else. When she got a few nods, she scuffed a line completely through the circle before stepping across it. "I'll come back later to clean up," she told her mother. "Right now, though, I feel like I need to just sit down for a few minutes."

"Rest, child," Braeth said, drawing the shadows back toward him. The room slowly lightened as sunlight filtered back into the room. "The energy you offered your mother was well-timed, but your body is already paying the price for it. I insist that you take a suitable amount of time to recover."

She lifted her chin a little. "I'm perfectly capable of doing that without sleeping."

The queen's eyes narrowed. "Elena."

"Don't make me." She met her mother's eyes. "Please."

"At least tell me you've been sleeping at night," the queen said, her voice soft.

Cam watched Elena, suddenly wondering the same thing. She'd have to be getting at least some sleep, or she'd have been stumbling around like a zombie after the first week. But there were all kinds of ways a person could cheat their way through a night's rest, especially when they had magic to back them up. "How long?" he asked, annoyed at himself for missing it before now.

Elena looked at him, surprised. He held her gaze, until she answered him. "I didn't sleep very well last night. That's all."

The first night since the long blackout, the one that had caught her while she was sleeping. As if losing consciousness at completely random moments hadn't screwed her up enough.

"Cameron." The queen's voice was quiet but firm, hitting some mother frequency that made his inner six-year-old stand at attention. "Make sure she gets some sleep. Please."

Elena whipped around to stare at her mother, looking horrified and a little bit betrayed. Before she could say anything, Cam hooked his arm through hers and pulled her towards the door. "You heard her, Princess. I'm not about to argue with a royal order."

~

"This is ridiculous." Elena glared at him from his bed, every inch of her body making it clear that she was sitting there against her will. Weirdly enough, Cam found the stubbornness comforting—even after everything she'd been through, it showed she still had plenty of fight left in her. "Switching beds won't keep me from blacking out."

"No, but it'll be easier to let yourself relax." He stood in the doorway to his room, mirror in hand. He'd call Laurel once he was sure Elena would at least try to get some rest. "You haven't been sleeping in your own bed because that's where you had the blackout, and a part of you panics every time you close your eyes. In a different bed, that won't be a problem."

She rolled her eyes. "I didn't know you were practicing to be a therapist. You should get advice from Dr. Flyte."

He winced at the thought of the mirror unleashing more therapy on him. "If you even think about making that suggestion to him, my vengeance will be more terrible than you can imagine." When she just kept glaring at him, he sighed. "The border guard isn't exactly like going to war. But stuff happens. You figure out how to get around it."

The glare disappeared, and he braced himself on the off chance some sympathy was about to erupt. Instead, she shook her head. "You're turning into your mother, aren't you? You just haven't wanted to tell anyone."

Dramatically, he pressed his free hand to against his chest. "You've discovered my secret." He pointed a warning finger at her in his best impression of his mother. "Now get some rest."

She rolled her eyes again, but obligingly let her head hit the pillow. Deciding that pushing for much more than that really would turn him into his mother, he shut the door. He stood there, listening for the sound of movement, but she was too smart to jump back up immediately.

He found a comfortable chair, saying his sister's name to activate the sequence for her mirror. After a few minutes, the swirling clouds disappeared to reveal a slender woman with dark blond hair cropped nearly as short as his. She smiled as soon as she saw him. "So, Dad driving you nuts yet?"

"I'm surviving." Even though an hour hadn't passed, Cam checked to see if he'd gotten either the map or list of charges. He probably should have waited to call Laurel until he'd received both of them, but he'd wanted to get things moving. "It helps that Mom's essentially confined him to the house."

"He'll get more restless as the cast gets closer to coming off," Laurel warned him, having broken more than a few bones herself over the years. "Still, Mom should be able to hold him back for a few more weeks while his leg gets back to full strength, and then you're free as a bird."

Cam froze for a second, stunned that he'd completely forgotten that little deadline. This was his Dad's job, not his, and he'd stretched things with the border guard just getting enough leave time to come back here in the first place. If he tried to stay any longer, odds were he wouldn't have a job to go back to.

Some of this must have come through on his face, because Laurel's brow lowered as she watched him. "Dad's not trying to suck you in to the bodyguard routine full time, is he? I know he thinks the other guardsmen are idiots, but I'm sure you're already getting bored."

"Nigel's hired muscle was a decent distraction." His mouth was working on auto-pilot, trying to give his brain time to recover. He could be okay with this. If they got Elena's aunt back here fast enough, they could probably have all this done in a few weeks. He could go back to the border knowing she was fine. And it wasn't like she didn't know how to use a mirror. His parents considered her family—no one would think it was weird if they still talked.

"Cam." Laurel's voice was firmer now, meant to get his attention. "What's going on? Talk to me."

It was the perfect opening. "I need a favor, actually," Cam said, pushing everything else aside. He'd deal with it later. "Have you guys finished cleaning up after that evil queen yet?"

"We've got a couple units doing final sweeps, but most of us are heading back to main camp tomorrow morning. You need me and Mason to do something?"

"More than that." Not that his siblings weren't the best at what they did, but they had no idea if the aunt would come willingly. He wanted them to have as much backup as possible. "As many people as you can convince your captain to let take a separate contract."

"You're hiring us?" Now her eyes widened. "Cam, what in all the gods' names have you gotten yourself in to?"

He refused to even think the answer to that particular question. "I'm not hiring you, the princess is. We—" No, that wasn't going to help. "She and the queen need you to bring in a sorceress who may or may not come quietly. There's a full list of charges and a royal order, and I'll send them both to you and Mason as soon as I get them."

Laurel just stared at him. "If the princess is hiring us, remind me again why you're calling instead of one of her official minions?"

"Because w—she needs this sorceress as quickly as possible, you guys are the best, and you'll be able to talk the captain around a lot faster than the queen could." He tried his best "you know you love me" grin. "And if I'd given out the code to your private mirror, even to royalty, you'd have killed me."

Now her eyes were narrowed like she was trying to see inside his head. "Get out of there," she said, sounding deadly serious. It was the voice she used when telling someone what they needed to do to stay alive, and it was the only reason Cam knew she wasn't joking. "I'll get Mason to push through the paperwork while I talk to the captain and round up the rest of the men we'll need. We'll be on the road tomorrow to get your sorceress for you, but only if you promise me you'll get out of there as soon as you can. I knew you were softhearted, but I had no idea this job would mess with you as much as it clearly has."

"Laurel."

"I mean it, Cam. Promise me."

"I'm fine." He fought hard to not get angry. "Like you said, body guard duty is easy enough to make people drop dead of boredom. Dad'll be back in a few weeks, and then there won't be any reason for me not to go right back to the border guard. My supposedly soft heart has nothing to do with anything."

She swore, far more fluently than Cam could have managed. "You still think talking a lot about something else will make it so people don't notice what you're avoiding. Look me in the eye and tell me you don't already care too much about this girl."

He held her glare for a moment, willing himself to lie. When he couldn't make anything come, there was a rattling noise from the other end that suggested she'd hit the table. Oh, I am going to kill him."

"Laurel." He gave up on resisting the glare, deciding it was better to focus his attention on not shouting. "It's not a problem. I can handle this."

In the grand tradition of big sisters, Laurel chose to completely ignore him. "If I'd known this was going to happen, I would have made sure it was me. I like the kid fine, but—" She stopped herself from finishing the sentence, then shook her head. "You know how terrible an idea this is, right?"

What was he supposed to say to this? "I am fine, Laurel. How many times do I have to say this?"

She glared at him. "If she breaks your heart, I'm going to have to kill her. No matter what Mom or Dad think."

"Laurel." He only barely remembered to keep his voice down. The last thing he wanted was for Elena to overhear the fact that his sister had completely lost her mind. "We're not a couple, so there's no chance of her breaking my heart. Now please go intimidate some big strong men and stop worrying about me. I'm not going anywhere, but I can promise you is that I will be totally, completely and one-hundred-percent fine."

Laurel kept glaring at him. "I'll have Mason call you before we set out tomorrow. But I meant what I said—I have no trouble with beating up on princesses, curse or no curse." She then cut the mirror connection.

Cam closed his eyes, rubbing his forehead against the headache he'd magically developed in the last few minutes. Hopefully, Elena was having better luck relaxing than he was.

CHAPTER 13

Sunshine and Bluebirds

"You look well rested, Elena," Dr. Flyte said cheerfully, as if nothing had changed between their last appointment and this one. They'd already chatted politely about the fact that he'd brought a few of his magical books into the office as decoration, and she supposed he considered this to be a casual segue."I take it you've been sleeping better."

Elena had been, but there wasn't the slightest chance she'd admit the reason. She and Cam had switched beds for the last few nights, which was completely ridiculous but had given her some of the best sleep she'd had in weeks. She's switched the blankets that morning, telling Cam that she wanted her very expensive bedding back. The truth was, though, that his bedding didn't smell like him anymore. "Yes, thank you." She gave the mirror her most polite smile. "It was simply the stress of the analysis that was keeping me awake."

"That's good to hear." Dr. Flyte's tone made it clear that he didn't believe a single word she said, but she hadn't given him much of an opening to push. Not that she'd been able to close it completely. "How has Cameron been sleeping?"

"I wouldn't know." Elena watched the mirror intently, trying to figure out where he was going with this. "He's just outside, though. If you're really interested, you can ask him as soon as the appointment's over."

"I presumed he must be, but I didn't see him when you came in." The doctor's tone now was pure therapeutic concern. "Is Cameron avoiding me?"

The question seemed genuine, making it harder to tease him. "I think he's afraid you'll try to analyze him again," she said carefully, deciding honesty was the kindest option. "I get the impression he's not really comfortable getting too many details about his psyche."

Dr. Flyte huffed. "I was simply expounding on the traditional sibling dynamics that were occurring right in front of me." He stopped himself, the projected image of his face bobbing a little in his frame like he was taking a cleansing breath. "Fair enough. All I can do is hope that his reluctance won't hinder him from seeking help if he needs it."

Elena's hands tightened on the armrests of her chair. "What does that mean?"

The mirror looked almost kind, which didn't help Elena's peace of mind any. "While you undoubtedly bear the brunt of the stress in this situation, my dear, there are repercussions for all of us. Cam has had less time to come to terms with that fact."

It was a stab, right through her heart. She wondered if he'd meant to hit quite so directly. "If he ended up needing to talk to someone, his parents are right here. You know how close the Merricks are." Not that she planned on dragging him any further into this than he already was. After his siblings brought her aunt here, the problem would be strictly magical. Whatever happened, the worst of it would miss him.

And if the worst didn't miss her, he would still be able to move on with his life. They had become friends, which would be hard on him, and he had his father's sense of responsibility. But Marie would help Alan, and they would both help Cam. All three of them were too strong for her to be able to break their hearts.

Elena took a deep breath, giving herself a firm mental slap. If she kept thinking like this, she was going to start crying. That was the last thing any sane person wanted to do in front of her therapist. "Besides, I'm not sure Cam could afford you. Didn't I hear you're doing long-distance consultations for Elves now?"

"It's not therapy, precisely." Dr. Flyte said lightly, giving her time to recover. Still, he watched her closely, as if waiting for any sign that her mind might wander off into dark places again. "Most Elves hate to talk about their feelings even more than Bishop, so the consultations actually fall closer to the realm of stress management. But you're right, they do pay well." He let just a hint of amusement creep into his voice. "I've been giving genuine thought to setting up a neat little blackmailing practice on the side. I haven't done so in years, but with some of the information I've been receiving it's a remarkably tempting thought."

Elena's own lips quirked upward in genuine humor. If Braeth heard Dr. Flyte talk like this, she suspected he would find the mirror slightly less boring. "I would think your therapeutic ethics would get in the way of really enjoying yourself, there. You're too good at what you do to muddy your reputation like that."

"It would, if I had a therapeutic relationship with any of

them. But since I'm merely a consultant, taking advantage of a lucrative opportunity is simply good business practices." Still, he gave a resigned sigh. "Of course, there's always the possibility that one of my blackmail victims would send an assassin to shatter me. I would have to hire bodyguards, and it's challenging to find ones who are willing to take me seriously."

"Turn them into frogs. I'm sure that would get their attention." She felt the muscles easing in her shoulders as she teased him. It was possible he was helping her to relax simply out of kindness, but it was also entirely possible that he was trying to lull her into a false sense of security before springing some deeply probing question on her. With Dr. Flyte, the two impulses were far from mutually exclusive.

Which meant that now was a good time for a distraction. "If we ever see Nigel again, I'll have him specially brought over so you can do the same thing to him."

Dr. Flyte chuckled. "Speaking of your and Cameron's pest, I was able to collect some of that information you were looking for. It seems that Prince Nigel is, in fact, the oldest son of the current king of Long Ago. According to the traditional rules of his country, he should be too busy learning how to run the kingdom to make trouble for us here."

"So what went wrong?" Elena tried to picture the scenario. "You said 'current king,' so it's not as if his family's been deposed or anything."

"No, but it appears Nigel himself has." Dr. Flyte turned slightly, checking some stream of information he was accessing. "Apparently, his father realized that Nigel would be such as disaster as king that he attempted to have the rules of inheritance changed. When that didn't work, he sent Nigel on a series of impossible tasks and named his younger brother regent until they could be fulfilled."

Elena snorted in disgust. "And let me guess—one of those tasks is to bring home an enchanted princess."

"I was unable to get confirmation on the specifics, since they mostly seem bent on pretending he doesn't exist, but that would be my guess," the mirror replied, voice thoughtful. "What I don't understand is why he simply doesn't move on and find a more willing princess. I suspect there are several who would be far easier to kiss awake, and at least a few desperate enough to accept him as the person doing the kissing."

She shook her head. "Most people arrange to get their sleeping curses in advance, and already have someone in mind to get them out of it. They and their families leak the information to the right people, the appropriate man or woman rides out, and as a result most sleeping curses are broken in about a week." Elena had long ago stopped being bitter about that fact. It was simply the way things were. "I'm sure Nigel would hear about a princess, and by the time he got to her she'd already be awake and in someone else's arms."

"True." He didn't sound happy about it, which she appreciated. "Still, I'm disturbed the fact that you're not actually asleep yet doesn't seem to bother him."

"Maybe he wants to be first in line." She rubbed a hand across her eyes. "If we can't turn him into a frog, maybe we can get my aunt to sleep-curse him when Cam's siblings bring her in."

The mirror's expression darkened. "Braeth should never have brought that up."

Her brow furrowed. She hadn't been referring to the wraith's suggestion at all, which made it all the more surprising that Dr. Flyte had immediately leapt there. "It was his version of being kind."

"Presenting that possibility to your mother wasn't a kindness. He himself recognized that deciding to wield it could break her, and with your father gone I'm not certain how well I could repair the damage." He sounded genuinely distressed, as if the thought had been weighing on him. "Braeth should have kept it to himself unless it became an absolute necessity."

Elena blinked, startled by the unexpected turn in the doctor's complaint. "Did you just say 'unless it became a necessity?'"

Dr. Flyte hesitated. "Well, we wouldn't want to eliminate any possible avenue of treatment, even one with as many negative effects as the one Braeth proposed. The psychological effect on your mother would be dramatic, but less harmful in the long run than to watch you fall to the curse." His expression shifted, as if gearing up for a lecture. "Still, with the new information we've received I'm certain there are other alternatives."

"Dr. Flyte," Elena interrupted, something heavy forming in the pit of her stomach. She hadn't rejected Braeth's suggestion outright when they were all in the circle, but that was mostly so she wouldn't hurt her mother. But if even the mirror was willing to consider something that could bring the council down on their heads "What Braeth suggested is probably a criminal act." She could hear the emotion in her voice, no matter how hard she tried to hold it back. "I don't want any of you to risk that kind of trouble for something that might not even work."

Now Dr. Flyte appeared startled, and he looked at her for a long, quiet moment. Elena hunched her shoulders slightly in an automatic protective gesture, not able to shake the feeling that he could see far too much.

Finally, the doctor broke the silence. "Are you planning on presenting that argument to your mother?" he asked quietly.

Elena lifted her chin, regathering her pride so she wouldn't have to think about the rock in the center of her chest. "I'm not an idiot, Dr. Flyte, or cruel. But I have just as much right to feel protective as the rest of you do, and it is your job to listen to those feelings and take them into account." It was a confession of sorts, true, but right now it was the only argument she had.

"Yes." Dr. Flyte's sigh held the weight of years behind it. "I suppose it is."

~

When the appointment ended, Elena escaped as quickly as possible. Cam was just shutting down his mirror when he saw her, and something in her face had him standing and ushering her out the door without a word.

Once they were safely out of the building, he moved close. "You usually have a weird half-satisfied, half-frustrated look when you come out of your appointments, like you've had a sparring match with someone who's a little better than you'd like them to be. Now you just look beat up."

She let out a long breath. "He went for more kill shots than usual. I should have kept my guard up."

"Want me to beat him up for you?" Cam held his arm out, and she slid her own arm through without hesitation. "Punching him would probably be fatal for at least one of us, but I'll get some pages to carry him up and down a flight of stairs until he's begging for mercy."

Elena laughed, the tightness in her chest easing. "I think we can spare him that particular torture, but thank you for that lovely thought." She moved a little closer to him as they walked.

"What you can do, though, is distract me. Has either your brother or sister called with an update yet?"

"Laurel did. I was just on the mirror with her while you were at your appointment." Something strange flickered across his face, disappearing before she could try to analyze what it was. "They're finishing up recon now on the estate where your aunt's living and expect to move in to pick her up in the morning."

"She's on the run and still managed to get her hands on her own estate," Elena said. "I know that sort of thing is supposed to be standard operating procedure for an evil sorceress, but it's rather annoying."

"Technically, it's not her estate. According to Mason, she married a widowed landowner with three grown sons. Your aunt's got a place to stay, but unless she gets him to change his will she won't inherit a thing."

"Maybe she wants gratitude money from us." Even as she said it, Elena knew the explanation didn't make sense. Anyone looking to get paid for a miracle would present his or her bill in advance. "Or maybe she's simply looking for a hobby while she figures out how to talk her new husband out of his millions."

"Have I told you that you can be annoyingly cheerful sometimes?" Cam asked. "Seriously, all this sunshine and bluebirds stuff is driving me nuts."

The corners of her own mouth curved upward. "I'll try to restrain myself."

"The takeaway here is that there aren't any big scary defenses for Laurel and her team to get through, and the company sorcerers say there isn't more than the basic magical shielding." He squeezed her arm. "Even if she puts up a fight, they have enough of their own spellcasters with them that it probably won't even take a full day to bring her in. Laurel and the team should be here with your aunt by the end of the week."

Elena refused to let herself dwell on how that particular confrontation would go. "I'll have the money ready for them as soon as they arrive."

That strange look was in his eyes again, lingering long enough that Elena recognized it as embarrassment. "You can have Bishop handle the actual transfer or something, can't you?" he asked. "Or someone else in the financial department. Mason enjoys talking to even the most boring people."

"Why are you suddenly so interested in making sure I don't speak to your older siblings?" Elena slanted him a curious look. "I have spent time with them before, you know. Not much—they were mostly grown by the time your father became my guard. But we were perfectly polite to each other."

Cam's expression made it clear he was sorting through a few different potential responses, then he shook his head and made an exasperated noise. "Laurel's gone crazed. I think Mason's probably safe, but I have a terrible feeling Laurel's going to try and get you alone in a corner somewhere. If you could help me make sure that doesn't happen, I'd appreciate it."

She studied him, more and more certain that he wasn't joking. "Is she mad at me for some reason?"

He opened his mouth, then thought better of whatever he'd been about to say and closed it. "She's just crazed," he said, sounding long-suffering enough that Elena was almost tempted to believe him. "Maybe it's some kind of berserker madness that hits people when they spend too long stabbing bad guys for a living."

"It's always possible." Obviously, he wasn't ready to tell her yet. She'd have to keep an ear open in case he let anything slip. "Will you be hiding as well, or am I the only one in danger of her 'berserker madness?'"

"Oh, I'll be right there with you." He grinned again. "So we should probably find a comfortable hiding place."

They were brainstorming different options as they made it back to the castle, navigating their way through the maze inside. Cam liked to have them take a different route each time they came back, expanding his map of the building without having to ask a maid for directions, and Elena humored him by coming up with longer and more twisting pathways. Secretly, she was pleased that he cared enough to learn.

They were winding their way through a nearly abandoned part of the castle when they were surprised by a door opening directly in front of them. They both stopped short, Cam automatically pushing Elena a little behind him, when Bishop stepped out with an enormous pile of paperwork. He jumped, they jumped, and half the paperwork scattered all across the floor of the corridor.

"We were looking for hiding places, too," Cam said, passing Bishop another handful of papers he'd recollected. "I take it you'd rather we find one not so close to your hiding place?"

"I would appreciate it," Bishop said. "I don't normally use it, but the finance meeting is tomorrow and all the department heads think they'll get special treatment if they plead their case to me in advance."

Elena headed down the corridor, collecting the stray sheets that had put the most effort into escaping. "Mother and I always did wonder where you disappeared to."

Bishop, who had been standing to re-stack the papers, hesitated. "Have you seen your mother today?"

The words stopped her short. "No," she said carefully, turning around to face him. Was this a subtle way of telling her that something was wrong with her mother? "Is everything alright?"

The elf was silent for longer than was at all comforting. "I had intended to ask you that question," he said. "I have kept myself too busy these last few days to speak to her privately."

"You've been avoiding her?" The thought sent panic flickering through Elena. She counted on Bishop to be there for her mother on an emotional level, needing it far more than anything the elf could ever do for her directly. If that changed . . . "I know it may seem like she's trying to distract herself with work, but that doesn't mean she doesn't need you there." She crossed the distance between them, starting to take the papers out of his hands. "We'll finish cleaning this up. Go find her and just sit in her office, or something. Bring paperwork if you feel like you need an excuse."

Bishop's grip on the papers tightened, and an echo of Elena's panic echoed on his face. "There's no need."

"Yes, there is," she said firmly, meeting his eyes. She wanted to tell him that it was alright, that she was happy that he cared so deeply for her mother, but it was hard to give him permission for something she wasn't sure she was supposed to know he wanted. "You don't have to say anything, Bishop. Actually, she'd probably rather you didn't. Just being in the room is enough."

The elf held her gaze, a muscle working in his jaw. "But I'm afraid I will say something," he admitted, voice low. "I won't intend to. I want nothing more than to dedicate all my energies to being everything she needs. But if I am alone with her now, when my emotions are riding so dangerously close to the surface—" He closed his eyes. "I won't be able to hide how afraid I am. I won't be able to hide anything. Your mother doesn't need that extra burden right now."

Elena had used the same argument herself too many times to have a defense against it. Cam would, she was sure, but he'd gone to get the scattered papers she'd abandoned. Apparently, he'd decided it was better that he not contribute to the conversation.

"It's okay, Elena," Bishop said gently, pulling away from her slackened grip. "Your mother is the strongest person I know. She doesn't need me."

"She's scared to admit just how much she needs you." The words slipped out of Elena's mouth without her brain warning her first. When Bishop appeared, suddenly intent, she plunged ahead before she could think better of it. "The reason she doesn't talk about you very much is because she's afraid of how much emotion she'll let out."

He went still. "You can't be sure she feels that way."

"I'm more certain than anyone who isn't her could be." Elena covered Bishop's hand with hers. "And if you don't want to make things harder for her, try to channel your worry into smaller arguments. Like making sure she eats when she forgets."

Understanding warmed the elf's eyes. "Or sleep when she hasn't been able to," he murmured.

Elena's cheeks colored. "Something like that." She gave Bishop a gentle push. "Go. Watch her face when she first sees you. You'll know everything you need to."

He went, finally. Watching him go, Elena blew out a relieved breath as she heard Cam walk up behind her. "Thanks for all your help with that, by the way. The famous Merrick emotional openness probably would have made that at least a little less horrifically awkward."

"From where I was standing, it looked like you did pretty

good." Cam moved to stand beside her, squeezing her shoulder. "One of these days we might even get you to start talking about your own feelings."

Elena looked over at him, thinking about silence and the things that mattered most. Surely life would let her keep this. Even if it was just for a little while.

She smiled. "Now who's starting to sound crazed?"

CHAPTER 14

Please, Worry About Me Now

"I usually try not to do this, but people's lives may be at stake. Did you say something to Laurel?" From the other side of the mirror, Mason gave Cam his best disapproving look. He didn't pull the "older sibling" card nearly as often as Laurel did, which only made it slightly more bearable when he did use it. "She keeps muttering and glaring at people, and the only thing I've been able to make out is your name."

Cam groaned. Now they'd both gone crazed. "Hold on." Leaving the mirror on the chair in the main area, he stood up and peeked into his bedroom to check on Elena. He'd gotten in the habit of staying up long enough to make sure she went to sleep okay, always carefully making sure it didn't look like that was what he was doing.

Now, though, there was no one around to see him stand in the doorway just long enough to watch her shoulders rise and fall with deep, even breaths. He quietly shut the door behind him, grateful she wouldn't be able to overhear yet another sibling decide to make his life harder. At least they had the decency to wait until Elena had gone to bed. The next time she stayed up late enough to go flying, all he had to do was accidentally-on-purpose turn the mirror off early.

Bracing himself, he sat back down and picked up his mirror again. "I only told her about the job, Mason. I promise." When Mason's expression didn't change, Cam tried harder to convince him. "Look, I was twelve the last time I accidentally did something to make Laurel mad. I'd like to think I've developed a few more self-preservation skills since then. And do you really think I was stupid enough to do something on purpose? I was trying to talk her into doing me a favor."

"Yeah, that's what I thought." Still not looking happy, Mason rubbed the bridge of his nose. "But talking to you was the only thing that happened between normal Laurel and scary Laurel."

"Come on. It's not like she hasn't been in a mood before." Despite the reassurance, Cam was starting to get uneasy. Apparently, he was going to have to pull Laurel aside before she worked everyone into a complete panic over absolutely nothing. "Maybe she's just mad about the extra work."

Mason shook his head. "Detaining that sorceress of yours wasn't any more work than picking up Gabby from a friend's house. Actually, I take that back—Gabby usually put up more of an argument." His mouth quirked upward a little. "Ariadne Coppin actually met us in the front yard, held her hands out for the cuffs, and asked when we'd be leaving. Her husband and stepson put up more of a fuss than she did. Naturally, that put us all on red alert for some sneak attack, but she's been quiet as a mouse the whole way."

"That's good." And probably comforting, unless he let his paranoia start working. Unless this was the first stage of a massive conspiracy, Elena's aunt sounded like she actually might want to help fix things. "You're basically getting paid for a babysitting job."

Mason thought about that. "Maybe she's disappointed it was so easy." He shook his head again. "I'll just have to pin her down and make her talk to me. If she accidentally stabs someone she shouldn't because she's like this, she'll just end up feeling guilty about it later."

"N—" Brain catching up just in time, Cam clamped his mouth closed to keep the word from coming out. As much as he didn't want that conversation to happen, trying to stop it would just get Mason on the scent. "Nice idea. You know how she likes to talk about feelings."

Mason's smile quirked again. "True. Maybe I'll frame it as a personnel issue." Then his expression got serious again. "Listen, if you ever need to talk."

"I'm fine," Cam cut him off, maybe a little more quickly than he should have. But everyone was acting like he had "Please, worry about me now" written across his forehead, and it was starting to piss him off. Elena was going to be fine. Therefore, so was he. End of story. "I know you feel it's your responsibility to make sure Laurel doesn't blow up and kill somebody, but you don't have to worry about me. I'm the cheerful, easygoing sibling, remember?"

"You're also the most stubborn person I know." Mason's "serious professor" face was back, studying Cam a little too closely for the younger man's peace of mind. "You're just remarkably good at making people forget that."

Before Cam had the chance to form a suitable protest—surely Dad and Laurel were at least tied with him in the stubbornness department, if not well ahead—Mason cut the call.

Cam considered calling back just to get the chance to argue properly, but he doubted it would help his case in the long run.

The problem was, he couldn't think of anything that would. Every option he came up with would get more people involved, which meant there was more opportunity for the worry to spread. He hadn't upset anyone's peace of mind for the first twenty-one years of his life, but apparently the universe had decided to make up for lost time.

Finally, Cam gave up and went to bed. He pushed it all out of his mind as he drifted off to sleep, secretly grateful that Elena had insisted on switching the blankets. She used a flowery-smelling lotion instead of perfume, and the smell of had started to fade from the blanket he'd been using. He'd never admit it out loud, but he'd missed it.

~

He woke up to the sound of the door closing, followed by footsteps in the darkness.

Cam didn't move, deliberately keeping his breathing relaxed and even. For a second he wondered if it might be Elena, coming to retrieve something out of her room, but then he heard the soft sound of a bag dropping on the floor. Slowly, silently, he slid his arm resting closest to the wall free of the blanket. If one of the castle staff had decided on a little light larceny, the person would find out that crime got you punched in the face. If whoever it was had something worse in mind . . .

He tensed, ready, as the footsteps approached the bed. Cam was already reaching by the time the person leaned over him, and there was just enough time for a strange male voice to swear before Cam grabbed him by the front of his shirt. He jerked his arm sideways, slamming the stranger's head into the wall and shoved both man and blanket aside as he rolled out of bed. There was more swearing, suggesting that the man was still conscious, and Cam dove toward the sound of it to finish the job.

The explosion of a flash charm, filling the room with blinding white light, put that plan to an immediate halt. Cam tried to shield himself, throwing an arm up in front of his eyes a second too late, but any night vision he'd had disappeared in a haze of dancing purple spots. The one saving grace was the continued swearing from the intruder, suggesting that he hadn't closed his eyes before he'd activated the charm. Also, it would be useful to track him until the other man was smart enough to shut up.

From the sound of it, he was trying to escape. Cam went for the tackle, slamming them both into the opposite wall and sending things rattling to the ground. The intruder smacked something into the side of Cam's head, probably one of Elena's books, and Cam shoved the flat of his hand upward against what he was almost certain was the man's jaw.

He heard the door open, but whoever it was had been smart enough not to turn any extra lights on. Cam had a second to wonder if his uninvited guest had a partner, but then he heard the quiet sound of a spell being prepped.

Before Elena had the time to use it, the man threw all his weight downward and pulled Cam with them. He half rolled them, giving himself enough leverage to throw a wild elbow that smacked into Cam's jaw. Cam finished the roll, landing a solid punch to the man's stomach. He knew he'd scored a direct hit when the intruder gave a pained grunt. Cam pulled back slightly, preferring the man conscious if at all possible. He was getting his night vision back, enough to start making out their unwelcome guest's face.

With a desperate sound, the man unfolded and lunged for him. Cam threw him back on the ground, pinning him down by sitting on him. "Who are you?" He pressed his hand flat against the other man's throat to make his point. "Did Nigel send you?"

The intruder's face was illuminated by a muted glow of light, and it was Elena's turn to swear. "That is Nigel." Her voice was hard as a knife blade as she went over and started examining the contents of the bag. "I guess here aren't any more thugs in the city as unintelligent as Bill was."

Cam looked down at Nigel, who was staring at Elena with wilder eyes than Cam was comfortable with. Seeing the look, Cam's brain started connecting the basic facts of the situation together. "You thought I was Elena." The little rat had just waltzed in there, thinking he could snatch Elena with her guard sleeping only a few feet away. Sure, she could have probably smacked him down as thoroughly as Cam had, but . . .

Noticing a leather tie around Nigel's neck, he yanked it free and tossed the charm that had been hanging on the end to Elena. "What does that one do?"

She held it up to the light. He could see worry flicker across her face, then fury. She flung the charm through the open doorway. "It shuts down any magic in the wearer's immediate vicinity as soon as it's detected," she explained, wiping her hand on her skirt as if she'd touched something disgusting. "They're meant to be a protection, but there are a number of places that severely limit their use. Some ban it entirely."

"Princess, I simply—"

Cam smacked the side of his head. "You don't get to talk yet." Then he looked up at Elena. "It can't be. Those nullify charms, too, and he used a flash one during the fight."

She considered it. "Did you hear the sound of breaking glass?"

"This idiot wouldn't stop talking. I could have missed it."

Elena went over to the bed, moving aside blankets until she found what she was looking for. "Bits of glass. He was probably carrying potions in a small bottle, and when he broke it they combined to activate the magic. The necklace would have nullified the resulting power surge in under a second, but the flash would have already happened." She turned back to Nigel, giving him a vicious kick in the leg. "If I'd tried a defensive spell, however, it would have shut me down the moment I started gathering power."

The thought sent something twisting in Cam's gut. "You still could have punched him in the face. I know Dad put you through more than the basic self-defense training."

"Oh, I would have done my best to make the toad bleed. But my first instinct would have been magic, so I would have wasted any chance at catching him by surprise. When you add a flash grenade to that, and everything else he's got in that bag—"

He went cold. "Hold him." Staying close only long enough for Elena to finish casting her freezing spell, Cam went over to the discarded bag and started looking for himself. He didn't recognize half the bottles rolling around inside, but there was one he knew immediately—they'd seized it off more than a few people trying to cross the border, generally before arresting them on outstanding warrants of some kind. It was a special, wildly illegal type of knockout tonic, preferred by professional kidnappers because it didn't use a shred of magic.

Cam tried to remind himself that he slept with his door open, and even if he'd been the one sleeping in his room he still would have heard Elena fighting. Together, they could take out anyone. She would have been fine. He wouldn't have been too late.

At least this time. Sneaking into the palace suggested a level of crazy that would only get more dangerous to Elena. He'd go straight to jail after this, but apparently he'd managed to slip through two dozen different guards to get here in the first place. For all he knew, Nigel would be able to get out of the jail cell just as easily.

Cam's hand tightened on the bottle.

Carefully setting it back in the bag, he walked back over and knelt down next to Nigel's head. "I have about fifteen more seconds, right?" he asked quietly.

"Maybe a little more than that.""It'll be enough to get me started." Putting his hand back over Nigel's throat, he put all of his weight into pushing down.

It took her a second to realize what he was doing. "Cam, no." She moved towards him. "He's not worth it."

"He waltzed right into the middle of the palace, thinking he could kidnap you and get away with it." A rage was burning inside him, but it did nothing to push away the chill. "From what you told me about his home life, no one will even miss him."

"You're right, they won't." Elena's voice was soft but urgent as she knelt down next to him, her light still illuminating the scene. "But I don't want to think about what this will do to you."

The rage didn't care. It kept pushing. "I'll say it was self-defense." His parents would never know. Even if they did, they'd have to understand. He was protecting Elena.

She put her arm acround his back, as if she was about to pull him close. "The only time I have ever heard you say you'll lie was with Mrs. Feeney, and even then you couldn't go through with it." She wrapped her other hand around his wrist, and it was only then that he realized she was trembling a little. "Don't have me be the reason you do something you'll regret. Please."

Somehow, that was enough to make it through the cold. Cam relaxed his grip just as the freezing spell ended, leaving Nigel coughing violently. Now the idiot's crazy eyes were being directed only at him, which Cam found infinitely preferable to the other alternative. "You would have killed me," he rasped, sounding shocked.

"Yes," Cam said simply, sitting on him again to keep him pinned. "Now, tell me how you got in here before I decide to go back to that plan."

"I bought a great deal of food and pretended I was a delivery boy hired by one of the palace guards." He sounded terrified, which was useful. "I gave some to everyone I passed, and they were too busy eating to ask me who I was delivering to."

Cam looked up at Elena. "Can I kill the guards?"

"Yes," she said, mirror in hand. She brushed her fingers against his hair as she left the room. "But don't do it until I get back. I want to help."

"So will Dad. Before we take care of that, though—" He turned his attention back to Nigel. "How did you get up here? The castle is a maze—you should have been lost after the first turn." If he had someone in the castle helping him out . . .

Nigel swallowed. "I did get lost. But then someone directed me to the kitchens without my asking, and after I stole a page's uniform I simply kept asking for directions until I found my way up here."

Cam felt a little more of the rage draining away at the sheer ridiculousness of the security loophole. "Fantastic." The one small comfort in all this was that it was definitely enough to give his dad leverage to overhaul the castle's entire security protocols. Not that an eight-year-old with a shovel couldn't manage to improve things at least a little.

Elena stepped back into the room. "The captain keeps swearing that they've heightened security like my mother ordered them to, but even if they did bring in new people they're just as incompetent as the old ones. Since it's clear the castle guard can't be trusted with anything more complicated than standing in place, I called the city guard to come collect our prisoner. They should be here in a few minutes."

"We'll give them the bag, too. They'll need it as evidence." He gestured towards Nigel. "Any questions you want to ask him?"

She gave him a long look, then shook her head. "Not any that I'd get a satisfactory answer to."

Cam lifted his hand, making Nigel start struggling again. "You can't kill me just because she didn't have any more questions! I've answered everything you asked, and you don't—"

The pleading cut off when Cam gave him a solid crack against the jaw, knocking him unconscious. "There." He moved off his temporary prisoner, sitting down hard on the floor next to him. "That'll give everyone a break from having to hear his whining."

"I knew you were clever." Voice gentle now, Elena walked over and sat down across from him. "I'm sorry, Cam." She squeezed his hand. "I didn't consider something like this happening when we switched rooms."

"Don't be stupid." He didn't think as he pulled her into his lap, instinctively wrapping his arms around her in a hard, tight hug that held everything that was left of his adrenaline and fear. He'd half-expected her to go stiff—he knew her family wasn't as physically affectionate as his was, but she settled against him like this was exactly where she wanted to be."If I could, I'd have everyone who wanted to hurt you come after me instead. Then you could swoop in and talk all condescending to them."

She slid arms around him. "Don't talk like that."

"What? You mean 'condescending?'" Cam's voice was light. The hug had chased away the rest of the rage, and the sheer relief was almost enough to make him cheerful. "I try not to use big words, but I'm pretty sure I got that one right."

"You know what I mean." Elena pulled back enough to glare at him. "It doesn't help me if you get hurt because someone was coming after me."

"That's kind of my job, Princess," he said softly, brushing her hair back from her face. "It's just convenient that it's also the best thing for my blood pressure."

She opened her mouth, ready to say something else, when they heard the sound of the door to the common area opening. The lights in the room turned on, making Elena's spell unnecessary, and Cam and Elena hurriedly helped each other to their feet as one of the castle guards stepped into view. "Your Highness, there's a group of city guardsmen at the gate, and they insist—" He choked on the rest of the sentence as he caught sight of the man on the floor. "What—"

And there went any chance at Cam's good mood. "That, you moron, is the man who waltzed right by all of you and tried to kidnap the princess," he snarled, blood in his eyes. The guard, who was a full six inches taller than Cam, took a few healthy steps back. "If the queen doesn't execute you as soon as she finds out, you should thank whatever gods you believe in."

"Oh, there are more creative options than execution," Elena said darkly, stepping forward. "If my mother doesn't want to take them, I'm sure Commander Merrick will. I'm requesting that he and his wife take immediate command of your entire unit."

"Captain Merrick?" The man's eyes widened even further at the mention of Cam's mother. Apparently, the city guard trainees had been telling stories. "But—"

Elena advanced on him. "So you'd prefer execution?" She was more than a foot shorter than the guardsman, but he scrambled away from her even faster than he had from Cam. "No? That's what I thought. Now send up the city guardsmen immediately. I need to talk to someone with a functioning brain."

As he ran off, Cam was surprised to feel the corners of his mouth turning upward. Apparently, he could be cheerful if he didn't have to talk to anybody but Elena for awhile. "See? You're excellent at being condescending. Why waste that kind of talent?"

She rolled her eyes at him. "You're an idiot."

His smile widened. "Like I said, pure talent."

CHAPTER 15

Less than Sanguine

Her aunt was scheduled to arrive that afternoon.

Elena and her mother had talked about how the initial meeting should go, at least as far as the elements they could control in advance. Would be better to sit formally in the throne room and make an early, dramatic show of power? Or would it be better to choose an out-of-the-way meeting room in order to maintain some semblance of secrecy? Should Elena do the talking so her mother wouldn't have to, or would that rob the queen of necessary power? They would take every magical precaution, but would it be wise to also have physical security present? There were advantages and disadvantages to every possibility, and the two women weighed and measured every option as carefully and thoroughly as possible.

The planning didn't stop either the fear or the hope that raged through them both, emotions that they each fought so valiantly to hide. But it also kept them from having enough time to think about either emotion, which was almost the same thing in the end.

~

"You look terrifying," Elena said approvingly, watching her mother make microscopic adjustments to her hair in the mirror. It was swept up in a much more complicated version of her usual severe knot, a set of sleek and sturdy metal hair sticks helping to hold everything in place. Alan had long ago sharpened the tips to razor points, capable of puncturing the skin to a depth of six inches.

The queen's eye makeup offered a far simpler intimidation, changing their color into the cold, intimidating gray of a sky in the bleakest winter. When combined with her mother's iciest glare, the one that Elena had seen reduce even the bravest men to quivering wrecks, it could be as powerful as a weapon.

Her mother smiled, eyes warming enough to ruin the effect of the makeup. "Flatterer." She brushed her fingertips against her daughter's cheek. They were alone in the queen's rooms, sitting before her dressing mirror as if they were primping for a party.

For a few precious seconds, Elena let herself cherish the odd intimacy. Their attempts to protect one another usually pushed them apart, but when they had a common enemy it only brought them closer together. "You taught me well."

The queen made an amused sound. "You look quite intimidating yourself, my love. You'd be a wonderful—" She seemed to catch herself, stopping what she'd been about to say. Her smile lost a little of its sincerity, and she pulled her hand away. "Never mind. I'm being fanciful."

Elena caught her mother's hand, giving it a brief squeeze. "Can you imagine the two of us together at meetings?" she asked lightly, pretty sure she knew what her mother had been about to say. "Any poor fool who caught a glare from both of us would melt on the spot."

The queen's expression warmed again. "We would be quite the duo, wouldn't we?" Then she took a steadying breath, blinking hard against the sudden wetness in her eyes. "And if I keep this up, I'll have to let Renae be the one to reapply my makeup. She was so disappointed I didn't let her help with it the first time."

"It's for the best. I don't think she quite understands the concept of war paint." Elena made herself turn away, checking her own hair and makeup in the mirror. The effect wasn't nearly as striking as it was with her mother, but she flatly refused to be the weak point in the equation. "Are you sure you want me to be the first one to speak to Aunt Ariadne?"

Her mother met her gaze in the mirror. "Would you prefer not to?" Elena could hear the protectiveness in her voice, quieter but no less solid than what she'd heard so often from Alan and Marie. She wondered how she could have missed it before.

Shaking off the regret, Elena took a deep breath. "I'm fine with it. I stopped being terrified by the thought of her years ago." She turned her head, meeting her mother's eyes again as she let some of her uncertainty emerge in her voice. "But I'm afraid it won't make as much of an impact coming from me. She's never even seen me, and I'm certain she'll be able to sense that you're a more powerful sorceress than I am. She has no reason to fear me."

Her mother pressed her lips together, not able to say anything. "I can't trust myself enough to be the first one to speak," she said finally, voice quiet. "I'm not certain enough of what would come out."

Elena knew how much such an admission cost. They were

both trying so hard. "Do you have any suggestions for what I should say? I'm tempted to actually try and write out a speech, but those are never good for more than a few seconds into the actual situation." She smoothed a hand down the edge of her sleeve, straightening it. "No matter how much effort I put into the preparation, I'm sure it will sound worse than useless the moment it leaves my mouth."

"Trust your instincts." The queen laid her hand over Elena's. "You had wonderful ideas during our discussions."

Despite the tension thrumming through her, Elena felt the corners of her mouth curve upward. It seemed to happen more and more often, these days. "They were easier to come up with when I thought you would be the one who had to say them."

Her mother stood, smiling as well. "You've discovered the secret of government." Holding her daughter's face in her hands, she pressed a kiss against her forehead. "We should go. We'll want to get into position before Cam's siblings arrive."

Elena took a deep breath, then pushed herself to her feet. "Is Bishop there already, or will he meet us?"

The queen's eyes flickered away briefly. "He's preparing the room for us."

Watching this, Elena hesitated. Her mother didn't seem upset, but this felt like too serious an issue to simply accept the silence. "Does he know he needs to stay?"

A faint flush colored the queen's cheeks. Seeing it, Elena felt immensely better. "He knows."

"Cam will meet the team bringing in Ariadne and guide them here. He'll send a page ahead to let us know that they're coming."

Her mother squared her shoulders. "Ready?"

Far from it. Still, she lifted her chin. "I'm ready."

~

Bishop had modified a meeting room into a more discreet version of the throne room, with the long table serving as a rough shield between the chairs and Ariadne. Bishop insisted on remaining standing, positioning himself at her mother's right hand.

A small eternity later, a page alerted them that the group was on their way. Elena had long ago locked down her emotions, making absolutely certain nothing would slip and lead to an unexpected crack in their armor. Now she focused on her personal shields, sealing and strengthening them against any unexpected attack.

They were ready when Cam opened the door. He stepped into the room first, followed by the rest of the team. She recognized Laurel, bringing in Ariadne by her magic-deadening cuffs. "Your Majesty." He nodded to the queen. "Your Highness." He nodded to Elena, then stepped to one side and unsheathed his sword. "Ariadne Coppin."

"Thank you." The queen motioned to Laurel. "You have fulfilled your contract well, but we have enough here to deal with her. You may go."

Laurel hesitated, then looked over at her brother. When he tilted his head toward the door, she and the rest of her team left the room.

Elena's first startled thought was that this stranger looked so much like her mother. Ariadne's hair was lighter, almost white, and the crow's feet around her eyes were deeper. But the shape of her face was nearly identical to the one who had sung Elena to sleep at night, her eyes the same shifting gray. It was foolish, but Elena hadn't been prepared for it.

A similar surprise was reflected in the woman's eyes, and

for just a second her expression went raw. "You look just like—" Ariadne stopped herself with an almost physical effort, wrestling her features back into the composed blankness she'd worn when she first stepped into the room. That, too, struck Elena as painfully familiar.

Rather than acknowledge what had just happened, Ariadne bowed low. "Your Highness. Your Majesty." Her voice caught, briefly, on the second honorific. "I am your servant."

Elena glanced over at her mother. The queen's jaw was like stone, her hands gripping the arms of her chair painfully tight. She looked like she wanted to close her eyes, but didn't quite dare.

Every protective instinct Elena possessed wanted to make certain all of her aunt's attention was on her. "Ms. Coppin," she announced, putting all the frost she possessed into the words. "Tell us why you're here."

Ariadne's eyes flickered upward briefly to take in Cam's presence, then met Elena's gaze with a look that seemed to ask if the younger woman was being entirely serious. When the only response was stony silence, the sorceress bowed her head again. "I am here to repair a grievous injustice I have committed, Your Highness."

It was exactly what they'd hoped she'd say. But they had no reason to trust the words. "Why now? Your injustice was committed nearly two decades ago. Did you perhaps get lost in the forest finding your way back to our door?"

Ariadne flinched at that, the reaction too sharp and immediate to be successfully hidden. It took a few extra beats for her to respond. "Does it matter?"

Next to Elena, the burst of her mother's tension felt like the moment just before a lightning strike. "How dare you say those words to me after everything that's happened between us?" the queen snapped, rising to her feet. She didn't shout, but each word still seemed painfully loud. "As if the last eighteen years were nothing more than a messy technical detail you didn't want to bother explaining to a client."

Ariadne didn't answer, her head still bowed. Elena tensed, torn between shaking some kind of response out of the woman and staying silent, letting her mother keep the reins of the conversation.

A second later, her mother decided for her. "Ariadne!" The pain in her voice scraped at Elena, who pushed it deeper under the cold. "Answer me!"

Her aunt jerked upright as if yanked, and for the briefest second the look on her face was as naked and bloody as an open wound. "I thought she was dead!"

The silence that fell after that was so thick that Elena could almost feel the weight of it. She glanced over at her mother, who was staring at Ariadne as if she'd never seen her before, then met Cam's eyes before she'd even realized she'd done it. He gave her an almost imperceptible nod, as if saying he was ready to follow whatever lead she chose to give him.

It was, Elena would reflect later, far more reassuring than it probably should have been.

She stood, attempting to project command with every line of her body. "Explain."

Ariadne's gaze snapped to Elena's, a dozen different emotions chasing each other across her aunt's eyes. Then the older woman clamped them shut, once again forcing her control back into place. "The curse was designed to slow down a person's bodily functions to a point near death. In an adult, the result would be a timed coma. In a child that had only begun his or her development, however, it seemed likely that the effects—" The word caught, ever so briefly. "that the effects would be fatal."

"They nearly were," Illiana bit out, the words icy enough to burn. For her mother's sake, Elena hoped no one else had recognized the faint tremor behind them. She knew she should be horrified by the implication of what had almost happened to her, but she was cold enough now to be numb to anything.

Ariadne flinched again, her newly-regained control already cracking and breaking. She took a step forward. "Ana, I—"

Everything happened at once. The queen flinched at the pet name, recoiling as if she'd been physically hit. Elena stepped forward, wanting to deflect Ariadne's attention away from her mother. Cam's arm shot out to block Ariadne's path, suggesting he'd do far more if she tested him. Her aunt whipped her head around to glare at Cam, her anger flaring wildly, and Elena started gathering her magic for a protective strike.

Ariadne's gaze snapped back around to face Elena, and she realized that the older woman had sensed the beginning stages in the spell. Elena stared her down, keeping the magic ready in a clear sign that she was more than willing to strike, if necessary.

"How much training have you had?" Ariadne asked.

It was such an absurd question, given the situation, and Elena could practically feel the anger rise up from both her mother and Cam. The chill inside her own chest, however, simply wanted all of this to be over. She needed this woman away from the people she cared about. "Why were you remotely accessing the spell?"

It was easier for Ariadne to regain her control, this time. "I only recently returned to this region, and it was soon after that I discovered you were still alive." She kept her gaze fixed on Elena, her voice as devoid of emotion as she could make it. "As time passed, I became more and more convinced that I needed to at least attempt to undo what I had done. Since I doubted I would be allowed access to you, I attempted to work remotely."

Elena knew the story couldn't really be that simple, but the truth was that everything Ariadne said was suspect. "How do we know you're not going to simply cause more damage if we give you access to the curse?"

Ariadne hesitated, as if her voice had failed her. "What further harm could I do?" Then she took a deep breath, slowly letting it out again. "I allowed your soldiers to bring me here because I need assistance. I didn't build a solid foundation for the curse because I never meant for it to be undone. The calculated instability of the curse was another defense—if someone tried to untangle it, it would collapse and cause even more damage. I need as many skilled hands as possible to help me hold everything together while I unwind it."

Elena watched her, thinking about her mother's reaction to Ariadne's attempts to manipulate the spell. "Did you know that breaching the shields would make you sick as well?"

For a second, it looked as though Ariadne was going to argue. Then she bit the words back. "No. I hadn't known." She sounded tired now, which Elena trusted more than the guilt. "I need both of you for that reason alone. There are no records of curses set through the blood bond. No precedents. If all three of us aren't in the circle when we break through into the heart of the curse, I truly don't know what will happen."

That seemed like a truth that was impossible to doubt or argue with. Elena glanced at her mother for confirmation, then spoke for them both. "Fine. We'll work together to clean up your mess, but know that you are here as a prisoner, not a guest." When Ariadne opened her mouth to speak, Elena lifted a hand to stop her. "Once everything's been prepared, we'll set up the spell circle. It will include the three of us, as well as another sorcerer and one of the original magic mirrors. Before that happens, you will give us all the information you have on the curse's construction and your plan of attack. We'll have them independently verified before we hold the circle."

That wasn't precisely true. Braeth was better at looking for magical traps than the rest of them, but what she really wanted him to do was help them understand the situation from as many angles as possible. She profoundly disliked surprises, and knowing all the possible alternatives would make it less likely that something would rise out of the darkness and bite her. Or, more precisely, yank her back down into the darkness with it.

It took a moment before her aunt responded. "I'll do what I can. I work more by instinct than specific procedure, so I unfortunately can't make any assurances on how comprehensive my initial round of notes will be. My documentation process has always been haphazard, at best." She paused. "If I could take another look at the curse to refresh my memory—"

Elena cut Ariadne off with a shake of her head. They had accepted that this was the wisest course of action, but they weren't about to trust her yet. "We look together or not at all."

Ariadne hesitated, as if weighing further argument. Next to Elena, the queen's fingers clenched. "Do not test us on this, Ariadne."

Her aunt's expression went blank again, and after a single frozen heartbeat she lifted her bound hands. Her gaze stayed firmly away from her sister's, as if catching even a glimpse of the queen would somehow be fatal. "It's difficult to write like this."

Elena motioned to Cam, and he used a key to unlock the connector between the two cuffs. Ariadne's hands could separate now, but the cuff around each wrist would still keep her from using magic. "We'll remove the cuffs before we cast the circle," Elena said. "Until then, keeping your magic locked away is the wisest course of action for everyone."

Ariadne hands never moved to her newly freed wrists. Her every movement was careful, as if designed not to startle. "Everyone?"

Elena kept her voice even. "It removes any temptation you might have to cause us concern. If you have any value for your continued health, you'll agree that this is the wisest course of action for you as well."

Rather than seem at all threatened, Ariadne gave her a thoughtful look. "I have a feeling you would have made a magnificent evil sorceress," she said, her voice carrying shades of fascination, pride and even wistfulness. "I suspect I would have enjoyed training you." Then, knowing the value of a good closing line as much as any evil sorceress, she turned to Cam. "I presume it's your responsibility to show me to my room?"

Cam's gaze went to Elena, making it obvious that he wasn't about to go anywhere without word from her, and she nodded. He hesitated for a beat longer, worry for her shining in his eyes, then he turned and ushered Ariadne out of the room. Slowly, Elena and her mother sat down.

Bishop was the first to break the silence, resting a hand on her mother's shoulder. "I take it Braeth completed the containment spells on her room last night?"

At the contact, the tension in the queen's body eased ever so slightly. "He used his entire repertoire, three of which are no longer approved by the Council." She lifted a hand to cover Bishop's. "I told him the Council would never have to know."

Elena closed her eyes, wondering if she should put in some

deliberate effort to try and push the cold aside. Even as she had the thought, a part of her knew it wasn't practical—she would need it again the next time they spoke to Ariadne. It was one of her strongest defense mechanisms, and her body had decided it couldn't be lowered yet. It made sense to listen to it, even her fingers felt cold.

"Elena." Her mother reached across the space between them, hand wrapping around her daughter's as if she had somehow heard that last thought. "Forgive me. I should have never put you in that position."

"As if I would have left you to deal with her alone." The warmth from the contact seeped into Elena, almost too much. But she clung to it. "There's something she's not telling us."

The queen's expression darkened, making it clear that she had recognized the same thing. Then she shook her head. "It doesn't matter," she said firmly, lifting her daughter's hand to press a kiss against it. "I would make a deal with a castle full of devils if it would mean saving you."

Elena squeezed her mother's hand, something hot and painful moving deep in her chest. Even the chill inside her couldn't seem to touch it. "As if I would leave you alone to deal with them, either."

MEMORY

Early winter, 19 years ago

"I know you feel like you need to be thorough, Ana, but this is getting ridiculous." Ariadne threw her hands in the air, giving them an extra little flourish for dramatic effect. Her tower was far more of a mess than it had been, now that Illiana was no longer here to clean up after her sister. "Just grab the man's blood and let me finish this! I'll curse him before he has any chance of catching you."

Illiana's hands were held tight behind her back, though it was entirely possible Ariadne wouldn't have noticed the way her fingers were clenching. She had been reporting by mirror for a month now, hoping to delay this particular meeting for as long as possible. Unfortunately, no delay tactic lasted forever. "It's more complicated than that, Ari. There are a lot of factors I need to account for."

Ariadne made an exasperated noise, pushing through the papers on a table as if looking for something. "You don't always have to double check everything, Ana. You'll never make a proper evil sorceress if you insist on obsessing every single little detail."

That hadn't been what Illiana meant, but she'd known her sister would interpret it like that. It wouldn't have occurred to Ariadne that her studious, obedient little sister would do anything that might be worrying enough to spy on. It was trust, in a way, and more than Ari gave anyone else.

Thinking of it twisted Illiana's stomach. But the thought of Thomas, the animation in his face shut down by her sister's curse, broke her heart.

"Besides, the client keeps coming around asking me how far along we are, and there are only so many times you can threaten a man." Her nose wrinkled briefly in distaste. "If he comes around again, I'll have to turn him into a frog and lose the commission on principle."

Illiana leapt on the comment, crossing her sister's workroom as she spoke. "Actually, that might be a smart idea. You'll get the reputation as being ruthless, and if we tell King Randall what the cousin was planning he'll probably pay you double."

She'd tried to keep her voice as calm and disinterested-sounding as possible, but Ariadne's gaze snapped to Illiana. Her older sister narrowed her eyes. "Where is this coming from?"

Illiana froze in place. Nerves caught in her throat, but she forced her breathing to stay slow and even. "It just makes sense." She'd worked through a dozen different possibilities for this conversation, and this was the only one that hadn't ended in complete disaster. "An evil sorceress of your caliber shouldn't have to put up with a client annoying her like this. If we get King Randall to reward you, you'll teach your old client a lesson and still get paid."

Ariadne straightened, turning to face her sister fully. "I don't get rewarded. I take what I want."

"Then we won't bother with King Randall." Illiana said each word with careful precision, as if they were runes she was inscribing in a circle. "Just turn the client into your animal of choice and take his money. If you wanted to, you could even turn the curse back on him."

Ariadne seemed to actually consider this, but then she shook her head. "No. It's unprofessional." A gleam lit in her eye. "Besides, a king is a far more worthy target for my skills than some ridiculous second cousin. Anyone and his troll can curse a pathetic hanger-on."

Panic pushed her further than her normal caution would have allowed. "We can find you a better target! Thomas's kingdom is so small it's hardly worth worrying about." She took a step toward her sister. "Please, Ari. Let's find you something better."

Ariadne stared at her little sister in complete astonishment. "I don't think I've ever heard you be that passionate about anything," she said, surprise melting away into interest. "Once we've finished this, maybe we can—"

Suddenly, Ariadne cut off whatever else she'd been about to say. Silence fell for a full thirty seconds, just long enough for Illiana to realize the mistake she'd made. When Ariadne spoke again, her voice was ice cold. "You called him Thomas."

The knot inside Illiana's stomach tightened to the point of pain. But her sister clearly wasn't in the mood for mercy. "That's his name."

"Which you hadn't used at any previous point in the conversation." Despite the chill remaining in her voice, anger was a simmering heat in Ariadne's eyes. "You were trying to con me, sister dear."

"No, I was trying to find a way out of this for all of us." Illiana took another step forward, no longer trying to hide the plea in her voice. "I didn't want to just throw myself at you sobbing. But there are options—"

"I have tried for ages to get you more involved in the work. Ages." Ariadne's anger had a hard edge to it, meant to cut, and Illiana took a step back without even realizing she'd done it. "I sent you out alone on this assignment to prove how much faith I had in your abilities."

"You sent me on that assignment because you hate doing the grunt work." Hearing the resentment in her own voice, Illiana pushed the feeling aside as quickly as possible. "I'm not asking you to abandon the case, Ariadne. Just change it!"

"Why? Because you've taken pity on some stupid helpless puppy of a king?" Ariadne's fingers moved, and Illiana realized to her horror that her sister was gathering magic. "Do you really think he cares about a little mouse like you? He's a noble, just like Mother and Father! You know as well as I do you'll never be enough for any of them!"

The words gouged, just as they undoubtedly meant to. "You don't know anything about him!" she snapped back, gathering her own magic. "You just decided he should be hurt because some sniveling little client came along and waved visions of glory in front of your face!"

Ariadne's eyes widened, full of shock and betrayal. "I've told you about those visions for years! How dare you suggest that little toad had anything to do with it!" Rage flared, along with a faint glow around Ariadne's hand. "I refuse to let you ruin both our lives just because your useless heart has finally figured out how to overpower your mind. Now go back there and get me the blood I need!"

When Illiana didn't move, Ariadne lifted her hand as if ready to throw the spell at her. Her own magic flowed around her, ready and waiting, but there was no spell strong enough to get through to her sister.

Powering down her magic, Illiana turned and left the tower.

~

Back in her room at the castle, Illiana stared at the collection vial sitting on her desk. Her options were painfully limited. More argument would only make Ariadne angrier, maybe even to the point of pushing Illiana away for good. Worse, it would do nothing to save Thomas—Ariadne would simply collect the blood another way.

If Illiana gave in and obtained the blood herself, she would at least get to keep her sister. This was her first real attempt at defiance, and Ariadne would probably prefer to forget it had ever happened. As long as it ended quickly, all would eventually be forgiven.

If she told Thomas what was happening, she would lose them both. But it was the only way he wouldn't be left helpless and in his enemy's hands for a century. Could she live with herself, knowing she'd let a wonderful man be sacrificed?

Could she slam the door on her sister, the only person who'd ever made room for her?

She was spared from answering either question by a quiet knock on the door. Wiping her eyes, Illiana hurriedly dragged her composure back into place. "Come in."

To her surprise, it was Thomas who opened the door. When he saw her, the worry on his face sharpened. "Are you all right?" When she stood, he moved towards her. "I saw you return this afternoon, but you barely spoke to anyone." He took her hands in his. "I know that look on your face. Tell me what's wrong."

Her normal reserve was helpless against him. "I'm just tired," she tried, voice already unsteady as she pulled her hands away from his. A second later, she already missed their warmth. "Perhaps I'm coming down with something. You should probably stay away from me the next few days. I wouldn't want you to catch it as well." By then, she would have thought of a way to tell him. It would break her heart, but to not do so would be so much worse.

How had she ever thought she had options?

The silence that followed was too loud. Finally, Thomas broke it. "What were you supposed to do to me?"

Stunned, she whipped around to face him. He was standing where she'd left him, expression solemn and careful as he dismantled everything she'd thought she'd known. "I presume that whatever it was should have happened by now, and your employer dragged you back to express his or her displeasure." The corners of his mouth curved upward a fraction. "And the first thing you do when you return is to tell me to stay away from you for a little while. I may be wrong, but it sounds very much like you're trying to protect me."

Illiana's knees threatened to give out. She sat down hard on the bed, staring at him with wide eyes. "You knew I wasn't a witch."

"There's a subtle difference in the way witches and sorceresses speak about magic. It's hard to pick up on unless you've spent a great deal of time talking to both types of practitioners." He sounded almost apologetic. "Clearly, you're intelligent enough that you could qualify as a scholar without lying, so I knew it wasn't merely to get into the library. I was the most logical target."

She spread her hands wide, lost for a response. "Then why didn't you arrest me?"

"On a suspicion?" Thomas shook his head. "You never once hurt me."

The words cut, but no more deeply than she deserved. He'd simply been waiting for evidence. "Blood." Illiana's voice was strained as she stood, reaching for her satchel. "I was supposed to get a sample of your blood to be used in a curse. After I leave, you'll need to be on the lookout for—"

Thomas intercepted her, catching her hands again. "You misunderstand me," he said softly, tilting his head to make her meet his eyes. "I could have arrested you. Kings are allowed to indulge in irrational abuses of power."

She tried to pull her hands away again, but he wouldn't let them go this time. "But you didn't, because you wanted to see what I'd do."

"No." Thomas's voice was soft. "I didn't want to lose you."

Illiana's eyes filled, holding onto his hands as tightly as she could. "I'm not worth holding on to."

"You're worth everything." He pressed a kiss against her forehead. "Stay with me. Please."

Her response was to throw herself into his arms.

CHAPTER 16

Complicated Torture Methods

The gossip was inevitable. Some of the whispers were about the mysterious prisoner, but no one who had seen her face clearly would contribute to the speculation. Those who had been in the castle long enough to speak knowledgeably about the situation were too loyal to discuss it with anyone who wasn't.

Besides, the Merricks were proving much more entertaining to talk about.

"Why is it not bothering you at all that you regressed back to a twelve-year-old at some point?" Cam glared at his sister, arms braced against both sides of the doorway to keep Laurel from getting through. She was still wearing her full uniform, even though there was no need, and he had a sneaking suspicion she was trying to make a point of some kind. "Because I'm pretty pissed off you think I suddenly turned into a twelve-year old."

"I never said you were acting like a kid." Laurel glared right back at him, jabbing a finger into his chest. "Though what you're doing right now isn't what I'd call mature behavior."

"Because you're about to make a fool out of both of us!" he

snapped back, causing a passing maid to perk up her ears in interest. Cam glared at her until she hurried away again, then went back to arguing with his sister. "I make my own decisions, Laurel. You know that. And you're still about to go yell at Dad for something I supposedly did!"

"You dope, I'm not mad at you. I'm mad for you." Affection leaked through the frustration, making it less potent. "Which means I get to go yell at Dad."

"No, you don't." A part of Cam understood that Laurel meant well, despite the fact that she'd lost her mind. He still wanted to choke her for it. "Would you want me to go yell at your commander because he led you into a situation I decided was too dangerous for you?"

"Try it and I'll—" Realizing that she'd just made his point for him, she stopped the sentence and made an exasperated noise. "Fine. But you can't stop me from being mad at him."

The concession seemed genuine, but Cam didn't dare relax his arms just yet. He and Laurel had sneak-attacked each other more than once, over the years. "If I don't get mad at him at least once a week, I feel like I haven't done my duty as a son. I just wish you were mad at him for a reason that's a little less insulting to me."

Laurel folded her arms across her chest. "It's not insulting. I'm trying to protect you."

"From who? Dad's mind-controlling powers?" When she shot him an exasperated look, he gave her his most serious expression in return. "I'm not kidding, Laurel. My tough-as-dragon's-teeth big sister is having a panic attack that I'm cooling my heels at the castle. Nothing about that makes any sense to me."

She glared at him a little longer, then it seemed to hit her that he wasn't kidding. When that sank in, she swore softly and let out a breath. "You always did have a talent for only hearing what you wanted to."

Now Cameron was really confused. "You know only girls speak in code, right? Not terrifying warrior women such as yourself?"

She gave him another "you're an idiot" look, but this time it was the sibling edition. "You said 'we.'"

"Still speaking in code here, Laurel."

"When you were talking about the princess wanting to hire us. You kept saying 'we.'" She stopped, shaking her head. "No, it's worse than that. You kept trying to stop yourself from saying 'we,' which meant that at least a part of you was smart enough to not want me to hear it."

"I was the one making the contact." He felt the worry spark inside him again, but this time it was harder to tell himself that his sister's insanity was to blame. "I decided the 'we' wasn't professional, so I kept trying to stop myself."

Laurel gave a disbelieving snort. "Don't give me that. You can't keep a girlfriend longer than six months to save your life, and you picked a job where you're never at the same guard station for longer than a year. Dad thinks you sabotage yourself to spite him, somehow."

He and Dad had talked about that before. Loudly. Cam wasn't thrilled that Laurel felt the need to bring it up now. "So first you're mad at Dad, and now you're siding with him?"

"No, because Dad's wrong about that, too. You're just careful about who and what you let matter." Laurel's tone gentled, which was oddly terrifying in context. "You backed Robbie one-hundred percent when he decided to just say no to the family business. You didn't even make Mom call you twice before you used up all your vacation coming out here. And when you talk about the princess, you say 'we.'"

Cam's fingers tightened on the doorframe. He could only imagine what his expression looked like, but it was bad enough that Laurel blew out a breath. "This is going to mess you up so bad, Cam," she said quietly. "And I'm scared to death for you."

"She's going to be fine." The words were out of Cam's mouth before he'd even had the chance to think them. The fact that his voice sounded strained didn't help his peace of mind, either. "If she's fine, I won't get messed up."

Laurel just stared at him. "Tell me you know how much trouble you're in."

Cam sighed, closing his eyes. "I'm getting the general idea."

"Good." When he opened his eyes again, Laurel was resolute. "I'll stay at least until our prisoner is back out of the castle. Once Mason realizes this is a family emergency, he'll stay, too."

Cam narrowed his eyes. "Tell him about the conversation we just had and I'll paint all your armor pink."

Laurel grinned. "That's the Cameron who used to jump out of trees at me." She took a step back. "Of course, you know if you even—"

Before she could finish someone barreled into Cam's back, and he managed to get out of the doorway just in time not to get trampled. Without a word, the man shoved past Cam and ran down the corridor. It was only after he'd disappeared that Cam realized the guy had been sobbing.

Laurel, who'd had to scramble out of the way as well, stared after the human cannonball with wide eyes. "Was that one of the castle guards?"

"Yeah." Cam glared after the man. "I told you Mom and Dad were given control of them after they'd screwed up and almost let Elena get kidnapped. Mom talked to the commander of the city guard, and he gave her a leave of absence pretty much immediately. Mom and Dad are both here as long the queen needs them to be."

"I know. Dad's been saying for years that they couldn't defend themselves against a cold." She turned back to the doorway, looking intrigued. "But I didn't know it was serious enough that Mom was making them cry."

Cam relaxed his arms. "How can you be so sure it's Mom? I know she can be scary when she wants to be, but Dad's willing to be more often."

Laurel shook her head. "Dad makes them shake. Mom makes them cry." Clearly coming to a decision, she gave him a friendly nudge backwards through the door. "Come on. Let's go see Mom and Dad torment people."

~

The scene in the courtyard was less interesting than they'd expected. The members of the castle guard were running around the outer perimeter—in full armor, mind you—though some of them were closer to staggering by that point. Occasionally, one of them would look longingly at the stone walls, as if dreaming of collapsing against the cool rock.

They didn't dare stop, however, because Dad was standing in the middle near the fountain, watching them with his arms folded across his chest and the most serious version of his death glare. His leg was still in splints, but no one had any doubt he could fully exercise his wrath should the need arise.

Cam and Laurel walked up to stand next to him. Before

either of them could speak, Alan glanced over at his middle son. "How's Elena doing?" he asked quietly.

"She's dealing." It wasn't the answer he wanted to give, but a more accurate one would take twenty minutes and suggest that he'd spent way too long thinking about it. "She's been holed up with Braeth, Dr. Flyte and her mother for most of the day looking over the notes her aunt put together. I haven't really talked to her much."

The only time they'd managed a real conversation was that morning, when he'd insisted she have something more substantial for breakfast than a cup of tea. He'd asked her the same question his father had asked him, and she'd gotten an awful faraway look in her eyes.

"It was strange, seeing her in person, but I'm more worried about my mother than anything." She didn't quite meet his eyes. "I'm fine."

He caught her hand, tilting his head until he caught her gaze. "I believe the first part, but that second bit sounds like a lie to me."

They'd stared at each other for a full minute, then Elena's expression eased. "I'll survive, then." She touched his cheek. "Thank you for being here. It makes—"

A sharp nudge from his sister jolted him back to reality. "Yeesh," Laurel muttered. "The minute Mason sees that face, he'll start taking bets on when you two get married. He'll get half the castle involved."

Naturally, Dad's selective hearing chose that exact moment to kick in. "Married?" He glanced back over at both of them again, the glare disappearing under the sheer weight of surprise. "Who's getting married?"

"One of the mercenaries in Laurel's company," Cam lied

quickly, glaring at Laurel to cut off any poorly-timed elaboration. He could tolerate genuine worry—if he had to—but if she got serious about the teasing he'd have to figure out a way to knock her unconscious and hide her in a closet. "Where's Mom? I thought we'd find both of you out here."

Alan's scowled as he turned his attention back to the guards. "She's testing their hand-to-hand combat skills one-on-one after I drain their will to live." He checked his watch. "She just got started on her current victim, so she should be back out in a few minutes."

Laurel looked over the group with a leader's practiced eye. "How many of them do you think you'll keep?"

"Not more than a third." The disgust in his voice was harsher than his usual dislike of the castle guard. Needless to say, he and Mom had been less than pleased to hear that the idiots had nearly let Elena be kidnapped. "After we've culled all the dead weight, it'll take at least a month to get the unit back into shape."

An idea sparked in Cam's brain. "You could probably talk the queen into giving you and Mom the unit on a permanent basis," he added helpfully, putting every ounce of effort into making his voice sound casual. "Then you wouldn't have to come back and do this again in six months when it all falls apart without you."

Laurel gave her brother a sharp look. "Don't you have a job to go back to?"

Dad was also looking at him, but with real interest. "You'd guard Elena on a permanent basis?"

Cam shrugged. "I like the idea of the castle guard no longer being raging incompetents. If I have to take over permanent duty as Elena's personal guard to make that happen, I'd be willing." As the words came out of his mouth, he was amazed at how much sense they made. It was a sound, logical reason, and even had the benefit of technically being true. The fact that the rest of the truth included the words "too far away" wasn't something he actually had to admit out loud.

Besides, Elena would just get into trouble without him around. Worrying about it from the border would drive him nuts.

"So you're just going to move in here permanently, as if I haven't said a single intelligent thing for the last twenty minutes." Unlike their father, Laurel's disgust was aimed directly at Cam. "You're right, it's not Dad's fault—you're just too stupid to live."

"Laurel, stop. You sound like you're five." Alan looked at Cam. "Did something happen you need to tell me about?"

Cam silently blessed his father's lack of emotional nuance. If Mom had been out here, she would have had a detailed analysis of the whole idiotic fight by now. "Can you and Mom get away tomorrow morning? The aunt hasn't tried anything so far, but when they start the spell circle she'll get her powers back. I'd like more people on hand who are capable of stabbing her."

"We'll be there," Alan said. He turned to glower at a woman on the opposite side of the ring who was seriously thinking about collapsing, then checked his watch again. "I'm surprised. I wouldn't have thought Jenkins would last this long."

Right on cue, Jenkins limped out of one of the side doors, holding onto his side like something terrible had happened to it. When he got closer, Cam could see the beginnings of what would become a really colorful black eye. Cam fought back a smile. Apparently, his mom had gone easy on the guy.

Marie Merrick followed, wearing her normal workout clothes instead of the full uniform his dad had chosen. She barely looked winded, but there was a grudging respect on her face as she watched Jenkins walk away. When she caught sight of Cam and Laurel, her expression warmed. "I hate that I haven't had the chance to talk to either of you today."

She pulled them both into a quick group hug, which he and Laurel happily returned. "I'm amazed Dad's letting you beat up all of them yourself," Laurel said as they all pulled away again. "Even with his leg, I'd think he'd want a turn."

"He doesn't want anyone to get off easily because he doesn't feel at full strength." Marie turned to her husband. "We want to keep an eye on Jenkins. He's not ready yet, but with a little more of a push he could be."

"You're the one with the training experience," Dad said. "I'll want to see him myself, but if you say keep him we keep him."

Mom shook her head. "I didn't say keep him yet. I said he might be worth keeping." That taken care of, she turned her attention to Cam. "I haven't had the chance to talk to Elena, either. How is she?"

"Cam says she's dealing," Laurel cut in, earning another glare from her little brother. She glared right back at him. "What? I just didn't want you to go drifting off in the middle of the conversation again."

Cam wished briefly that they were both kids again, so he could kick his sister in the shin like she deserved. Picking up on this, Marie gave her son an odd look. "Is everything okay?"

"Yeah," he grumbled. "Like Laurel said, Elena's managing."

"I wasn't talking about Elena." Now that he was looking more closely, Cam could definitely pick up the worry in his mother's tone. At this point, he was amazed that people weren't stopping him on the street to ask him what was wrong. "How are you handling all this?"

It was an unwritten law in Cam's head that it was wrong to get annoyed at your mother. To make sure he followed this, he took a few extra seconds before responding. "I'm mostly just standing around useless, wishing I had something to stab."

Dad clapped a sympathetic hand on his shoulder. "You'll feel that a lot, being a bodyguard. It's good preparation for fatherhood."

Mom laughed as Laurel looked at Dad like he was nuts. Cam decided that silence was the only safe response, not wanting to say anything that might get Laurel started about him and Elena again. It was a decision he was doubly thankful for when all of the guards averted their eyes from him at exactly the same time. For a brief, panicked second, he wondered if they'd all been listening enough to realize what was going on.

Then he told himself not to be an idiot and turned to look behind him. Elena had followed his and Laurel's route into the courtyard, and as she walked toward him he couldn't stop the corners of his mouth from sneaking upward. He just liked it better when she was there. "If you're looking for some peace and quiet, this probably isn't the place to get it." He started moving towards her. "Mom and Dad are torturing people for their own good."

"I know. It's probably wrong that I find it soothing." She scanned the still-running guards, none of whom were willing to meet her eyes. Clearly, his parents were including some well-deserved guilt as part of their training. "But one of the maids told me you were out here."

"Did you need something?" He'd stopped lurking at the doorway of Braeth's room because he hadn't wanted to be a nuisance, but if she'd needed him and he hadn't been there—

"Yes." Elena didn't elaborate, instead moving close enough that her shoulder pressed against his upper arm. They stayed like that for a moment, not moving, before she spoke again. "I know I've said this already, but thank you."

She'd been doing that a lot since her aunt had arrived. It might have been enough to worry him, but it was worlds better than the cold he'd felt radiating off her during her initial confrontation with Ariadne. "I'm not going anywhere." He placed a hand on her back, herding her over to his parents. They'd be good about not fussing more than she could handle, but if they didn't get the chance to at least see her they'd never forgive him. "Now spare me some future grief and come say hi to Mom and Dad."

Elena hugged both of them, then exchanged a polite nod with Laurel. "Alan says we've been invited to the spell circle," Mom said, giving the princess the same scan she often gave her children.

"Yes." Elena moved back to stand next to Cam, once again making sure their arms were touching. "It's just a precaution, of course."

"Of course." Dad said. "You look tired."

She shrugged. "I have a great deal on my mind." When he looked worried, she smiled a little. "Don't worry. Your son's been making sure I get at least a little sleep."

Both his parents looked at Cam approvingly, while Laurel surveyed all of them as if plotting a sneak attack in the immediate future. Cam sent her a covert look that promised a whole host of creative deaths if she said anything inappropriate.

Mom smoothed a hand over Elena's hair one more time, then glanced over at the still-running guardsmen. "They're starting to collapse," she murmured, absolutely no concern in her voice. "Much more and they'll be completely useless."

"We might as well move onto the next phase," Dad said, his voice heavy. He waved to the three of them before moving towards the guards. "Attention, everyone! Corridor hunt-and-find starts in one minute exactly!"

Mom smiled at the three of them. "Don't worry. We'll make sure not to leave any bodies lying around." With a quick hand-squeeze for both Cam and Laurel, she followed her husband.

Laurel, on the other hand, didn't look like she was about to go anywhere. "So," she started, the deliberate pause making it obvious that no one was going to like where she was headed. Her hand rested on the hilt of the sword hanging at her side, such an obvious intimidation tactic that he kind of wanted to smack her for it. "It's been awhile since you and I talked, Princess."

Cam wrapped an arm around Elena to keep her from encouraging his sister's idiocy at all. Elena looked up at him, her expression making it clear that she would have understood without quite such an obvious prompt. Then she smiled her cool, dangerous smile at Laurel. "That's true, but not terribly surprising. We've never had a great deal in common."

Laurel smiled back, equally dangerous. "Now we do."

"Laurel, stop." He'd been holding onto exasperation as long as possible, but now it was sliding fast into anger. "I thought we'd settled this."

Elena glanced up at Cam, then gave Laurel a long, measuring look. "You have," she said firmly. When Laurel met her gaze, ready to argue, Elena shook her head. "My guess is that you're angry at me rather than your brother, and he's simply made himself a target in an attempt to protect me. Stop tormenting him now, and I promise you we'll have the conversation you're so clearly looking for once I've dealt with my aunt."

Cam was oddly touched, but he couldn't let her do this. "Elena."

She looked up at him again. "No, you don't get to keep taking harassment for me. I make your life hard enough as it is."

After a brief burst of surprise, Laurel watched them both with a thoughtful look. "Fine. But I'll be watching." She turned, hand still on her sword, and disappeared back into the castle.

Once she was gone, Elena let out a breath. "If I have to turn her into a frog, I promise it will be purely in self-defense."

Cam grinned at the image. "There's no need to limit yourself like that."

CHAPTER 17

Solid Purchase

Elena hated swimming.

She'd tried it once, in an ice-cold pocket of a lake that was the kingdom's only significant body of water. Her mother had done her best to teach her the basics, but all Elena could remember about the experience was the feeling of constant floundering. She had clung to her mother, her toes constantly seeking for some solid purchase. True, that went against the entire point of swimming, but to Elena's mind it would have been far less terrifying to simply learn to breathe underwater.

Now, with her aunt in the castle, she would have given anything to have only mere water to deal with. She was so tempted to just give up, stop struggling and peacefully sink to the bottom, but this time her mother was floundering, too. They couldn't help each other from the bottom, so they were both trying hard to stay above the surface.

Little more than a day later, Elena was already exhausted. Her patience was proving to be the first victim.

"You're being deliberately vague here," she snapped, jabbing her finger at the offending section of notes. She glared at her aunt across the worktable. "The connection between the shields and strands is one of the most important parts of curse construction. I refuse to believe that you remember so little."

Ariadne narrowed her own eyes, apparently emboldened by the lack of guards in the room. "I could give you detailed notes about the condition of the structural ties when I created the curse, but those would be useless to us now. I spent weeks battering the thing apart—there's no way to tell what they look like until I've seen them for myself."

"Which means we might have to partially re-construct the curse in order to take it apart safely." Her mother leaned forward, the words outwardly more calm than Elena's. But it was still possible to hear the old anger in the queen's voice, far more dangerous than impatience. "If that happens, knowing everything we can about how the structure ties together will be vital."

Ariadne's jaw tightened, and she took a deep, steadying breath through her nose. "Fine. But we're wasting time."

"And who was the one who made my daughter's eighteenth birthday the deadline?" The queen met her sister's gaze, enough chill in her voice to make even Elena shiver. "Write out the notes."

There was complete silence as the two women stared at each other. There was no question in Elena's mind who would back down first, and a few seconds later her aunt proved her right. "Fine," Ariadne said, eyes escaping back down to the notes. "I'll give you everything I have."

"Even if we won't remember all the information, Dr. Flyte will," Elena forced her own voice to be even as she re-gathered what was left of her patience. Not that there was much of it—she needed to find some excuse to duck outside for a few minutes.

Just a joke or two from Cam would do wonders. "He'll be monitoring both me and the curse while everyone's working to take it apart. I have a personal stake in making sure he's as prepared as possible."

Ariadne's eyes widened a fraction, as if she'd just realized something. "Dr. Flyte? Was he the mirror you used to—" She stopped herself, eyes flicking over to her sister before dropping back down to her notes.

There was just enough vulnerability in the words to make Elena suspect that her aunt regretted opening her mouth at all. She glanced over at her mother, who was staring at Ariadne with raw eyes, and Elena squeezed her mother's hand. "You'll meet everyone when it's necessary."

Ariadne's nod was relaxed, and focused entirely on Elena. There was something in her eyes that looked almost like gratitude, and Elena was appalled to realize it was directed at her. It was exhausting battling her temper, but she also had no interest in offering the woman anything, either. If something that neutral could be seen as a kindness, she would have to watch her words even more carefully.

She pulled herself back from her thoughts in time to hear her mother's next question. "Are you sure there's not a less violent method for destroying the curse's shields?" This time, the queen's voice held more concern than anger. Unfortunately, the change wasn't particularly comforting. "I'm aware that overloading them is less violent than using brute force to smash through them, but the energy release could cause its own damage."

Something almost like fondness flashed across Ariadne's face. When the queen looked away, no longer willing to meet her sister's gaze, Ariadne closed her eyes. "Any method we have of destroying the shields will require a certain amount of violence.

The energy overload has the advantage of not putting any undue stress on the structures beneath."

The words were carefully vague enough that Elena was immediately suspicious. "What structures?" She looked back and forth between the two women, both of whom were carefully not saying anything at all, and she had a terrible feeling she already knew. "Me." She took a deep breath, ignoring the way her stomach twisted. "Getting rid of the curse could destroy the strands of my magic tangled up in the middle."

Ariadne's jaw tightened. "Even if that's true, it might be no more harmful than dismantling a spell."

The queen's eyes narrowed. "You may be willing to take risks with my daughter's life, but I am not."

"I agree," intoned a far deeper voice. Elena turned as Braeth appeared in her mother's workroom, hovering behind her the shadows swirling around him like malevolent clouds. He'd picked up the habit of flowing into a room through some nearly invisible crack, rather than do anything so mundane as actually open a doorway. Elena hadn't even known that particular trick was in his repertoire, and suspected this was his version of grandstanding. "Her life will not be damaged, Ariadne Coppin, even if I have to drain yours to assure that she remains sufficiently strong."

Ariadne's eyes widened briefly at his surprise appearance, though she pretended they hadn't. "There's no need to threaten me." She met the wraith's gaze, voice firm and more confident than it had been in hours. "Despite what you may think of me, I assure you that we have the same priority."

"If that is truly the case, then do not think of this as a threat," Braeth said calmly. "I am simply telling you what will happen if your priorities change." He then turned to the queen. "When shall we perform the binding spell? I would do it immediately, but the good doctor feels that the magic-draining restraints your sister is currently wearing will blunt its impact."

"A binding?" Ariadne asked, her voice sharpening. "I need to be at my full strength when I work on the curse, not under the influence of outside magic. Restrictions of any kind may hamper my ability to attack the spell, or deal with an unexpected problem as it arises."

"If it hampers you from hurting my daughter, I'm quite happy to take that risk." The queen's voice brooked no argument, an attitude Elena shared completely. Ariadne made a small sound, caught somewhere between hurt and frustration. "Why would I come here if my goal was to hurt her?" Her shoulders were tense, like she was prepared to either throw a punch or defend against one. "There's no reason for me to expose myself like this if I didn't truly want to help!"

"How am I ever supposed to trust you again?" The queen's voice was an equal mixture of fury and grief. "You attacked my daughter in order to punish me for falling in love! How can I ever believe another word you say?"

"I—" Ariadne looked stricken, her voice failing her. To Elena's ears, her mother had simply repeated the basic facts of the situation, but her aunt looked like the imagined punch had hit her square in the face. It made no sense that the woman's feelings would still be this raw. Surely she'd made some kind of peace with a decision she'd made so deliberately.

Elena filed the discrepancy away as she regained control of the conversation. "We'll take all the necessary precautions as soon as circumstances call for it." Her voice was firm enough to cut off any unnecessary conversation. "Until then, we have more important things to worry about."

"Indeed." Braeth almost amused as he turned to Elena. "I must temporarily requisition your guard, princess. The doctor wishes to be returned to his room, and Cameron's only task at the moment seems to be studying the stonework on the opposite side of the corridor."

The queen's eyebrows lifted a fraction. "I thought Cam was with his family."

"Cam is completely capable of making his own decisions." Elena knew her voice sounded just a little too casual to be believable, but the heavens help anyone who dared call her on it. "You need to ask him, not me."

"I did. He seemed to feel that you would have something to say on the matter."

She felt her cheeks heat. Cam had indeed been with his family, at least until she'd hunted him down. After assuring Cam more than once that he hadn't been in the way, he'd gotten the hint and followed her back here.

And she would be strung up by her ankles rather than admit any of that out loud.

"How long do you think it will take?" she asked Braeth, making sure she didn't meet anyone's gaze.

"That depends on who we can find to assist him. Cameron's younger brother is in classes right now, and he seems quite determined not to ask either of his older siblings."

"I'll help." It wasn't the most dignified exit, but seeing Cam suddenly seemed far more important. "If nothing else, I can keep Dr. Flyte from psychoanalyzing the poor man."

"But we still—"

The queen shook her head, cutting Ariadne off. "The meeting is done. Get us the rest of the notes by tomorrow morning. I want to have the spell completed by nightfall." Her voice gentled as she turned to her daughter. "Go. I'll let you know if there's any new information."

Elena touched her mother's arm in silent thank you. She left just as Braeth and his shadows slipped out of the room.

~

"Are you sure mirrors can't gain weight, Doc?" Cam muttered, adjusting his grip on the mirror to accommodate Elena's shorter height. There wasn't a great deal of distance between her mother's workroom and the room that had been set aside for Dr. Flyte, but there were enough turns to make the walk a slow one. "Maybe you've been snacking on magic cupcakes while we weren't looking."

"Cameron, I feel it's time for a humor intervention," Dr. Flyte said, voice as serious as it was in sessions. If you didn't know him, it would be impossible to tell that he was joking. "I hate to be the one to break it to you, but you're simply not as amusing as you think you are."

Cam chuckled. "Poor guy. You ended up with Mason's sense of humor." He looked at Elena. "You seriously haven't tried to help him with that before now?"

"Who says I haven't?" She put on her best innocent face. "A few years ago, his sense of humor was hopeless enough that he might have actually found you funny."

Cam made tsking sound as he shook his head. "She's in denial, Doc. You've got to help her."

Dr. Flyte sighed dramatically. "You poor, delusional boy. Mind the stairs, please."

Elena helped Cam maneuver the mirror up the stairwell, enjoying listening to the banter between him and the mirror.

She'd been ready to deflect any unwanted therapy Dr. Flyte might try to unleash on Cam—sometimes the mirror couldn't help himself—but Cam had been ready with the jokes from the very beginning. Since then, he'd kept a guiding hand on the entire conversation, keeping the doctor busy while tossing enough openings to Elena to make sure she didn't drift off someplace unpleasant.

If she called him on it, Elena suspected Cam would deny he was doing anything but making stupid jokes. The fact that she knew better felt like a secret shared only between the two of them, a piece of Cam that no one else had.

It was an embarrassing thought, but she cherished it.

"I know I'm probably the hundredth person to ask this, but aren't there transport spells that would make this easier?" Cam asked, walking backwards around a turn. "I mean, normal people buy them in individual batches to move furniture short distances."

"Transport spells interact poorly with my inherent magic," Dr. Flyte explained. "The one time I attempted it, my entire frame left without me. Needless to say, it was unpleasant."

Cam winced. "I can imagine."

"Braeth's offered to make him specialized transport charms, but nothing like that's ever been done before," Elena said. "Dr. Flyte would have to be an experimental test subject."

"Most true magic mirrors are content staying on one wall their entire lives," the doctor said. "My profession has caused me to lead an unusually adventurous life."

Elena smiled. "But not adventurous enough to test Braeth's sense of humor."

Cam gave the mirror an awkward pat. "I don't blame you there, buddy."

They made it to Dr. Flyte's room, setting him down in the stand without any undue jostling. Once he was in place, the mirror sighed in relief. "Thank you both. I won't need further assistance until we establish a time for the circle." He looked at Elena. "I have a meeting with your mother in the morning, but it will be held here."

"Good." Elena said, casting about for any excuse to linger even a few more minutes in the little bubble of peace Cam had made for her. She couldn't be too obvious about it—they would start to worry—but the thought of tearing herself away was painful. Surely she could have just a little bit longer.

Cam watched Elena, his mouth opening to say something, when Dr. Flyte spoke to him. "Cameron, please apologize to your parents for the fact that I haven't spoken to them since their arrival at the palace. I'm aware they're as busy as I am, but the lapse is unforgivable."

"Don't worry about it," Cam answered, any sign of what he'd been about to tell Elena vanishing from his face. "Smacking the palace guard into shape is taking all their time, but they love it. When I talked about them maybe taking the job permanently, Dad almost got excited."

Dr. Flyte looked intrigued. "Your mother would stay?"

Cam shrugged. "She really likes working with the kids at the city patrol, but the queen said she could still consult for them. And Dad's been itching to do the job for years."

Elena blinked, the words finally sinking in. "Your father's taking over the palace guard permanently?" The sense of peace vanished abruptly, leaving her feeling lost. She'd known Cam would leave—he had a life to go back to—but she hadn't prepared to be disconnected from the entire family like this.

Cam flushed. "Sorry, cart before the horse here. We haven't talked to your mom or anything."

"I'm sure she'd approve. I think she would have offered him the position already if she'd thought he'd take it." Elena tried to keep her voice calm, but she felt her stomach sink as her eyes escaped to anywhere but Cam's face. She was going to lose them both. "I'll have to hire a new bodyguard, but I'm sure your father would be willing to oversee that."

Cam, who had been moving towards her, froze at that. "You want someone else?"

It was the anger in the words that made her look up, focusing on Cam's face. Elena was thrown by how furious he suddenly looked, heat flaring up behind the wall of cold, and she lost whatever she'd been about to say next. "Cameron, I—I thought—"

Dr. Flyte, who had been listening to all this, sighed. "Cameron," he said gently, "I believe what she's trying to say is that she didn't know you intended to stay."

Elena took a deep breath, trying to collect herself. "Dr. Flyte, this isn't—" Then she realized what he'd actually said, and sheer astonishment overwhelmed everything else. Her gaze flew to Cam's. "What?"

Cam stared right back at her, looking just as confused as she felt, then rubbed a hand across his face. "I thought it was obvious," he said, voice flickering between amusement, exasperation, and something else she couldn't read. He gave her an odd half grin. "Think your mom would approve?"

She couldn't seem to make her brain work correctly. "You have a job to return to. On the border."

"I'd probably have to go back for a few weeks, because it's kind of tacky to use up all your vacation and then quit on someone. But I'm sure Mom or Dad would keep an eye on you until I got back. Then it'd just be you and me."

Elena stared at him. Was he really saying what she thought he was saying? "You hated having to take this job."

"That's when I thought you were some stuck-up ice princess, and you thought my purpose in life was to make you miserable. Are we really going to drag all that back up?"

She searched his face, trying to find an explanation for the impossible things he was saying. He was too stubborn to give up his entire career for his father, no matter how much he loved him. And there was nothing for him to feel guilty for.

But she hadn't even dared wish for this. And nothing so far in her life had suggested the universe was capable of being this kind.

Cam's expression closed off, apparently taking her inability to speak as some kind of answer. "Fine." Then he turned, heading for the door.

Later, Dr. Flyte would tell Elena that he was glaring at her so furiously it was a wonder she hadn't burst into flames. At the time, however, all she could see was Cam's retreating back.

"Wait." She caught his arm before his hand reached the door handle. "You really want to stay?" Just saying the words made something hot and light rise up in her chest, unfamiliar enough to be incredibly dangerous.

He looked at her like she was an idiot. "That's what I've been trying to tell you." His expression softened at whatever he saw in hers. "I think we make a pretty good team."

Elena swallowed, throat tight. "Yes, we do." She squeezed his arm, filled with the sudden, wild urge to hug him again. Cam was staying. "I'm sure my mother will approve this, too."

Cam let out a relieved breath. "If not, hopefully you'll sweet-talk her for me."

"After." She'd never really let herself picture a world where the curse had been safely broken, let alone plan for it. But if Cam was going to be part of that world, she would have to be as well.

That thought made the hope slightly less terrifying. "I'll talk to her after all of this is settled."

"Good." Voice tender, he brushed his knuckles against her cheek. "I can't think of anyone I'd rather have watching my back."

She threw her arms around him before her brain could try to argue, holding on as tightly as she could. His warmth seeped through her, like hearthstones on a cold day, and she pressed her face against his neck.

Cam's own arms were steady and sure, and they felt as unwilling to let go as hers were. As long as he was here, it seemed impossible for her to drown. "You know, we don't have to save this for special occasions," he murmured. "You're free to do this whenever it strikes your fancy."

When they broke apart, Dr. Flyte cleared his non-existent throat dramatically. "As grateful as I am that this has been cleared up," he said, "I do have some further studying to do. Trying not to interrupt the two of you with helpful insights is proving to be rather distracting."

Both Cam and Elena laughed.

CHAPTER 18

Terrible Timing

Cam's brain had known exactly how big a mess his heart was getting into. They'd just agreed not to talk about it.

Right now, though, it was getting harder and harder not to face up to the facts of the situation. All Cam had to do was look at Elena to remember how her arms felt around him, or see the light in her eyes when she'd finally gotten it through her head that he wanted to stay. He wasn't about to admit it to Laurel, but he could at least admit it to himself—he didn't just want to be Elena's bodyguard. He wanted to be hers, period.

Which just proved that love had a lousy sense of timing.

The only thing Elena needed to be worried about right now was getting the curse fixed. She had a morning consultation with the rest of the magic experts in less than an hour, and if everything went well they'd start setting up for the spell right after that. Cam's only job in all this would be to stay out of the way, catch Elena when the blackout hit, and stab Ariadne if the situation called for it. Poorly-timed declarations of romantic intent would have to wait.

Complete silence, however, was too much to ask for.

"I decided a whole tray would be a lost cause, but you have to at least eat this," he said, tossing her the apple he'd saved off his own tray. "It's never good to worry on an empty stomach."

Elena caught the fruit. She was at her desk, reading her notes about the curse for the fiftieth time. As it was just past dawn, it was time for a distraction. "I'm not—" She stopped herself before Cam even had time to give her the look, shaking her head. "It's really annoying that you don't like it when I lie to you," she said, taking a dutiful bite. "If this comes back up later, I hope you know that it's going to end up all over you, too."

"As if you'd ever give anyone that much proof that you're not completely cool and collected." Cam watched Elena's face, which was carefully made up despite the fact that she planned to spend most of the day in her mother's workroom. "Besides, you'd mess up your makeup."

Elena's expression turned rueful. "I know it was probably ridiculous to bother with it, but—" She shook her head, swallowing a second bite before answering. "My mother always taught me to think of it as war paint. It seemed appropriate."

"It's not ridiculous. Laurel used to wear Dad's gauntlets every time we had to go visit our great-aunt." Cam sat down on the edge of the bed, close enough that his knee nearly touched Elena's. "Though please don't tell her I ever told you that. She's still tall enough to get me into a headlock."

Elena's lips curved upward briefly. It wasn't as much as Cam had hoped for, but he'd take what he could get. "Your secret is safe with me."

"See, that's just more proof that you're a lot nicer than you pretend to be. You could have stretched that out and blackmailed me for all kinds of favors." He leaned forward, one hand on the bed. "You know you'll be fine, right? One more unpleasant day of dealing with your aunt, a session of complicated magic I only sort of understand, and then all of this will be over."

Elena met his eyes as if searching for something. "You sound awfully sure about that."

Cam had to be. Anything else was going to break his heart. "It's easy to be sure when you know you're always right." He grinned when she rolled her eyes at him. "Hey, I may not be a sorcery genius like the rest of you, but I've been listening at enough doors during your planning sessions to know that you guys know what you're doing."

Elena looked guilty at that, even though that was the last thing he'd meant. "Sorry. I would have wanted you in the room, but I just—" She shook her head. "I don't like my aunt being able to study you. She's got enough ammunition on my mother—the last thing I want is to find someone else to target."

Cam was oddly unsettled at the thought of Elena trying to protect him. With everything else on her plate, he was the last thing she should be worried about. "Your aunt can't say anything that's going to hurt me. The only thing I care about is being where you need me."

She relaxed a little at that. "Sure, now you feel like being obedient."

"A favor you should repay by eating more of that apple."

Her smile was stronger this time as she took another bite. "Actually, I was thinking about taking you flying once all this over. You know, as a way to say thank you for all the time you've spent standing in corridors and listening to longwinded technical discussions."

It took him a second to realize what she meant. Once he did, he couldn't help but laugh at the picture that formed. "Not that I'm doubting your skills, but I don't think that harness of yours could carry both of us."

Elena gave him an amused look. "Of course not, though I'm sure your family would pay good money to see us try. But it wouldn't be too hard to make you your own harness." She looked back down at the apple. "Since the magic is in the leather, you should even be able to guide it yourself."

Cam's first response was the instinctive "no" of anyone who didn't enjoy looking like a fool in public, but the smarter parts of his brain pushed that thought aside. He'd kind of invited himself on her nightly flying sessions, but now she was offering to invest a significant amount of time so she could share them with him. It was a pretty big offer.

Also, would it count as a date? Cam really wanted it to, and Elena covertly asking him out would be a comforting thumbs-up for his long-term plans. But he was pretty sure she hadn't dated much, if at all, and to her this might be nothing more than two friends spending time together. Last time they'd gone out to do something—dinner at his parents' house, usually a fairly significant step in the whole dating process—he was pretty sure he'd been adamant about not even wanting her as a fake girlfriend. Hopefully, she—

"If the answer's no, you can just tell me."

Elena's voice jerked Cam out of his thoughts. Her hand gripped the apple a little too tightly as she watched him, like she was trying to figure out what he was thinking. Since sharing his thoughts would be a bad idea on several levels, Cam cleared his throat. Focus on the matter at hand, idiot. "Sorry, just picturing myself running into trees. But if you can keep me from doing that, then sure."

She looked relieved, and Cam mentally kicked himself for

worrying her. "There's a clearing I used when I first practiced," she said. "You might crash the first few times, but it won't be into trees."

He covered her free hand with his. "That's okay. I'll just tell anyone who asks that you beat me up."

Elena shook her head, taking another bite. "You're the only person who'd actually believe that."

"That's because no one else knows you like I do."

~

Cam was prepared to wait in the corridor for the morning meeting, but Elena gestured him into the room. He stayed by the door while they talked, taking up the traditional guard stance, and distracted himself by trying to make sense of the technical chatter. When he caught Ariadne watching him, he gave her a little wave and then ignored her.

Bishop showed up just after the meeting ended, standing close enough to the queen that they could hold a quiet conversation. Cam's parents arrived as the circle was being prepared, and his mom helped Cam move Dr. Flyte into position while his dad took position by the door. The mirror monopolized most of the private conversation, but Marie still found a moment to pull her son into the relative privacy of the corridor. "Where do you want us?" she asked, voice low enough not to carry through the door. "If we're all within striking distance of Elena's aunt, we'll get in the way of each other's swords."

"I definitely want you both within striking distance, but you should also be able to see the queen. She'll be your best indicator that something's wrong." Other than screaming, of course, but he wasn't going to let himself think about that. "I'll be sitting inside the circle with Elena, so either you or Dad will have a better shot at Ariadne if we need it." He'd already taken off his swordbelt, knowing there'd be no room for him to draw it properly.

His mother hesitated. "Why," Then she stopped. "Ah."

Cam tensed. He'd known she'd figure it out quicker than his dad. "We don't actually have to talk about it, right?"

She pulled him into a sideways hug. "I'll spare you until all of this is over."

By the time they made it back inside, everything appeared to be ready. Elena, standing in the middle of the circle, scanned her work one more time. "We should get started," she said. "Cam, if you'll please remove my aunt's cuffs?"

His mom and dad moved into position behind Ariadne, but the sorceress ignored them as she held her wrists out towards Cam. "My niece's protector," she murmured, sounding amused.

He held her gaze as he sketched out the unlocking sigil on the underside of the cuffs. "Look at her wrong, and I'll stab you before you can blink." When they clicked open, he handed them to his father. "Hold onto these. We might need them in a minute." Then, as Braeth's shadows darkened the room, he unsheathed his dagger as sat down cross-legged in the middle of the circle.

As the illumination spell activated, Elena sat down as well. "I should have known you'd find some way to be armed," she murmured, settling close enough that her hand rested on his leg. Around them, the circle briefly flared as the protection spell kicked in.

"A good bodyguard is always armed." He followed Elena's gaze upward as the tangled knot of the curse formed above their heads. It still looked as menacing as ever, but at least it was less of a surprise this time. He felt Elena's hand tighten on his leg, her entire attention fixed on the writhing mass that was tangled up inside her.

Ariadne was staring at it as well, something in her eyes that looked like horror. She shook her head sharply. "Remember, the more we unwind the outer layers of the curse, the better we'll be able to see the core. None of the strands will be completely freed, but get them as out of the way as you can."

"And be careful." That was the queen, shooting her sister a stern look. "Smashing our way towards the shield will cause more harm than good."

The knot flared with red, teal, purple and silver light as the four magic users began to work. Elena's hand half lifted, as if tempted to add her own magic, then she tightened her fingers into a fist. She'd decided not to officially participate in the spell, since the blackout would knock her out just before the really complicated part hit. It was the sensible decision, but not an easy one.

The work was painfully slow, but Cam wouldn't have wanted anyone to hurry. Dr. Flyte focused on the already loose strands, glyphs appearing on the surface of his mirror as he used his magic to move them out of the way. That freed Braeth to work on the more tightly knotted sections, quick and methodical. The wraith's magic moved through these tangles, making the individual strands shrink away from its red glow.

The queen had grabbed one of the strands with her magic, using it to unpick other parts of the knot. Ariadne sent out brief pulses of power to jostle the strands loose, then pushed them out of the way. Soon, she started discreetly loosening the strands near where the queen was working, careful to make it clear that she wasn't intruding on her sister's space. The queen hesitated, not touching the loosened strands for a moment, then began unpicking them without looking at Ariadne. Soon, the two were working together.

Whenever one of four pulled too hard on something, Elena would flinch. Cam couldn't tell whether the cause was mental or physical, but he wrapped an arm around her and tried to brace her as much as he could.

Now they could see portions of the core's shield. It seemed thicker than the remnants of the outer shield had been, shimmering deep beneath the surface. At the sight of it, Elena tightened her hand on Cam's leg again.

Outside the circle, the queen took a deep breath. "Once everyone has charged their strand, hold until I say ready. We'll all need to release the charge at the same time if we want to have the greatest chance of completely obliterating the shield."

The chosen strands glowed more and more brightly as they were moved into position. Next to Cam, Elena laid her head on his shoulder. "Make sure they don't stop halfway," she whispered. "I want the curse gone, whatever it takes."

"I'll do what I can." It wasn't a promise. He didn't have the authority to make these people do anything they didn't want to do, and Cam suspected that he and Elena had very different definitions of "whatever it takes." But he didn't want her to go under without some kind of reassurance. "I want the curse gone, too."

Above their heads, the queen started the countdown. At her signal, the strands touched the core and sent up a brief, blinding flash of light. Elena slumped bonelessly against him, the blackout taking her, and Cam pulled her just a little closer. He pressed his cheek against her hair, reminding himself that this was all still going according to plan.

Once the light cleared, the shimmer of the shield was gone

as well. Now, he could see faint blue lines in the depths of the knot, the same color as Elena's magic.

Ariadne blew out a breath. "It's more tangled up in her powers than I thought it would be." There was enough regret in the words that Cam resisted the urge to punch her.

"Which means that we need to be that much more careful when we unwind them," Dr. Flyte said firmly. "This will take some time, so I suggest we begin immediately."

This time, the work was even slower. Everyone started using the queen's unpicking technique, slowly untangling the strands that tied Elena to the curse. Whenever they managed to free one completely, it faded out of existence. Cam started counting the strands that disappeared, clearing thirty before their absence made a noticeable difference. He knew the queen was suffering her own effects from the curse—she was paler than normal, mouth tight—but it didn't seem to affect her focus at all.

He could feel the tension in the air, the strained focus of people doing vitally important work over far too long a time period. Cam felt even more useless than he had during the analysis, and he would have been happy to donate his energy to anyone who needed it. Actually voicing the offer, however, might distract someone at the worst possible time. On top of that, he wasn't a magic user—they might not be able to even use anything he had to give.

"If a particular strand refuses to release, move onto another one," Braeth reminded everyone. "Do not force it."

Still, something must have been happening, because Elena flinched in Cam's arms. At first, he thought he'd imagined it, a sign his worry was making his hallucinate. A few minutes later, though, he felt her flinch again.

The third time, Cam studied what everyone was doing with

the same intensity he used to watch for bandits. Soon, he noticed one of the blue threads straining as Ariadne slid one of the curse strands free. As the thread stretched, Elena made a small, helpless sound.

Cam held her closer, raising his voice loud enough to be heard. "Every time you do something to one of the blue threads, it hurts Elena."

He felt everyone in the circle go still. "We discussed this," Ariadne said, voice quiet. "This is bound up tightly enough with her magic that discomfort can't be avoided."

"She shouldn't be able to feel it," Braeth said. "It appears to be a biological response, not a magical one."

Silence fell. The queen cleared her throat. "Elena wouldn't want us to stop," she said, and Cam didn't know if the strain in her voice was from the curse or the decision she was making. He wanted to reassure her that she was right—this was what Elena would want, no matter how much it was killing them both to see her in pain. "But please, be extra careful."

They continued unwinding the curse, clearing away as much of it as they could. Finally, only about twenty strands remained, wrapped together in a tight central knot. It was thick with Elena's magic, the lines crisscrossing each other so often that the entire thing seemed to glow with a faint blue light.

Ariadne eyed the knot in frustration. "All of the work we've done should have at least partially loosened it." Purple magic skimmed lightly over the tangled surface, sending out little pulses. As far as Cam could tell, they had no effect. "Maybe I could—"

The queen shook her head. "It should be my responsibility." Fashioning her magic into a needle of light, she carefully slid it underneath one of the blue threads and pulled upward.

Elena jerked against him, making a sound that left no doubt that she was in pain. Cam's own chest felt like it had been hit, and the queen froze as if she'd had a similar response. An instant later, the needle disappeared. "We didn't discuss this." The threat in the queen's voice was lessened by a faint unsteadiness. "If such a small movement hurts her that much, untangling the rest of the curse from her magic might kill her."

Ariadne looked genuinely worried now. "There shouldn't be such a direct physical effect." She magnified the projection of the curse so she could examine it more closely, her expression turning frustrated as she shrank it again. "Magic is energy flow. Disrupting that energy may hamper its ability to be channeled, but it has no effect on nerve endings or pain receptors."

Dr. Flyte looked grim. "Could it have something to do with the fact that you used shared blood to activate the curse?"

Ariadne lifted a hand. "I don't see how. It's not as if—" She stopped speaking suddenly, and even from inside the circle Cam could see that the woman had gone pale. "Elena hadn't finished developing yet."

The queen unconsciously placed a protective hand to her stomach, a horrified understanding on her own face. "It grew with her." As Bishop moved close enough to touch her back, the queen's voice cracked. "Ariadne, what did you do?"

"I didn't mean for this to happen, I swear. I didn't even know—" Ariadne cut herself off abruptly.

Cam just needed to know what was going on. "Someone needs to fill me in here."

"When a witch or sorceress is cursed, the curse normally attaches itself to the victim's magic," said Dr. Flyte. "Like calls to like."

"But since Elena was still developing, her magic hadn't yet

completely differentiated herself from the rest of her," continued Braeth. "The threads you see are Elena's magic, but the curse tangled them too early. They're snagged in her physical body as well, and when one of those snags is pulled it causes her pain."

Rage flared in Cam's chest at the sheer unfairness of it. "So you can't finish undoing the curse without killing her."

"No," Ariadne said quickly. "If Elena was awake, she could guide the untangling process more safely than we could."

"So she'll hurt herself instead of you guys hurting her?" Cam asked. "How is that any better?"

"Her awareness of her own magic will make her far more precise than we could ever be," Ariadne explained. "There will be discomfort, but she should be able to spare herself pain or debilitation."

"Only if she's awake," the queen said quietly.

"We may have no choice but to use the spell I discussed," Braeth said, his bony fingers curling inward as he spoke. "If we reflected the result's curse onto another, Elena would be conscious even when we attack the core. Since the spell merely alters the results of the curse, not the curse itself, she would remain conscious enough to do what was needed."

"That spell is meant to punish not heal," Dr. Flyte said, his spectral face pressing closer to the mirrored surface. "We have no idea whether it will even work like that."

"Do we have a choice?" Braeth asked.

It was the queen who finally answered him. "No." She sounded tired. "Start closing the spell, everyone. There are things we need to discuss."

CHAPTER 19

Making Things Clear

She should have known.

It was the only thought circling through Elena's mind as she listened to everyone what the next step was. When she'd first opened her eyes, she hadn't even needed to ask whether the curse had been broken—the answer had been painfully apparent on everyone's faces. There had been quick reassurances, talk of snags and Braeth's reflecting spell, but she let it wash over her in a wave of words. Inside, all she felt was cold.

She should never have let herself hope. She was smarter than that.

"Elena." The queen's voice was sharp, commanding her daughter to return to the conversation. Her mother's gaze was equal parts worry and anger, though Elena wasn't sure who or what the last emotion was directed at.

They were all sitting at her mother's worktable, as if this were just another planning meeting rather than a dissection of her inevitable fate. Even worse, she was struggling to keep her eyes open, the effects of the curse having drained most of her energy. Still, she forced herself to focus as the queen continued. "You need to listen to this. When we restart the spell, your part will be the most important."

Too bad I'll be unconscious. Elena bit her tongue to stop herself from saying the thought aloud. Hurting her mother wouldn't help anything. "I need to follow my magic closely enough to unsnag it at key points," she dutifully recited. "It sounds similar to what you did in untangling the spell, except I would be working by feel rather than sight."

Of course, that would only be possible if they could make Braeth's spell work. What had struck her as so unnerving a mere week ago seemed like nothing more than a fantasy now. The old evil sorcerers had cared so little for the mechanics of how certain spells worked that Braeth wasn't entirely sure how the reflection spell worked. If the magic was a shield ready to deflect, it might be useless against a curse that had already been cast.

And even if it did work, who would they get to take that kind of risk? You couldn't force someone into a spell without an appalling level of compulsion magic. Whoever it was would have to voluntarily accept the risk of the curse never being broken, of sleeping for a hundred years and losing their entire life in the process. No one in their right mind would take that on, and she would be unforgivably selfish to ask it of them.

"Elena." It was Dr. Flyte who spoke this time, using the same carefully measured voice he usually saved for particularly tense therapy sessions. "We want you to be a part of this." He didn't have to explain how. "You may have been a passive victim of the curse, but you can be an integral part of its destruction. We need your insight as we move ahead."

Resentment spiked inside Elena, a jagged crack in the middle of the cold. "What insight can I give?" Her voice wasn't quite as controlled this time. She looked around the table, carefully skirting past the eyes of everyone who had been in the circle. Cam and Bishop were standing behind her, mismatched guards who had stationed themselves on both sides of the door. Cam's parents, thankfully, had gone. "Until we actually test Braeth's spell, everything we're discussing is pure speculation. I have no more facts than anyone else here, which means my theories have as little relevance."

"Do you have a theory? Any theory?" Braeth asked. "Relevant or not, I believe it would comfort us all to believe that your brooding had produced some vaguely useful result."

Resentment heated into anger, but a shouting match would change nothing. She bit her tongue, forcing herself to be content with a glare.

Ariadne looked up from the spell book she'd been studying. "If we want a useful response, then we should be looking for a willing subject instead of discussing magical theory." She looked at Elena with a mixture of sympathy and frustration. "Brooding or not, she's right about one thing. We need to test Braeth's spell."

"You can't test it," Elena snapped, switching her glare to Ariadne. "Unless I've wildly misinterpreted Braeth's description of the spell, it can't be undone once you've cast it. If the plan doesn't work, I've simply condemned some poor innocent person in my place."

"What else would you have us do?" Braeth said quietly.

Elena bit her tongue again. Logic and harsh reality aside, she wasn't enough of a monster to say the truth where her mother could hear it.

Miraculously, Ariadne stepped in. "The curse doesn't activate until your eighteenth birthday, Elena. Even if Braeth's spell doesn't work, we haven't come to the end of our options or the time we need to work on them." She turned to look at everyone else at the table, meeting everyone's gaze but her sister's. "But we won't know what step we need to take until we know whether this one works."

"Which means we need to find someone willing to take the burden of the curse's effects from Elena." Dr. Flyte's voice was solemn, but it was evident he didn't disagree with everyone else's assessment. "The spell requires someone of similar biology, which unfortunately eliminates Braeth and I from the running."

Elena's stomach knotted tight. How had she not realized they would volunteer themselves first? She couldn't let any of them risk themselves for something this pointless. Especially not—

As if she'd heard Elena's thoughts, the queen opened her mouth. "I—"

"I'll do it."

Everyone turned at the sound of Bishop's voice, which was as calm as if they were discussing the monthly budget. The elf hadn't moved from his position by the door, but the way his gaze had locked with the queen's made Elena afraid to see the look on her mother's face.

She forced her voice to function. "Absolutely not."

Bishop turned to look at her. "It's the most sensible option. If the spell is successful, your mother's skills will be needed to aid in undoing the curse." The brief unsteadiness in his voice made it clear he'd known how close her mother had been to offering. "This way, I can be of use as well."

"What if it doesn't work?" Elena felt the panic rise in her chest. She stood, pushing away from the table so that she couldn't even see her mother out of the corner of her eye. "Is it any better that you fall asleep for a hundred years?"

"You make it sound like those are the only two options," growled Cam. Since she'd woken up again, she hadn't met his gaze once. It was too painful. "Like Dr. Flyte said, this isn't the end. Even if this doesn't work, there are other things we can do."

"I'm not sacrificing myself for you, Elena. I'm risking myself." Bishop's smile was just a little sad. Elena knew the elf was looking at her mother. "There's a difference."

There was no help for it. Elena turned, facing her mother. "I don't want this." The words caught in Elena's throat. "You shouldn't have to sacrifice him just to keep me safe."

There were tears in the queen's eyes. "I would burn the world down to keep you safe." She locked gazes with Bishop, her voice thick with emotion. "How can I help but love someone who would risk so much do to the same thing?"

A hush fell. No one dared to speak and break the moment, no matter how much it cheated her mother and Bishop to have it happen in such terrible circumstances. Grief and resentment at the unfairness of it all twisted in Elena's chest, making it ache. This wasn't right. She was the only one who was supposed to be at risk here. She'd known the curse was coming for so long that there was nothing left for it to snatch away, but she refused to let it start stealing from other people as well.

That, she was willing to fight for.

"No." Elena's voice was calmer now, a new sense of determination helping her wrestle back her control. When everyone looked at her, she lifted her chin. "Bishop, I am deeply grateful for your offer, and if worst comes to worst I may have to take you up on it. But if I heard Braeth correctly, the person who takes my blackout will also feel the pain that comes every time I untangle something."

"I am aware," Bishop said, obviously trying to reassure as

he turned to look at Elena. "But the pain is also likely to be far less than what you experienced."

Elena blew out a breath. "But I'll have to watch myself hurt you, which for me will be worse than actually feeling the pain. I'm going to need all my concentration for this, and I won't be able to do that if I'm making someone I care about suffer."

Privately, she still didn't believe they would ever get to that point. But she would do whatever she had to in order to keep them from getting any more hurt than they already were.

She turned to Braeth, hoping he would be the most practical. "If you're still insistent on doing this, surely there's another pool of candidates we could draw from. The crown has enough resources to make it worth the risk they'll be taking on." Callous, yes, but if someone had to be a risk she would rather it be a stranger than someone she loved. "I also feel I should once again point out that even if this doesn't work, the candidate isn't necessarily condemning themselves to anything," Ariadne interrupted, showing more than a hint of impatience. "To a prisoner, for example, the risk/reward ratio might be entirely feasible."

"So we start walking through the prison and ask murderers if they want to save Elena's life?" The disbelief in Dr. Flyte's voice made it clear what he thought of the suggestion. "Even if any of them could be trusted, we couldn't in good conscience let any of them back out on the streets."

"Don't be dramatic, doctor," the queen said, sounding far steadier than before. "It doesn't have to be murderers. But there are lesser crimes that still carry hefty sentences, some of which wouldn't necessarily pose any risk to us. If we found someone that seemed reliable, I would have no qualms about freeing them. There's a long tradition of royalty pardoning anyone they like when it's in their best interests."

"In my experience, the phrase 'service to the crown' covers a vast amount of sins," Braeth added, turning to Bishop. "You must get us the prison records."

"Of course," Bishop said. Elena noticed the subtle but definite signs of relief on his face, making the knot inside her loosen just a little bit. "I'll have to make a few mirror calls, but I can get them to you within the hour."

"Or we could just ask Prince Nigel," Cam said, catching everyone's attention. He was standing by the door, pretending to be a simple guard, but Elena could feel the frustration radiating off of him. When she tried to catch his gaze, he firmly avoided looking at her. "His crime was directly against the princess, which means that helping save her would balance out the scales."

"That's true, but wouldn't he be less likely to agree?" the queen asked. "His focus was on activating Elena's sleep spell, not freeing her of it."

"Yeah, but only because he'd screwed things up at home enough that they told him he couldn't come back until he brings home an enchanted princess," Cam explained. "He still doesn't get to bring Elena home this way, but you can give him some kind of official documentation saying he freed a princess from her sleeping spell. He seemed pretty desperate to get that checked off his list."

"If he requires more incentive, we may be able to aid him in completing other tasks on his list as well," Braeth said. "Between us, we have resources he is unlikely to find anywhere else."

"It's a good idea, but I'm not too thrilled with the idea of trusting Nigel to be logical," Elena said, still watching Cam. She didn't care about the suggestion one way or the other, but she needed him to look at her. He was more than simply frustrated with her, and it stung in a way it shouldn't have.

"I suppose chaining him to the floor is an option," Ariadne offered. "If we're careful about the metal the chains are made of, it shouldn't interrupt the spell."

"We will not chain someone to the floor," Dr. Flyte said firmly. "That's the sort of idea only someone truly evil could come up with."

"Says the mirror who assisted dozens of evil sorceresses with their work over the decades," Ariadne shot back.

"I consider you a level below them," Dr. Flyte returned, an uncharacteristic amount of venom in his voice.

"Children." The command in the queen's voice silenced them both. She turned back to Cam. "Do you think you can persuade Nigel to see reason and agree with this?"

"Yes," Cam said, looking at Elena. She'd been ready for the anger, no matter how much it bothered her, but the sheer hurt in his eyes broke her heart. She was the one who had done that to him.

Worse, there was no way she could safely explain. How could she admit that she hadn't dared look at him after she'd opened her eyes again, too afraid that she'd shatter completely. There was no safe, socially acceptable way to tell another person that he was a reminder of everything she'd been stupid enough to hope for.

Still, there were undoubtedly other things she could say. "We both will," Elena announced.

From the surprised looks everyone gave her, it was evident the conversation had moved on. "You want to examine the inmate lists?" the queen asked.

"No. Cam and I will see Prince Nigel together." She looked at Cam, daring him to protest. Instead, he gave her a small nod that suggested he knew exactly what she was doing. It was the one sure way they would have a chance to talk—argue, most likely—somewhere out of everyone else's earshot.

She turned back to the rest of the group. "I'll trust your judgment on the inmate lists, but if Nigel doesn't agree I'll want to meet the possible candidates in person."

"Of course." The queen looked at both Elena and Cam, as if she knew exactly why her daughter had invited herself along. "I would never choose someone without your full approval."

"It will be easier, however, if you can simply persuade this Nigel person to go along," Ariadne added. She looked sternly at her niece. "Perhaps you should let your protector do the talking. I suspect he'll put more effort into convincing our target than you will."

Annoyed, Elena met Ariadne's eyes with her best coolly disinterested look. "I'll do what I need to."

Her aunt lifted her hands. "Because you've been so enthusiastic up to this point." Her voice was sharp, with genuine anger rather than the mocking Elena had expected. "You clearly can't even manage to convince yourself of the plan, so forgive me if I doubt your ability to do the same to anyone else."

"Why do you care?" Elena stared at her aunt in disbelief. "I still don't understand what you're even doing here! Fine, maybe you were upset by the thought that you'd accidentally killed an infant. But as you can see, I'm not dead." Her voice was just as edged as her aunt's had been, not caring if she wounded. "The curse worked out exactly as you'd intended it. There was no reason for you to suddenly regret all your hard work."

Everyone else in the room was silent, watching the scene unfold. As Ariadne's jaw tightened, Elena remembered her aunt's odd reaction from earlier. She leaned forward, focused on the other woman. "Unless there's something I'm missing." The words were as much a threat as she could make them.

The tension in the room was thick enough she could feel the press of it against her shoulders. Dr. Flyte was the only one brave enough to risk breaking it. "Elena, I don't think—"

Ariadne cut him off. "Yes." Eyes still on her niece, she pushed herself to her feet before anyone could argue. "I presume there's an empty room nearby where we can speak?"

That certainly didn't help calm down the rest of the table. "Ariadne, sit down," Braeth commanded. "Elena, don't."

"We're just going to talk, Braeth." She kept her gaze fixed on her aunt, wondering if that was really true. The anti-magic cuffs were back on Ariadne's wrists, and if it came down to a physical fight, Elena was far from defenseless. If the battle turned emotional, Ariadne was one of the few people in the room who didn't have the power to cause her pain. "It will ease my mind."

The queen's expression was brittle as she turned to Ariadne, but her eyes were so full of feeling they almost burned. "Anything you can say to her you can say to me."

Her sister flinched away. "No, I can't."

The queen absorbed this in silence. "I don't need to tell you what will happen if you hurt my daughter."

Ariadne's face went tight. "No."

No one else protested as they headed for the door, but Cam stopped her briefly with a hand on her wrist. "You're not planning on doing anything stupid, are you?" he asked under his breath. "Killing her might be stress-relieving, but it will just make things harder later."

Elena surprised herself by smiling a little. "I'm really a much calmer person than you think I am."

Cam made a disbelieving noise, and it was comforting when he followed them to the spare meeting room. He stood guard outside as Elena shut the door, then turned to her aunt. "No more games. You have nothing to lose by telling me the truth and nothing to gain by feeding me a pretty story. Once you found the curse hadn't malfunctioned and killed me, what made you decide you had to undo it completely?"

Ariadne just watched her. "What do you want, more than anything?"

Elena blinked, thrown by the question. "Is this where you offer to buy my soul?"

Her aunt scoffed. "I'm being entirely serious. Name me one thing you would give up everything to have."

Elena stared, offended by even the idea of the question. Nothing she wanted was worth everything. "What business is it of yours?"

"Your mother nearly died saving your life."

Stung by the implication, Elena's eyes narrowed. "You're the last person who has any right to accuse me of being a bad daughter."

There was a flicker of amusement in Ariadne's eyes, quickly gone. "No. But I don't think you understand that the curse was intended to activate immediately. The only reason you could have possibly survived as long as you have was because your mother must have poured enough energy into you to create a reserve that kept you alive."

Elena's eyes widened at the news. So it had taken the sacrifice of someone she loved to get her even this far. It seemed like a particularly cruel joke. "I'm sure you found that hilarious."

Ariadne flinched. "A long time ago, I thought I wanted my sister back." She closed her eyes, hand moving to grip the back of an empty chair. "But I didn't want her enough to risk my pride, and even if I hadn't made the worst mistake of my life I would have still lost her."

The last thing Elena wanted to do was believe her. But the pain in her voice had been too raw to be an act. "And you think she'll forgive you now?"

Her aunt took a deep breath, opening her eyes. "No. But I want it badly enough to risk everything I have."

Worry and anger tightened Elena's chest, and she moved away from the door toward her aunt. "Even her?"

The surprise on Ariadne's face made it clear that Elena had let too much of what she was feeling bleed into the words. "I swear to you I will die before I let your mother come to any more harm than I've already caused her," her aunt vowed, her gaze far too understanding. "But you have a choice to make."

"I've already made it." Elena's fingers curled. "I won't let them be hurt because of me."

Ariadne looked at her like she was an idiot. "Do you really think that losing you to the curse won't hurt them far worse than any spell from me could manage?"

"That's not—" The words froze on Elena's tongue, and she tried to force out a different variation. "They've prepared for that."

"Ah, the great lie, that one pain is kinder than another." The thread of bitterness in the words was far more convincing than sympathy would have been. Ariadne moved toward the door, patting her niece's shoulder as she walked by. "It seems we're more alike than we thought."

As the door closed behind her aunt, Elena was left with the sneaking suspicion that Ariadne had left with far more answers than she'd given.

CHAPTER 20

A Convincing Argument

Cam really wanted to punch something. If that ended up being his big sister, then so be it.

"Just tell me you're not going to do anything stupid," Laurel said again, watching her brother strap an extra dagger sheath to his thigh. There was no need for it—it would take eight arms to properly use all the weapons he was attaching to himself—but Nigel was probably too stupid to know that. And if Cam needed to intimidate the guy, he'd be ready.

No matter what happened, he wanted to be ready.

Laurel scowled at Cam's silence. "Listen, I'm not saying you shouldn't do this. I just want to hear you say, out loud, that you're not going to do anything that would get you arrested if law enforcement saw it."

Finally, he stopped long enough to glare at her. No matter how little she clearly thought of his emotional self-preservation, she usually trusted him to hold up his end of a fight. "I won't do anything you wouldn't do in my place," he snapped, wishing she'd go back to being the dangerous hothead he'd grown up with. "Is that comforting enough for you?"

"Of course not. Why do you think I'm worried about this in the first place?" When he didn't respond, she broke eye contact first. "Fine." She shook her head with a quiet curse. "At least let me go with you."

"So you can get arrested instead of me? No."

Lauren swore more loudly this time, slamming the flat of her hand against the hallway's stone wall. "You can't expect me to just stand here!"

Wholeheartedly understanding the sentiment, Cam throttled his anger back. "There's not much of a choice when you're dealing with magic. This is the first useful thing I've been able to do all day."

She sighed, temper draining out of her. "I know." Stretching her now-sore fingers, Laurel gave her brother an assessing look. "There's room to stick another dagger or two in your boots."

Cam huffed out a laugh, some of the pressure inside his chest easing. "I would, but I ran out."

"Amateur." Pulling a dagger out of her own boot, she flipped it around and handed it to him handle first. "Ever pick up Mason's little trick with one of these?"

"Those one-handed, mid-air spins he used to do? Not unless I keep my eye on it the whole time, which kind of misses the point." He added the dagger to his own arsenal.

"Doesn't mean you should abandon the idea completely. Just do one spin with it as you walk in. You can keep watch out of the corner of your eye for that long without the guy noticing." Her smile was dangerous. "If you can time it so the blade catches the light, it'll be even better."

Cam felt a rush of affection for his big sister. "You're scary."

"You always were a flatterer," she said, shaking her head. "I'm thinking Mason and I should head out in the morning. I'm not going to worry less if I'm back with the unit, but at least I'll have something to do to distract me."

He watched her, not sure what response she wanted. "Makes sense."

"As much as I hate it, there's nothing I can do here to back you up. And, I will admit, I have no right to try and drag you off the battle line," she said. "This is your fight."

She looked so sad and proud of him, all at the same moment, that Cam instantly felt uncomfortable. "Remember, I'm mostly window decoration at this point." He made the words more joking than he felt. "I probably won't even get to stab anybody."

"Oh, there's always hope." Genuine humor lit her eyes. "This Nigel sounds like enough of an idiot to need persuasion."

~

Elena was waiting for him just outside her mother's workroom, clearly listening to the discussion going on inside. As the two of them left the castle, she filled him in on the new developments. "If we can't make Nigel work with us, there's an embezzler who we might be able to use in the spell. Apparently, elves own several of the accounts he stole from, and he's terrified that they'll find him once he gets out in a few years."

Cam listened with only half an ear as they left the castle, trying to figure out what was going on inside Elena's head. He thought she'd offered to go with him so they could talk, but if they were going to keep pretending like nothing was wrong, she might as well go back to the workroom. "Sounds safer than picking someone who's in for a violent crime."

"That was the general consensus." Elena hesitated, then seemed to come to a decision. "I'm not sure he's our best choice, though. He doesn't think ahead, so he might agree without thinking through all the implications."

That sparked his temper. "So could Nigel," he shot back. "That doesn't mean we shouldn't ask them."

She gave him a sideways look that said too much for Cam to translate. "So you are upset with me."

The little restraint he'd had left snapped completely. "Of course I am!" he shouted, making the few people who were out on the street turn to stare. He'd spent the entire miserable day trying to be good. He'd let her keep her distance, no matter how much it had hurt, because he knew how fragile she must feel. He'd wanted to go beat his knuckles bloody against something, but he'd stayed close because he'd remembered how much it had mattered to her before.

But Elena hadn't been licking her wounds and getting ready for the next round. She hadn't cared about him being close, because she'd been ready to push them all away for good.

She might as well have kicked him in the stomach.

For a while, neither of them spoke. Then Elena cleared her throat. "I'm sorry." She paused again. "I wasn't avoiding you because of anything you'd done. It should have occurred to me how rude it would seem to you."

Cam's jaw tightened at the completely misdirected apology. Knowing he was going to shout if he said anything, he fixed his eyes straight ahead and kept walking.

Elena accepted this for about ten steps, then he felt her glaring at him again. "Listen, I thought we came out here so we could talk about this. I told you I was sorry, but if you need to shout at me than go right ahead." When he didn't respond, she reached out and grabbed his arm to stop them both. When he tried to pry her hand off his arm, she only tightened her grip. "You're the one who hated the ice routine so much, which gives you absolutely no right to do it now. Talk to me."

Cam pivoted around to face her. He'd been wrong about the glare—there was challenge in her eyes, not anger. He imagined she'd have a similar expression if she was facing down a dragon.

The fact that he would have killed to see it on her face an hour ago made his chest hurt. "You wanted to give up."

Elena froze, her eyes widening. "What?"

"Earlier. If your mom hadn't been there, you would have argued to not use Braeth's spell at all." Cam's voice was strained. "You didn't even argue that they should have kept the first spell going. You would have been wrong, but I would have at least understood where you were coming from."

Still looking shell-shocked, Elena hunted for something to say. "Cam, you have to understand—"

"No. I don't." He met her eyes, needing her to see how much he meant what he was saying. "I don't care if you try to keep Bishop from risking his neck for you. We all know the spell's dangerous, and if there was a better option I'm sure everyone would jump for it in a heartbeat. But you can't expect me to be okay with the fact that your life seems to be at the bottom of your priorities list."

Elena just stared at him, a dozen different emotions flickering in her eyes. She swore under her breath. "I'll show her how 'alike' we are," she muttered, pivoting around and striding down the street. Everyone's eyes followed her, then looked back to Cam as if he could offer some explanation.

He held his hands out helplessly, no more sure of what was going on than they were. Then he hurried to follow her.

~

Cam had been to the kingdom's one and only prison plenty of times—watching its perimeter was one of the border guard's responsibilities. It was half built into the mountainside, jutting out like the stone itself had reached out. A few prisoners always tried to escape—digging through the mountain was always popular, and only took about forty or so years to manage—and it was the guardsmen's job to round them up. It was generally more polite than letting the terrain kill them.

Thankfully for Nigel, he was still being kept in one of the row of jail cells down at the city guard headquarters, which was located in an old, sprawling building near the market. There was a minor stir when Cam and Elena arrived—the princess was an unexpected sight in this part of town. Though they'd mirror-called Ross, the sergeant apparently hadn't told anyone else they were coming.

"Your Highness!" The rookie on duty at the front desk went bug-eyed when he recognized Elena, scrambling to his feet and smoothing his uniform out into some semblance of order before saluting. "Welcome to the city headquarters. We didn't expect—" He cut himself off with a blush, caught without any kind of script. "I'm sorry. I didn't—it's just—"

"It's okay." Elena kept her voice gentle, clearly feeling as bad for the kid as Cam did. "We're here to see one of the prisoners."

The rookie looked confused at the word "we," obviously having not registered the presence of anyone else but the princess. When his eyes fixed on Cam, a familiar face to anyone who'd seen his mother's photo collection, it seemed to steady him a little. "Right away, Your Highness. I just need to get the paperwork from Sergeant Ross, and I'll be right—"

Before Cam could answer, Ross himself stepped through the doorway. "You don't bother royalty with paperwork, Palmer," Ross boomed, the same cheerful tone he used when delivering even his most colorful threats. It generally terrified the new recruits, which meant that he and Cam's mom got along wonderfully. "Let 'em through so they can get down to business."

"Thank you, Sergeant." Elena was in extra-gracious mode, which usually meant she was nervous. Now, though, Cam suspected she was trying to make some kind of point. "Both of you are wonderful examples of the kind of city guardsmen we can all be proud of."

The rookie blushed again, but Ross just laughed and waved them on. "Your man's in the cell on the end, Your Highness. Only one we got in lockup right now, so it'll be just the three of you." He met Cam's eyes briefly. "Figured you two could handle it yourselves?"

Understanding the unspoken offer, Cam nodded and guided Elena back toward the cells. Nigel was right where Ross said he would be, sitting on the edge of his cot with a vacant look. When he caught sight of Cam, he scrambled backwards hard enough that he kicked the cot out from under him. It shot forward, sliding until it hit against the metal bars and leaving Nigel to drop hard onto the cold stone ground.

Elena closed her eyes, pressing a fingertip to the bridge of her nose as if she could already feel the headache coming. Cam did nothing, having decided that even reaching for the handle of a weapon might give the idiot a heart attack.

Finally, Nigel managed to get upright again. "You can't kill me." The defiance he was trying for was ruined by the tremor in his voice. "There are officers just at the end of the hallway. They'll hear me if I scream."

"I didn't see them come running in when you had your accident," Cam said, voice mocking.

Nigel had already drawn in a breath, ready to keep talking. Cam could almost see the air freeze in the other man's lungs when he realized Cam was right. "Elena, stop him." Nigel sounded strangled as he pressed himself flat against the back wall. "You know this isn't civilized!"

"He's simply making conversation, Nigel," Elena soothed. "I would think you'd appreciate it after being locked away in here all by yourself."

"I'm not an idiot. I know a threat when I hear it." Genuine temper sparked in the prince's eyes, enough to make him forget that he'd been attempting to flee. "My father made threats all the time, pretending he was teaching me how to be a good son. He said it was for the kingdom's sake, but I knew better." His mouth settled into a pout, ruining whatever dignity his anger might have given him. "He was just resentful because I was so much more popular than dim little Frederick."

"Of course, he is." Elena's voice was sugar-sweet. If she'd tried using that tone with Cam, he would have known not to trust a single word that came out of her mouth.

Thankfully, Nigel didn't seem to notice. "It's a test. That's all it is. Young noblemen are given quests all the time, and it's only right that a king should have experience with this sort of thing." Nigel was pacing now, talking more to himself than either of them. "All I have to do is come back with the list all complete, an enchanted princess on my arm."

"Which is where I might be able to help." Elena spoke just loudly enough to cut off Nigel's monologue. "Do you need to bring the enchanted princess home with you, or do you just need to save her from a terrible fate?"

"Does that really matter?" Nigel threw his hands up in the air, completely missing Elena's insinuation. "You're the only cursed princess in the immediate vicinity, and the only one for miles who doesn't already have a prince or randomly heroic woodsman hanging off her arm!"

Elena put on her best sympathetic expression. "Unfortunately for you, that appears to be true."

Relief blossomed on Nigel's face at the thought of someone finally agreeing with him. "Exactly! And every time I try to have a civilized conversation with you about it, you sic one of your savage watchdogs on me!"

Cam smirked inwardly at the "savage watchdog" comment. He'd have to pass that one on to Dad. "So you're definition of 'civilized conversation' involves kidnapping and hired thugs?"

Nigel squawked a protest, but the much bigger surprise was the sidelong glare Elena shot him. "I'm handling this, Cam," she said. "If you can't be polite, perhaps it's best that you wait outside."

For just a second, Cam thought that she'd picked the stupidest time in the world to be mad at him. Then Elena's gaze flickered to Nigel before returning the glare, and Cam realized that she was trying to discreetly inform him that he had better stop screwing up her plan.

Which meant she'd cared enough to come up with one.

Fighting a sudden urge to grin, Cam bowed dramatically and took a step back towards the opposite wall. If she was ready to start fighting, he was happy to do whatever was necessary to back her up. "My apologies."

"Yes, well." Nigel sniffed, lifting his chin as he took his own step back. "My point was that I'm only here because my father put me in an impossible situation."

Elena took a few moments to respond. Cam could imagine her counting out the right number of dramatic beats in her head. "What if we could change that?"

Nigel's entire body froze, a wild light in his eyes that Cam remembered from the aborted kidnapping attempt. Cam's hand moved to the hilt of his sword, ready for anything.

Elena edged back slightly, giving Cam room to get between her and Nigel if necessary, but showed no sign of worry. "I find myself in the need of some princely assistance." She'd turned the sugar back on, full blast. "And if you'd be willing to help, I'm sure we could work together to convince your father to let you return—"

Nigel leaned forward before she'd even finished the sentence, lips puckered as if planning to kiss her through the bars. Elena stepped even further back as Cam moved in, reaching between the bars to grab Nigel's tunic. When his forward momentum was stopped by a fist, the prince looked confused. Then awareness came back into his eyes. "What is he doing?" Nigel squeaked, sweating a little as he tried to pry Cam's fingers off him. Any time he accidentally glanced at Cam, his eyes would dart away again. "You said you needed princely assistance!"

Behind him, Cam could hear Elena take a few slow, deep breaths, the kind that usually meant she was talking herself out of homicide. Only then did she touch his shoulder, a warning before she moved around him. He stepped sideways to give her more room, relaxing his grip only a little.

Once Nigel had stopped struggling, Elena tried again. "I'm afraid the task set before you is rather more complicated than a simple kiss." Though still encouraging, her tone was far more formal now. "I need your help with a spell."

Nigel stared at her in absolute confusion. "I'm not a witch or a sorcerer. I don't do spells."

Cam could feel Elena's hand tighten briefly on his shoulder. "I don't need you to cast the spell, Nigel. I need you to be the hero who protects me from it."

Comprehension seemed to dawn in Nigel's eyes. Then he opened his mouth and ruined it. "Does the spell involve a kiss?"

Cam thumped Nigel against the bar's just enough to make a point before letting him go again. "Stop asking stupid questions. She needs you to save her life."

The threat of danger in the last sentence had been a risk—the man clearly knew how to cower—but heroic fantasies would fit right in with the prince's usual delusions. Nigel's eyes lit. "Will I get a sword?"

Elena looked briefly upward at the ceiling before responding, as if praying for strength. "I don't think a sword will be necessary."

Nigel's expression turned mulish. "I want a sword. How can I look princely without one?"

Yeah, that was never going to happen.

"Then I'm sure we can arrange one for you." Elena lied, leaning forward slightly. "Now, are you ready to take on the quest?"

"I—" Nigel hesitated, then a rare burst of coherent thought hit. "Did you ever tell me what the quest was?"

Elena shook her head in mock regret. "Sadly, I can't tell you. It's a secret quest."

Nigel looked offended at that. "But how will everyone adore me if I come home after fulfilling a secret quest? I can't tell anyone if it's a secret!"

"Part of your reward for successfully completing your quest

will be a magnificent story to tell everyone," Elena said easily. Given how little time she'd had to work all this out, Cam was impressed by the level of detail. "And the fact that you saved a princess of the realm and received the grateful thanks of an entire kingdom will be entirely true."

That awful light was back his eyes, making Cam clench his fists. If Elena didn't need the creep for her plan . . ."And you'll come back to my kingdom with me?"

"Sadly, no. I'm afraid that would ruin the story."

Nigel pouted, then tried again. "But I can tell them anything I want?" he asked, moving close enough to wrap his hands around the bars.

Elena tensed at that, clearly less than thrilled by the possibilities that left open. "Only if I get your word, sealed by magic, that you will follow all of my instructions to the letter. Spells are precise, and if you step at all out of line it could ruin everything."

This time, it was Cam's turn to tense. If Braeth's spell was really that fragile, then suggesting Nigel had probably been one of Cam's worse ideas. The one thing the prince had proven any good at was causing chaos.

But Elena hadn't seemed willing to drag one of the other prisoners into this. And if he stopped her now, who knew if she'd be willing to look at other options?

Nigel hesitated. "You're not going to make me slap myself or anything embarrassing like that, right?"

"No," Elena said, her voice exasperated.

Nigel shrugged. "Fine. Now release me."

Elena shook her head. "Not without sealing your vow. Spit on your hand." When Nigel recoiled at the thought, she narrowed her eyes at him. "Do it."

Reluctantly, Nigel managed to spit a tiny amount of saliva

into his palm. He moved to stick his hand through the bars, flinching back when Cam stepped forward again. Elena made an exasperated noise, then grabbed his wrist and tugged it through the rest of the way.

"Now repeat after me. 'I will follow all of Elena Randall's instructions to the letter until I am released from my vow.'"

After he repeated the words, Elena murmured a phrase and sketched a symbol in the air over his palm. As she completed it, the spit glowed white and sank into his skin. Nigel jumped, shaking his hand violently. "What did you do?""It's a simple sealing. If you don't hold to what you've promised, the spell will deliver a powerful reminder shock." When Nigel eyed her with growing unease, Elena reassured him. "Not that you'll need it, of course. We just want to make sure that everything goes perfectly for your triumphant moment."

Nigel's face settled, and Cam told himself everything was going to be fine. Elena had thought of the same thing he had, and she'd made sure a contingency plan was in place. They could do this.

They had to.

MEMORY

Spring, 18 years ago

It was a week before Ariadne received a letter from Illiana, a single sheet of paper delivered via owl service so it would arrive more quickly. The words were simple, a seemingly calm explanation of her impending marriage and refusal to continue helping with the spell, but someone looking closely could see that many of them were tear-stained.

Ariadne was in no mood to look closely.

She raged, at first, sweeping things off tables and tipping shelves full of her sister's beloved books until it all came crashing to the ground. Then she sent a windstorm roaring through the tower, not caring what she left destroyed in her wake. She shouted. She cursed. She cried.

But for once, there was no one to listen.

Once she'd wrung herself dry, Ariadne paced back and forth through the destruction as she began to plan how to best make the king suffer for his crime. Even if he promised her all the jewels in his treasury, it would not be enough to atone for the fact that he had taken her sister.

Illiana had always been so quiet and shy—Ariadne should have known she'd be highly susceptible to the kind of romantic nonsense nobles were so good at. No matter how smart Ana was, she wasn't wise to the ways of the world. The king had blinded her, stolen her away.

That had to be the reason she'd turned away from her beloved sister. From her only family.

Ariadne merely had to find the best punishment for him, something worthy of the crime he'd committed against her. She sorted through the chaos she'd made, digging out her spell books for inspiration. Death would be viscerally satisfying, the more gruesome the better, but murder was illegal even for "evil" sorceresses. Torture ran into the same difficulty, proof that the WSG had defanged them all in an attempt to make them more commerce-friendly.

Unfortunately, she didn't have the power to go against the ruling body of all sorcery, which meant she was forced to play by their rules. Curses cast outside of a binding contract annoyed them severely, and they policed their ranks with a viciousness that made outside punishments pale in comparison. Still, the risk might be worth it if it could quell the rage and pain burning in her chest.

Unless, Ariadne stopped, struck by a possibility. She'd been hired to curse him with a century of unbreakable sleep—doing so would simply mean she was following through on her original, fully-authorized contract. True, it wasn't nearly as much suffering as she'd hoped to inflict on the man, but it would effectively remove him from Illiana's life.

Her sister would be hurt by the loss, of course, maybe even to the point of tears. But hadn't Ariadne been hurt? Hadn't she shed her own tears? Illiana would see reason in the end, and they would both forgive the other of their crimes. They were sisters, after all.

The only problem with this plan was that Ariadne still didn't have a sample of the king's blood. Acquiring one meant facing her sister head-on, a battle she had no interest in beginning. Ariadne knew she would win, of course—creativity beat out studiousness every time—but there was no pleasure in defeating part of your own heart.

Ariadne's mind caught on the last thought, examining it from all angles as she would a spell projection. Basic curses worked using biological triggers, but that was only because they were the most obvious representation of the target's essential nature. Most obvious certainly didn't mean only. In fact, there might be a better alternative, and the only reason no one else had found it was because they hadn't bothered looking. The world was full of people who were less clever than Ariadne was.

Still, even clever sorceresses couldn't just snap their fingers and make something revolutionary happen. Ariadne spent weeks studying emotional representation in spells, trying to find a stand-in that would let her reach out and curse the king. She relied more on experimentation than research, feeling hobbled that Illiana wasn't there to do her part. Rumors came of wedding plans between the king and his mysterious new bride, further inspiration for Ariadne to continue her research.

Finally, she found the key—heart's blood.

Ariadne drew the circle, clanking one more time at the childhood trinket of Illiana's that she'd incinerated to test her idea. Curses and binding spells often worked through physical ties, but emotions were generally the trigger used to break them. Why couldn't it work the other way? Or even better, combine the two and utilize the power in each. Shared blood and emotion tied Ariadne to her sister. Shared emotion tied Illiana to the king. If she was clever enough, Ariadne could use them both to create a channel that would arrow the curse straight into the king's treacherous heart.

She was always clever enough.

Ariadne stood in the middle of the circle, using a word and gesture to activate the projection of her original curse. Then, reaching inside herself, she spoke a simple spell she had written herself and called forth another thread of magic from deep inside her own chest. When she pulled it free, it was possible to see little flickers of her sister's blue magic in the middle of Ariadne's own purple light.

Then she wove it into the knot she had already made, speaking out loud to focus herself as she adjusted the aim on the spell. "I bind you to the newest star in my sister's heart," Ariadne murmured. "Send the new invader into the darkness and leave her free to come home again." She repeated the words, over and over, as she worked.

When the morning came, she was done.

~

Ariadne used the engagement party as cover. Knowing Illiana was smart enough to have put up magical protections, she slipped in using a magic dampener, careful makeup, and a stolen invitation. She felt a faint shiver as she passed through the shield, but the dampener made her read as a mere mortal and she passed through unharmed.

The party was exactly the kind of glittery nonsense their parents had always abandoned them for, a fresh betrayal on top of all the others. A backwater little kingdom like this one had barely enough nobles for a tea party, so there were plenty of business owners and other solid citizens dancing and snacking on plates of hors devours. It was ridiculous, and so far beneath her sister she could strangle someone.

She watched Illiana and the king mingle with their guests, noting the guarded look in her sister's eyes. Perhaps Ana was already questioning her decision, realizing that she'd made a mistake to trap herself in this ridiculous twisting castle in some mountainous backwater. Cursing the king would make Ana stubborn again, Ariadne suspected, but in the end she might even see it as a relief.

And if she didn't, Illiana couldn't care too much yet. She'd known the man barely any time at all, and she'd known her sister her whole life. She'd forgive her eventually.

Ariadne felt a flicker of doubt, quickly swallowed by a rush of hatred for the man who'd forced her to feel this way. She wanted the king to taste fear before the blackness took him.

Ariadne waited until formal receiving of gifts, shedding the magic dampener that had kept her hidden. The power returned as a visible blaze, clearly a part of the spell her sister had set up, and the crowd gasped appropriately and backed away from her.

From the twin thrones, the king rose. "Guards, seize her." His expression was furious, and he moved to stand in front of Illiana as if he had the right to do so. "I know your sister ruined your plans, but I won't let you hurt her."

"She's not the one I want to hurt!" Ariadne shot back, anger erasing any mocking speech from her mind.

"You can't touch him, Ariadne." Illiana stepped around the fool, her gaze hardening. "All offensive spells have been blocked by my magic, which means you won't even be able to stop the guards."

Ariadne lifted her chin, hurt that her sister would let her be dragged away like a common thief. "I've found the one avenue you weren't able to block, sister dear." She raised her hand, activating the curse.

The king should have collapsed. She'd seen it a thousand times in her mind, dreaming of this moment. Savoring it, knowing the sight would be the only revenge available to her.

When the moment came, however, it was Illiana who dropped to her knees.

For a second, Ariadne could do nothing but stare in horrified shock along with everyone else. Her little sister curled around her stomach, clutching it, as Ariadne's mind raced to figure out what could have happened.

Then Illiana looked up, eyes full of stunned betrayal, and mouthed a heartbroken question at her sister. My baby? Why?

Only then did Ariadne understand the full weight of what she'd done. Illiana wasn't far enough along to show yet, but the curse wouldn't have cared about that. All it knew was that there was an even newer star in her sister's heart.

One that would never survive a sleeping curse.

Ariadne reeled in horror at what she'd done. There would be no forgiveness for this. No reunion with the sister she'd so longed to have back. Even her career was in ashes, since she'd just murdered an unborn child. Her unborn niece or nephew.

Ignoring the heartbroken screaming inside her head, Ariadne vanished from the room.

CHAPTER 21

Risks and Rewards

She had drawn so many protective circles in the last few weeks that she'd started seeing them in her dreams.

Elena carefully finished the final glyph, trying to convince herself that this current circle would be her last one. It certainly qualified as her most complex, incorporating a few command glyphs used by the ancient evil sorcerers and a secondary protective circle often used by witches. She'd shut herself up in her mother's workroom early that morning so she would have extra time to work on it, the necessary reference books laid out open around her. The result was as close to perfect as human hands were capable of.

Of course, the circle wasn't what she was worried about. The sealing spell had been a last-minute addition to a hastily put-together plan, most commonly used to add more weight to a witness's statement in a court case. Unfortunately, it had fallen out of favor because it didn't work on people who truly didn't believe they had broken their vow.

She wasn't sure how even Nigel could manage that particular

trick, but she'd failed to predict what he was capable of before. Either way, it was a risk she would simply have to be ready to deal with on her own. Their current plan wasn't great, but she wasn't sure she had the courage for another one.

Elena sighed, sitting back on her heels. Honestly, she hadn't truly felt brave enough for even this attempt. But she would have done just about anything to stop the pain she'd seen in Cam's eyes.

You wanted to give up.

She took one more look at the picture of the witch's circle to double-check that her mirroring was accurate. The adaptation she'd made was listed in the spell book's notes, but it was so rarely used the author hadn't thought to make an illustration of it.

Shaking her head, she brushed away one of the tiny lines and redrew it with a small adjustment. If by some miracle she survived all this, Elena promised herself she'd have a talk with author.

She heard the door open, then a familiar voice. "Even Dame Kadrey would have to be impressed with that circle."

Elena looked up from her work, smiling at the sight of Robbie standing in the workroom doorway. She hadn't wanted to include him in the spell itself—too many people were already too close to danger—but she'd asked for suggestions about what elements to incorporate. "Come take a closer look." She waved him over. "I'd like to get a second opinion."

He looked surprised, then pleased, and quickly closed the door behind him. "You've worked with mixed magic more than I have." Still, he crossed the room and knelt down by the circle, giving it a thorough study. "I like how you structured it. The two circles should work together rather than draining each other's energy." He moved a hand closer to the chalked patterns, fingers hovering over one of the witchcraft-based elements. "You don't see the thorn circle used a lot. Witches don't tend to pull that one out unless they're going to battle."

She heard the question in his voice, phrased carefully enough that she could ignore it if she wanted to. "I thought it worked best with the glyphs Braeth gave me," she explained, gesturing to one of the symbols in question. "Their energy is dark enough that I needed a protective spell that wouldn't be overwhelmed."

Robbie nodded, ever the attentive student. "That's a lot of protection, though." When Elena didn't respond this time, he lifted his head to look at her. "The thorns are in both directions. That means you're watching out for offensive spells inside the circle, too."

More unspoken questions, harder to evade than the last ones. If Robbie ever decided to abandon witchcraft and join the police force, he'd be an intimidating interrogator. "Not that anyone was willing to provide me with diagrams. I had to do the mirroring from written notes, which was incredibly frustrating. You'd think no one cared about properly educating future generations."

"Elena." Robbie said her name exactly like Cam did when he was being serious, which was the last thing her control needed right now. "If you're worried that your aunt might try something, or the sealing won't be enough to keep Nigel in line—"

Elena shook her head, cutting him off. "I'm fine," she tried to assure him, not quite meeting his eyes. She hadn't made a promise not to lie to Robbie. "I'm just being paranoid." She didn't quite dare risk a smile, but she kept her voice light. "With two people who have made attempts on my life in the same room with me, it seemed like the smartest attitude to take."

She could feel him still watching her, solemn and more

insightful than she would have liked, and she wished fiercely that she would get the chance to finish seeing him grow up. She suspected it would be a sight to behold.

Throat tightening, Elena returned to her work on the circle to hide whatever expression might be on her face. When Robbie spoke, it seemed the questioning was done. "I made you something."

Taking a deep breath to steady herself, looking up at him again. "Please tell me it's a charm to make Cam less argumentative."

"Sorry, even magic doesn't have the power to silence the Merricks." He fished a small bottle out of his pocket and handed it to her. "It's a potion meant to help people think quickly and clearly. It's one of the first things a witch learns how to brew." He looked faintly embarrassed. "We tend to use it for tests, but I thought it might help when you're untangling the curse."

"Thank you." She took the bottle, touched. "I'm sure it will."

Robbie's cheeks colored a little, and he cleared his throat. "I made one for your mom and aunt, too." He straightened. "I gave your aunt's to your mom. I'm not ashamed to admit she terrifies me a little bit."

Elena raised an eyebrow, letting herself enjoy the teasing. "My aunt, or my mother?"

As he left the room, he shot her one last grin. "I'll leave that up to your imagination."

After he was gone, Elena accepted the fact that she'd have to follow him relatively soon. She'd stretched out drawing the circle as far as she reasonably could, but Cam was more than likely awake by now. She'd already broken their unspoken agreement that she be there by the time he opened his eyes.

Standing, she lifted her skirts and carefully stepped outside the circle. Examining it one final time, she sketched a quick shape in the air and murmured the words of a basic preservation spell. Now there was no risk of the shapes being smudged or washed away, at least until the original enchantment had been lifted.

Looking down at the bottle Robbie had given her, she smiled a little and downed it in one long swallow. Then she squared her shoulders, getting ready to face everyone downstairs. All she needed was a few more minutes.

When she heard the door opening behind her again, Elena realized she'd stretched her window of time too far. She stole a few extra seconds to school her features. "I'm sorry I've been up here so long. I'm afraid my perfectionist tendencies took over."

"Or you were hiding."

Elena turned at the sound of Cam's voice, surprisingly free of the frustration she would have expected from such a statement. It was, however, far too solemn, which was worrying in its own way. "Of course I was. Braeth and Dr. Flyte have been squabbling so much about the technical details that I've been tempted to keep score."

He smiled briefly, hair still a little mussed from sleep. She curled her fingers in, fighting back the impulse to cross the room simply to smooth it down. Just to touch him. "If you keep score, that also means you need a referee," he said, thankfully unaware of her thoughts. "No one would be dumb enough to take on that job." As he spoke, he moved close enough to study the circle she'd just made. "I really need to steal some of Robbie's spell books."

"Feel free to make use of mine as well." Elena watched him, biting her tongue against the impulse to explain the different elements she'd used. She'd never been tempted to drag his father into the day-to-day details of what she did, but the thought of being able to discuss her magic with Cam was far more appealing than it should have been. "Some get bogged down in technical minutiae, but I can point you to the authors who remember they're speaking to human beings."

"I'll still probably need you or Robbie to translate." He crouched down, fingers tracing the air just above one of the inner thorns, then looked up at her. "You're worried Nigel will find a way to get around the sealing spell, aren't you?"

Elena's confusion immediately transformed into annoyance as she realized what had happened. "It seems as though Robbie's already doing plenty of translating. Did you ask him to do some reconnaissance, or was that all his idea?"

Cam's look was entirely unrepentant. "He's worried about you. He also knows how worried I am about you, and it was either distract me with this or watch me wear holes in the stone floor downstairs." He straightened, carefully stepping around the circle towards her. "He opted for this."

Elena scowled, not finding anything in his explanation she could argue with. Frustrated, words slipped out she hadn't intended to say out loud. "Do you know how incredibly difficult it is to be worried about by so many—" She cut herself off, surprised and a little appalled by what had slipped out.

Cam, however, nearly smiled again. "Have you met my family?"

Her eyes narrowed. "Then you should be more sympathetic. And, by extension, less annoying."

"Tough." Eyes still bright, he moved around the rest of the circle. They were only a few steps apart now, and she moved to close the distance between them without even thinking about it. "Because as much as I wanted to hit my sister over the head with something heavy, your family has the right to completely lose their minds wanting to protect you."

The sudden tenderness in his voice caught in her chest, making it ache. Fighting was so much safer than doing something absurd like burst into tears. "So your family's response to crisis is to officially adopt me? I hate to say it, but your self-preservation instincts are terrible."

Suddenly, the humor disappeared from his face. "They're better than yours."

"Oh no. You don't get to do that." Elena stepped towards him, jabbing a finger into his chest. "I've been trying."

"How hard?" Cam snapped back. "If you were this worried about Nigel doing something, why didn't you tell me? And if you didn't think I could do any good, why didn't you tell someone else who could? You're not alone in this!"

"I should be!" Elena cursed herself for the sentence as soon as it came out of her mouth, and she cursed herself for being an idiot as she moved to lock the door. Then, for good measure, she threw a quick silencing spell around the room. It would only make things a thousand times worse if her mother overheard any of this.

The fact that Cam had heard it was going to cause her enough problems. His expression had gone hard again, eyes full of so many emotions she couldn't pick them apart enough to identify them. "I'm going to pretend you didn't just say that."

Elena was so unspeakably grateful for his response that she forced her temper back into submission. "You're overreacting about Nigel. Of course there's a possibility that the shocks won't be enough to get him to listen to my instructions, but even if he doesn't we'll just start the spell over again. The only time it would even be a problem is if he steps out of alignment and the spell misaims. The protective circle should keep the rest of you safe, but if the spell reflects back at me it might reverse—"

Elena finally managed to get her mouth closed, barely resisting the urge to clamp her hand over it. She hadn't known she'd even been thinking that last bit, but now that she'd said it the logic was undeniable. If the magic reflected in just the wrong way, it was possible that the spell could end up binding Elena to Nigel rather than the other way around. If that happened, she didn't know if they could ever get Braeth's spell to work properly.

Of course, the other option was to remove the protective circle and leave one of her family at risk of being bound to Nigel.

Cam watched the horror bloom across her face. "Tell me this is the first time you've thought of this."

Not trusting herself to open her mouth again, Elena just nodded. The original evil sorcerers had probably used mind control to solve the problem, but those spells had been eradicated from the books more than a century before. Even if Braeth could remember it, they'd be committing an even worse crime than the one that had left them in this mess in the first place.

A muscle tightened in Cam's jaw. "And why have none of the other mighty sorcerers and sorceresses downstairs thought of this?"

Unfortunately, that question required something more than a yes or no answer. "Robbie gave me a potion to help me think more clearly."

Cam cursed, closing his eyes a second. "I'll have mom and dad take Nigel back. We'll go with one of the other prisoners."

"Absolutely not." More time was the last thing any of them needed. "There's only a small chance the spell will go wrong in exactly the way I described. And don't even try to tell me you didn't plan for Nigel doing something ridiculous. You probably have six different contingency plans, depending on the particular flavor of idiocy he attempts."

"Of course I did. But those plans are to stop him from hurting you, not stop him from accidentally tying you to his dangerously incompetent self for the rest of your life." He stalked towards her, the frustration in his voice seemingly aimed as much at himself as it was at her. "I thought if he tried anything, we could just whack him in the head and start over again. But the look on your face made it clear that's not going to work."

"It might." Unless her mother and aunt took Robbie's potion, and realized the same things she had. She'd have to figure out a way to steal them back. "I was thinking of worst case scenarios. It could be fine."

"See, I can't even tell if I really am overreacting or if this is some secret suicide tendency of yours I can't figure out!" Cam's voice was climbing by the second, the words hitting Elena hard even if he wasn't thinking clearly enough to aim them. "I need to be able to trust you!"

"How dare you!" Livid, she shoved at him. The fact that he barely moved only made her angrier. "Who in all the gods' names do you think I'm doing this for? Do you know how hard it is to keep trying like this? It took years for me to make peace with the fact that my life was over, and now I—I—"

When her brain caught up with what she had said, Elena gave in and clamped her hands over her mouth. Obviously, this was a sign that she should just stop talking permanently, since any kind of brain-to-mouth filter she'd once had access to had vanished along with the ice inside her.

Cam just stared at her, all traces of anger replaced by sheer, unadulterated shock. "Who are you doing this for?" he asked, voice far less steady than it had been.

All she could do was stare back, horrified to realize her eyes were filling. Elena didn't dare move her hands away from her mouth, not at all certain what would come out next if she did. She thought back to all of those careful conversations with Dr. Flyte, all those times when he'd seemed almost desperate to get some kind of strong emotional reaction out of her.

Clearly, all he'd had to do was shove Cam into her life. The man had made her lose her mind.

The shock on Cam's face had melted into something almost like wonder, and his own eyes were suspiciously wet. "Elena," he asked again, gently enough to break her in half. "Who are you doing this for?"

She squeezed her eyes shut, the tears leaking down her cheeks. Slowly, carefully, she felt Cam pull her hands away from her mouth. "I'm sorry," she whispered.

"Don't be sorry." Cam's voice was rough with emotion. "Don't ever be sorry for something like this." He lifted one of her hands to his lips, placing a gentle kiss against the palm. He chuckled against her skin, the sound just a little wild. "I was trying to figure out how to tell you myself."

Elena's eyes flew open. "What?"

"Oh, don't play dumb like that with me." The wry humor on his face didn't hide the way his voice shook a little. And his eyes, his eyes held everything. "I'm amazed you didn't pick up on it before now."

She swallowed, still capable of doing nothing more than staring at him. The potion Robbie had given her was completely useless now, her brain stunned enough to be beyond even magical assistance. She'd long ago decided that romantic love wasn't something she could afford to have in her life, and now that it had suddenly appeared she found herself entirely unprepared for it. "You could have given me a hint," she managed finally,

A challenging light flared in his eyes. Then, after a single, breathless moment, he bent down and kissed her.

The feel of Cam's lips against hers, the taste of him on her tongue, was as wonderful as all those stupid romances said it would be. He tried so hard to be gentle, but Elena would have liked nothing more than to disappear entirely into the rush of feeling he sent coursing through her. No more curse, no more deadline, just this moment stretching on for eternity.

His hands cradled the sides her face, his touch utterly tender as he showed her everything she'd never even imagined. Weightless with the light and heat of it, she clutched him as if he was the only thing keeping her from flying away.

But such wonders couldn't last forever, no matter how much she wanted to. When the kiss ended, Cam seemed as reluctant to pull away as she was. "Does that work?" he murmured.

She was horribly embarrassed to feel her eyes filling again. "You cheated," she whispered, wrapping her arms around him and holding on for dear life.

Cam let out a breath as his own arms came around her. "If I'd known it was an option, I would have cheated a long time ago."

She wanted to laugh, even though it didn't make the slightest bit of sense. What had just happened had raised the stakes for the spell infinitely higher than she'd ever wanted them to be, and it would only make dealing with everything that much harder. According to any kind of logic, admitting she loved Cam was almost as terrible an idea as falling in love with him in the first place.

But that wasn't enough to stop the wild, bubbling happiness inside her. Cam loved her back. Now everything mattered so much more than it had just a few hours before.

She pulled back enough to look up at Cam, thinking furiously. "I can use the freezing spell on Nigel as soon as he steps into the circle. It doesn't last very long, but if I have everything prepared in advance I might have just enough time to finish before he unfreezes. That way, he won't have the chance to try anything."

Cam looked worriedly down at her. "If he sees you toss a restraining spell at him, he may try and jump you no matter how hard the sealing spell shocks him."

Not to mention the fact that Dr. Flyte would raise a protest that would waste valuable time. But she wanted to live, more than she had in a very long time, and she didn't see another option. "We aren't going to be able to completely eliminate my risk in all this, Cam."

An intent look came into his eyes as he lifted his hands to cup her face again. "No, but there's a way we can lessen it."

CHAPTER 22

Battle Royale

Cam took a deep breath. "I'll take Nigel's place in the spell."

On the surface, he knew that the idea sounded stupidly self-sacrificial. That was his first thought when it had occurred to him somewhere in the middle of his and Elena's argument, and he'd initially rejected it as part of the nonsense people always spouted when they were in love.

But it made tactical sense, and the part of Cam's brain that could still think clearly knew that. The only way to completely eliminate the risk was to make sure that everyone involved would do exactly what they were supposed to. They had to want it as much as Elena did.

More, probably.

Elena, naturally, didn't feel the same way. For a second, she looked absolutely terrified. "No." Then she wrenched away from him, fury flooding in to replace the fear. "Never."

"It's our best option." He reached for her, then decided it was probably a bad idea. "It's the best shot we have of making sure the spell goes perfectly."

"Which means that you'll be the one the curse gets redirected at!" She stared at him as if he'd lost his mind, fingers curling like she wanted to physically shake some sense back into him. "Even if everything goes exactly according to plan with Braeth's spell, all that happens is the deadline falls on your head instead of mine. We're trying to fix this, not make it worse!"

"You'll fix it." He tried to put all his determination and faith into what he was saying. "If we can make this work like everyone thinks, sending me under gives you the best conditions for being able to untangle the curse like you talked about."

"But what if that's still not enough? What if I still fail you?" Her eyes filled again, and she swiped her hand across them to get the tears out of the way. "And what about your parents? Your siblings? They love you just as much as I do, and it won't even be their fault!"

Every word was a kick to his heart, just like he knew she'd meant them to. But if he had to, he'd face everyone he loved down and explain just like he was trying to do with Elena. "Risking our lives for the greater good is the family business. They won't like it, but they'll have to understand."

"I don't!" She was fierce now, her entire stance screaming defiance. "If I wouldn't let Bishop put himself up on the chopping block, do you really think I'm going to let you risk your life over this?"

Cam's instinctive stubbornness immediately protested the word 'let,' but the rest of him smacked the thought into silence. Instead, he held his hands up in a supplicating gesture. "Explain to me how this is different than someone coming at you with a sword."

That seemed to throw her for a second. "This is a magical

attack," she said, grabbing for the first answer that came to her. "When that happens, it's my job to protect *you*."

He almost smiled at that. "Want me to get out the document outlining my job description? Because I can promise that little detail isn't written down anywhere."

"It should be," she snapped back, eyes narrowed. "And it will be, even if I have to throw a sleeping spell at you and shove you in a closet for a week."

He had no doubt she would do exactly that if she felt she had to. Unfortunately for her, she'd need backup in order to be able to pull it off. "Won't work. You know every single person in the circle is going to agree with me on this. They'd be able to undo anything you threw at me."

Fear flickered back across her face as she realized he was right. She squeezed her eyes shut again. "Don't do this," she whispered. "Please."

Needing to touch her, Cam walked over and put his hands on her shoulders. "I'm not doing this as your bodyguard," he said quietly, voice thick with all the worry and hope of the last few days. When she opened her eyes, he bent his head enough that she'd have to meet his gaze. "I'm doing this as the man who's already planning his collection of embarrassing pictures of our future children."

Her eyes were wet. "You'll be alone."

"Not at all." When she shot him a disbelieving look, he pressed a kiss against her cheek. "I have you watching my back."

She inhaled shakily, bracing her hands against his sides as if she could keep him in place. "There might—"

"I am apparently woefully behind in the castle gossip. I had expected to interrupt a shouting match."

At the sudden sound of Braeth's voice—the wraith had a really bad habit of using his shadow trick to melt into rooms while other people were distracted—Elena flinched as if realizing what she'd been about to say. Shaking her head, she yanked herself backwards and away from Cam again. He let her go, knowing that holding her wouldn't help things any.

"A shouting match isn't the only reason to put up a silence shield." Elena glared at Braeth, turning away from Cam just enough that there was no chance to even make eye contact. "And we seriously need to figure out a way to put a bell on you."

"I look forward to your attempts." The wraith's hood shifted as he looked back and forth between the two of them, as if weighing the sudden change in emotional temperature. "I suspect, though, that you were discussing matters far more serious than romance."

Cam considered whether getting Braeth on his side would help matters or just make Elena more determined not to listen. "We were talking about—"

Elena stepped forward, raising her voice to talk over the top of his. "Did you need one of us for something, or have you simply gotten bored of arguing with Dr. Flyte?"

Cam pushed ahead before the wraith could respond to Elena's question. "We were talking about the possibility of Nigel moving at the wrong time and the spell echoing off one of her protective circles. She's afraid it—"

She shot him a furious look. "I simply said it might—"

Cam raised his voice. "She's afraid the spell will reflect and make her Nigel's shield instead of the other way around."

The invisible wind around Braeth stopped moving for a second. "There are measures we can take," he said. "If we require him to take an oath—"

"She did, and followed through with the sealing spell I'm sure you're about to suggest," Cam interrupted, keeping his eyes on Elena. "She thinks there's some way he can get around it."

Braeth turned to Elena, who tried to look anywhere else before responding. "The sealing spell sometimes doesn't work if the person doesn't believe they've truly broken their vow." She sounded like the words were being dragged out of her. "I'm not certain enough how Nigel's mind works to be sure."

"True." The wraith made a sound that might have been a sigh. "It's been centuries since I cast a compulsion spell, but I'm certain it would take me only a few minutes to remember the specifics."

"No." Elena's voice was firm. She was doing the same thing he was, talking to Braeth while her glare was only for Cam. "Those leave the person too suggestible, which means he'll try to follow anything and everything that sounds even vaguely like a command. Besides, this is all an overreaction. I can handle whatever magical risks Nigel might cause, and just as well as Cam can handle the physical dangers."

"There's enough risks in all this as it is," Cam responded. "Now is not the time to be taking on more."

"Exactly!" There was a brief light of triumph in Elena's eyes. "Especially if the person taking on the risks wasn't in danger in the first place!"

"It seems wisest to take this discussion downstairs," Braeth cut in, bony fingers gesturing towards the door.

Elena whirled on him. "My mother does not need to be involved in this."

The wraith just looked at her for a moment, not responding, then turned to Cam. "I was referring to the fact that your parents have arrived with Nigel. They are waiting in the throne room until we have further instructions for them."

By the time Cam looked back at Elena, she was already out the door. He indulged himself with the most creative curse he could think of, then glared at Braeth. "You couldn't have waited five minutes?"

The wraith didn't threaten him with lightning, which was probably as close to an apology as he ever got. "You offered yourself in the prince's place," he said instead.

If he was about to get lectured in "romantic nonsense," he was definitely going to have to hit something. "It's our smartest option right now."

"Yes, it is," Braeth agreed, surprising him. "I will inform the others."

That was Cam's cue to head for the throne room. He ran the first part of the way, but after the first few panicked looks from the staff he forced himself to slow to a quick walk. Running guardsmen were the first sign of disaster, especially if they were in uniform.

When he got to the throne room, he found Elena had closed (and possibly barricaded) the throne room doors behind her. Cam steeled himself for the fight he knew was coming. In comparison, taking part in the actual spell would be a piece of cake.

With that less-than-happy thought, he pushed the doors open.

The throne room was relatively small, functional rather than ornate, decorated only by a few tapestries on the wall. There were no barricades, but the four people waiting inside would be enough trouble on their own. Nigel was standing next to Cam's father, scanning the room with the disdain of someone already making plans to redecorate. Given the fact that he was still wearing his prison uniform, and smelled like he hadn't bathed in a week, he really had no room to talk.

Elena was in the opposite corner of the room talking to Cam's mother. His mom was in uniform, just like his dad, and Elena was still in her work dress. Whatever they were talking about must have been pretty serious, their voices low and Elena's hands gripping Marie's arms tightly. A dozen different emotions shifted across his mother's face, one after the other, and Cam looked away before he could identify any of them.

Instead, he headed over to his father and Nigel. The prince, catching sight of Cam, immediately started trying to back away. Since Alan had a firm hold on the chain linking the handcuffs, however, all that happened was he nearly ended up falling backward over his own arms.

Both Cam and his father ignored this. "Nigel won't work for the spell," Cam told Alan, deliberately using his "making a report" tone of voice. "You should take him back to the station."

Nigel, having some trouble finding his feet again, protested. "You can't have these heathens drag me all the way here only to be dragged back again! The princess specifically requested my assistance!"

Alan, who had been watching Marie and Elena's discussion with an intensity Cam knew wasn't good, turned back to his son. "I'll need a few more details than that."

"It turns out that if Nigel moves at the wrong time, he could screw up the spell so completely we won't be able to cast it again." He pointed at Nigel, finger only a few inches from the man's nose. "And if a wrong step is enough to make that happen, think of all the other damage he could accidentally do."

Nigel drew himself up to his full height, looking offended. "A prince does nothing they don't intend to."

Both men ignored him. "Elena said something about having a magical contingency plan," Alan said. "Has that gone into effect?"

"Apparently, there's a way for Nigel to get around it just by being himself." Cam decided it was safest not to go into detail. "Elena seems to think it's a real possibility."

"Don't talk about me as if I'm not standing here!"

Not looking at Nigel, Alan weighed what his son had told him. "What if one of us stayed in the circle with him?"

"Unless he knocked us off balance for a second, or we accidentally jerked him back too hard. Then we'd just be another potential factor that could cause the knife to slip, or the spell to be misaimed." Cam shook his head. "Without knocking them unconscious, it's hard to keep someone absolutely still. And if we knock him unconscious, he apparently can't do his part of the spell."

"You're not going to knock me unconscious! That wasn't part of the agreement!" Nigel insisted. Then there were a few beats as his brain finished working. "Wait, there's a knife?" His voice went higher. "I'm certain no one mentioned a knife when this was described to me."

Both men ignored him as Alan kept thinking. "Could Robbie focus on freezing Nigel while everyone else is working on the binding? If he had to, you could hold onto Nigel while he froze you both. Then you'd be there in case there's a gap between the spell castings."

Even in the middle of what was potentially the worst day of his life, Cam couldn't help but be impressed. "Does Robbie know you pay that much attention when he talks about magic?"

The look on his father's face made it clear that he wasn't about to be distracted. "Answer the question."

"Someone needs to answer *my* question," Nigel cut in, though no one else was paying any attention. "And I did not say I would be frozen! How am I supposed to properly save the princess if I'm stuck there like some idiotic statue?"

Cam shook his head. "You know as well as I do that the more moving parts a plan has, the more opportunity there is for one of those parts to go wrong and make the entire plan backfire," Cam tried, taking refuge in the fact that he was still being completely honest. "Elena says that sorcery, especially on a spell like this, is all about absolute precision, and witchcraft is all about instinct and the ebb and flow of nature. There's no predicting how the two types of spells will interact with each other, and right now we don't have time to test it."

Alan's jaw went tight, as if the words confirmed something he'd already known. "You're determined to take Nigel's place."

Nigel started laughing. "That's absurd."

Cam watched his father's face for any sign of reaction. "Tactically, it's the best move we have."

"But that's not the reason you're doing it," Alan said flatly.

It wasn't an accusation, which would have angered Cam but not entirely surprised him. It felt more like a demand, and Cam knew his father wouldn't back his play unless he knew the exact reasoning for it. Out of the corner of his eye, he could see Elena and his mom still in intense discussion, and he realized the only answer his father would accept.

Cam took a deep breath, hoping he wouldn't have to keep doing this. "If this was happening to Mom, where would you want to be?"

At first, there was no reaction. Then Alan's body sagged slightly, as if accepting the weight of the last news he'd wanted to hear. Before he could answer, Nigel took advantage of the distraction.

His father reached out, making a grab for them, but the prince scrambled out of the way. The cuffs missing Alan's fingers by less than an inch.

Cam made his own grab for the prince, catching him by the upper arm. It was only then that he realized that his father had relaxed his grip for a split second, too affected by his son's news to pay his usual strict attention. His father made a frustrated sound, then grabbed for Nigel again. He connected this time, making sure to get a firm grip before scowling at both the prince and his son.

"Really?" Not sure if he should be angry or hurt, Cam narrowed his eyes at his father as Nigel struggled. "You're not even slightly pleased by the possibility you might get grandchildren out of this?"

Nigel huffed. "As if she'd want you to father her children."

Alan shot them both another glare. "We're not having this discussion here."

Nigel yanked himself sideways so hard that the fabric of his sleeve tore, but it was enough to get him free. The two men lunged again, but Nigel scrambled out of the way to stop well beyond arm's reach. "Someone needs to start listening to me now!" the prince announced, loudly enough that it caught the attention of Elena and Cam's mother as well. Abandoning their discussion, they hurried over.

"Oh, we're listening," Alan said, voice cold. He shifted his weight, looking ready to charge if needed, but Cam knew he technically shouldn't even be out of the splints yet.

"Nigel, stay right where you are," Elena ordered. "We need to talk about this."

Nigel took a wary step backwards. "Don't—" That was as far as he got before his hand jerked with the sealing spell's shock, and he pouted as he cradled his hand against his body. "Fine. We should talk."

Elena put her hands on her hips. "You agreed to do this, Nigel. You gave me your *word*." she said, any attempts at gentler persuasion abandoned.

Nigel, following long habit, missed the menace entirely. "You told me you needed me to be heroic, not that you were going to be using a knife anywhere near my person." He sounded breathy and more than a little panicked. "Weaponry of any kind was most certainly not mentioned when we initially spoke!"

"It's a simple prick with the tip of a knife blade," Elena said, her voice cool. "Far less than anything you'd face on a real heroic quest. I assumed that a prince of your experience would be familiar enough with swords that a knife would barely make you blink."

Out of the corner of his eye, Cam could see his mother circling around to take Nigel from his blind side. Cam started slowly inching sideways, ready to cover him from the opposite side.

Nigel looked flustered at Elena's declaration. "Well, of course, but—" He floundered briefly, looking for an acceptable way to end the sentence. "But I should have been informed beforehand. That would have been the dignified thing to do."

"Now you have been." Elena stepped forward just enough that Cam could see her out of the corner of his eye. "Since that's been settled, you need to come with us to the upstairs workroom so we can get started."

Nigel took another step back. His hand twitched like it had been shock again, but it clearly hurt him far less than it had last time. "I'm no longer sure that I do."

Elena's face shifted like she'd just mentally kicked herself. "I am instructing you to come upstairs with us, and reminding you that you vowed to follow all my instructions." There was an iron formality in her voice. "If you do this, you'll finally be able to go home."

"Not like this! I'm supposed to go back a hero!" Nigel kept moving backwards, and despite Elena's corrected language the sealing spell didn't activate at all. Cam shifted around, ready to cut him off, but Nigel saw him and stumbled sideways.

Unfortunately, he caught sight of Marie standing far closer to him than he'd expected. He changed direction quickly enough that he nearly tripped, running in the opposite direction.

He could hear Elena murmur a quick spell, and Nigel froze mid-stride, Elena's spell catching him with one leg lifted. Momentum and lack of balance caused him to tip forward gently, crashing face-first onto the floor. Cam wished the idiot had hit the ground harder.

Muttering insults that seemed as much at himself as at Nigel, Alan bent down and hauled the prince's dead weight back into a relatively upright position, leaning Nigel against his body.

"We have thirty seconds before the spell wears off," Elena announced, then jabbed a finger in Cam's direction. "Don't say a word. If I hadn't phrased the first command so poorly, this wouldn't have happened."

"It's not your fault. Nigel could have pulled something like this at any time, which meant we would have been doing that little comedy routine in the middle of the spell." He was torn between sympathy and frustration, landing in an uneasy spot in the middle. "Which you would have been right in the middle of."

"I'd rather deal with that than the fear that I'm going to leave you unconscious for a century!" she snapped back, reaching for Nigel to yank his frozen form out of Alan's hands. When he didn't let go, Elena shifted her glare to him. "Don't you dare tell me you'd rather put Cam at risk than this idiot."

Alan's gaze flickered over to Cam before returning to Elena. "I understand why he's doing it," he said quietly, then his voice firmed. "And he is right about Nigel being dangerous. Since the contingency plan didn't work, it's too much of a risk to try the spell with him in it."

Expression mutinous, Elena didn't respond. Instead, she pulled harder on Nigel, putting all of her weight into it. She was still doing it when the spell ended, the no-longer-frozen prince going lax suddenly enough to catch Elena and Alan by surprise. When he dropped, they went with him.

Cam and Marie ran forward as the three struggled, but Nigel showed a moment of rare intelligence and landed a solid kick straight at Alan's still-sore leg. A second kick made him let go, and Nigel escaped the pile and ran for the exit before either Cam or Marie could grab him.

As they ran to follow, Cam caught Elena's eye. "This one's your fault."

She ignored him.

CHAPTER 23

Welling Up

Elena knew they should call the castle guards, but that would only serve to make the entire mess more embarrassing than it already was.

Also, there was a fairly significant chance she was going to burst into tears sometime in the next half hour, and the fewer people who were there to see that the better. She was horrified at how she'd spoken to Marie, but she suspected she'd end up saying far worse before all this was over. Her potion-sharpened thinking kept trying to agree with Cam—including Nigel in the spell would be far too risky—but the desperation crawling up her throat didn't care.

If they didn't find Nigel, though, she'd have no choice. She, Cam, Alan, and Marie headed for the exit, which was where any sane escapee would go, but there was no sign of him. None of the castle staff had seen someone desperately fleeing, and the newly cowed guards were still standing guard at the front gate.

Marie's eyes were furious as they headed back into the castle. "If he's hiding somewhere—"

"I doubt it." Alan shook his head, his lack of expression a sign that he was even more furious than his wife. "They lock most of the doors when they're not in use, and Nigel doesn't have the luck to stumble across the handful of rooms that are open."

"You mean like the luck he'd need to escape three armed soldiers and a sorceress?"

Alan grimaced. "Fine. I'll start on this floor. Each of you take one of the above floors and we'll work our way up."

Marie took the next floor, and Cam and Elena hurried up to the third floor. "You take this one, and I'll head upstairs," Elena said quickly, hurrying up the stairs before he could argue. She couldn't risk him trying to convince her again, not until she had Nigel back and Cam's parents close enough to help with a counterargument. Alone, she was far too susceptible to him.

She heard him hurry up the stairs after her, catching her wrist before she could make the first turn. "Elena—" When she tugged her arm out of his grip, he caught it again. "Elena, wait."

Elena stopped moving, but didn't turn around. Her heart was pounding for reasons that had nothing to do with physical activity, a metallic taste rising up in her throat. "I can't. We need to find Nigel."

His grip tightened briefly, thumb stroking along the soft skin on the inside of her wrist. It took real effort to repress the shiver. "Elena, don't do this. Please."

"First you get mad at me because you didn't feel I was doing enough, and now you're upset that I won't stop." The words were a last, desperate defense, designed to wound. "You need to decide what you want out of me, Cameron."

Cam pulled on her wrist firmly enough to turn her around. His face was stony, just like his father's, but his eyes were raw.

"You. Alive and safe and next to me. That's all I've ever wanted out of this."

She knew the helpless pain in his voice, a twin to the jagged ache in her own chest. "And you're willing to risk everything for it." Her voice was ragged. "But what about me?"

He looked incredulous. "I don't want you to risk anything."

"You're asking me to risk you." Elena could feel the desperation inside her collapse into pure, unadulterated grief. "I would rather risk my own life a thousand times over than lose you. And if the mirror spell works and I can't break the curse, you'll fall asleep without me." Her voice cracked, eyes filling with all the tears she'd been holding back. She'd always considered sleeping for a hundred years to be the worst possible future, but having to stand aside while Cam slept for a hundred years would be far worse. "Don't make me be the one who's left behind."

Cam's eyes widened, and he opened his mouth to speak just as Elena heard someone thundering down the stairs behind her. He let go of her wrist, and they both turned around just in time to see a maid come hurrying around the last corner. "Princess, there's—" The girl stopped as she took in the tear tracks on Elena's cheeks, looking back and forth between her and Cam in an awkward panic. "I'm sorry, but I, I thought I should—"

"It's fine," Elena said firmly, her tone quelling any potential questions as she swiped away the wetness in as business-like a manner as possible. "What did you need to tell me?"

The permission seemed to bring the maid immense relief. "I saw that strange man who the constables dragged out of the palace before." She pointed upstairs. "I didn't know he wasn't a delivery man the first time, but when I saw him up by your chambers again—"

Before the girl could finish the sentence, Elena had already pushed past her and up the stairs. Cam was right behind her as they both hurried to her chambers, where Bishop and one of the pages were pushing firmly on the closed door. When the elf saw Elena, he stepped back. "Nigel's barred himself inside," he murmured, low enough that it couldn't be heard through the door's thick wood. "According to the maid, she was about to ask him if he'd gotten lost when she recognized him. She gasped, he panicked, and barricaded himself in your chambers."

Cam made an exasperated sound. "Of course he did." At Bishop's confused expression, he sighed. "You know what the castle is like. When he couldn't find the way out, he ended up following the only other route that looked familiar to him."

The one he'd used when he'd attempted to kidnap her. Not only did it make a ridiculous amount of sense, it also filled her with the very reasonable desire to strangle Nigel. Given everything else she'd felt in the last half hour, it was a wonderful relief.

Sliding past Bishop, she pounded firmly on the door. "Nigel, come out here and speak to us properly!" she shouted, keeping her tone chiding. "Hiding in a lady's chambers is no way for a prince to behave!"

There was only silence on the other side. After a second, Cam leaned in close. "Do you have a spell that would take the door down?" he asked quietly. "We can take it down physically if we need to, but that's solid oak. It would take more than just me and Bishop to pull it off."

"Not yet," she whispered back, then pounded on the door again. "Nigel! I insist that you behave like a gentleman and leave immediately! You're disgracing your title with this behavior!"

There was a noise from inside that sounded like something

large getting knocked over, then Nigel cursing loudly. A minute later, he spoke from just the other side of the door. "You disgraced your title by not telling me you wanted to freeze me and take my blood!" he shouted back, voice high and scratchy. "A gentleman should be warned of these things!"

Behind her, Cam made a rude noise, but she shook her head and he went silent again. Then she leaned closer to the door, keeping her voice crisp and efficient. "We only brought up the freezing spell because it sounded like you were going to go back on your bargain. I apologize for not telling you about the blood, but it's a small enough amount that I assumed it would be irrelevant to someone of your obvious nobility."

Bishop leaned forward. "Subtlety, Elena," he murmured. "Laying it on too thick can destroy the entire lie."

"Only when you're lying to someone intelligent," Elena whispered back. Still, she kept the thought in mind when she raised her voice again. "We'll just need a few drops, your highness. I'll make a small cut on the palm of your hand, and after we're done I'll heal it so fast you won't even know it was ever there."

There was no response from the other side of the door, but Elena resisted the urge to keep cajoling. Finally, Nigel spoke. "Surely you can use something other than blood," he tried. There was something in his voice that made him sound like he was close to hyperventilating. "Spit, or hair, or even—"

"Nigel," Cam said sharply, cutting off the list of suggestions. Elena couldn't be angry at him for it, even though Nigel's awareness of his presence would make negotiations more difficult.

Nigel, ever predictable, immediately proved her correct. "You have no place—"

"It has to be blood," Elena said, pulling the prince's attention back to her. "Nothing else is strong enough to carry the spell."

Except her aunt had proven that emotion could carry the same strength. And when you combined blood and emotion together, you could do things that no sorceress was supposed to do. A sister's love, and a mother's love for her child, had bound them all deep into this mess. Did that mean an equal measure of love could help undo it?

I'm not doing this as your bodyguard. I'm doing this as the man who's already planning his collection of embarrassing pictures of our future children.

Elena shook the thought away, fingers gripping the wood far more tightly than necessary. She wasn't about to trust Cam's life to theory unless she absolutely had to. "Open the door, Nigel. I'm tired of trying to talk to you like this."

It took far too long before Nigel spoke again. "How many people will be watching when you take my blood?"

Elena hesitated, not having expected that response. The simplest—and most satisfying—thing to do would have been to knock him unconscious, but then she'd have no choice but to agree with Cam. And just when she might have finally gotten him to understand how much she didn't want to risk losing him . . .

She turned to Bishop, hoping he'd have some clue to what the prince was really trying to ask.Bishop leaned close enough to whisper in her ear. "The more of an audience he has, the more people he risks shaming himself in front of."

"He already had a nervous breakdown and put us all through an absurd clown routine," she whispered back. "How much more embarrassing can he get?"

"Cam and his family are commoners, which means they don't matter in his eyes," Bishop explained. "You need something from him, and are at least willing to pretend that the previous incidents never happened. He can't get the same assurances from anyone else who might be in attendance."

Elena bit back a less-than-polite comment, feeling a headache start to form. Her treacherous thoughts kept telling her things the rest of her didn't want to hear, and the amount of patience she had left for Nigel was burning away by the second.

She took a deep breath. "There will be other sorcerers and sorceresses there," she admitted, working to keep her voice unthreatening. "But it will be over soon, Nigel, I promise. Please let me in so we can get ready."

There was another long, silent stretch, then Elena heard the sound of the lock being clicked open. Resisting the urge to shove her way in, she signaled for Cam to wait a little while before following her and carefully stepped inside.

The common area was in better shape than she'd expected, only a table knocked over and a few cushions out of place, but Nigel himself hadn't fared so well. He was standing against the far wall, breathing hard and holding something half behind his back. A closer look told her it was the spindle he'd tried to attack her with more than a month ago, which she'd transported onto one of the shelves in her room. The fact that Nigel had apparently been searching her closets was not a good sign. The fact that he thought the spindle might still be of some use to him was less so.

"Nigel." Staying where she was, Elena waved Nigel toward her. "I need you to come with me and help us get ready for the spell. I promise you no harm will come to you except for the cut we need for the spell."

Nigel swallowed. "About that." He lifted the spindle into view, and behind her Elena heard both Cam and Bishop step forward.

She held up a hand to stop them both. If Nigel tried anything, she could throw a freezing spell before he got anywhere near her. "You know that hurting me won't get you anything, right?"

The prince looked appalled. "I wasn't going to hurt you! How can you even think that?" He lifted the spindle up higher, holding his other hand up so that the palm was parallel to the spindle's point. "But if I get the blood now, we won't need to do it in front of everyone else."

That might be bad. She took a step forward. "Nigel, we really need to do this in the circle."

Nigel had the gall to actually scoff. "Only because no one else has been intelligent enough to do it this way." He looked down at the spindle, confidence fracturing as the panic flickered in his eyes. "I can do this. I'm a prince."

Elena had known she'd have to protect herself from Nigel with a freezing spell, but she hadn't expected to have to protect Nigel from himself. As his hand came down she lunged forward, Cam only a step behind her, but they were both too late to stop Nigel from plunging the spindle into his hand. The metal sank into his hand almost an inch, the blood welling up red and thick around the edges of the wound.

Nigel stared at his hand as if he couldn't believe what he'd done. "See," he said, voice already wavering. "There was no—"

Before he could finish, his eyes rolled back in his head and he collapsed to the floor in a dead faint.

Elena stared at the unconscious man, then turned around and kicked a chair hard enough to knock it backward onto the floor. Out in the corridor, she could hear the sound of footsteps on the staircase.

Bishop cocked his head as if he could hear them as well, then sighed in anticipatory exhaustion. "Forgive me, Elena," he said quietly, studying Nigel as if he could somehow discover how he'd missed this particular eventuality. "Shall I send for pages to carry him upstairs before our company arrives?"

"There's no point." Elena closed her eyes, rubbing the bridge of her nose as if that would somehow be enough to chase away the headache. She could cast a spell to get rid of it, but unless her life radically changed in the next few minutes it wouldn't disappear for long.

She opened her eyes just as Alan and Marie stepped into the room, their gazes going to Nigel's unconscious form. Marie's eyes then flickered to Elena, and it took all the bravery Elena possessed not to look away.

Thankfully, Bishop took their attention. Elena turned back around, needing the escape, and Cam moved to stand close. She tensed as he laid a hand on her shoulder, her thoughts from earlier spinning together with all of the arguments Cam had made. "I know this proves your point, Cam, but I still—"

"I wasn't going to keep arguing," he murmured, the faintest hint of amusement in his voice. When she raised an eyebrow at him, he even smiled a little. "I swear I wasn't." He squeezed her shoulder. "You kind of looked like you wanted to hit something, which I decided was probably my cue to try to be comforting."

She couldn't stop herself from leaning into him a little, or wishing that it was an appropriate time or place to ask for another hug. "Wise man."

"I try." As if he'd read her mind, wrapped his arm around her. "We'll figure this out, Elena. Even if you don't use me, we'll come up with something else."

Elena leaned her head against Cam's shoulder, feeling better than she had since Cam had first suggested she use him in the spell. Even though he'd been the one to upset her in the first place, his support steadied her better than anything else she'd ever found. With that steadiness came strength, and a will to do things she never would have been brave enough to attempt otherwise.

Together, emotion and blood were enough to bend the rules of magic. They had the emotion, and her potion-sped brain was happy to suggest any number of alternative ways to use the blood.

Don't make me be the one who's left behind. But if she could go with him—

Taking a deep breath, Elena looked up at Cam. "Do you trust me?"

She could see the flash of surprise in his eyes, chased away by certainty. "With me? Absolutely."

Lifting her head, she made herself step away from him and walk over to his mother.

The strain was still evident on Marie's face, and Elena felt her throat tighten as she touched the older woman lightly on the arm. "I won't use your son as a mirror," she whispered. "He's too important for that. But what I need him to do might be even more dangerous."

Now every eye was on her. Still, it was Marie who spoke, her voice far steadier than it had been. "You have a plan."

Elena could feel Cam walk up behind her, laying a hand against her back. She squared her shoulders, trying to sound confident. "I want to form a blood bond with him, as formal and magic-infused as possible. My aunt proved that emotion can have an effect on magic, and when you combine emotion and blood together you can get around rules everyone thinks are absolute. I need him in there with me."

Bishop looked skeptical. "Why did no one bring this up in the planning discussions?"

Elena decided it would help nothing to admit that Nigel had technically given her the idea. "Because it's never been tried before, and I'm not even certain what effect it will have on the spell. But it should keep me awake as well as the mirror spell, since there will be two people to absorb the backlash instead of just one. After that—" She lifted a hand in silent apology for her lack of answers. "We'll work with what we find."

Alan's face was emotionless, but his gaze was intent. "Why do you trust this more than the mirroring spell?"

Elena hesitated, trying to lay a framework of logic around what essentially amounted to a gut feeling. "With the mirroring spell, I would be using Cam as something of a human shield. He would take the brunt of any attacks, but not much more than that. With a blood bond, however, the magic should see each of us as an extension of the other."

"And the curse will envelop both of you," Bishop said.

"I'm fine with that," Cam said quickly.

Elena's throat tightened at the thought, but she forced herself to speak. "I don't believe he'll get the brunt of it, like he would with the mirror spell. The connection came after the curse was already cast, so the only part of Cam that should be inside the boundaries of the curse is his connection to me." She showed the others the layering effect with her hands. "He won't be with me in the curse. He'll be anchoring me to safe ground outside of the curse."

Alan and Marie looked at each other for a long silent moment, then back at Cam. "It wasn't our decision either way," Alan said quietly.

"I'm with her," Cam said, pressing a kiss against Elena's hair. "No matter what."

Elena swallowed. "But I want to know that you both forgive me for agreeing to this."

Startled, Marie turned back to meet Elena's eyes. "There's nothing to forgive," she said, laying a hand against Elena's cheek. "We knew this was going to happen one of these days." She looked over at her son, expression rueful. "We just wish it hadn't happened quite this dramatically."

"Hey, it's Dad's fault," Cam said, voice deliberately light. They were all trying. "He's the one who introduced us."

Alan held his hands up in a cease and desist gesture. "Don't try to pin this one on me."

Bishop rubbed his chin, looking thoughtful. "Your logic seems sound, but I'm no sorcerer. What will your mother say about this?"

"We're not changing our plan of attack against the curse itself, and if she was willing to risk you to keep me safe, I doubt she'll complain about this," Elena said. "The theory is as sound as everything else we've tried."

Which, translated, meant that it was nothing more than a desperate shot in the dark. But this one, neither of them would be taking alone.

Bishop nodded. "Then we should tell the others." He ushered everyone toward the door. "On the way up to the workroom, remind me to find a page to take care of Nigel. There will be legal difficulties if he bleeds to death on our property."

CHAPTER 24

Brace Yourselves

Cam may not have understood magic as well as he liked, but knowing Elena had taught him one important thing about sorcerers and sorceresses—there was nothing they liked less than going into a situation blind.

He wasn't surprised, then, when they didn't take Elena's explanation of her new plan very well.

They all sat around a table in the queen's workroom, giving each other weighted looks that Cam couldn't decipher. Finally, Dr. Flyte was the one to break the silence. "I see your logic, Elena, but what you're proposing has never been tested. Braeth's plan was dangerous, but at least the mechanics of the spell were understood well enough that we knew what would happen in theory. Here, the way you're planning on utilizing the blood-emotion connection is wildly different than the way Ariadne did. We have no idea what the effects will be."

"We had no real idea what the effects of the mirroring spell would have been," Elena said, iron determination radiating out of every line of her body. He was sure she had the situation in hand, but she wasn't about to sugarcoat anything. Cam couldn't help but be grateful his parents had left with Bishop to deal with Nigel. "If it registered my blackout as a physical condition or a defense mechanism rather than an attack, then it would have failed to redirect it and we'd be left with nothing. This way, at least, I can be absolutely certain neither Cam or I will face the curse alone."

Ariadne shook her head. "It won't work. The blood and emotion work together as a conduit for magic. Your guard is powerless, which means he'll give you nothing."

The dismissal sparked Cam's anger like a match, but he wrestled it back down. He didn't have much to argue with, and he knew it—Elena herself didn't seem entirely sure how his presence in the spell would help her. But if there was a chance she might need him, he'd follow her through each and every one of the thousand hells.

Especially when she stared people down with that fire in her eyes. "You guess." Elena told her aunt, voice cooled just enough to carry a warning. "But you've guessed wrong before. Personally, I'm far more willing to trust my instincts than I am yours."

Ariadne's eyes flashed, but then she gave her niece a small, tight nod. Elena, accepting it, let her expression ease slightly. "We all know how experimental this is," she continued, now addressing everyone. "But all of our options at this point are experimental. And this is the only one that doesn't leave me absolutely terrified."

Her voice didn't change, but her fingers pressed against Cam's in a silent request. He closed his hand around hers, holding on for all he was worth, and she shifted imperceptibly closer.

"Indeed," Braeth said, his attention flickering between

Elena and Cam as if he'd watched their wordless exchange. "Unfortunately, the only other blood-bond ritual I am familiar with is used to bind a servant to a master. Those of us in the darker arts tend to see such a tie between equals as little more than an impediment to world domination."

"I know one." The queen spoke for the first time, her voice brimming with about a dozen different emotions she refused to let all the way out onto the surface. When she looked at her daughter, however, Cam could see the shimmer of tears in her eyes.

Next to him, he felt Elena lean forward ever so slightly as if she was resisting the urge to stand up and go to her mother. "Mom." Her voice caught on the word. "I have—"

The queen smiled, lifting a hand to stop whatever her daughter was about to say. "I'm not about to argue," she said, voice thick. "I'm just happy to see you want something this badly."

Elena tried to answer, but the words seemed to catch in her throat. Abandoning the attempt, she took a deep breath and dashed a hand across her eyes. "Well." She let out a long breath, hand still tight in Cam's. "We should get everything set up."

~

The bonding spell, it turned out, was simple enough that even Cam could understand it. All they needed was a ritual knife, the circle Elena had already drawn, a candle, a glass of water, and a bit of dirt from the castle gardens.

He and Elena were standing together in the middle of the circle, facing each other in preparation for the binding spell. She held the ritual knife against her chest, her other hand firmly wrapped around Cam's own. Braeth, Dr. Flyte, the queen, and

Ariadne were standing opposite each other on all four sides of the circle, the glyph that represented their chosen element on the ground in front of them. They were discussing the finer points of the spell, wanting to make sure they got it right the first time.

Elena was busying herself explaining it all to Cam. "The mechanics will be similar to what we've been doing with the curse—a physical manipulation of our magical energies—but it will be less tiring because the ritual helps us direct it. We also won't be casting a projection spell, because there are certain projection elements written into the binding. I'm not sure if it's for the sake of theatricality or simply that the casters wanted proof of what was happening."

He'd figured most of this out already, but there was just enough nervousness in the words to suggest all this focus on detail wasn't really for him. Still, distraction was probably in order. "You know, you're cute when you go into lecture mode," he said. When she blushed, then scowled at him, he reached over and pulled the hand holding the knife into his grip as well. "Hey, I'm not complaining. I probably would have liked school a lot better if I'd had you in one of my classes."

She squeezed his hand. "I just want you to be absolutely sure you know what you're doing."

"I'm sure." Cam bent forward enough to kiss her hand, a little surprised at how calm he felt. He'd been wrestling with frustrated adrenaline often enough the last few weeks that he'd expected to be chomping at the bit right now. If nothing else, it would have made sense to feel some of the charge that always hit when he knew he was about to catch the bad guy.

Instead, he felt like he was in a life-or-death battle with someone just a little better than he was. When you were in those kind of fights, all that mattered was what you did next. If you didn't make the right choice then nothing else really mattered.

Dr. Flyte, lighting the candle in front of him with a murmured word, smiled slightly. "I did some quick research while we were setting up, and it turns out that the dragons still use a variation of this spell." He paused a beat, for effect. "They often pair it with poetry and incorporate it into their marriage rituals."

Delighted, Cam winked at Elena. "I'm sure I can remember a poem or two," he murmured, grinning when she blushed again.

The doctor, for once, seemed to be entirely oblivious. "Oh, I doubt you have the vocal chords for draconic poetry. Some of the most moving passages mostly consist of snarling."

"Thank you, Doctor," Elena said, shooting the mirror a quelling look. "I'm sure we're all fascinated."

The queen cleared her throat to get everyone's attention, but there was an amused look on her face as she activated the illumination spell. "Positions, everyone."

Once the circle lit, the queen spread her hands wide and murmured a phrase in what Cam had always privately thought of as "secret magic language." Then she blew gently into the circle, the air turning into a silvery cloud of light as soon as it crossed the barrier.

It was Dr. Flyte's turn to speak, making the candle flare at an unnatural angle and cross the circle. Droplets of water rose from the cup at Braeth's portion of the spell, and when Ariadne spoke a thin stream of dirt rise into the air. After each element crossed the circle, it transformed into a silvery light that slowly filled the circle.

The entire time, Elena was whispering the translation to him. He'd asked before they'd started if it would cause problems with the spell, but apparently magic didn't recognize Common. "alone, fragments of a true whole. Only entwined can they become themselves."

At Ariadne's final word, the circle flared with green light. That was his and Elena's cue to begin their portion of the spell. Reluctantly letting go of each other, they both took a step back. Then Cam held out his hand, and she used the tip of the knife to sketch what looked like a compass rose against the skin of his palm. A silent apology in her eyes, she pressed the knife into the center of his palm just deep enough to draw blood. When the first red drop welled up, the entire pattern flashed green.

Cam was fascinated enough that it took him a second to remember his line. Elena had taught it to him phonetically, and so far it was the only line he knew in "secret magic language." "Inimeserjetaure da vaka." My heart is bound to yours.

Then Elena sketched the same design in her palm before drawing a drop of her own blood. Her pattern flared blue, the same color as her magic in the earlier spell. "Kenmu a tauledus-jeaedno." Our souls are tied as one.

The queen then drew a symbol in the air, ending in a wide circle that she closed by joining her hands together. As she spoke a final word, he and Elena pressed their palms together. The flash of light was bright enough that he shut his eyes, blue-green spots still dancing behind his eyelids.

A second later, he opened one eye and risked a peek at Elena. "Are we done?"

She hesitated, as if considering the question. "The spell's over. I don't feel any different, but there's no reason I necessarily would."

"Not unless your bond was put to the test," Braeth said. Before Cam could react, the wraith flicked a small jolt of electricity straight into Cam's right ear. He flinched, grabbing the now-sore appendage, and next to him Elena did the same thing to her own right ear. A second later, he realized that the electricity hadn't hurt quite as much as he'd thought it would.

Two seconds later, he realized a potential problem. He grabbed Elena's hand, forcing her to meet his eyes. "So if I get stabbed in the chest at some point saving your life, this means you're going to feel it anyway?"

Elena stared at him, completely incredulous. "I think you have more important things to be concerned about right now."

Annoyance was not helping him be any less worried. "No, I really don't."

She stared at him another moment, then kissed his hand. "Only you," she murmured, the wealth of affection in her voice doing dangerous things to his heart. When she met his eyes again, though, there was a serious warning in them. "Now you know you'd better not let yourself get stabbed."

"Given his profession, that's not exactly a feasible restric—" Dr. Flyte began, only to be cut off by a rattling noise that sounded like someone giving his stand a firm kick. Cam sent a silent but heartfelt thank you to whoever had done the kicking.

When he looked up, he saw the queen moving away from the mirror and back to her original position. She was as solemn as someone about to go into battle. "I see no reason not to move on to the next step immediately," she said, gaze sweeping over everyone. "Are we agreed?"

Cam watched Elena go pale, his eyes never leaving hers. When she nodded at him, he squared his shoulders. "We're agreed."

As everyone else cleared the remains of the binding spell, Cam pulled Elena down onto the floor next to him. "Now, if all of this goes like it's supposed to, I'm the only one who should be blacking out in the—"

She shook her head, cutting him off. "No. If this works out, neither of us should lose consciousness."

"Okay, I'd prefer that," Cam continued, pulling her closer. "But either way, it's probably safer if we start this a little closer to the ground." He scanned the circle, measuring out his height and relative angles in his head, then scooted them both closer to one edge. "If I do end up collapsing like I'm not supposed to, I'll try to make sure I don't fall over onto the runes and screw everything up."

Elena brushed an imaginary bit of hair off his forehead. "Oh, your head will explode long before that happens," she said.

He smiled at her, knowing she was trying to play. "I have no idea why no one else can see this evil side of you."

Before she could respond, everything was ready. As everyone moved into position, the universe displayed a truly horrible sense of timing by letting the door open. Silently, his parents and Bishop walked into the room.

Cam had no idea what the expression on his face might have been, but Elena read it well enough to squeeze his hand. "They belong here, too."

He glanced back over at his parents' seemingly emotionless faces, far too aware of how much pain they were hiding. "While I'm not admitting that you were right at all," he whispered. "I'm starting to understand your side of our earlier argument."

As the illumination and projection spells activated, the corners of Elena's mouth curved upward just a little. "Eventually, you'll learn that I'm always right."

She'd said "eventually." Cam grinned despite himself.

When the image of the curse flared to life above their heads, however, all he could do was stare. The knot that had tangled Elena up so painfully tightly the last time he'd seen it had started to move again, the strands straining and twitching as if they were trying to get away from whatever was at the center. The strands of Elena's magic seemed to push in the opposite direction, trying to draw back in to the core, and every time the two threads strained against each other Elena winced. It took Cam a second to come to the quite horrible realization that, unlike Braeth's little trick with his ear, he wasn't feeling a thing.

"Why isn't the bond working?" He took Elena's face in his hands, trying hard not to sound desperate. "We're supposed to be sharing the pain, remember? Tell me what I need to do."

Ariadne said something over his head, the words sharp, but Cam didn't bother paying attention. Elena looked like she trying to figure out the answer to his question, and he was going to listen to her opinion before anyone else's. "I don't know. I think—" The words were cut off by another wince. "Maybe the effects of the binding are only automatic if it has a parallel to work with."

And he didn't have any magic. Fantastic. "Then how do we make it work?" His own brain raced, trying to come up with its own answer. "I don't have magic, but I have energy. Use that."

"Cam." Elena winced again, then let out a long breath. "This isn't that significant a problem. I'm not going to steal your energy just to make myself more comfortable."

More talk happened above their heads, but none of that mattered. "Elena, this is why I'm here." Determination rose up inside him, as if his energy could reach for Elena all on its own. "If it's this bad now, you're going to need it later."

"Then I'll use it later—"

The conversation above them coalesced into the sound of his mother's voice saying his name. "Cam. Look up."

He obeyed, but it took him a while to understand what had happened. The strands of Elena's magic, originally bright blue, were shimmering with a faint green light that made it look the same color as her mother's. The curse strands were moving even more violently now, not pleased by the new development. Cam wasn't sure he was pleased, either, since just looking at it seemed to be giving him a headache.

Then Elena, who was also staring up at the knot, squeezed his arm. "It doesn't hurt as much anymore." There was something close to wonder in her voice. "Cam, what did you do?"

"I have no idea." But now that he concentrated, he could tell that the headache was really a series of faint aches piled on top of each other.

"Fascinating," Dr. Flyte said. "It seems that Cam somehow forced the binding spell to recognize his energy as an appropriate comparative for Elena's magic."

Testing the theory—at least, that was what he was going to tell Elena if she started yelling at him—Cam focused on trying to push more energy at her. The knot flared again, the pain in his head sharpening into more distinct individual jabs, and Elena's eyes narrowed at him. "That's enough." She lifted her hands to touch his face. "You have less energy to work with than I do."

"That's true, Cameron," the queen confirmed. "Elena's father and I attempted a few things when she was a child. When you use life force for both physical and magical energy, you're drained twice as quickly." She paused, sounding oddly wistful. "His energy was green, too."

"I need you with me through all of this," Elena said firmly, the warning clear on her face. Since she was also obviously in far less pain than she had been before, Cam decided silently that he'd been proven right and left it at that.

Deciding he wasn't going to try anything stupidly heroic for the next few minutes, Elena looked back up at the knot. "So, you said that it was the destruction of the inner shield that made me black out last time. Since that doesn't seem to have renewed itself, do we have any guesses as to what might trigger it now?"

Every head turned to Ariadne. "I never experimented beneath the inner shield," she said, a careful rephrasing of what Cam guessed had originally been "I have no idea." "The simplest answer would be an attack of equal strength, but it's likely that the core will be even more sensitive to attack than the rest of the curse. Anything might set off a defense mechanism."

Cam saw Elena's mouth move, muttering what he was pretty sure was "Well, that's helpful," too low for anyone to hear. Then she took a deep breath and reached up toward one of the blue strands. "There's one way of finding out."

Lightly touching it with the tips of her fingers, Elena closed her eyes. She curled her fingers to the right just a little, as if she was attempting to carefully nudge something into place. Cam felt a faint ache inside himself, like an old bruise being poked at, but he ignored it.

"She's following the line of her magic," he heard the queen say, though he was pretty sure neither he nor his parents had asked a question. Maybe she explained things when she was nervous, too. "She's tangled too deeply into the curse for us to do a great deal, but the more she can free herself the more easily we can work on removing it."

A moment later her hand nudged again, this time in the opposite direction, and as she tensed Cam felt a stronger twinge of pain in his chest. Then she stopped, her body tensing as she opened her eyes. "Cam," she said quietly. "Get ready."

When he squeezed her arm in response, she looped her

finger around the visible strand. Then, with a quick jerk, she yanked it free.

Pain blossomed in Cam, sharp and hot, but that wasn't nearly as bad as the wave of dizziness that crashed into him. He swayed, feeling Elena do the same, and braced them both. It took some effort, but they both kept their eyes open.

Elena held onto him tightly. "I won't do it that abruptly again, I promise." He could hear the leftover strain in her voice. "But now we know."

Cam steeled himself for what was coming. "Now we know."

CHAPTER 25

Sacrifice and Glory

The work went painfully slow, with far too much emphasis on the last two words.

For the first little while, Elena was working mostly alone. The writhing had loosened the knot, giving them more leeway to work with, but there was still far too much of her magic in the way. The jostling was constant enough that the pulses of ache blended together, and though Cam was a steady, quiet presence next to her she could imagine every slice of pain inside him. It made her want to hurry, to get him safe and away, but her experiment had already shown what would happen to him if she moved too fast. She forced her fingers to be patient.

The silence in the room had a weight. Everyone watched her work as the time slipped away from them, each second stretching out until it seemed endless. Occasionally, the others would catch the curse strands with their magic, either holding it in place or move it aside to make her work a little easier. She was certain they wanted to do more—she remembered how hungry she'd been to help the last time they had done this—but they didn't dare until she'd cleared more room. A thousand threads would have to disappear to make any real difference, and it took a small eternity to unwind each and every one. Even then, there was always another one waiting.

Every needlepoint project she'd ignored over the years mocked her.

The writhing curse strands both helped and hurt matters. They gave her desperately needed room to work, but they put just as much strain on the strands of her magic as impatient fingers did. Her own pain was distracting enough, but the knowledge that Cam was hurting as well did even more damage to her focus. It should have made her focus even sharper, her love for Cam transforming her into the kind of woman with the power to save them both, but she had failed in the romantic heroine department.

"Talk to me," she murmured to Cam. There was something unforgivably rude about the request, as if no one else was in the room, but she needed to get away from her own thoughts if she wanted to have any hope of finishing this.

Cam hesitated, a more relaxed stillness than when he was bracing them both, then leaned just a little closer to her ear. "Any idea why the binding spell made the curse panic like this?" The last few words carried some strain in them, timed perfectly with a fresh jab through her own ribs. "Or is it something else entirely that's set it off?"

"It was you," Ariadne said, completely ignoring the fact that she hadn't been invited into the conversation. Her aunt's fingers twitched, unhappy with the helplessness that pinned them in place, and she hooked her magic around one of the curse strands and began to work it free. "I can't be certain without more experimentation, but from what I saw the curse recognized you as an invading presence in the center of its magic. It wasn't happy."

"You're suggesting it sees Cameron's energy as a threat nearly equal to the combined force of all our talents?" Braeth asked, finding his own strand only seconds after Ariadne had claimed hers. "For that to have any chance of being true, your curse would need to be as insanely possessive as its creator."

There was no response from her aunt, and Elena wondered if the wraith's insult might have a seed of truth in it. They'd proven that emotion could affect magical bindings, and if that was true, maybe it could also alter the very shape of a spell.

She heard her mother say Braeth's name quietly, an unspoken reminder that now wasn't the time to argue, and Elena let the thought go momentarily. You're not talking enough," she whispered to Cam, eyes still on the curse. He leaned closer to her ear. "I'm just going to set everyone else off again, and I don't think that's the kind of distraction you're looking for," he whispered back.

She hesitated only briefly before the admission slipped out. "I need the sound of your voice." The words were as brisk and practical-sounding as she could make them, the last remnants of pride that hadn't yet thrown its metaphorical hands up and accepted the hold that Cam had on her. "I don't care what you say, or how anyone else feels about it. But I need you to talk." Another brief pause. "Please."

He didn't say anything at first, but he did shift close enough to eliminate the few scraps of air that had managed to squeeze between them. Tightening his arms around her just a little bit more, he leaned down so that his lips were close to her ear but his breath wouldn't tickle her skin. "Article 3, subsection 2: Each member of the border patrol shall be issued one full set of leather armor, fitted as closely as possible to the wearer given the armor currently in stock. One standard-sized crossbow, though the patrol member may also outfit themselves with—"

Elena smiled slightly, promising herself that there would be time to ask him why and how he'd come to memorize what sounded like a part of the border patrol handbook, and resumed her work.

Soon, her mother and Dr. Flyte joined in as well, wrestling the curse strands into submission. Time continued to crawl, the knot disappearing far more slowly than it had the last time they had battled the curse. At one point Cam apparently came to the end of the handbook, leaving him scrambling for a moment before moving on to detailed descriptions of his own patrol routes.

All Elena could do was continue the patient taming of her own knotted magic, surprised at the way it had been so bent and twisted by the curse. She had never felt any limitations on her power, any handicap that had kept her from reaching her full sorcerous potential, but surely this much of a mess had created some sort of negative effect.

If not on her magic, on her health. Every jab of pain seemed more than enough confirmation that it was somehow snagged in her physical body, though the limitations of the projection spell meant that she couldn't see it. It was a great waste of research opportunity, she knew—she had never heard of such a thing happening, and it was an unparalleled opportunity to gather data—but she had no desire to spend even a second longer in the middle of this tangle than she had to.

Suddenly, the thread of magic she had been working to free was pulled out of her hands, pain digging deep as something inside her was jarred. She opened her eyes, trying to figure out what had just happened, only to stare at the curse strand now lying snugly across the thread. She could have sworn her mother had lifted it out of her way only seconds before.

Elena stared in horror as another strand appeared, wrapped crosswise over the first. Her hands stayed frozen in midair, incapable of movement as she watched all the hard work everyone had done slowly but surely disappear before her eyes. More pain came, the threads of her magic compressed and twisted anew under the weight of a curse that seemed to be rebuilding itself, but right then it was the least of her worries. Far more wrenching was the helpless sound torn from her mother's throat, or the way she felt Cam tense behind her as if he could somehow absorb the blows for them both.

By the time she managed to rip her eyes away from the knot, everyone else had turned to glare at Ariadne. Elena's aunt was staring at the curse in blank-faced shock. "It's not supposed to do this," she said, answering everyone's unspoken question. She turned to the queen desperate. "I swear to you, I—" Ariadne stopped, looking appalled, and turned back to stare at the curse. "It was supposed to last for a hundred years." Her voice had dropped to a whisper. "Energy degrades after a time, and I didn't want him to wake up early, so I—" She swallowed. "I forgot. It was such a small thing, intended for such a different context than this. I never meant—"

"That doesn't matter," Cam snapped, the anger in his voice cutting through the room like a knife. "All we care about is what you're going to do to fix it."

A wave of exhaustion washed over Elena, and for an instant she thought it was simply despair once again rearing its ugly head. When she felt Cam sag just a little, however, she realized the truth was far worse. "It's getting its energy from us," she managed, clutching Cam's hand as if she could keep him awake through physical force. "The curse is pulling from me and Cam to remake itself."

Ariadne made a choked sound. "It wasn't supposed to pull enough that anyone would notice! Just enough to renew itself against the natural ravages of time. But assault—" The words trailed off again, as if she couldn't bear to finish the sentence.

Out of the corner of her eye Elena could see her mother's fingers curl, as if she was fighting the urge to lunge for her sister, but Bishop stepped forward and put a steadying hand on her shoulder. Alan stepped forward as well, positioning himself between the queen and her sister. "Think." The word was an order, aimed at Ariadne with all the force of a blow. "There is no apology in the world that can save you if you let these two die."

"Speed is the only answer," Braeth said instead, turning his magic into a clawed hand and yanking away an entire handful of the cursed strands. As soon as they disappeared he dug into it again, ripping at the knot as if the secrets of the world lay on the other side.

Just as the second handful disappeared, however, Elena could see the strands from the first knot reappear. As Braeth's skeletal hand reached for more she felt another wave of energy leave her, with Cam's head dropping against her shoulder as if he could no longer hold it upright. Still, he kept flinching at pain she could barely feel, as above them both the knot pulsed green. He barely had the energy to sit up, pouring all of it into the knot so he would hurt instead of her. She reached back to grab him as if she could physically pull him up out of the energy-sucking tangle her mouth forming the words to tell Braeth he was killing them both.

Before she could tell him, Ariadne stopped the wraith by grabbing the arm of his cloak. She yanked her hand away, burned by the freezing cold radiating out of him. "You'll never be fast enough, and then their deaths will be on both of our hands," she said, every ounce of her regained control wrapping the words in iron. "We need to cut off all of the curse's magic at once, so it doesn't have time to renew itself."

Dr. Flyte gasped, but Elena's brain was too battered and desperate at this point to understand what was so shocking about what Ariadne had said. Elena's mother, at least, seemed to have a piece of it. "You want to use the spell they put into the charms that nullify magic," she said, voice strained. "But you know just as well as I do that they don't nullify curses. All it would do was shut down the projection spell and keep us from having any idea what's happening to them. It's useless for something like this."

"When it's used as a surface charm, yes." Ariadne's voice was empty, and she looked everywhere but at her sister. "But we would be injecting the spell straight into the heart of Elena's and the curse's magic. Since the curse is entirely made of magic, there won't be anything left of it to re-boot itself."

The queen's eyes flickered to Elena, then back to her sister. "You have no idea what it will do to my daughter's magic, do you?" When Ariadne didn't respond, she turned to Dr. Flyte. "Do any of us?"

The mirror hesitated, clearly not wanting to answer. "The briar pattern Elena used in the protective circle should keep the spell from touching the rest of us, so we'll at least be able to maintain some control."

The queen's voice was cold as she turned back to her sister. "That's not what I asked."

Braeth stepped in. "It's impossible to calculate the dangers of something like this. I consider the blood-binding spell to be far more harmless."

"I don't care." Elena nearly shouted the words, the effort of forcing her lungs to work pushing itself out all at once. "I can't take this anymore, and if the choice is between Cam or my magic I will pick him every single time. Do it."

Cam lifted his head, his self-sacrificial tendencies once again giving him strength at the most inopportune times. "No." The word was a rasp, making her afraid for him all over again. "There has to be another way."

Elena turned her head just enough to glare at him, covering his mouth with her hand. "No. If you're the one who gets to value my life, I get to value yours. You don't get a say in this."

She saw the surprise light his eyes, even as exhaustion overtook them. The curse was still pulling from them both, trying to recover from their hours of work, and it was killing him. She tried restoring the balance, pushing her magic into him to take more of the load, but there was no corresponding flare of blue light. Here, apparently, his stubbornness would not be bent.

Screaming at him inside her mind and loving him so much she could barely breathe, Elena turned back to her aunt. "Do it. Now."

She turned around, the better to hold onto Cam, as her aunt sketched the necessary symbols in the air. She lifted her hands out in front of her, as if pressing them against the surface of the protective circle, then pulled them back again. "No. This isn't close enough." Taking a deep breath, she stepped inside the protective circle and dug her fingers into the center of the ever growing knot. The reappearing curse strands wrapped around her, as if simply adding her to its mass.

Cam's own eyes were nearly closed now, but the knot still

flared green again as if he knew what was coming. Elena pressed her lips against his hair, pulling him even closer against her. "Stop it, you idiot," she whispered, her eyes filling. "Please."

Ariadne murmured the final incantation. The inside of the circle flared white, the result of the spell attempting to do its work in a far more magically volatile environment than it was ever meant for. Elena felt like she'd been hit physically, a chill sweeping through her, but she just wrapped her arms tighter around Cam.

When the light cleared, the projection had disappeared entirely. Her mother re-cast it quickly, the runes safely outside both the protective boundary and the effects of the magic-nullifying spell, and thin green threads reappeared almost instantly. There was a flickering blue in their depths, and for a second Elena was foolish enough to think everything would be alright.

Then the green light started to fade, and an area of shadow she hadn't noticed before started solidifying into a curse strand. "Again!" The word was torn out of Elena's throat. "Harder!"

Ariadne's entire body seemed to flare with purple light, and the part of Elena's brain not screaming about Cam realized that she was drawing almost all of her power to the surface. The nullifying spell would hit her almost as hard as it would Elena. Maybe harder, since she didn't have Cam standing in the way.

Elena felt more jostling, likely the result of her aunt sketching the necessary symbols straight onto the curse strands themselves. There was the faintest pulse of green light as Ariadne said the incantation again, making the entire inner circle flare bright enough to blind.

By the time the spots had cleared from Elena's eyes, her mother had already recast the projection circle. The blue threads were there, as strong and straight as if they'd never borne the weight of a curse, but the green light that had nearly covered them before had faded until it was almost impossible to see.

The curse immediately forgotten, Elena tilted Cam back onto the workroom floor. His heartbeat was slowing down, the feel of his breath against her palm faint enough that she wasn't certain if she was hallucinating. Not caring about anything else, Elena tried to shove energy at him through the bond. He was no longer conscious enough to stop her, and she felt weakness take her as her energy moved to fill in the terrible deficit.

"If there was anything left of the curse, it would have started to return by now," Ariadne said, sounding as exhausted as Elena felt. "It's done. She's finally free."

When Elena looked up again, however, she wasn't looking at the empty spaces where the curse had once been. She was looking for the green light, still barely visible. It wasn't fading anymore, but it wasn't growing any stronger.

She swayed, then felt her mother reach out to grab her shoulder. At the same time, the teal glow of her mother's energy flowed into her, restoring her strength. She pushed that on as well, and the green light above her head brightened just a little. Soon gold light joined the teal, the two colors twined together by a careful hand. Elena looked up at Bishop, who had silently offered her mother use of his energy as well. The elf smiled at her, as if he heard the "thank you" she wished she could say.

Then Cam's mother stepped forward, her husband only a step behind her. "Us, too," she said, and Elena reached out and murmured the words to carefully draw out their energy as well. It came twined together as well, grey-blue and vivid yellow, and she channeled it all into Cam. She could be more methodical about it now, the draining sensation fading as his body recovered, and Elena could have cried at the sight of the green light above her growing brighter.

When Cam's energy was as vivid as it had been before, she ended the spell and stopped pulling energy from his parents. Her mother cut off her own spell soon after, and Elena silently sent enough energy to all of them that they felt nothing more than a lingering tiredness. She kept less for herself, but she was more than strong enough to yell at Cam just as soon as he opened his eyes.

But it wasn't happening. His body was fine, nearly pulsing with all the energy she'd fed it, his breathing steady, but when she laid her hand against his chest his heartbeat was still far too slow. Regathering her magic, Elena prepared to start the process all over again.

Then Braeth moved closer. "Let me." He leaned forward, lightly touching the tip of his finger to Cam's chest. She felt a jolt near her own heart, an echo of what he'd sent into the man she loved, but that was nothing compared to what filled her when Cam's eyes flew open. He gasped, jerking upright into a sitting position, and before he could say a word, his arms were full of Elena.

She wrapped her own arms around him, burying her face against his neck as he tightened his arms around her. Elena felt dizzy, still reeling from the sudden absence of the weight and worry that had been a part of her life for so long.

No, not dizzy. She felt like she was flying.

Cam's head moved, and she could tell he was looking up at the now-clean projection. "That looks like we did it," he said, voice rough. "Tell me that means we did it."

Elena closed her eyes, tears of happiness catching in her throat. "We did it."

NOW

Illiana was the second person to hug her daughter, holding on as tightly as Cameron had. The thousand things she needed to say caught in her throat, coming out only in tears that were dangerously close to sobs. Elena, her own cheeks streaked with tears, seemed to understand.

Then the parents switched children, Cameron's releasing him into Illiana's embrace while they enfolded Elena into their arms. She had shared her daughter with them for a long time now, too grateful for their strength to let herself resent the hold they had on Elena's heart, but now the families would be stitched together formally. In a way, they would be hers now as well.

Cam seemed surprised by the strength of Illiana's hold, but he hugged her back as tightly as any son who had been well-trained by his mother. When they pulled back, Illiana held his face in her hands. "I think I will very much enjoy having a son-in-law," she whispered, her voice thick with emotion.

His eyes were wet. "We can team up against Elena when she's being too much of a handful."

Illiana laughed, hugging him again.

Then she hugged the Merricks, both of them wrapping their arms around her in the exact same embrace they had given the children. No words were needed here, though she knew they would have many in the weeks and months that followed. She'd been as bound by the curse as Elena was, the idea of making friends impossible when all that was good in the world hung by such a slender thread, but now a future stretched out before her as well.

As they pulled away, Marie squeezed her hand. "Let me give

you my mirror code." She grinned, the expression remarkably similar to her son's. "I'm sure you already have Alan's, but he's a terrible conversationalist."

Alan simply smiled, the joke clearly an old one between them, and Illiana felt her throat close up with emotion as she squeezed both their hands. "Let me give you the one for my private line as well. I don't want to miss anything."

She wrapped Dr. Flyte up in a hug as well, frame and all, and smiled at Braeth in a silent acknowledgement that she would do the same to him if it were physically possible. Elena had pulled Bishop into the exchange, throwing her arms around him with an exuberance she was certain the elf had never seen from her daughter. He hugged her back just as tightly, looking at Illiana with a wonder that threatened to make the queen's heart burst from her chest.

Surely she had the courage now. Illiana turned, ready to speak to her sister. She wasn't quite certain if she was ready to embrace her—there was still so much between them, even after the successes of the last few moments, for anything so open and simple. But Illiana knew what Ariadne had offered up in that last, desperate burst of effort to save Elena, and why she had not participated in the energy sharing to save Cam. There could at least be peace between them, if nothing else.

But when she looked, Ariadne's space in the circle was empty. Her sister was nowhere in the workroom, the celebration having given her plenty of opportunity to slip away without anyone noticing. It was the simplest way to end things, with actions replacing the words that neither of them would ever say. Ariadne's debt was repaid, if not precisely erased, and their place in one another's lives could fold gently into the past.

Illiana touched Bishop's arm, drawing the attention of both him and her daughter. "I'll be right back." Then she hurried out of the room.

Ariadne was outside in the sunlit courtyard, just as Illiana had suspected she would be, making arrangements for transportation to a coach service that was headquartered in the city. When she saw her sister approach, Illiana thought she saw the barest flicker of sorrow in her eyes. "Everything is well, isn't it?" Ariadne asked, the tremor of worry in her voice not entirely masked as she slipped her personal mirror back into her pocket. "The projection spell was still active when I left, and there was no sign that the curse had returned. I know I have gotten a great many things wrong in all of this, but here at least I have the physics of magic to confirm my hypothesis."

Overcome, Illiana crossed the rest of the distance between them, reaching out to take her sister's hands. "I know what you did," she said softly.

Ariadne took a deep breath. "It was nothing. Given the time window we were facing, half-measures would have been even more harmful than doing nothing."

She no longer knew what to say to her, the anger inside her drained away to make room for the new joy. She wasn't used to wanting to say anything kind to her sister, the feeling of instincts she'd thought long dead slowly creaking back into life.

The words that came weren't the ones she had expected. "Your magic will come back," she reassured Ariadne, not certain whether or not she was lying. No one had ever released a negation spell of that strength with the heart of their power so exposed. Cam had protected Elena's magic—another debt she owed him—but Ariadne had taken the full brunt of it. "It just needs a little time."

Ariadne smiled a little, her face open in a way Illiana hadn't seen for a very long time. "It doesn't matter whether it does or not." She sounded tired, but her smile widened slightly. "My power is the least of what I owed you both. If I can look at my husband and step-granddaughter without a weight upon my heart, it will be enough."

"Thank you" seemed like the wrong thing to say somehow, the words both inadequate and not entirely true. There were other words, however, that might end up meaning more. "You could write." Illiana pushed the words out in a rush, worried her resolve would fail her. "The castle gets very good letter service."

Ariadne froze, as if she couldn't quite believe what she was hearing, then closed her eyes. "Yes," she breathed, squeezing her sister's hands painfully tight. "I will write you."

When she slipped away, Illiana to watch her go. Once Ariadne was gone, the queen let herself smile at the wonderfully familiar presence behind her. "I didn't intend to pull you away from the celebration," she said, turning to look at the man who had come to mean so much to her

"I know," Bishop said quietly, his voice happier than she had ever heard it. "But I prefer to be near you always."

Tears that had barely had time to dry welled up again, and she took him in her arms in a way she hadn't been brave enough to do for so long. His arms came around her as well, as steady as the mountains that surrounded the kingdom.

"As I would prefer to be near you, my love," Illiana whispered against his shirt, marveling that she had been granted such a gift twice in her life. She wondered, at times, if Thomas had sent him to her. "Stay with me."

He pressed a kiss against her hair. "There is nowhere else I would be."

EPILOGUE

Many Happy Returns

They waited until the day after Elena turned eighteen to officially celebrate her birthday. It was Elena's idea, but no argument had been needed to persuade everyone else. Cam himself hadn't slept very well that night, finally giving up an hour or so before dawn. He debated whether or not sneaking into Elena's room to check her breathing was allowed per the unofficial fiancé rules and regulations. Before he could decide, her door opened.

Cam let himself just stare at her for a minute, knowing he was grinning like an idiot but not caring. He hadn't ever let himself think too much about this last, lingering bit of shadow in his heart, the fear that they had somehow missed something. But with the deadline safely behind them, he felt like dancing. "Hi."

"Hi yourself." She closed her bedroom door behind her, moving closer. Her smile was bright as the sunlight. "You look uncommonly cheerful for a man who sounded like he spent most of the night pacing."

"You're exaggerating. I only spent a third of the night pacing.

I was tossing and turning for the rest of it." He moved toward her, sliding an arm around her waist. "Of course, I notice you're up ridiculously early yourself."

"Maybe I simply wanted to put my overprotective but somehow oddly adorable fiancé out of his misery." She laid one hand on his shoulder and wiggled the fingers of the other. "Dance with me?"

Taking her hand in his, he twirled the woman he loved around the room.

~

"This is your fault, you know," Elena said under her breath later that morning, waving at the crowds of people lining the streets. Her smile was taking on a faintly homicidal edge, but Cam was pretty sure no one else recognized it. "No one in their right mind says the word 'parade' at a committee meeting."

"I didn't think they'd take me seriously," Cam whispered back, pushing an enormous papier-mâché flower back into place before it fell and gave one of them a head injury. They were on a float that looked like an enormous mutant garden, the words "spring into hope" emblazoned on the side in ornate, glittery script. Sadly, it was far from the most ridiculous float in the parade. "What I really want to know is how you talked them into letting you drag me along for the ride. We haven't officially announced the engagement yet!"

"I told them you're going to be king one day," she murmured, giving him an amused glance before turning her attention back to her subjects. He should really not enjoy the wicked gleam in her eye so much, especially when the torment was being directed at him. "You need the publicity practice."

"Are you sure I can't just be a consort or something?" he

asked, the same question he'd tried a hundred different times since he'd heard about this particular quirk in local law. The only person who seemed to understand how he felt was Bishop, who would get saddled with a kingship himself as soon as he and Elena's mother officially tied the knot. "Her Majesty's Royal Muscle and Personal Houseboy?"

Elena pressed her lips together, eyes dancing as she fought the urge to laugh. "My mother wasn't royal, and she ruled the kingdom single-handed for six years. We'd have to dismantle centuries of tradition to keep you from having to sit next to me on the throne." She reached over with her free hand, squeezing his. "So man up, Merrick. You're not going to get out of policy meetings quite that easily."

"I don't mind the policy meetings, as long as they keep letting us go to the same ones," he murmured. "I will make you laugh in the middle of a tax debate, one of these days."

She smiled again, but this one was genuine. "And you wonder why I dragged you up on the float with me. Now start waving, Royal Muscle and Personal Houseboy. My arm is getting tired."

~

Dinner, thankfully, was just for family.

"This table is exactly fifty-five footsteps long," Gabby announced, having decided sometime in the last week that her destined career was going to involve measuring things. She wasn't entirely certain what real job would allow her to do that, but Bishop was trying valiantly to help her with the research. "And the room is three hundred and fifty footsteps long." She looked at the queen. "I always thought this room was really big. Why do you have such a big room?"

The queen looked amused as she took a careful spoonful of soup. "I'm not sure, exactly. It was already here when I moved in."

"I believe it was built this big to accommodate state dinners," Bishop offered. "There hasn't been one here for decades, but the records suggest that Elena's great-grandfather was particularly fond of them."

Cam eyed the room. The ten of them were bunched together on one side of the table, with a lot of empty space left on the other side. And if you brought in enough tables to actually fill the room, "That's a lot of mouths to feed."

"Oh, they probably didn't fill it," Mason offered, reaching for a particularly complicated looking salad and passing it over to their mother. "Anything ridiculously large is good at intimidating the enemy. It's basic battle tactics, used at the dinner table."

"Which is why Laurel's so terrifying to the enemy, I'm sure," Elena offered, smiling syrupy-sweet at Cam's oldest sister. "Her swollen head would be enough to frighten anyone."

"We should get you out on the field some time," Laurel shot back, matching Elena's smile. "With your ego and my swollen head, we could conquer the world."

Both women laughed as both Marie and the queen aimed a chiding look at their respective offspring. Robbie, shaking his head in a gesture that looked far too old and wise for his actual years, passed Cam the basket of rolls. "You do realize you have surrounded yourself with women who are scarier than you are, right?" he asked his brother.

Cam took a roll, then passed the basket on to Gabby's eagerly reaching fingers. "I had picked up on the subtle signs," he replied cheerfully, not at all bothered by Robbie's smirk. "Not my fault, though. Dad passed the gene onto all of us."

Alan shrugged. "It's true. Merrick men are instinctively drawn to women who will run them ragged." He smiled a little. "Your future wife will probably blow things up as a hobby."

As Robbie looked horrified, Cam grinned. "Elena's already taken that slot, remember?"

"It was one pair of socks. One!"

~

Cam finally got Elena alone again later that night. Unfortunately, he wasn't quite as excited by the activity as he was by the company.

"It's like you don't trust me," Elena chided, adjusting the straps of his harness one more time. "I used the exact same routine to make your harness that I did to make my own. I am starting you in a safe, well-protected clearing, where you won't have to worry about either falling from a great height or the potential mockery of others. And you still look as though I have a loaded crossbow pointed at your head."

Cam took a deep breath. "It's not you I don't trust." He rubbed a hand along the back of his neck, helplessly calculating all the ways he could make himself look like an idiot over the next few hours. "Are you really sure I can't just stay on the ground and watch you be magnificent?"

"I will never understand why this is the one thing you think you won't be able to do," she murmured, stepping back and giving the harness's fit a critical once-over. She tightened one of the leather bracelets,.

Cam watched her work, letting himself be distracted by the concentration on her face. "There has to be something. The odds against me get stacked higher with each new thing I try."

"Somehow, I think you'll survive the experience." She kissed his cheek, stepping back as he pulled his shirt back over his head.

The disappointment in her eyes was extremely gratifying, but the nights were getting cold and there was nothing less sexy than hypothermia. "Just follow my lead, don't get ahead of yourself, and you'll be flying just like a cute little bird."

"You know you're the only person in the world who I'd let get away with calling me something like that, right?"

Elena raised her eyebrow. "I think your mother could manage it."

Cam considered this, then nodded. "Okay. One of only two people who could call me something like that."

She laughed. "I'm honored."

They took each other's hands, holding on tight as Elena murmured the words of the spell. Cam could practically feel the magic gathering in the harness and bracelets, a subtle lift that suggested they were now holding themselves up completely independent of gravity. Even after all the magic he'd seen, it was both amazing and just the slightest bit terrifying.

Seeing something in his face, Elena squeezed his hands. "Just trust me."

"I do." He lifted her fingers to his lips, the same silent promise they'd made to each other dozens of times over the last several months. "I wouldn't be out here if I didn't."

"Good." She smiled, taking a step back without letting go of him. "Now, we're going to jump on the count of three. One . . . two . . ."

Together, they flew.

ACKNOWLEDGEMENTS

It takes a village to make a story. First, thank you so much to my fans. You guys are amazing, and I love each and every one of you. My eternal thanks to my mother, who will always be my first and best editor. This time, though, I had extra help. Heather De Puy, Noie Duckgeischel, and GhostWriterLost were with me from the first chapter to the last, giving me an invaluable perspective outside of my own head.

And for Rachel, both a thank you and an acknowledgement of your suffering. I know you went further inside your head than you ever wanted to for this one, but I think I can safely say that it won't happen again.

Jenniffer Wardell is a fantasy author and fairy godmother extraordinaire who thinks the world needs more happily-ever-afters (and a better sense of humor). She's written two previous books, *Fairy Godmothers, Inc.* and *Beast Charming,* and in her free time is an award-winning arts and entertainment journalist. She lives in Salt Lake.

33557620R00210

Made in the USA
Middletown, DE
18 July 2016